ALSO BY JAIDA JONES AND DANIELLE BENNETT

HAVEMERCY

SHADOW MAGIC

DRAGON SOUL

DRAGON SOUL

JAIDA JONES

 AND

DANIELLE BENNETT

SPECTRA

BALLANTINE BOOKS
NEW YORK

Published in the United States by Spectra, an imprint of The Random House Publishing Group, a division of Random House, Inc., New York.

Spectra and the portrayal of a boxed "s" are trademarks of Random House, Inc.

Library of Congress Cataloging-in-Publication Data

Jones, Jaida.
Dragon soul / Jaida Jones and Danielle Bennett.
p. cm.
ISBN 978-0-553-80769-1 (acid-free paper)
eBook ISBN 978-0-345-52168-2
1. Dragons—Fiction.   2. Brothers—Fiction.   3. Imaginary places—Fiction.
I. Bennett, Danielle.   II. Title.
PS3610.O6256D73 2010
813'.6—dc22   2010010116

Printed in the United States of America on acid-free paper

www.ballantinebooks.com

2 4 6 8 9 7 5 3 1

First Edition

Book design by Lynn Newmark
Map by Neil Gower

To my dad, who still wants to visit New Zealand
—*JJ*

To Grandma Marjorie and Taid,
for spoiling me rotten and fighting to stay awake
when I wanted "just one more story"
—*DB*

ACKNOWLEDGMENTS

A thousand thank-yous to our amazing editor at Spectra, Anne Groell, and our tireless agent, Tamar Rydzinski. Without either of these two fine ladies there would be no book. We are also eternally grateful to our sharp-eyed copy editor, Sara Schwager, and our assistant editor at Spectra, David Pomerico. As always, we owe just about everything to ruthless Mom—whose ruthlessness is next to godliness. And who could forget the efforts of the province of British Columbia, so rainy that we are forced to stay in and write all the time? Special thanks to all the members of our families who make allowances for our weird hours and who don't make fun of us for not changing out of our pajamas all day; to Dr. Schmirer (he knows why); to Jean Lerner (she also knows why); to Mylanta, down-to-the-wire beverage of champions; and, once more, to everyone at the livejournal community Thremedon. You guys are incredible and we are incredibly grateful.

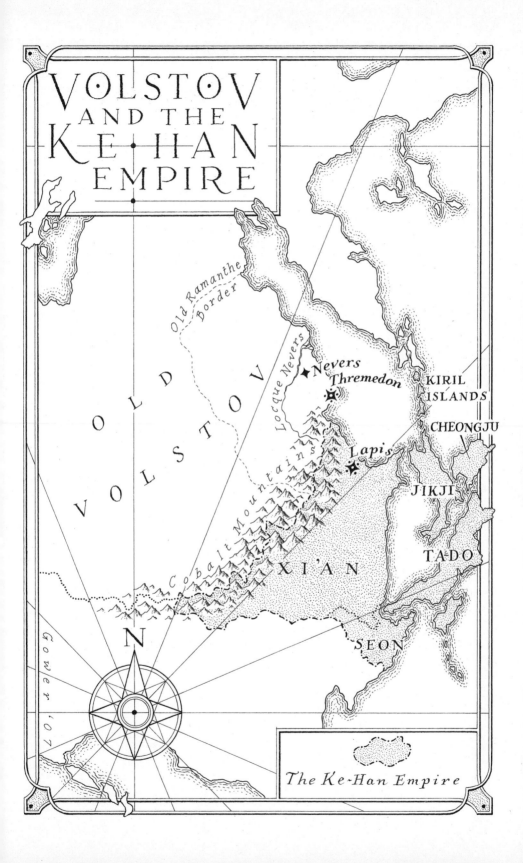

DRAGON SOUL

CHAPTER ONE

THOM

On the day Rook became my brother again, I turned into a liar.

Balfour was the first to ask, once we started up a correspondence, whether or not I had any memories of my older brother. Our time together had been so distant, and to fondly remember a brother only to be confronted years later with the reality of *Rook* was bound to be a nasty shock.

The question surprised me, but I'd found myself writing an answer nonetheless.

Of course I remember John, I'd said, clutching at the few specifics that I knew to be true. They were enough to make these memories convincing to others and—after a time—I too became convinced.

After that, it was too late. When others asked me whether or not I remembered my older brother, I always said "Of course," as though it was a foolish question, and didn't bear thinking about. I'd always prided myself on my honesty—a rare virtue, since it was always the first thing a Mollyrat cast aside—and that I'd stifled it so quickly was a notion that troubled me.

"So you two are brothers?" the innkeeper asked. He was a short, provincial man, with one of those recognizably provincial accents: blurring his *h*'s and his *e*'s together, and rounding off his *r*'s, as though his tongue couldn't quite shape them in time to get them out. I wondered if I could ascertain his place of birth and whether or not he had been raised there. To me, it seemed clear that he had been born in Hacian, just on the border between New Volstov land and the Old Ramanthe, but I never offered a theory on birthplaces unless I was a hundred percent sure. You never knew whom you'd offend, and among this man's properties I noted a certain strength of arm, if not of character, that I myself did not possess.

I would let the matter go, though I would make note of it in my travel log.

We were far enough into the countryside that no one knew Rook by sight. We were anonymous travelers, with the mystery of the open road before us—though when I'd shared this sentiment with Rook he'd threatened to take my logbook and stick it somewhere where I need make no further entries. There was nothing to intimate that my brother was one of the greatest heroes of our time—the famed pilot of the dragon Havemercy, who had saved this country.

Not single-handedly, but for some reason Rook had a way of sticking in people's minds like an irritating burr.

"Yes," I told the innkeeper. "We are brothers."

"Don't look anything alike," said the innkeeper's daughter. She wasn't looking at me. She was staring straight at the window, out toward whatever place Rook had disappeared to earlier. The excuse was that he intended to stretch his legs, but we'd been walking for half the day, and personally I would have found it more relaxing to take a hot bath, have a hot meal, and compile notes about what we'd seen.

"Ah," I agreed, not trying to offend her either way. Searching for some other topic, I happened upon the only matter on which I was an expert. "I notice that you have an accent of peculiarly—"

"I'd best be seeing to the horses," she said, hurriedly fixing a strand of her hair before disappearing out the door.

"Now, you listen here," the innkeeper said, reaching across the desk and grabbing me by the collar. "I don't want any funny business in my establishment."

"She's just gone to see—"

"The horses?" the innkeeper said. "Horses my left nut. She doesn't need to fix herself up for any horses. You find that brother of yours and you make sure nothing happens."

"I will do my utmost," I promised. It was the liar in me reasserting himself—though it wasn't a true lie, since I did intend to try my hardest.

I just wasn't particularly optimistic about our chances—mine or the innkeeper's.

But what was most shocking to me was that anyone seemed to think that *I'd* have any influence on the situation. Despite what had changed since the time of our meeting in Thremedon—a time I preferred to examine in private, like poking at a bad tooth—it was fair to say that I still had very little influence upon what my brother chose to say and do.

To his credit, thus far Rook had managed to avoid any behavior that would have gotten us thrown out of a night's accommodation, but this was hardly the first time I'd been threatened in this manner. And it seemed that all the innkeepers we'd encountered were under the misapprehension that I had some control over my brother.

This was far from the truth, but I found myself marching off to avert disaster as best I could—a lone sandbag against the coming flood.

The horses were liable to grow spoiled, with three people heading out to see to their needs. Except that it was only Rook who'd set out to look—myself and the innkeeper's daughter were there for another beast entirely, and one that didn't go about on all fours.

I had barely reached the stables before I heard his voice. Whether he'd lost the best of his hearing during his time with the Dragon Corps, or whether he just didn't care who heard him, I had never been able to ascertain, but Rook was loud and it carried. He had no reason to quiet himself since, for Rook, reason was akin to desire. If he didn't desire something, he found it completely unreasonable.

"We can do this easy or you can be difficult about it, but it's *gonna* happen, so you might as well be a good girl and keep your mouth shut, all right?"

A sinking feeling settled into my stomach. Visions of being thrown bodily from the establishment, of sleeping on the hard ground in the cold with no respite for either my tired muscles or my grumbling stomach, flitted through my mind. I hoped the innkeeper was still inside, or at least tending to matters that would keep him there for a while, for I was in no mood to consider giving up the bath I'd been fantasizing about all day. I picked up the pace.

Fortunately, it was a short enough distance across the courtyard that I didn't have time to call up anything too lurid in my mind. Perhaps it was because the circumstances under which I'd been reunited with my brother had been so particular, but I found myself consistently expecting the worst.

As Rook had kindly suggested, offering his opinion on my "nerves," I was a grim little fucker when I set my mind to it.

When I reached the stables, he was bent double, digging a stone out of one of the horses' hooves with his pocketknife. The innkeeper's daughter was standing as close as she could without chancing a stray kick. She held her hands clasped nervously in front of her. It was as innocent a scene as I could have hoped, and I couldn't help feeling some perverse disappointment, as though I'd somehow been tricked.

"Picked up a stone, did he?" the innkeeper's daughter asked.

"She," Rook grunted, his attention on the horse, who didn't seem bothered in the slightest, though I knew that if I'd attempted the same trick, I'd have received a good kick to the chest for my efforts. Rook's hands had that effect on animals—and women too, I sometimes thought in my less charitable moments, but I prized myself on being too much of a gentleman to voice the comparison. "Not her fault. *Some* people have a hard time followin' the trail."

He'd added that last part just for my benefit; he must have, since Rook was of the opinion that it wasn't any fun listing my shortcomings unless I was in the room to hear them. I thought I'd been rather quiet in entering—not knowing what I was about to walk in on—but apparently my best was still not enough to catch Rook off guard.

I should've known, but that didn't stop me from trying every now and then.

"That wasn't a *trail,* it was the side of a mountain," I sniffed, crossing my arms. "And if I'd known you were going to declare your own shortcuts every ten miles, I'd have prepared myself better."

The innkeeper's daughter spooked like a startled horse. *She* hadn't heard my approach, nor did she know enough of Rook to know when he was needling someone in the shadows, and she proceeded to glare at me as though I'd interrupted the most intimate of encounters.

Fortunately, I'd survived glares more withering than hers.

She was a strapping sort, and it was obvious that, despite her father's precautions, she could take care of herself. Only Rook wasn't the sort of man you could take care of yourself against, no matter who you were. The countryside had never been prepared for him. He was like a walking natural disaster—one for which the Esar provided no compensation or monetary relief. In fact, since the dissolution of the Dragon Corps, I was sure he wanted nothing to do with Rook, and the sentiment was entirely mutual.

"Hungry," Rook said, more like a grunt than a word.

The innkeeper's daughter didn't miss a beat. "I'll bring in some supper," she supplied, moving past me as though I weren't even there. I could hear her feet crunching the hay, and the whinnies of the horses as she hurried off.

"Amazing, isn't it," Rook said. He whistled, a low sound to soothe our horse, then dug the pocketknife in deep and, with one fluid motion, eased the stone out.

"That is *one* word I'd use to describe it," I admitted. "I wonder if she'll bring two plates."

"You didn't fucking ask," Rook pointed out. He flipped the stone over in one hand, the nails of which were cracked and muddied, before he held it out to me with a grin, knowing full well that I'd recoil. "Memento? Souvenir? You're always asking about 'em."

"Rook," I began.

"Didn't think you would. Can't put this kinda thing down in your book, can you?"

I couldn't, and it was impossible for him to understand. The beginnings of a headache—not unfamiliar to me now, as all my days ended with them—were creeping toward my temples from the bridge of my nose. I recognized the dull pain instantly, and knew there was only one solution: a hot bath, a full meal, and a good night's sleep.

"Sure is taking a long time to get the fuck out of this country," Rook muttered, giving the horse one last soothing rub before clapping her, in an unsettlingly recognizable way, on her rump. Even she allowed these offenses with a pleased whinny, and I gave up hope of ever convincing anyone that Rook's abuses were not misplaced signs of affection. It was all too easy to fall into that trap with Rook. Whether it was conscious or not, he encouraged that response—the angry sort of person fools believe themselves capable of calming.

I had assumed—quite miserably presumptuous of me—that things would change when we were on the road, but every muscle in Rook's body was tightly wound with such thrumming, anxious tension it seemed at times he would snap like a metal coil and ricochet with violent speed in an unknown, dangerous direction. He was no longer openly hostile toward me, however, and I was grateful for even this smallest of changes.

Logic said you couldn't change a person, but I was committed to trying.

"Well, Volstov is very large," I reasoned, shoving my personal thoughts aside in an attempt to soothe him with facts. I always found facts very soothing. "I could show you the map again, if you'd like."

"I thought I told you to take that map," Rook began. Before he could finish, he nearly ran into the innkeeper's daughter—which on any other occasion wouldn't have stopped him, but she was carrying a plate of the most incredible countryside food. The very smell of it was so delectable I found myself transported to another time and place, and my stomach rumbled so loudly I couldn't help but be embarrassed.

"I prepared it for you myself," the innkeeper's daughter said, somehow managing to support the heavy-looking tray on one arm while twirling a stray lock of hair with her finger.

"All the loving care of home, huh?" Rook asked. "Well, this idiot's hungry. I'm sure he'll appreciate it."

"What?" I asked, snapping back to reality a little more rudely than I might have wished to under the circumstances. Someone had to defuse this situation, and it certainly wasn't going to be my brother.

"Pardon?" the innkeeper's daughter managed, fluttering her eyelashes with what seemed to be a nervous tic.

"Been listening to his stomach growl for near on an hour now," Rook said, taking the tray from her hands as though he wasn't drawn in the *slightest* to its symphony of aromas. "It's grating on my fucking nerves."

"Oh, I'm sorry," said the innkeeper's daughter, in a way that really meant she *was* sorry, but it was only because I was there at all.

Rook shrugged, thrusting the food at me without as much as a cursory glance. "He's too stupid to say anything. Got dropped on his head as a kid and he's never really been the same since. Hard traveling the country with a brother that slow, but we've all got our burdens."

Excuse me, I wanted to say, but my mouth was full of bread and turkey gravy, and I couldn't quite form the words. It was rude not to speak when spoken to, but ruder still to speak while eating.

"Oh, I didn't realize," said the innkeeper's daughter, looking at me with a sudden sympathy. "Have as much food as you like. It tastes *delicious*," she said, the words drawn out and slow as if she was teaching an infant to speak.

Rook chuckled as though he'd found a silver lining in the cloud after all, then clapped me on the shoulder. "That's all right. He's just like a big animal, really. Real sweet-tempered until he gets into one of his fits."

Once again, I tried opening my mouth to defend myself, but all I could manage was a kind of grunt in protest.

"I'll just show you to your room, then, shall I?" Hands free once again, the innkeeper's daughter brushed her skirts out and eyed Rook in a way that suggested hope sprang eternal in the hearts of some women.

"Sure," Rook said, starting off like he knew the way better than she did. "Come on, Thom. You can finish inhaling that bird when we get there."

I followed in his wake, careful not to choke myself with the dual purpose of eating and walking.

It was strange to be addressed—in that voice—by a proper name after Rook had put so much time and energy into thinking up the most caustic, personal insults. Stranger still were the times when we forgot ourselves and slipped into John and Hilary—though this happened rarely, after a mutual decision on both our parts.

"It's just too fucking weird," Rook had said, which meant that it was too fucking weird when *other* people called us by names we had long since put aside.

I'd agreed. It was one of the few instances I could recall that we'd been on the same page regarding even the simplest of issues.

"We're crowded tonight," the innkeeper's daughter explained, skirts swishing as she followed Rook up the stairs.

I hadn't seen many other guests about, but then we'd arrived at the inn rather earlier than I'd expected, on account of Rook's little shortcut. Inn traffic, as I'd made note of in my travel log, seemed to pick up most at night after the sun had set and travelers realized they hadn't planned ahead to where they'd be staying. One had to strike first in order to secure the best accommodations, and if one was lax in his preparations, one found himself sleeping under the stars.

It was an unsettling way to go about things, but it seemed to have worked out well so far.

Rook, of course, thrived on it, as he thrived on all things where there was a chance of being eaten or drowned or falling off a cliffside.

The innkeeper's daughter unlocked the door to our room and stood back to let us survey the surroundings. I tucked the tray of food a little closer against my chest, following Rook inside. It was a fairly standard room, bare but well tended to. Clean. No bugs that I could see, and therefore superior to most of the lodgings I'd taken in Thremedon.

"Bathroom's just through there," she said, still behaving as though Rook were the only guest for the night. "I'll be showing guests in for the rest of the evening, but if you need anything at all, my room's second from the left on the first floor, and local people know not to bother me much past eleven."

I couldn't help but wish that Rook's particular charisma worked half as well on the innkeepers as it did on their daughters. We might have had extra gravy, or perhaps a discount.

Rook surveyed the premises with the same bored, slightly derisive air he'd had for almost everything we'd seen up until this point. The innkeeper's daughter twisted that stray lock of hair in her fingers again, anxious to know whether he'd heard her and not entirely willing to ask.

"I'm gonna take a bath," he said, nodding when he'd decided that the room was suitable. "Bring me up some dinner when you get a minute, will you? He doesn't really know when to stop, and I don't think there'll be much left when he's through."

"You poor thing," the innkeeper's daughter murmured, staring at Rook with such rapture that you'd have thought he'd up and announced he was joining the Brothers of Regina.

I'd been mentally compiling my update to our log, but this was enough to make me pause.

"I *beg your pardon*," I began.

"That's all," Rook said to the innkeeper's daughter, still hovering in the doorway.

"I'll have it right up," she promised, smiling as Rook disappeared into the bathroom.

We were left together, staring at one another, completely at odds.

"Thank you," I began, but my pleasantries were too late; she swung the door closed behind her without a second look at me.

"Am I invisible?" I demanded, going over to the bathroom door once she'd gone and there was no chance of her overhearing me. It was ironic, really, as there had been numerous times in my life when I'd wished for nothing *but* the power to be invisible. Now that I had it, such treatment was beginning to wear on me.

"Not the way you've been eating," Rook snorted. "Get out, Cindy. You ate my dinner. I'm taking the first bath."

"Please," I said. "That language."

"Look," Rook said, not for the first and no doubt not for the last time. "I'm tired and I've been traveling just as much as you. You wanted to come along, so you play by my rules. Eat your fucking turkey and leave me be."

Once again, a door was shut unceremoniously in my face, and I was left alone. The room smelled of gravy and horses and the mud of travel but also of clean sheets. There was only one chair, and one of the legs was shorter than the others, so that when I sat the thing nearly went out beneath me.

To soothe my spirits, I took out my travel log and began to write of that day's adventures. No matter how minor, I did wish to remember them.

ROOK

The only problem I had with the fucking Hanging Gardens of Eklesias was actually getting there.

I repeated the same thing over and over to myself, trying not to rip any throats out. *You try traveling with someone who spends more time talking about what he's seeing than actually seeing it and you'll know what I mean.* It was like dragging a lame horse along behind me, helping it out because of sentimentality instead of shooting it like I should've done, and I never had too much patience for that shit in the first place.

Now he was tired, now he was hungry, now he was *a bit fucking parched*—there were any number of fucking problems that could make a good day's traveling take three instead. Stopping to talk about a ruined wall or a pile of stones or an old farmhouse wasn't my style. I didn't care if this was the famous spot where Absalom the Gentleman had killed himself only to reappear months later in the Arlemagne countryside, and I *definitely* didn't care that this was where some Ramanthine revolutionaries had made their last stand.

"Perhaps some of Ghislain's relatives," Thom'd said, in that hesitant way he had that made me want to smack him.

"Sure," I'd said. "Whatever."

I didn't want to think about Ghislain's relatives—or Ghislain himself, to be perfectly honest, since then Thom'd wonder why I wasn't "keeping in touch" or whatever the fuck it was he thought he was doing with that cindy Balfour. I couldn't see much point in thinking too long on things that'd already passed, and everything that I'd had in common with the other members of the corps had gone out with our girls.

What I really missed these days—what was really getting under my skin—was how quick things used to go. How quick you could get from one place to the next when you weren't stuck to the ground. When you were flying.

Horses were fucking slow, and they felt all wrong beneath you. The sounds they made were animal sounds—the kind of noise you had to tune out just to hear yourself think. Horses never asked you for an opinion and they never told you where to fucking shove it when you were going the wrong way. Fuck that. I was so tired of looking at horses, buying horses, trading horses, putting horses down for the night, shucking fucking pebbles out of horseshoes, and making sure horses didn't see snakes on the road that I was this close to leaving and doing things by myself, trusting my own legs and no one else's. The only fucking problem was sitting outside the bath, eating the local gravy, and writing about it in some idiot book he thought about more than he did about real people. That fucking problem couldn't move like I could, and wouldn't ever if he kept eating the way he did.

Yeah, I'd made a big mistake. And now I was suffering for it.

That made it even fucking worse—knowing it was my fault and not knowing how to get rid of it. Sure, I could just fucking leave him where he was. He'd probably find his way back to Thremedon, eventually, where all the walkways were paved and you couldn't spit without hitting a building, and there were as many books in the libraries as there were people in the city. He'd be in his element again, talking to professors and experts, coughing up theories, and never going to any of the places he was chattering about.

I closed my eyes. The water was starting to get cold and I was starting to get pruny. The fucking braids in my hair took forever to dry, especially in the countryside, and especially at night, when everything got damp as—well, as fucking horses.

But I didn't want to go outside and deal with the gravy, and I certainly didn't want to go downstairs and deal with the bitch who'd made the gravy. I had an itch that fucking couldn't fix and fucking would only aggravate it. And it wasn't thinking of Thom getting in my way, or thinking of the problems it'd cause, or thinking of anybody's *feelings* that was stopping me, either.

Point was, I just didn't fucking want to. And that'd never happened before.

"Don't expect you to believe me, but one day, Airman Rook, you'll appreciate things beyond rutting with the loudest girls Our Lady has to offer," Chief Sergeant Adamo'd said once, back when he was still Chief Sergeant and before he turned into some kind of fucking professor on us. Or so Thom's letters said; I hadn't wanted to stick around long enough to see what the boys did with themselves after the war, and Chief Sergeant Adamo turning professor on us was one of the reasons. At least it didn't bother me to think about Adamo the way it did some of the others, and anyway I had bigger fucking problems right now than feeling squirrelly over the guys who were long past feeling anything at all. Anyway, I didn't see as how what Adamo had said could be it at all, since I wasn't even halfway toward appreciating any of the things we'd seen so far. We were moving too damn slow.

In fact, I didn't remember any of our journey, excepting that time we'd taken the shortcut and the horse'd spooked and sent Thom straight into the blueberry bushes. Wasn't the same as a handprint on his face and *he* sure as shit didn't appreciate the memories as much as I did, but it'd kept me laughing all the way to that night's inn.

But that "incident"—which was what he called it—had all been a couple of weeks back. After trading horses—what kind of an idiot could keep his hold on a *dragon* and not a horse, I wanted to know—I was getting mighty sick of traveling with the forgotten thirteenth wonder of the world: my fucking brother, the talking blueberry.

I twisted the braids back from my face—only thing more fucking annoying than damp hair was that same hair hanging in my eyes—and braced myself for whatever barrage of questions lay waiting for me on the other side of the door.

On a full stomach, Thom's brain was more daunting than the entire bastion-damned Ke-Han capital laid out bare and blue. I opened the door.

"She bring the food up yet?" I asked. Talking first was the only way to get the drop on him and it was near on fucking impossible to get a word in edgewise unless you came out swinging.

Fortunately, I had a lot of experience there.

He was writing, so of course he didn't answer me right away, which was just another layer of icing on the fucking cake. We'd been through this before and he said it broke the flow of whatever he was writing and that he had to get his sentences down first before he forgot them, or the point he was making. Damn waste of my time is what I called it, and *he* was the one who got mad when I started throwing things to get his attention.

"Whatever," I said, tucking in my shirt, then untucking it again, which pissed me off because I didn't know why I'd done it in the first place. "Fine. Don't let up on chronicling your fucking eating tour of Volstov's piss-poorest inns. Guess you won't miss me when I drop dead of starvation."

The gobbler made a funny sound, almost like a snore, and his head drooped lower to the desk. I couldn't believe it. He hadn't been writing at all. He'd fucking fallen asleep.

"Guess you weren't that eager for a bath after all," I said, taking the liberty of moving the tray so he wouldn't wake up with his face in it.

It took a special kind of witless moron to fall asleep with his head on a plateful of turkey, but that was my brother for you. At least he hadn't gotten any gravy in his hair, except that saving grace was only because he'd taken the liberty of eating it all first.

I cracked my neck and pulled a jacket on over my shirt. Looked like I was gonna have to brave the wilderness of downstairs without him. What a fucking shame. With any luck the bitch'd stay in her room, waiting for my grand appearance—her getting ready for it was probably why she hadn't brought us our second dinner—and meanwhile I could have myself a real night off.

She'd gone and told me where she'd be, after all, so I knew just what to avoid.

Of course, helpful little priss hadn't told me anything useful, like where the kitchens might be, but unlike some people, I was resourceful. I followed my nose.

The common area was about as crowded as I'd been expecting, full of bearded men and their wives—who were less noticeably bearded, but not exactly picks of the litter, either. The conversation died down a little when I showed up, which was just fucking peachy by me since the last thing I wanted was someone striking up a conversation about my hair while I was trying to choke down a late fucking dinner.

I sat down on my lonesome, pretty set on avoiding anything that had both turkey and gravy since I'd seen and smelled enough of that for one night. I was far enough away from people that they'd know to keep their distance, but the whole place was small enough that I'd still have to listen to them talking.

That was fine. I'd tuned out raid sirens to sleep, so I could tune these bastards out.

"Let me *see* it, just once. I've always been so curious," said one of the travelers' wives. She was wearing some sort of bonnet over her hair, which was—according to the walking encyclopedia peacefully making drool stains on his travel log upstairs—a sign of chastity out here in the southern country. Her husband had a bored, red-faced look about him, and there were bits of turkey caught in his beard.

Not that I was interested, but after looking over it was pretty clear that most of the inn's patrons were gathered together in a group, chattering among themselves like hens and roosters, and about that much brainpower among them, too. At the center of the group was some poor pockmarked bastard with milky-white eyes and drooping ginger hair. It made me laugh, since he looked about the same as if someone'd taken th'Esar and run him through a printing press. He moved like he'd had one bad fever too many as a kid and never quite bounced back, and every now and then his fingers twitched. A gruesome fucking sight if ever I'd seen one, but these country folk couldn't seem to get enough of whatever story he was serving up. He was holding something in his hands, but I couldn't see it over the top of somebody's bonnet.

After that woman'd spoken up, asking to see "it," a murmur of excitement rippled through the crowd—whispered comments and the creak of chairs being pulled forward as people jockeyed for a better position.

Take the bonnet off, bitch, I thought, and—despite how much I hated them all—I leaned a little closer myself. That was mob mentality for you, and even I couldn't resist it all the time, even when I saw it coming. The trick to avoiding it was sticking to what was important. In this case, what mattered more than country gossip about people I'd never met was eating my dinner and getting out of here.

Turkey Beard muttered something and rolled his eyes. I was with him, particularly since the serving girl'd brought me a proper plate of food and I had something else to turn my attention toward.

Ginger Hair clearly felt differently. The more he was pressed by the squabblers around him, the more important he became to himself, making a big to-do of going through his pack, drawing out a smallish metal box, and unlocking it with a key he was keeping—like it even mattered, like anybody fucking cared what he was hiding—around his neck.

Someone gasped. I took an extralarge bite off of whatever poor animal they'd served me up instead of fucking turkey and let out a belch. Just to even things out.

"Only eyes, please, no hands," Ginger rasped in a reedy voice, like straw breaking. "Not that I don't trust your company, but I paid good money for this, so don't muck it up."

"From one of th'Esar's *dragons,*" murmured one of the bonnets, only I didn't really catch her face. It was what she'd said that mattered.

"I don't believe it," sniffed a little man, who wasn't quite man enough to have sprouted his own beard yet. "Why would it be here? In the hands of someone like *you,* to boot? It ain't real."

"Jealousy's disgusting in a child," Ginger replied. "I'll tell you what the peddler told me: Even if history doesn't appear in the books yet, one should still be mindful of it."

"Everyone knows the dragons went down in the middle of the battlefield," the little man said, but he was just as interested as the rest of them. My teeth were so tight my jaw was about to crack.

"And then they were destroyed," said a woman. "Everyone knows *that,* too."

"Destroyed, or merely disposed of?" Ginger asked. These weren't his lines; he was too gormless for that. Someone'd fed him a story—a story they were all eating up. Someone was out there selling bits of shit and telling country suckers they were off *my fucking girl.* All of a sudden, I could hardly hear anything over the roar of my pulse thumping away in my ears.

I stood up, leaving my half-finished dinner on the table, since I didn't have anything even remotely resembling an appetite anymore.

"I'd like to fucking see that," I said.

Everybody stopped talking, which had been the fucking point. The bonnets and the beards alike all looked at me like I was a barnyard animal suddenly asking them to please pass the fucking potatoes, their jaws hanging open and their eyes glazed over.

"Am I speaking fucking tongues?" I asked. "Last I checked, I was in fucking Volstov."

Ginger must've known which way the wind was blowing—not in his favor—because he nudged the bonnet sitting next to him out of the way. *Damn right,* I thought, but I didn't take her place, just shoved in to stand over him so I could see what the fucking deal was.

In the box was a scale. It'd been pretty badly burned, of course, but one side of it hadn't taken too much damage, and on top of that, it'd been polished to look like it was pristine. Some of the gilding was worn away because of it, so it caught the light all wrong. Silver, so it wasn't mine, but I'd seen that color before. I'd know it even if I was asleep.

"Chastity," I said.

Everybody was looking at me like I'd gone crazy. Maybe I had. But I couldn't take their gawking for another second. I was going to start knocking heads together, beards and bonnets alike.

"The fuck are you looking at—" I started.

"Rook!" Thom said, from across the common area.

"Rook?" a bonnet said.

That name was starting to be a fucking problem. I didn't have time to be recognized or sign anything. I didn't want to tell stories, or answer stupid questions; I didn't want any of these idiots to know how things *really* were because unlike some people I didn't know how to explain it. I didn't know how to explain anything. The whole mess just was, and it wasn't for anyone to know about but the people who already knew. It was why I'd left in the first place. Maybe I'd been a hero for this country but now I couldn't stay here one fucking second longer, and even *that* was starting to be too much.

Without thinking about how much Ginger paid for it or even how he'd shit his breeches, I elbowed him in the face and grabbed the box from him—everybody else still too dumbfounded to make a move against me or figure out what I was doing before it was too late. Someone in the crowd let out a shout, but I was already turning away.

Thom's face was blotchy and horrified, with an ink stain under his nose like it was bleeding. I could've punched him right then, but I could've punched *anybody* at that point. Who it was didn't matter.

"Are you *stealing*?" Thom demanded.

"Can't steal something that didn't belong to a man in the first place," I snarled. Everyone was shrinking away from me now, but I didn't care what they were thinking. "Someone's selling *our* girls. Piece by fucking piece."

MALAHIDE

It was twelve o'clock, of the midnight variety, when the Esar called me in to speak with him. I had not been at the same party as the others—not rubbing shoulders with those of high standing and high society, that is—but rather waiting for when I would become necessary.

I bowed my head before anything else. Protocol had to be observed, even in these more peaceful times. My liege was troubled; I could see it in his eyes, in the deep lines around his mouth, obscured for the most part by his reddish beard but recognizable to those who knew him best. I had a good sense about these things. When one could not speak, one listened very carefully to what everyone else had to say.

"Malahide," the Esar said, after the formalities were over, "I have a favor I must ask of you." His tone was weighty and somber, and the seriousness of the situation delighted me. There was something of great importance for which I was needed. Such occurrences were as rare as disasters were commonplace these days. I knew how it disturbed him, yet I could not help it when my nostrils flared.

It was always difficult—even for a ruler—to speak with someone who could not hold up her end of the conversation. It put most men and women at a distinct disadvantage, and those who were not accustomed to the discomfort tended to ramble.

But the Esar was not someone who minced or wasted words. His time was precious, and I could already see how moved he was by tonight's business.

I sat down at the opposite end of the table from him. Despite how careful he was to hide his uneasiness around someone as queer as I, I could nonetheless sense it, a hunting dog smelling a fox's fear.

"There is a box before you," the Esar said. "Open it."

There was indeed. It was a simple, wooden affair, with a catch. Half expecting to need a key, I found it already unlocked, and caught the top as it swung open. Within the box was a twisted piece of metal.

I looked up at the Esar. How fascinating. I could tell from the scent of the metal that it had been through many fires. If I had been a superstitious sort, I would have been afraid to touch it, for fear it was still hot.

"You may touch it," the Esar said.

I shook my head. I would never have marred its pristine condition with my own fragrance. During my work, I always wore gloves, but I hadn't been working when I'd arrived. There had only been the hint of duty, a promise of my coming necessity on the dry palace air, and so I'd waited to be called, hands bare and fingertips pressed together.

I had to press them tightly together just now to keep from touching the prize. It was *very* tempting. To be told what it was would almost spoil the surprise, but I knew that very question was what the Esar awaited from me. A lesser agent might tire of the little games we played with one another, but I never had.

I looked up, features arranged into polite confusion—the expression he expected from me.

The Esar glanced from right to left, as though expecting to see listeners at either corner. He was a sensible man for the most part, but living so long with no viable heir had made him more paranoid than the average gentleman.

"Do you have any idea what this is?" he asked me.

I had my guesses, though they were nothing more than that. Small, vague theories had formed in the few seconds since I'd opened the box. I was trained to think quickly, but I also knew not to volunteer guesses when my liege was leading the show. I would not offer anything but certainty to the Esar—something he knew as well as I did. I shook my head.

"It's a relic from another time," he said, voice worn around the edges in a way I'd rarely heard from him. Under normal circumstances, he possessed too much self-control.

My instinctive deduction was correct, then: It must be an artifact from the war.

I tilted the box toward me, letting the metal fragment within catch the dim, private light. No one on this side of the mountains had lost so much as the Esar in that war—not when it came to political advantage and technological development. There was only one sort of metal that the Esar would keep, twisted and ruined as this was, for he was not a sentimental man. All at once I felt a tight clutching in my belly, of excitement and anticipation. To what end was I gazing at a piece of one of Volstov's destroyed dragons?

Only the man before me would be able to answer that, and he'd been watching my face carefully to gauge my reaction—a task I knew was particularly difficult. I made it that way on purpose though my deception was not intended specifically for my liege.

Once, during wartime, I'd worked with a partner—a man to speak for me so that all this interplay might be avoided—but the war had claimed him just as surely as it had claimed the Esar's dragons. And for both of us, a replacement seemed impossible.

"Malahide," the Esar said, and I took my eyes away from the scrap of metal. "We have reason to believe that key elements of those dragons we lost during the war did not 'disappear' as claimed."

I nodded, and bade him to please continue with a gesture of my hand.

"*Parts,* it seems, are popping up everywhere you look. Some are counterfeit, and some—like this piece—are not. There's a black market for everything these days, and our royal guess is that they were simply waiting for the terms of the provisional treaty to get laid down before they began to—what is the phrase? Ah yes." His tone was grim. "Hawk their wares."

I had never heard the Esar sound so angry. I knew somehow that he never would have spoken so in an audience chamber, with servants and officials present, but my meetings with the Esar were always unofficial and therefore we were always alone. If I hadn't been such a queer thing,

I'm sure such clandestine trysts would have made the Esarina suspect us—though as one palace guard had put it, *You can't be much for kissing with no tongue in that head.*

I smoothed my skirts, straightening them over my knees while I thought about how to put my question. My now-deceased partner had made things travel at a much quicker pace. *All the more regrettable that he'd died,* I thought.

It was evident why the Esar had called me here. His intent was always straightforward: I was to track down those responsible for selling the charred remains of his dragons to the public. Not for sentimentality, as I already knew he was not a sentimental man, but for safety and security. Pride, too, was a factor, but the Esar was not what moralists would call a bad man, nor one foolishly governed by his own feelings.

If Volstov's enemies happened to get their hands on what had once been our prize, the consequences would not bear thinking about.

The provisions of wartime that had allowed the Esar to commission the dragons in the first place presumably no longer existed. And while the members of the bastion argued with the members of the Basquiat, our neighboring enemies all would scramble to re-create what had once been our most efficient weapons. How unfortunate that would be. It was now in my hands, this ability to avoid more unnecessary conflict; the tragedy of needless, violent deaths; the escalation of tensions between border-sharing countries. Even above my duty to the Esar, I was a patriot down to my bones. This task suited me well.

I had a special skill in tracking. I did not tire with the same frequency as men sent to do the same tasks, and I had given up my speech for skills immeasurably more useful than simply talking.

"We want you to find them," the Esar went on. "If you are helped by smaller, trifling pieces such as this, then you are to collect those as well, but know this: It is not for simple scraps that we send you. After the destruction of our dragons, certain key parts remain *missing*. Chief among these was a piece entirely unique: the soul of a dragon."

If I'd had a tongue, I'd have found difficulty in holding it here, suggesting that instead my lord might seek a Brother of Regina to accomplish this task, if taking hold of a soul was involved. If I had no confirmation of my own, how would I know a dragon's when I saw one?

He seemed to know what I was thinking, as he often did. It was part of why we worked so well together.

"We are looking for one in particular. In light of this, we have ordered blueprints up from the bastion, that you might study them and know what it is you're looking for. Return to us what is rightfully ours. We cannot make ourselves any clearer."

I'd done far more difficult things in the past. Indeed, despite the gravity of his words, and the current imperiousness of his affectations, the Esar had almost made this task too easy for me. He had given me something to go on—a piece of one of the dragons themselves.

The stench of the burned, warped metal filled my nose, but there were countless other scents at play as well: the cold of the Cobalt Mountain Range, their deep blue rocks laced with dolerite, and the countless excited hands passing over its twisted features. The land of the Ke-Han Empire . . . and places yet farther south, spiced with the flavors of the desert.

That was where I would begin my search.

There was only one problem, one I had nearly forgotten in the giddy rush of smells emanating from my task. With no partner, it would be next to impossible to gather information of the sort I needed. Tracking the culprits depended strongly on word of mouth, and I could not trust enough in luck to hope I would always be at the right place at the right time to overhear all the information vital to my mission.

I would need a voice, but I had no partner to give me one.

Besides that, I had a difficult nature and wouldn't work easily with just anyone.

I passed my hand over my throat, bare of the jewelry that was so in fashion these days, since the scent of metals and stones interfered with my thinking.

The Esar, not the most observant man I'd ever known but nonetheless one of the shrewdest, seemed to understand at once.

"We have not yet located a replacement for your partner. As time is short, we had the magicians at the Basquiat cook a little something up for you that should give you the assistance you require without the troubles of partnership."

He reached for something hidden in shadows at his end of the table. I'd noted it upon entering, then allowed it to slide from my mind as the conversation proceeded and the Esar made no reference to it. Every man should be allowed to keep his own secrets, and men such as the

Esar demanded that respect. I was only a silent observer; I wooed not through flattering speech but through the conscientiousness of my efforts—a silent flattery that required more observation than most could muster.

The Esar gestured, peremptorily, that I was to stand. It was the closest we had ever been, and I made note of the fact that his precious Antoinette was not currently with him. Had she been, she would have brought the box to me rather than allowing me to get so close.

He was uncomfortable with me beside him. I was not the sort of woman who put him at ease, despite all my attempts to reassure him. Still, he needed me, and that went a long way toward making him accept my presence.

It was humorous, I thought, that a man such as he would smell of country dishes beneath his cologne. Even though he wore the most expensive silk—imported, I could tell at once, from Seon—he nonetheless smelled of stew, the main ingredients of which were tomatoes and eggplants, which at once felt homely and relaxed. Whatever he had dined on, it was not the same dishes that were currently in fashion and which the members of the bastion—and those pretentious socialites in the Basquiat—currently swooned over.

I bowed my head to hide my smile.

"I'd never have imagined I'd be giving such an item to you," the Esar said, with the same ruefulness as an innkeeper offering his wife a token of the many years of their marriage. The item in question was a second box—one with equally little ornament, but its contents were far more complicated. I knelt beside my liege and observed him as he took from the box a sweet little necklace.

The Esar knew I did not wear jewelry, but only the faint scent of deep water came forth from this trinket.

He fastened it around my neck and it settled, all at once, in the hollow where my two collarbones met. I could feel it sinking against the skin—an uncomfortable sensation, not unlike being choked.

"Speak, Malahide," the Esar said.

That was impossible, or so I had always assumed. A brief blossom of fear awoke inside of me—I had bartered my voice for my powers, and this would be akin to cheating whatever gods had made such bargains possible in the first place. I had been a quiet child, weedy and recalcitrant, even for an inhabitant of the orphanage in which I'd been brought up. When my own seedling of Talent was discovered, after I'd taken great pains to make sure it blossomed in the first place, I was brought in front of the Esar. He'd been searching in his own quiet ways for children of a certain caliber who might be trained to work for him outside the influence of the Basquiat. With no friends to speak of, and little to occupy my time, I'd jumped at the chance to have something to apply myself toward. To have a purpose in life was a wealth that could never be measured. It was one for which I had been willing to make any sacrifice in order to hold on to. It was something that other people found difficult to understand, but for me the decision had always been easy.

I swallowed and was reminded of the heavy bead digging into my flesh. A strange warmth overcame my throat.

"My liege," I said, speaking for the first time in ten years.

The sound of my own voice did not come out with rusty hesitance, nor did it startle me. In point of fact, it seemed so distant and so foreign from my own conception of myself that I was not bothered by it at all, though I would have to learn to use my mouth to pretend I was forming the words. The voice itself echoed up through the depths of my throat, like some distant puppeteer casting his voice to his puppet, and it seemed fitting that the Esar would be behind this sleight of hand. His magicians were capable of truly commendable work.

The Esar observed me with his head tilted and his eyes bright—a handsome man, though far from my type. It was a stroke of luck that I was far from his.

"A pretty voice," he said. "It hardly suits you."

"I will have to make it suit me," I said, and was dismissed.

MADOKA

On the border between Seon and Xi'An territory, nestled between marshland and the desert, was the village where I was born. It was shit and everyone knew it, but we had some kind of deep-down Ke-Han pride that always kept us thinking of it. Even those of us who were lucky enough to get away from it and find ourselves in what city folk would have called *a real city* couldn't wash it off our skin.

After all I'd seen, though, I didn't much care for real cities one bit.

I'd been in the capital when the dragons came, and I'd seen every weakness that a city had to offer. Buildings that fell because the ones beside them had already fallen; the earth shaking the towers above it, turning years of hard labor into fine dust; men and women trampling their neighbors to protect themselves; walls, designed to protect, keeping their charges from escaping to safety. And, most deadly of all, fires that spread faster than a man could run, from one district to the next, leaving char and ash in their wake, bones and wood alike burned into blackness.

It wasn't a pretty sight.

You could sum it up with poetry or you could put it out of your mind, and the longer I dwelled on it, the less time I slept. So I tried not to think about where I'd been or what I'd seen. If I gave it enough time, everything would be rebuilt—like nothing had ever happened at all, and I hadn't been burning my hands picking debris from debris days after the fires had finally died down.

I was asleep, dreaming of sunlight glinting off sand, when the old woman woke me. We'd left the capital at around the same time heading south, and ended up traveling together when I'd caught her going through my bags for food.

"Madoka," she said. "They're rounding up the scavengers."

"Shit," I said, still half-asleep, and the old woman smacked me in back of my head hard enough to take care of that.

"Watch that mouth," she told me, tugging at my arm and all but pulling me out of the pile of rags and discarded garments I'd turned into a bed. It wasn't as comfortable as it could have been, but it sure as shit beat sleeping on the ground.

The old lady was as shriveled up as a dried leaf, but not nearly so fragile, and when she had a mind toward doing something it was best just to go along with it.

I shook her off and started scooping clothes off the ground, pulling them on one by one—layers of cotton and silks discarded for the scorch marks on them. The old woman said it made me look like a madwoman or a minstrel—neither of them being a desirable identity—but I liked to travel with everything I'd need all at once in case I ran into any difficulties—difficulties like this one. I tied my sash at my waist, cinching everything together, then hoisted my pack up over my shoulders.

One day, when people had money to buy things again, all this would be worth something.

"Any point in trying to get a head start?" I asked, already knowing what the answer'd be. There was no point in trying to run from the emperor's soldiers since they'd take your own family just as gladly as they'd take you.

I'd left most of my family behind a long time ago, but that didn't mean I was looking to get an unpleasant reminder. Important men didn't like it when someone made them feel unimportant, and they'd do all they could to remind you just how important they were.

"Even *you* aren't as foolish as all that," the old woman said, fixing my hair like I was the hopeless case she'd always called me. What good would fixing my hair do when I looked like this? I was a big girl—taller than all my brothers and broader than some of them too. I wasn't, as the old woman was fond of saying, the marrying kind, but I guess I was all right with that. If I'd been born some flittering little moon princess, I'd hardly have managed half so well on my own in the Ke-Han countryside. "Go on. Maybe one of those handsome soldiers'll take a liking to you and you can move out of this hole in the ground."

"Just what I've always wanted," I said, pulling a face and dropping low to avoid the swipe of her hand. It was a harder feat to accomplish with the pack on my shoulders and so many layers making me slow, but I managed it somehow.

The old woman pushed the tent flap aside and bright light flooded in. Outside, hard-faced men in disciplined lines were organizing us into groups, digging through bags and storming into the half-ruined houses without even knocking. They weren't shouting—they'd probably gotten enough of that during the war—but they managed to have the same effect. We'd long since been warped by years of tradition and wartime duty to do whatever an official told us.

A convenient system for our emperor, no doubt, but one that spoke very little of the will of the people under him.

It made me sick, but I was a part of it too, and like my village I could hardly cut it out of my being. Even if it *was* shit.

I shouldered my bag and strode out into the sunlight, sand crunching beneath my sandals and last night's grit caught between my toes. I could see now that there were caravans, big ones, meant for transporting people as well as cargo. I didn't like the looks of them, or what it meant that they were there in the first place, but I had enough brains in my head not to run at the first sight of something that spooked me.

"You there," said one of the soldiers.

"Me here?" I asked, pointing, but he just took me by the elbow and pushed me into one of the scattered lines slowly being formed.

Soldiers never listened to what the common folk had to say, but that had never stopped me from trying to say it. It was an attitude that would one day land me in more trouble than I was looking for, according to the old woman, but I'd gotten lucky so far. I planned on staying that way.

Plus, I was pissed at being interrupted right in the middle of a good dream for some last-minute examination. All we had was trash anyway—nothing the higher-ups would ever want to use. It was funny how the emperor hadn't given a shit what we took from the capital back when it'd still been burning and he didn't want to dig through anything himself. But now that other people had gone and done the dirty work for him, he could just follow after them and collect what he liked, simpler than sifting through a whole pile of dirt.

In short, the whole deal pissed me off, but there wasn't much I could do about it now. I spat on the ground and adjusted one strap on my pack. Maybe if I looked angry enough—and stupid enough, on top of that—they'd think I was a waste of time and go right by me. It was a long shot, but I was willing to take whatever I could.

I wasn't about to let them get ahold of what *I'd* found.

Besides that, I wasn't too keen on giving up the little things either.

We could use this crap—make clothes, wrap our babies in it, see to it that kids had proper shoes. Up at the top of the heap, all it would do was gather dust at best; at worst, it'd burn. But wasn't that just like power? Someone had to make sure things stayed the way they were— poor people having nothing and rich people having even the things they didn't want or need.

At the end of my line was another soldier sitting at a long table; he was wearing a hat, which meant he was more important than the others even though he looked a hell of a lot younger from where I was standing. I could tell what kind of man *he* was without him having to say a word—shirt neatly pressed, cuffs stiff and clean, medals gleaming like he polished them every morning alongside his shoes. Only the young ones had the energy to be that spic-and-span about every little detail. What someone like *him* was doing in charge of this operation was beyond me, but there was no money to be made in speculating so I didn't waste my time doing it.

When he lifted his head I could see the poor bastard had a long, ugly scar running up through the center of his cheek and—mercifully—just to the left of one eye. It was the kind of thing you got when something tried to rip half your face off and didn't quite succeed, which I guess was why he was so young and so important in his hat and all. If he noticed me staring, he didn't say a thing, only folded his hands together on the table and lifted his chin like he was real sure of himself and used to it.

"Open the bag," he barked.

Being an obedient little lady of the realm, I swung it off my shoulders and onto the table with a thump. The soldier looked angry, which meant that I'd taken him by surprise and I felt pretty satisfied about that. Less satisfied came afterward, when he snapped his fingers and two soldiers set to undoing the buckles and tabs that kept my pack together, not to mention keeping everything inside it.

I bit down on the inside of my cheek. It wasn't my stuff anyway, not to begin with. Besides, I was a woman and a peasant, and I had no rights even to things I'd been born with, like hope and dignity and pride. The old woman was always saying my tongue'd be the death of me if I survived the war. Thinking about the smug way she'd laugh if she turned out to be right was all that kept me silent while the soldiers tore through my findings—like patterned cloth too big or still too torn to wear, and things I'd thought to send to my mother once I got the time and the money. There were other things too, smaller and more fragile, bundled in the fabric to keep them safe from the kind of treatment they were getting now.

One soldier pulled loose a smaller bundle I'd made, strips of deep, heart's blood purple wrapped around my prize. I stiffened, hands clenched behind my back, and if they'd thought to have soldiers holding me they'd have noticed straightaway, only they hadn't planned for that. Because I was only a woman, probably, or maybe because they just didn't have the manpower for that anymore. Whatever the reason, I was seconds away from leaping across the table and snatching what was mine back from that soldier's hands. The only thing stopping me was thinking up the best way to do it.

What they unwrapped was a hunk of metal, scorched black along the back and twisted from the heat of the fires I'd found it in. There was a clock face set into the front—I'd grabbed it at first because I'd thought it was a watch and maybe if I got it working again I could use it to tell the time—but instead of numbers there were only symbols, strange and foreign. I'd been about to throw it back when the pieces had started moving. What I'd assumed to be the hands for telling time, a sculpted arrow and a broken spring, suddenly aligned like the hands of the weirdest damned compass I'd ever seen—the other two were still—and both pointed toward the wreck of the magician's dome, where the fires had burned the hottest and most scavengers still feared to go.

That was where I'd discovered my real treasure: the shiny, smooth scales of a Volstovic fire-breather, those monsters that had decided the war for good. I'd turned up three scales and one mean-looking claw; I'd sold the claw first and the others pretty quick after that, once word started to spread.

Even if there wasn't money for food, there was still money enough for *that*.

I wasn't some kind of sentimental fool out to keep a memento of the monsters that'd ruined us, and if some idiot wanted to feed me and my family for the privilege of sentiment? Well, that was fine by me.

The hands on my find hadn't so much as twitched since I'd left the capital, but that didn't mean I wasn't still checking it regular, every night before I went to bed and every morning when I woke up, and periods in between when no one was looking too.

"What is this?" The soldier with the scar snapped to, all of a sudden, taking my prize in his hands and holding it up to the light, blunt fingers twisting the hands around like he was trying to set it to the right time.

The clumsy oaf was going to break it.

A fool would've hit him, but I had better control over myself than that. I shrugged, trying not to look like I cared one way or another. "I found it," I said. "I don't know what it does."

"Perhaps you haven't heard, but there's a rumor going around about scavengers selling government-owned property on the black market," he said, like we were on speaking terms all of a sudden when he hadn't so much as said "boo" to me this whole time we'd been standing across the table from one another. *Soldiers.* Arrogant as peacocks, the lot of them, and none so handsome. He'd probably been waiting for just the right time to impress upon me who was in charge and who wasn't. "Things that *should have* fallen under the terms of the provisional treaty. That sort of action is treasonous."

"I wouldn't know anything about that," I sniffed. Maybe once things'd been settled in the capital it'd start spreading outward, but I wasn't holding my breath.

"It would be convenient for you if I believed that," he said. "I think we'll take you along with us."

"To the capital?" I asked, before I remembered I wasn't supposed to speak. The old woman would've got me good with her stick for that one, and I would've deserved it.

The soldiers exchanged a look. They'd started shoving things this way and that back into my bag, but I noticed they were still holding on to my prize—like they didn't plan on giving it back to me ever. I didn't like to admit it, but I was getting anxious. And anytime I was anxious, I got pissed off.

"Somewhere much closer than that," my friend in the hat answered me, finally. He pulled me close by one of my seven sleeves, all of them layered like I was some kind of princess straight out of a fairy tale. At least I was tall enough that he didn't tower over me, and I did my best not to stare right at that giant scar. "Tell me, country girl: Have you heard of the magicians' city?"

I wanted to tell him all that was a bedtime story. Shit like that wasn't real anymore, and maybe it'd never been real to begin with, either. But I bit back on my anti-national way of thinking and looked away, off toward the cracked dome of the magician's tower, lying overturned in a heap of its own rubble. Hatty'd take my drift.

"Commoners," he said, and shook his head as he pocketed the one piece of treasure I'd ever held in my hands. "You're coming with us."

I had no choice, so I went.

CHAPTER TWO

THOM

This was not the first time I'd ever been a part of a barroom brawl. However, it was the first time I had ever participated actively in one.

It was difficult to deny Rook when he issued a command—something he'd learned, no doubt, from Chief Sergeant Adamo and saved only for special occasions. There was more power behind an order when it was bellowed in unfamiliar tones, making a man who'd otherwise remain neutral fall into a sudden alliance from which he could not withdraw. It was, in some ways, the most basic strategic lesson I had been given, inside the 'Versity or out.

And so I had allowed myself to become a hooligan.

While it wounded my pride, the main source of hurt was in my knuckles, which were swollen beyond my capacity to move them.

I didn't even remember the face of the man I'd struck—it might just as well have been a woman, save for the faint imprint of what seemed to be a beard spread across my stiffened fist. If we were arrested, which we might well be, I had no excuses or even any explanations. I had simply punched a man because Rook had told me to, and it was all over some item, now tightly secured in Rook's hands, which I couldn't even identify.

"Didn't know you could fight like that," Rook said moodily, the sound of his voice cutting through my troubled thoughts and bringing me, somewhat miserably, back down to earth.

"You forget my upbringing," I replied.

Rook snorted. "I wasn't there for it," he said. Then, perhaps because that was too much even for him, he fell silent again.

We were in our rooms now, after being mobbed by an entire innful of country folk incensed at being insulted. And why shouldn't they have been, I asked myself, since Rook had called them all thieves, liars, and the women whores. No one would take very kindly to that treatment, and they had only reacted as they saw fit. Besides which, he had confiscated something of theirs.

I didn't blame them, but still I had fought them tooth and nail. Even now, I felt it necessary to apologize, or at least to offer the innkeeper payment. At this very moment, he was no doubt calculating the extra cost to us for staying in his establishment and doing our level best to tear it down before we set out to our next target.

"Rook," I said, drawing in a steadying breath. "Since I have now been involved in actions I . . . am not entirely proud of . . ." Rook snorted again, and I tried to ignore it. "I'm waiting for an explanation," I concluded at length. "Any reason at all for why we . . . Anything, really, would suffice."

Rook's face was twisted into an expression of such deep unhappiness that, at first, it might have passed for anger. In point of fact, even I drew back, before the sum total of his features—his hard jaw, his tight lips, the redness around his eyes and the whiteness around his mouth—brought me up short.

I had misread the situation—somehow—and on top of that, I was not the sort of partner he'd wanted.

Of course not. I wasn't one of the boys. Brawling was *not* my specialty, and I did not enjoy the rush of simple pleasure brought on by physical fights.

But there was some other key element lacking—something that had to do with camaraderie—and when I thought too long or too well upon the subject, my heart began to hurt.

I tried to move my hand to distract myself. That pain was simple and immediate, and it was a momentary distraction. A dirty tactic, but for the time being it would serve its purpose.

"Like I said before things went to piss," Rook muttered, "they had a fucking piece of Magoughin's girl, all right?"

I glanced down at the box in Rook's hand, trying to follow. His words had barely made sense—and then someone had made a grab for the box, and he'd thrown the first punch, and after that all was chaos. Hitting and kicking and clawing—all manner of action that drove real thought straight from a person's head.

He'd said that before—*our girls*—but it hadn't occurred to me at the time what he was actually talking about.

"Chastity?" I said.

"Yeah," Rook agreed. His mouth twisted to the left, then resettled into its grim, hard line, like the slashed mouth of a ritual mask from the distant south. Those masks were meant to frighten away the curses placed upon a family by one's ancestors. I would have explained the dark humor to Rook if I hadn't already known the outcome: *Shut up, Professor. Shut the fuck up.* "You've still got all that memorized, huh?"

"You do, as well," I pointed out.

"That's different," Rook snapped, and he was right.

I steadied myself to be brave enough for my next question. "May I see it?"

"It's nothing special," Rook said. "Just a fucking scale, nothing important. What good's looking at it gonna do? Fuck me." He lifted the box, though, as if he were about to slam it down on the table in front of us, then set it down gently, popping open the top. There it was, a scale indeed, though I personally would never have recognized it. I knew very little of the dragons themselves—I'd been given no real time to study them, and mechanics had never been my strong suit. In point of fact, what little I did know was of their riders. If this was Chastity, then it was as much a piece of Magoughin as it was a piece of metal.

I reached forward to touch it with my bad hand, and Rook whistled.

"Looks like that hurts," he said.

I sniffed. "It does. Quite a bit, actually."

"You bunched your fist too tight, that's why," Rook explained. "You made the muscles too tight. You gotta make your fist go loose—less bruising that way."

The theory made anatomical sense. "I hope I never have to put that advice into practice, in any case," I said.

"Well, don't say I never taught you anything," Rook muttered.

"I wouldn't exactly say that."

Rook got real close to me, his eyes crazy in a way I hadn't seen them get for a long time. "That some kind of insult?"

"A compliment," I managed, voice coming out distinctly strangled. "I believe I intended it to be a compliment."

"We're getting sidetracked anyway," Rook said, wheeling away and stalking to the window. "What the fuck do you think about that thing?"

"About the dragonscale?" I asked, knowing already what the answer was. But I was buying time to think my answer over, foolishly convincing myself that if I put enough thought into it, I could divine the *right* answer, the one that would assure Rook he hadn't been completely out of his mind to take me along.

I stretched my hand uneasily, trying to keep it from getting too stiff. I was treading on unsteady ground, and the hard lines of Rook's back were as unforgiving as they'd ever been—even back in the days before we'd known what we were to one another. I stared at the dragonscale on the table, trying to mold my thoughts around the twisted shape of it.

The problem was, I'd never been as close to the dragons as I'd been to the men—one had to call them men, even if other words were preferable—who'd ridden them, and I'd been somewhat reluctant to raise the topic during my time spent traveling with Rook. How did one broach such a delicate subject? Thus far, we'd never addressed the dragons or what had happened to them at all, to say nothing of those members of the corps still living—or those now lost to us forever.

I'd written letters at first, and shared the responses willingly enough with Rook, until he'd pointed out that he didn't give two shits whether Ghislain had bought a ship or not, or what classes Adamo was lecturing in. After that, it seemed best to keep both my letters and my theories to myself.

Rook had left Thremedon, and, it seemed, all thoughts of Thremedon as well.

All that, however, had been before I'd been foolish enough to get myself involved in Rook's business as though it really were my own. The delicate throbbing in my hand told me it was too late to retract my support and, what was more, I'd spent enough time stalling.

I could hear his teeth grinding together in impatience from where I sat.

"Well," I said, clearing my throat when my voice came out too dry for my liking. "During the last attack on the capital, there were only four dragons that made it back to Thremedon . . . And then *you* came back, of course, but not . . ." Rook grunted and I switched gears immediately. "What I mean to say is that, assuming things progressed as they'd initially been decided, the Esar would have had what remained of those four surviving dragons . . . destroyed, in keeping with the provisional treaty. And if that's the case, that still leaves ten dragons that went down in or around Xi'An's capital. I'm sure they would have done their best to recover and destroy the majority of the . . . ah, bodies. I hear from Balfour that most of those vital remains have been recovered. And it's my understanding that after the destruction of the dome, the population of Ke-Han magicians was considerably depleted. I'd imagine that's their chief concern right now, as opposed to gathering up the fallen pieces of dragons. However, it's possible that pieces here and there went overlooked. In war and in recovery, there is always something left unaccounted for."

"So," Rook said, and I fell silent once again. "What you're *sayin'* is that there's a chance someone out there's got pieces of our girls all carved up to auction off to the highest bidder."

"Not exactly," I said, fingering the scale while I thought. Its edges were sharp, whereas Magoughin had been all blunt corners. It was strange for me to have such vivid memories of men I'd never considered my friends—sometimes far too vivid for my liking, infiltrating my waking hours as well as my dreams. Thinking about them made me feel strange, like missing the bottom step upon a staircase or returning to a series of notes I'd made, only to find them all in disarray, the contents shuffled and some missing entirely.

I couldn't imagine how Rook felt to think about it, but I hadn't yet worked up the courage to ask.

"You gonna elaborate on that thought, or are you just waitin' for me to come over there and *extract* it?" Rook turned around, features ablaze, lip curled in a snarl.

I put the scale down quickly. Fortunately, I was too frightened of the consequences to drop it.

"I think it's likely that . . . certain smaller parts, such as this, may have escaped the initial cleanup," I explained. "I've read from certain accounts that there are often scavengers who turn a profit on rare items like these, and that's likely where our friend downstairs obtained his piece. It seems to me that such tasks would be best accompanied with a liberal side of secrecy, however, since if the emperor were to get word of such a business getting under way . . . But no doubt it has a great deal to do with rumor, authenticity, that sort of—"

"I don't give a shit about any of that," Rook snapped, looking as though he was regretting not throwing me out the window. He stalked back over to me, picked up the box that held the scale, and slammed his other hand down onto the table for emphasis. "What I want to know is if some rat bastard is out there with bits and pieces of *her,* showing 'em off for kicks in some backwater shit hole like this. That question plain enough for you, Professor?"

I should have known it would come to this—insults and nicknames recycled from a time we'd never quite escape.

I resisted the urge to draw away, since that would have been akin to retreat and Rook knew all too well how to scent blood in the water. Instead I forced myself to think the matter over as quickly and carefully as I could, knowing what the outcome would be no matter what I said.

He was angry; he was desperate for someone to blame. And I was the likeliest candidate since I was already there.

"There's a chance," I said at last, a faint band of regret forming tight around my heart. "There's always a chance. To my knowledge, Havemercy was never recovered, and : . ." I trailed off, the name sounding like blasphemy on my lips.

More than anything, I did not want to send my brother on a wild-goose chase to try to recover something that had long since been lost. False hope, no matter its intentions, was never kind. But Rook was a grown man—perhaps slightly overgrown in some respects—and it was hardly my place to tell him what to do. He could decide for himself where he went and why, and would no doubt do exactly that no matter what I said to him.

"*Fuck* the hanging gardens," he said, shutting the box top and picking it up. "I'm gonna go have a little chat with the man that gave me this and see if we can't learn a little more about *exactly* where it came from."

I stood up, muscles aching in protest over what I'd already put them through. "Are you sure that's a good idea?" I asked. As always, it was only a formality. I had developed a new instinct when it came to my brother's actions—a kind of self-preservation born of desperation. It was necessary, for our sanity—and, at times, for our survival—that I be prepared for the punches he threw my way.

He barely spared a glance in my direction.

"Get in my way and I'll leave you here. I mean it this time."

I didn't doubt him. "Is there anything I can do?" I asked, sounding desperate even to myself. Despite all my protestations, I was his younger brother, and I wanted, more than anything, to be useful.

Silly Thom, I thought. *You haven't changed.*

"I'll do the talking," Rook said, pocketing the box with one hand and jerking his other toward my travel log. "You can write things down."

MADOKA

Where was I?

That was a damn good question. It was also a question I didn't have a proper answer for, seeing as how my friends the cleanup brigade had blindfolded me nice and gentle and kept a knife in my side as insurance. On the one hand, I hated being kept in the dark; but on the other, it might've meant I'd get out of this alive, now that I had absolutely no real information about where I was or how I'd gotten there. Hopefully, I could wiggle my way out of this one on the strength of being stupid, but it didn't seem likely. It was the best defense I'd cultivated, and not even years of being poor and a woman had managed to strip that from me.

They sure had me good, though, taking me by wagon, then by foot, turning me this way and that so my head couldn't focus on any one direction. All I really had to go by was the sound our feet made on the ground once we'd gotten down off the cart, and even that wasn't giving me much. All I really knew for certain was that we weren't outside anymore when we finally stopped for good, and the air itself was damp and kind of cold. The rest was silence. I tried to make like I was too dumb for paying attention, so maybe, in the end, I could go back to the rest of the world and laugh at everyone, telling them I could make it out of anything alive. Just like a rat. The old woman'd probably clout me a good one with her stick, but I could even look forward to that if it meant getting out of here in one piece.

Footsteps signaled the arrival of some new asshole. I braced myself.

"You are being treated quite poorly," an unfamiliar voice said. "I apologize for that."

"Sure," I said. "Sounds great."

"You should not deny what small kindnesses we allow you," the voice said, falsely sympathetic, and I bit the inside of my cheek. "You are in a disadvantageous position. Please, take off her blindfold."

Aw, shit, I thought, *don't go doing that,* but it was too late and now I could see everything: dim light and shadows and rock, like we were in some kind of storage cellar. If this was the famous magicians' city, then I was one disappointed commoner right now. Then again, maybe Hatty had been full of it when he'd told me that was where we were going.

I'd never seen a magician up close before, but if I had to guess, I'd say I was looking at one right now. The man standing in front of me was dressed simply but I knew by the way he held himself that he was somebody important, even with how young he was. He was holding my treasure—I guessed I should call it a compass, not having any other name for it—and I focused my eyes on that because it was something I recognized, at least.

"I suppose it is clear by now that we wish to know where you found this," he said. His robes were blue, the color of a real Ke-Han patriot, and his head was shaved down to the bone. That look worked on some people, but his skull had too many knobbly bits.

"It's garbage," I told him. "Some people collect that."

"You're a profiteer," he said. "You seek to benefit from the empire's loss."

"Somebody needs to, all due respect," I replied.

His lip twitched at the corner. He wasn't a soldier and he wasn't nobility, because he had real facial expressions—the sort of thing you never saw in people who carried themselves like he did. "There is no respect in that," he said, touching the curved body of the compass gently, in a way that made me uncomfortable. He could stop making love to it anytime now and I'd feel a whole lot better. "You've sold parts—parts like this one?"

"Not really," I said, and gritted my jaw. "No use in selling the good stuff."

"And why is that?"

"I think," said my old friend, Hatty with the scar, "she hopes to make a greater profit when there is greater profit to be had."

The stranger whirled on me without further warning—he was trying to intimidate me physically, and he had the element of surprise on his side, so damn me if it didn't work. "Do you have, or have you had, in your possession, any pieces similar to this one?" he demanded.

"Nothing like that," I said. "You want me to swear on something?"

The stranger smiled. "Your life will serve."

Great. A fucking crazy person was in charge of me now. At least with Hatty I'd known where I stood since it was easy to know where you stood with a soldier: Keep quiet and they'll usually do the same. Safest thing to do with a crazy person, I reasoned, was to go along with whatever craziness he was spouting and hope he didn't change directions midthought just to trip me up.

I held out my hands, palms down like I was bowing, only I wasn't about to get on my knees in a place like this. No telling *what* was on the ground in a storage cellar, even a storage cellar that attracted men as fancy as this one.

"On my life," I said. "I *swear* I only found that one. But it seems to me like it's the sort of thing you only find once, if you don't mind my speculating."

"Indeed," my interrogator said thoughtfully, turning my prize this way and that, the way a squirrel might fiddle with a nut until he found the best place for sinking his teeth in. "So there is some humility in that head of yours, after all. Still, perhaps I ought to have phrased my question better."

He raised his head. I hadn't looked into his eyes before, but just as I did it seemed to me that something passed over the surface of them, flickering and pale as a ghost. I'd have jumped backward if Hatty hadn't been standing beside me, that knife stashed away but not forgotten. I wasn't giving him any excuses to use it. Still, there was no denying those eyes. Every kid in Xi'An knew how to pick out a Ke-Han magician. They bargained with the spirits to get their powers, and they ended up with ghosts in their eyes. I was glad the old woman hadn't been taken along with me now, since she probably would've dropped dead of shock right on the spot. Even I felt a little weird about it. I'd thought all the magicians had been killed in the dome.

"By your word, this piece is the only one of such rarity that you've discovered, is that correct?" He went on without waiting for an answer, just another man who liked to hear himself speak. "I will ask you, then, whether or not the reason you have *kept* this piece instead of selling it off is that you feel it will be of a greater profit in your hands."

I wanted to ask why he thought he was the one who could be asking questions in the first place, some magician with goddamned ghosts in his eyes, but I was still playing stupid and that meant not drawing any attention to myself. It was probably just some trick to intimidate me, mixing it up so it wasn't *just* his height and his creepy, sudden movements. He'd thought this out. Either that or he'd been at it a long time, and either way it didn't bear much thinking about.

It was what it was. He was fucked up.

I didn't want to let anyone in on my little secret, but I didn't want to die down here in some forsaken storage cellar either, with no one to write home to the people waiting for me.

That was why they'd taken me in the first place, I figured. No one to come looking for me if things turned bad quick.

"I don't know what it does," I said, just so we were all clear on that up front. "I'm no genius like yourself or anything. I just picked it up because I thought it looked interesting. And that's all it was, at first."

"At first," he repeated, seizing on that like an eel on some hapless fish. "Which means that your understanding of the object changed from the time of your first theorization. Oh, no; I'm not interrupting you. I wouldn't dream of it. Please do continue."

If Hatty hadn't been such a slaphappy bitch to deal with himself, this was where he and I might have shared a look of camaraderie, because this guy we were *both* dealing with was clearly out of it. In a big way.

"Right," I said, because my mother always told me it was safest to agree with a madman. "That's what I said. Only when I picked it up, the little hands started flying all over the place. I thought it was broken for sure, but then they stopped . . ." It pissed me off, but right about now, I didn't know how else to explain it.

"They aligned, didn't they?" The stranger had started pacing again, his back to me and my escort, hunkered down over my compass like it was the emperor's feet and he just couldn't wait to pay his respects. "Like the hands of a compass, only it wasn't true north they guided you to. No; it was something far more elusive than that, wasn't it?"

He startled me again by looking up; his gaze hit me like a strong wind, unexpected and chill.

"I . . . guess you could say it was like that," I said. We were getting into information that I wasn't all that comfortable sharing with other people, but I supposed between that and a quiet death underground, I'd take a little discomfort any day. Besides, rats survived so well because they *were* rats. They knew when to keep quiet and they knew when to squeal.

"What did you find when you followed it?" the madman asked, bringing his ghost eyes up close to my face this time. He smelled a little strange, sweet and bitter at the same time, the way madness might have smelled if it could've taken a physical form. Or maybe it was just whatever he'd eaten at lunch. Either way, the combination was making my stomach turn.

"Other pieces," I said, wrinkling my nose and hoping it wouldn't show in the dark. "Nothing like that, like I said before, but little things. Small prizes. That thing's like a ready-made treasure detector, if there's treasure to be found."

"Ah," said the madman. He was breathing on me, and I wanted to ask if he'd ever had a mother who'd taught him about manners and personal space and all those little niceties men seemed to plumb forget about when they were outside the capital. I held my tongue, but it was tough going. "It led you right to them, didn't it? Like a helpful little bloodhound."

"Never had a dog," I said, "so I wouldn't know about that. But as for the rest of it . . . yeah, you could say that. I don't know anything about how it works, though, so if you're looking for more answers, I'm all out."

"Of course you wouldn't. It's incredibly precise." The madman brushed me off with a gesture of his hand, retreating once again to fiddle with my compass. I took a grateful breath of stale cellar air while I could. Meanwhile, he was muttering to himself—things that I couldn't quite catch and might not've understood if I had been able to, but his fingers never stopped moving, roving over the metal's surface and shaping the sharp point of the one unbroken hand like a blind man who thought he could memorize the thing.

"Do you know what this is?" he asked at last. "Do you know what you've brought us? *You*, of all people—a scavenger bird making your nest upon the corpse of his imperial reign? You're no better than a filthy animal, no matter how many fine fabrics you swathe yourself in . . . and yet here you are, with the greatest treasure I could ever hope to see in my lifetime."

"It's no good for finding gold," I said, to take the edge off how offended I was, which was: *plenty*. It took a lot of nerve for someone conducting meetings in a storage cellar to call someone *else* a filthy animal. At least I didn't spend my time in a hole under the ground—and on top of all that, *he* was the one who didn't have any common courtesy about him. "It doesn't find jewels either, just hunks of dragon, and then you've got your work cut out for you trying to convince anyone that's really what you've got and not a heap of twisted old scrap metal."

The madman clutched at his head like I'd hit him somewhere soft and vulnerable.

"Your stupidity pains me," he said. "Do I look like the sort of man who wishes to profit from selling spare parts to grasping fools?"

I could have told him *exactly* what sort of man he looked like, but I wasn't playing that kind of stupid.

I was nice instead, if a liar, and said, "No."

His fingers twitched as he held up the compass. Its hands were whirling in uncontrollable circles around its ash-clogged face, unable to find even a moment's rest. If he kept this up, he was probably going to break it—unless he knew exactly what he was doing, which scared me even more. There were some people in this world who were too smart for their own good, and this guy was one of them.

"Let me tell you a story," he said, eyes locked onto the compass like he couldn't drag them away. "Doubtless its countless nuances will be too much for a mind like yours to grasp, but I find myself compelled nonetheless, and it doesn't do to ignore one's compulsions—no, not at all. The story begins this way: Once there was a cellar mouse, the lowest form of creation with a spine. His mother was favored by the emperor, and even though the mouse was illegitimate, good for nothing, and would doubtless have benefited more from being smothered at birth, the emperor favored him too. They were even happy for a time, the mouse, his mother, and the emperor. But as everyone knows, happiness is a fleeting sensation, and those who aspire to owning it are met only with despair." He paused with his fingers on the face of the watch, though he didn't look up at me. "The rodent's mother died, and with her some part of the emperor himself. No longer could he bear to look at his child, who so resembled the woman he'd lost. Thus the mouse lost both his parents in swift succession." The hands on the compass face started spinning again, more rapidly than before. "One might *think* that to be the most crushing blow a man could suffer, but that was before the end of the war. Even though he'd been cast aside by the father he loved, the mouse felt his allegiance burning in him stronger than ever. The loss of the war was a mortal wound to the emperor, but the mouse vowed to restore his kingdom all the same."

I was starting to get a bad feeling about this guy, and not for the first time. Behind me, I could feel Hatty tense up like a dried squid and I knew that whatever he was thinking, it was along the same lines as me. Which said a lot, because weren't they supposed to be on the same side?

When you couldn't trust your own allies, what was the world coming to?

I was getting a little too theoretical for my own liking. I was pretty sure this story wasn't something he'd just made up out of the blue, either, and people who talked about themselves like they'd read a tale in a book were more than a little bat-shit crazed. I needed to get out of here, back to a world with dangers I could understand, like getting robbed in the night or losing a friend to disease. They weren't small by any means, but at least they made sense. They were predictable. This guy wasn't.

"What was Volstov's great advantage in the war?" the magician asked, drawing something out from behind his back while my heart hammered in my chest.

It took me a minute to realize I'd seen this thing before, even though recognizing it threw me for a loop at first. I'd been the one to find it—and, after that, I'd been the one to sell it, for a pretty fucking price, at that. So I knew before he got to his grand finish what it was he was planning on showing us. The closer to the compass he brought the piece—at first glance it was a hunk of twisted metal, the surface dull and burned on one side and fiercely polished on the other, exactly the way I'd found it—the wilder the motions of the hands became until, at last, they scissored to a stop. All four of them pointed to the piece of metal, curved and sharpened at one end like a lotus leaf.

I was pretty tempted to say something to the effect of *Yeah, I've seen that, and before you ever did too,* but I managed to restrain myself. I deserved a fucking medal.

"All right," I said. "That's pretty incredible."

"Your lack of imagination . . ." the madman began, then trailed off, like he didn't even think chastising me was worth his time.

"I've got a lot of imagination," I countered, just because I was too stupid to hold my tongue. "It's free, isn't it?"

"Then imagine *this,*" the madman said, thrusting the twisted hunk of metal right up into my face. "Imagine what the Ke-Han Empire could do if they harnessed the power of the dragons. Even a mouse could restore us, given the right materials for *re-creation.*"

A shiver ran down my spine. He was crazy all right; only a madman would dream of trying to start up a war it'd taken us one hundred years to end in the first place.

"What does that have to do with me?" I asked, holding my voice steady. "Why didn't you just take the thing for yourself and leave me to live out the rest of my uneventful, un*imaginative* life?"

"We find things for a reason," the madman said. "I believe in destiny. That you are so well suited for this task must be the trick of an ill-humored god, but I have never been one to ignore the signs. Unless, of course, it works in my favor."

If you believe in destiny, I thought, *then what do you think about our city now? Or the people starving in the streets for all anyone cares? Why not let the dragons be?*

Destiny wasn't the sort of thing I had any reason to believe in. And the people who did believe in it pissed me off something fierce. I eyed Hatty's dagger, wondering if I could get it away in time to arm myself and make a break for freedom.

Even if I could, that would've been too fucking stupid, even for me. Where did I think I'd go after that?

"All right," I said again. "I'll play this game. You want something from me. Let's get it out in the open."

"Aha," the madman said. The ghosts over his eyes settled into the shadows, coloring them faintly gray, and if that wasn't the creepiest sight I'd ever seen in my life, then I was prepared not to live much longer just so I wouldn't have to see what could top that. "The way I see it, matters are simple enough. You have two choices."

"And those are?" I asked, with more courage about my prospects than I felt.

"One: You die here," the madman said, simply, like he was telling me how much it'd be for that pound of rice. "You've seen enough of something far too important to continue your life as it is—and there's no doubt in my mind that you'd sell the information to the highest bidder, no matter what I might tell you of the repercussions." He paused to let that sink in, and I paused to agree with him. He was right, in a way. I'd sell that information, but not just for the money—I'd do it for a personal grudge as well, just to sink him in deep shit.

Next to me, Hatty cleared his throat, probably bored with proceedings and ready to get back to his wife and kids, or whatever it was he had at home. If he'd been as scared as I was before, he sure as hell wasn't showing it now.

"I see you're impatient," the madman continued. "Well, I will oblige you. We all have business to attend to. Very well, then; your second option is to give yourself up in service to your country after so much of your life has been devoted to matters *other* than patriotism. As you might have guessed, we are currently short on manpower. Tragically short, in fact. Most of us who still operate do so unbeknownst to his imperial greatness." He tilted his head, like he was imparting some big secret to me. "It's rumored that the first man among us who can restore the empire to its former glory will be honored for five generations. With such a prize on the line, you can hardly blame us for not working together."

"Real honorable," I said, but at least I didn't spit on the floor. "Why don't you send my friend here? He seems sturdy. He could probably handle it."

At my back, Hatty stiffened. *Ha-ha,* I thought. See how he liked it.

"Soldiers are suspect in these distressing times," the magician said. "We cannot deploy them as we might wish to, especially with an embassy from Volstov arriving at our capital in a matter of days. For this mission, we are in need of someone less impressive, less memorable, than a real hero. We are in need of a dung beetle."

It bothered me less that he'd called me a bug and more that he was referring to a mysterious "we"—like he could've been talking about anyone, and the last person to know who I'd be in cahoots with if I signed up for this shit was *me*.

I looked around nervously, momentarily caught Hatty's eye, and shared something with him I wish I hadn't: sympathy.

I ignored it. "You have no reason to trust me," I said. "Whatever you want me to do—I mean, supposing I even *could* do it—what tells you I wouldn't just up and run?"

"I've taken precautions against that," the madman said. Then, before I had time to react to that, he grabbed my hand with one of his and pressed the compass into my palm.

Light flashed through the room, about as sharp and bright as the pain that flashed through my hand. It was like reaching down for a piece of scrap metal that hadn't yet cooled off from the street fires, only about ten times worse. I could feel the burning in my blood, scorching white. And then, as soon as it had started, it was all over.

"I require a very special part of the Volstov dragons for my plan," I heard him say. "Only one survived the crashes at the end of the war. Some foolish creature ran off with this part after the capture of her pilot—thought he'd sell it, no doubt. The trick of it is he actually managed to unload the thing before I caught up with him. *That* is what I need, and it is the only thing I need, aside from your fair personage, of course; I can't be distracted by every discarded talon and scale scattered about our fair countryside. I've calibrated this device to find what I desire, and *only* that. Even a dung beetle should be able to handle so simple a task."

I blinked, tears sparking in the corners of my eyes. I wasn't about to let anyone see me cry, certainly not these bastards, but it was my body reacting to pain and not my heart reacting to any deeper hurt.

For there, implanted into the palm of my hand, was my treasure. It was the perfect size.

"You're going to need some gloves," the madman said.

ROOK

The facts, as my fucking blabbermouth brother was so fond of saying, were these:

That idiot with the broken face knew even less than I'd given him credit for. Either that, or he was the best liar I'd ever seen, but considering some of the shit I'd threatened him with, I doubted it. He didn't seem like the fucking type.

He'd bought the scale off some guy living in the Cobalt foothills— the kind of rat bastard who made a profit off of everyone else's misfortune. When pressed—my boot on his neck and the sound of Thom's pen scritching away at the page as he took notes like this was a fucking 'Versity class on how to shit-kick information out of somebody—he added that *that* rat bastard had said something about the scale coming fresh from the Ke-Han capital, which was where all the good stuff was being sold these days.

That was when I'd yanked Ginger up by his collar and held him there until he started turning all sorts of pretty blue and purple. It was a rare fucking son-of-a who could lie through something like that, and I wasn't about to go waltzing back into Ke-Han territory based on information some Cindy trying to save his own ass fed me.

And that was pretty much where the transcription had ended too, since Thom had some kind of prissy problem with writing down words when they were being choked out of a prisoner. Prisoner my ass, since Ginger deserved what he was getting, and worse, but in the end none of that mattered.

He wasn't lying and he'd told me all he knew.

He could get out, get lost, get a bunch of his friends to come after me, get revenge, whatever he wanted. I could deal with that; I'd dealt with a whole lot worse.

Anyway, I didn't even have to prepare myself because I'd done enough to make Ginger piss himself sideways trying to get away from me, and still I refused to let him go. After the little mother-licking piece of shit fainted I let him drop, storming out of the room and waiting for Thom to follow.

"What do you think?" I asked. I didn't have any more room for getting angry, since I'd about taken up all the room in my body already. But if I *had*, I'd have been pretty fucking pissed that I'd stooped to asking my kid brother his opinion on something to do with the corps and my girl.

Fuck me, but I didn't have anyone else to ask.

He was busy folding up his notes like he was just as surprised to get a consult on the subject as I was, but his head flew up like a startled fucking rabbit's once he caught on. At least he'd held his own in that brawl downstairs, but barely. And my attentions were divided the entire time because *I* needed to be looking out for *him*, which wasn't anything like brawling used to be.

"He had little reason to lie to us," Thom said, rubbing his sleeve over his mouth. There was still ink under his nose, but fuck if I was gonna be the one to point it out. Hell, I wasn't gonna be around forever, and eventually he'd have to start picking up on these things for himself. "Men tend to lose their reticence once their bladder's done the same, if you'll pardon the allusion."

I didn't know what the fuck he was asking me to pardon since I was the one who'd made the guy piss his pants in the first place, but I figured playing along'd be faster than starting another argument. My teeth were gonna be powder by this time tomorrow with how tight I had 'em clenched. I deserved some kind of award just for keeping a civil tongue in my head, but bastion if I didn't hate all this prancing around.

"It does make sense," Thom continued, stopping up the inkwell he carried around with him and rubbing his thumb over the top nervously. I folded my arms over my chest and waited for him to start making sense.

"Well, it makes sense that contraband items would be appearing from the conquered territory," Thom continued. "Not to sound like a lecture—I know how much you hate that—but all the Ke-Han's resources are no doubt currently quite strained; they can't attempt to rebuild their city, recall all their soldiers from their stations, deal with the chaos currently visited upon their capital, *and* keep a sharp eye on everything that enters and leaves the city, all at once. The black market thrives even when conditions are prime for stopping it. And besides . . ."

"There's a whole lot more they can sell now," I finished. Lecture or not, that was something I could understand.

"It is a curious question," Thom murmured, suddenly lost in his own little 'Versity world. I wanted to tell him to snap out of it right away, but it was finally a topic that was halfway useful. "One would assume that all the major parts *have* been returned to Volstov—the Esar issued strict commands on that matter. But Balfour *did* say there was a great deal of protest—"

"Politics," I muttered. "None of my fucking business. Better than having 'em in a museum, anyway. They wouldn't've wanted it."

"It is troubling," Thom concluded, looking up at me. "A great many things about the past few hours have been exceedingly troubling, but I mean this more on a hypothetical level."

"You mean what," I said, with enough bite to my words to make him rethink the gobbledygook he was currently spouting.

"There's a difference between sitting back and watching as you help a man to piss his breeches for information," Thom clarified, "and wondering what will happen to the world if the technology behind such weaponry is being sold to whoever is capable of paying for it. Do you see the difference?"

Bastion help me, but I almost fucking laughed.

"In any case," Thom went on, looking away from me to attend to his collection of fucking quills, "it would seem that the scale you have now must have come from the Ke-Han capital. The route it traveled is conjecture; we can't trace its trajectory beyond knowing where it began and where it ended up."

"So you're saying we gotta make a detour into Ke-Han territory?" I couldn't think of anything I wanted to do less if I was being perfectly fucking honest with myself. My skin twinged just thinking about it—a whole mess of scars left neat as you please across my back like *I'd* been the one thrown from my horse into some nasty fucking blueberry brambles, only these weren't by accident. There wasn't much love lost between the Ke-Han and me, and I was pretty sure they knew what I looked like a little better than some backwater Volstovic farmhands.

"I . . . Oh," said my genius brother, catching up with the lead dog in the race at fucking last. "I suppose that *is* what I'm saying, isn't it?"

Not one word about the Hanging Gardens of Wherever, either, and I had to give him credit for that if nothing else.

Thom drew in a deep breath, so I knew that whatever he said next, it was going to be something real stupid.

"Do you really think that's wise?" he asked finally.

"No," I answered.

He frowned. "If you would take just a moment to—"

"The Ke-Han hate me," I said, "and they have every right to. I hate them, too. I'm not going there thinking it'd be easy. But if they're selling off pieces of her, then I'm going to be there, plain and simple. I'll track down every last rat bastard who thinks they can do something like that and live, and I'll teach them all the lessons their mamas didn't." I grinned, but I didn't feel like I was smiling. "And I'll finally see a little piece of the place I've been fighting all my fucking life too. Pretty funny, isn't it?"

"But what do you hope to *accomplish*?" Thom asked miserably.

"I'm taking what's mine," I told him. It was as simple as that. "She deserves to rest the same as anyone when they're dead and gone. And no one *else* out there has any right to touch her."

We were quiet after that, though I wasn't stupid enough to think I'd won the argument. I wasn't the sort to hold by any kind of tradition, so maybe I'd just stunned him silent by telling him I wanted to lay Have to rest, but this definitely wasn't over. There was no winning with some people, no matter how fast you talked.

From outside in the hall, where I'd tossed Ginger after I'd finished with him, I heard a low groan, which meant he was waking up. He'd have to explain how he'd ruined his breeches to his wife, if he had one, and I tried to think about that instead of whatever was happening on the other side of the mountains. It was bad enough she'd been busted to pieces, but the other thoughts I was having were even worse. I had to start moving to stop thinking them.

"I'll go with you," Thom said, a little too loudly, like he'd forgotten how to control the volume of his voice.

"Who said I wanted you to come?" I asked. It couldn't be that easy.

"Well, it's like this," Thom said. "You're going to need someone who has . . . connections. I could write—right now, right here—to the people I know at the 'Versity. The dragons weren't my specialty, but I know a few students who *did* study them, and—more important—I know their professors. I know a man who studied the black market. There's so much I could do to help you, and . . . you're going to need *help*, Rook," he said at last. There was pleading in his eyes, in his voice, in the stubborn set of his mouth.

I clenched my fists, but he was right. I wasn't used to working alone.

That didn't mean I could work with just anybody, either.

"In any case, we obviously can't stay here tonight," Thom said. "So we're just going to have to finish up our business and leave."

"You mean sneak out before we pay for fucking this place up?" I asked. I didn't believe it. My baby brother, suggesting we skip town? Never. He was too fucking self-righteous for that.

Thom flushed. "That's hardly what I—I would *never* in a thousand—Rook, such behavior is downright wrong, and we—"

"I sure as shit don't have the money," I said.

Thom wilted like a daisy. "Neither do I. I suppose there's always..." He turned his back on me to fish around in his pack. It took him a while to find whatever he was looking for, since the bag was stuffed with papers and reading material and that bastion-damned quill collection—all of which he was gonna have to ditch if he really planned on coming with me—but finally he must've found what he was looking for, because I saw his shoulders slump. "Here," he said, holding out his hand. "I'm just as much to blame for the ... *position* as you are, and it's time I started paying for myself in these situations."

He looked too damn much like a kid—so much that I didn't even move to take whatever it was he was holding out for me. It was like he'd found a ha'penny on the street and he was proud of himself; the money was his, but he wanted me to have it. I'd seen this already and I'd never wanted to see it again.

"*Here,*" he repeated, and I snapped out of it.

The object in question was his badge of honor. It was gold, and it was worth more than this entire place.

Gestures like this were either stupid or self-centered, and in his case, I had to believe it was a combination of both.

"Don't do that," I said. "Don't make fucking sacrifices."

"But I thought—"

I shook my head. "We're sneaking out. You keep that. I'll figure something out. Why don't you write to th'Esar and say, 'Your esteemed hero broke some tables, and in recognition of his service to the crown, could you kindly reach into your deep fucking pockets and bail him out?' Something useful he could do, for any of us, anyway."

Thom snorted. When I looked over, I realized he was laughing. "I wish I could," he said finally. "But like you'd say ... I don't have the balls."

"And I can't write," I said. "So I guess we've gotta get out of here, huh?"

"Sooner rather than later," Thom admitted, closing his hand back around the badge and shoving it somewhere into his bag, so I knew that I'd won *that* argument, at least. Good. Anything less'd be bad for my ego. "Though before we skip town *entirely,* I'd like to make use of the postal service—send off a quick letter to someone trustworthy, just to alert them to what we're doing and to ask if they've any advice to help us along. I . . ." He hesitated. "*I* think it's a good idea."

"Right," I said, ignoring the fact that my kid brother was the sort of person who thought we had time to write letters before we ran out on our inn bill. "Fine. Whatever." The only thing we had to worry about at this point was Piss Pants waking up and rousing a few of his friends, but I could take care of whatever the country had to throw at me.

I'd show 'em what it meant to have even a piece of a dragon around.

"I thought I might write to Adamo first," he said, when it became pretty clear I'd finished with all I had to say. "He's the only *mutual* acquaintance among our experts, and Balfour says . . ."

"Do I look like I'm in the mood for a game of Balfour Fucking Says?" I asked, somehow managing not to kick our room door open, since that'd have attracted more attention we didn't need. "Write the damn thing, I don't care who to. Just make sure they know their ass from their ball sack and don't waste time."

"All right." Thom nodded, looking momentarily hurt that I didn't care to hear the entire contents of whatever cindy love letters he'd been writing back and forth between here and the capital. He sat down at the desk, pulled out a sheet of paper, and picked out a quill from the bunch—the one he used all the fucking time, so that I didn't know why he'd even brought the other ones along in the first place.

I couldn't sit—I was too fucking keyed up—so I settled for pacing back and forth, probably distracting him, but the letter didn't have to sound pretty. It just had to make sense.

Meanwhile, I planned our escape.

We could probably get to the stables easily enough from our rooms, but the innkeeper'd have to be an idiot not to lock his horses up at night. *I* had no problems going it on foot, but then I wasn't weighted down with a collection of Volstov's finest quills and ink like some people too stupid to know what it meant when you said "pack light." I had a blister on my palm and I started picking at it angrily.

"Tell him about the scale," I said. "And how we're goin' in no matter *what* he says and if he thinks he's keeping me from going after her, then he can take this letter and stick it up his—"

"Dear Adamo," Thom said loudly, already writing, though I was pretty fucking sure he wasn't putting in anything I'd said.

"Tell him to use whatever fancy 'Versity clout he's got to help us, understood? No point in turning fucking professor on us if he's not gonna help when it really counts. I know you've got your own experts and shit to write to, but it wouldn't hurt to have him grease the fucking wheels for us before your letters get there, would it?"

"Oh, for the love of— *Honestly,*" Thom said, scratching something out and reaching for another piece of paper. "This isn't at *all* how you dictate a letter."

"Gee, I'm so sorry, Professor! Guess all those little missives I expertly composed while saving the fucking *country* from the Ke-Han hordes never reached you," I snapped. It turned out I did have a little bit of extra temper in me after all.

"Mm," Thom agreed. Shameless little Mollyrat wasn't even listening to me, but scribbling away like writing a letter took his whole focus. Maybe it did. Hell if I knew.

"Hurry it up," I said. Lucky we'd never really unpacked in the first place, and *one* of us had gotten a little sleep in. Then I stopped pacing. "You thought about how Adamo's gonna write back to us now that we're skipping town?"

That paused his quill sure enough, but only for a minute, then he was back to writing like I hadn't even said anything. "I have a friend who left Themedon to study languages in Tarkhum. It's a little farther south—desert country, you know—but it runs close to Ke-Han territory. I'll tell Adamo to send his response there, and we can aim to make it our next destination."

It was a good plan, and it actually made sense.

Maybe taking him along wasn't gonna be a complete waste after all.

MALAHIDE

Down in the dirtiest part of Molly was where the fishermen netted bodies out of the water. They sold fish, of course, but also rings torn off bloated fingers, scraps of leather not too badly damaged by the water, and whatever information they'd heard from whatever corner they'd been lurking on the night before, and all the rest of the news that had come in with the tide. Molly specialized in certain truths—inescapable truths about poverty and wretchedness—but there was something to be said in praise of idle gossip. For the longer you held it up to the light, turning it this way and that like a piece of glass, the closer it approximated a diamond in the rough.

All it took was patience and the proper angle.

The only difficulty with heading down to Molly was trying not to look like you were anything more than broken glass yourself. But I was fond of masquerades, and this was one of my favorites. It was close enough to my own meager beginnings that the thrill of pretending to be who I really was coursed subtly through my veins, and ached at the metal box placed within the hollow of my throat, through which I now cast my unexpected voice.

I had practiced it alone in my quarters—in lodgings as far as could be from Mollyscum—like a puppeteer whose puppet was herself. The Esar's commands would not afford me time to become accustomed to the proper way of it, but I could not allow myself to sound rusty or unusual, either. It took an entire night before the full-length mirror to remember how it was to speak, but at last I'd managed to make this act seem natural, compensating for differences in pitch, feeding the mechanism with false emotions.

It all reminded me that I was not what any man would call a beautiful woman. My nose was too strong, my neck too thick, and the rest of me too slim and unshapely. My lack of beauty but my wealth of composure was what disconcerted the Esar so much when we were together—and indeed what concerned most men with whom I spent any amount of real time beyond the most perfunctory curtsy.

But this was all conjecture, my theories on why I was treated as I was. These insights helped me in my charades, but little else.

I had money—a great deal of it—and the dragonscale. Now, dressed in breeches and boots that were rotten enough not to be stolen off my feet, I found myself in Molly all over again, listening to the fishermen gossip on the wharf while a few Mollyrats eyed me, wondering if I was worth the drop or not.

The fishermen didn't recognize me; no information would flow until I'd broached the topic myself, offering them an olive branch, or at least something to go on.

Pitching my voice deep, I said, "Evening."

"Evening," one of the men said to me. They smelled of brine and salt and aged skin, weathered beyond repair. And so young. I leaned back on the rotting wood, as though anyone could ever be comfortable in a place like this. "You're looking for something, then? It'll cost you."

"Pity no one here has money," I said.

We all shared a friendly, bitter laugh. You could approach someone worlds apart from you by offering them, like a handshake, a simple truth from their own lives. I kept with me like a memorized prayer a list of every truth, belonging to every sex and race, from high and low, marsh and desert and country farm. This was where I excelled. I kept my smiles hidden and my eyes on the water, an uncomplicated rhythm.

"I'd drink to that if I had drink on me," the fisherman said.

"I have something else for you," I said. "I'll be honest about my purpose, but here it is."

Out of the folds of my peacoat I took it, the scale, wrapped in paper to keep it smelling clean. The fisherman closest to me leaned in tight and I couldn't risk him touching it, so I unwrapped a little corner like it was a toffee and let him see the color of it.

Down in Molly, everyone recognized a dragon. No matter what form it took, no matter how small or how big. They were a possessive lot. I covered my clue back in paper and hid it once again on my person like a magic trick, pretending I was pocketing it while I slipped it into a fold inside my sleeve.

"I'm selling," I said. "One day, I'll be rich. And when I am, I'll come back here and buy you all a round. But that's only if I can sell."

The fishermen whistled together in unison. "That'll either make or break you," one of them said. "Th'Esar'd cut your throat for peddling that."

"Did I tell you, Nor," one of the fishermen told his friend, "about the time I bounced that boy on my fucking lap? Didn't go by Rook then, did he, but he's still one of ours all the same."

"I remember 'im," Nor answered. "And there wasn't no bouncin', either."

"Where are you selling that piece to, anyway?" the fisherman asked, eyes on me without warning; they were gray and keen, the only sharp part of his whole blunt face. That would matter to them. "You thought about that?"

"Money's worth about as much as honor, these days," I answered, all part of the plan. "I wouldn't sell the second one for the first, though, I promise you that. I just want to know what the market price is."

"So you're lookin' for a key to the market, hey?" Nor asked.

The fishermen were quiet for a long minute, listening to the river. Somewhere, in the far distance, it spilled out into the sea. I could smell that, too, despite how little pleasure it gave me.

"I'll vouch you," Nor said finally. Something moved in his pocket; it was a knife, and he was threatening me. "So don't let me down, newf."

"Thanks, Nor," I said.

"Don't mention it," he said, in a way that meant he expected me to mention it quite often. Talk was cheap in the city's first and second tier, but in Molly it was just about all anyone could afford. They couldn't get enough of it. "This way, then."

I followed him, letting my worn boots fall heavily on the uneven cobblestones and tramping straight through puddles of muck that, under normal circumstances, I'd be going out of my way to avoid. I wasn't bothered by these things the way most other women of my standing might have been, however, which I supposed was one of the elements that made me so good at my job. I allowed Nor to walk ahead of me, since even in the dirtiest Molly alleyways, all Volstovic men liked to feel they had something up on the younger generation. But I didn't mind walking slowly, since it would aid me in memorizing the area. If it proved necessary, I could return here at any time I liked without Nor for an escort.

He paused before a ramshackle building, this one given the distinction of having brick walls instead of wood, though the mortar between them was crumbling and their red color had faded into a dreary shade of gray. It was the most unimposing building I'd ever seen, as though it had been assuming since it was built that time or calamity would tear it down again.

I waited, hands in my pockets, as Nor knocked on the door, then took off before anyone could answer, looking at me over his shoulder and gesturing for me to follow.

"Been raided by the Provost's wolves a couple times," Nor explained. "Seems old Dmitri's had more time on his hands now that the war's over and all. Can't be too careful; everyone needs a trick or two in case the wolves start sniffing."

I nodded, mindful of my surroundings as we stepped off the main street in case there was some mischief at hand. I was well acquainted with Provost Dmitri. In fact, we'd grown up in the same home for unwanted children, smack-dab on the border between Charlotte and Miranda, though not so obviously that it would remind the more frivolously minded citizens of the consequences of visiting Our Lady of a Thousand Fans too often. He'd been something of a companion to me in my lonelier times, and though I'd never sought out companionship, I couldn't call it anything other than that.

More than our distinguished background, however, we also shared a common bond in that our value as citizens of Volstov was measured in direct correlation with how useful we could prove to the Esar. Dmitri was a handsome man, if overly serious, and he refused to ignore the darker corners of Molly the way a sane man might have. I liked him, or was at least somewhat amused by his stubbornness, but my opinion was not a popular one among these people. Instead of offering it, I spat into the street. Such gestures had an eloquence of their own, and I felt it would be the sort of response Nor could appreciate.

The path he was leading me down was little more than a space between buildings for housewives to throw the day's piss and shit. Rats ate their meals and orphans made their beds here, and I was grateful for the dim light that filtered in from above the rooftops, if not the smell.

"Watch your step," Nor mentioned, and I was only too grateful to oblige.

When he halted, it was in front of a heavy-looking metal door, the bottom of it crusty and laced with rust. It looked like one solid kick would send it to pieces.

"This here's the real door," Nor said, giving it a sharp thump with his knuckles. "You knock once on the front to let 'em know to expect you, *then* you come around here. Door won't be unlocked otherwise, and like enough if you come straight here, they'll assume you're sniffing 'em out, if you know what I mean."

"Easy way to a quick end," I agreed. "I'll remember that."

The door gave a heavy groan and Nor stepped backward quickly as it swung open. The inside corridor wasn't lit, which made it difficult to see, but lamps were rare below Charlotte, and to burn one during the day was an unheard-of luxury. If there was someone who'd opened the door, in any case, I couldn't see them now, and Nor didn't greet anyone as he stepped inside, clearly expecting me to follow.

I did, cataloging the things I'd learned thus far. Unlike most buildings in Molly, this one was made of brick, which meant that the sounds of whatever happened inside would *stay* inside instead of becoming fair game for any passerby to eavesdrop upon. In addition, there was a fairly primitive system of checks in place, though evidently there was more to it than I'd been shown—provisions made for if someone *didn't* know the proper steps—but I was not the sort of person to forget such things. As I thought this over, my nose began to prickle, and the sensation spread irresistibly to my throat. Drifting in from some hidden room was the unmistakable scent of incense—a sandalwood blend that was far too expensive for any Mollyrat worth his claws. This particular variety was of interest especially because it was a *foreign* smell. Sandalwood was preferred by Ke-Han magicians for use in clearing their minds, and as far as I was aware, the practice had not yet spread to our fair shores.

In time it might have become all the rage, but it was certainly not the sort of practice that would rise from the bottom up.

"That smell," I began thoughtfully.

"Reeks to high heaven, don't it?" Nor agreed, from somewhere in front of me. "They think it classes up the joint when really all it does is stick in my craw something fierce. Leave it to the Ke-Han to think they can improve on good, clean air, huh?"

"Indeed," I said, making a show of clearing my own throat.

We came to a curtain, a heavy velvet affair that was thick with dust. Nor paused before drawing it aside and I could tell that he was enjoying himself. In his hands he held the power to reveal another world, as it were, to someone lower than himself. Mollyscum didn't get much chance to feel better than anyone, so as long as he didn't waste *too* much of my time, there was no harm in allowing him the delight of drawing the moment out.

"It's Nor," my guide said. "Nor by Nor'east today. I've brought a guest for you."

"What's his number?" a man asked.

"He's decent," Nor said. "I shook him down myself."

"Buy or sell?"

"He's selling, I think," Nor replied. "Funny little bugger."

This was my cue, and I drew the scale out of my secret pocket as the curtain was drawn back fully.

Whatever I'd been expecting to see, it certainly wasn't what lay behind that curtain: a smallish, shabby room that someone had taken great effort to decorate in their idea of the Ke-Han style. There was the incense, in a curious bronze dish shaped like a tiger, and various standing screens were scattered here and there, in direct antithesis to the Ke-Han principles of austerity. Most folk in Molly hardly had enough things to fill up a room, let alone decorate it, so one could hardly blame them for going a bit overboard with such a wealth of exciting, foreign items at hand.

"You the seller?" The same man who'd asked the questions glanced over, looking me up and down. He was a geometric breed of person— square head, straight shoulders, and a rectangular body—and he was seated in a Volstovic-style chair, though I noticed he'd seen fit to decorate it with an elaborately embroidered Ke-Han cushion.

"That's me," I said, the metal of the scale warm against my gloved palm.

There weren't any other chairs in the room, but there were more cushions. They were plainer than the one the man had chosen to adorn *his* chair, but that was to be expected. I sat, crossing my legs beneath me.

"Saw you admiring my tiger," the square-shaped man said, in a way that told me immediately which piece was his favorite. Men could be so predictable at times. "Had a monkey that came with it, but that went last week."

"What if I told you that I've got something in my possession that'll blow monkeys and tigers right out of the water?" I said, laying the scale bare and holding it out like an offering, without hiding anything like I had down at the docks.

Trying to be coy here would only make it look as though I was trying to pull a fast one, and it would be doing an unkindness to Nor by Nor'east to make myself out as a person of questionable motivation.

The man's eyebrows shot up as though they'd been fired from a cannon and he leaned forward, his interest plain and the chair creaking beneath his weight.

"Where'd a slip of a thing like you get a piece like *that,* hey?" he asked. "I'm not so bold as to think all Ke-Han junk comes through me first, but I pride myself on getting the best of the goods—my own joke, there."

"So I've heard," I said, sidestepping the question.

"You don't look like a soldier," he said. "Where's it from?"

"I wasn't, but my brother was," I said. "He's dead. It's a memento from the war, and I'm looking to sell."

The excuse seemed to satisfy him. "You won't get its worth trying to pawn it off on your own, that's for certain," the man said, stroking his square chin in thought. He had a three days' beard growing, not yet at the stage where it was substantial, and there was a scar on his chin that marred the effect somewhat.

"That's why I'm here," I answered, sitting up straight but not *too* straight. "Easier to move a piece with the right connections, and I hear you've got quite a few."

"Can't be beat," he said, looking as proud as if I'd just complimented one of his children. "I could probably find some idiot from the Basquiat with more brains than sense to peddle it off to, but doing business in *dragon* parts is tricky up near Miranda. Dangerous work, if the wrong man overhears," he added, and drew his finger across his throat in the universal gesture for losing one's head.

"I'm quite attached to my head," I said. Here was where I had to be careful and influence the conversation in the direction I wanted it to go. I couldn't afford to sell the scale the Esar had given me *within* Thremedon itself; I'd worked out already that my best bet would be to try to get a foreign buyer, which would at least lead me to the point where those in Thremedon traded off with those from other nations. It wasn't a gamble, but it was also far from a sure thing. "I want to buy a big house next to th'Esar's palace, not end up buried underneath it."

"That's the only way most of us'll ever end up in Miranda," the man said, then laughed a wheezing sort of laugh that was more like a cough. "You're right, though, and I'm not that keen on losing *my* head either. Be better off with a foreign investor, someone with no ties to Volstov *or* the Ke-Han. Can't let something like that fall into the wrong hands, now can we?"

"Do you already have someone in mind?" I asked, rubbing my thumb over the blackened surface of the scale. It had a curious feeling to it, hard yet with a bit of a give if you pressed against it—almost the way flesh would have.

But of course, there was no telling with magicians.

"Not someone," the man said. "More like, a whole *lot* of someones. And whoever I pick, it's his lucky day, you understand?"

"I see," I said. "All foreigners?"

"Yeah," the man said. "Listen, I'll let you in on a little secret of the market, because you're a first timer and Nor vouched for you and all. Since the war ended, even countries that weren't involved—*especially* countries that weren't involved—want themselves a little piece of the history that took place. No one ever thought the damned thing *would* end, so now that it has, everyone's in a celebrating mood. And when people celebrate, their purse strings get loose. Everyone's looking to turn a profit, but to do that, you've got to shell it out first."

"Fascinating," I breathed, and meant it. There was nothing I enjoyed more than learning a new fact about the way people operated, and mentally I filed this bit of information along with the rest.

" 'Course some folk are on the lookout for more than just mementos, but I wouldn't bother you with that lot. They're *real* particular. When it comes to a piece like yours," the man continued, "a real part of one of Volstov's *dragons* now, I'm not even going to have to put it on the open market. I'll pass the word to a few choice contacts, real classy gentlemen, and soon you'll have more suitors than you can shake a stick at, friend."

"And what do I owe you for this kind favor?" Only a fool did favors in Molly without expecting something in return, and it was up to the recipient to ask up front or else *he* was the fool. I neatly skirted around his mention of *particular* customers, not knowing whether that was a warning to me, that he'd perhaps sensed something off and wanted to see if I'd nibble.

No such luck. Even in Molly, I was a well-trained professional.

"I get a cut of whatever you make. Twenty percent is standard on high-ticket items, and I can't say as things get any higher ticket than this."

"Done," I said, without compunction. The Esar provided me with an allowance, as well as covering any costs I incurred while working for him. Money was no object. I would cheerfully pay off this man out of my own pocket—or the Esar's own pocket—in order to achieve my ends.

What *was* objectionable, I realized, was the idea of anyone unsavory getting wind of this deal before it was finalized. Like the man had said, word spread fast over something this hot, and if Dmitri's men were to hear of the deal and shut things down before they got under way, I ran the risk of losing my only lead.

I certainly didn't cherish the idea of having to return to the Esar to ask if he happened to have any other spare parts lying around that I could use, nor did I think Nor would be so open-minded to strangers in the future, no matter how neat my next disguise was.

The man sitting in the chair got up and held out his hand. I switched the scale to my other hand and took it, shaking once firmly as I'd practiced so many times, then releasing him.

"Nice doing business with an interesting chap for a change," he said, with a glance at Nor that I supposed meant *he* fell into the uninteresting category. "Nor here'll be in contact to let you know when we've got a buyer. As a personal favor, I'll weed out any offers that I don't find worth our time."

"Very generous of you," I said, the understanding between us that he was also being generous to himself.

With a short bow to the man and to Nor, I left.

Soon, I hoped, depending on how quickly the market's lines ran, I would have a point from which I could start. After that, I would trace the trajectory from Thremedon until I came to the point of origin of where these parts were being sold. In the meantime, it looked as though I'd be spending my time in Molly. Still, my game didn't have to be all waiting, not now that I'd discovered some further business that required attending to.

I didn't much cherish the idea of conducting said business in my current attire, but there was nothing to be done for it.

I had to go speak with the Provost.

CHAPTER THREE

THOM

Another night camped out under the stars and I was going to lose my mind.

My hand had healed, as had some of my wounded morals, but my back was what troubled me now. The weather was turning hotter and drier as we headed south toward the deserts, and the inns in these parts were few and far between.

And I couldn't trust Rook with people, given his present mood.

I didn't count; I was his punching bag for the time being, and I could consider myself lucky that such abuse was merely verbal and emotional, and had not yet turned to fisticuffs. It was easy enough to assume I would lose should matters ever come to *that,* but I did wonder how deep the vein of Rook's anger ran, that even the extreme amounts of physical exercise we endured was not enough to cool his temper.

My travel log was full of notations—not merely on my surroundings, which was to be expected, but I found I was falling back on old habits, making note of each grunt and scowl Rook tossed my way like a master tossed his hunting dog scraps. Matters had been worse before—even I could admit that, despite how depressing they were now—but now I had no one else to talk to. There was only the fire, the soil, the open road, and Rook. The first three couldn't speak, and the fourth refused to.

Days of traveling had taken their toll on me, and I wondered if this was an endeavor that could have been accomplished by carriage rides. How did normal people travel, I wondered to myself, and with what comforts and expenses?

Yet if I considered it all fieldwork—if I reminded myself that *Excursions with a Hero: A Travel Diary* might become a fascinating treatise on a sort of modern-day walkabout—it was almost bearable.

Luckily for my sanity, we had found ourselves a campsite.

There were such places along the best-traveled routes to and from the major cities in Volstov, and those outside of Volstov's domain that nonetheless were both friendly and major sites of trade. It was the possibility of visiting such metropolises that truly thrilled me, and our next stop would be just outside the famed caravan oasis of Karakhum—where my 'Versity friend Geoffrey Bless was, I could only hope, expecting our arrival.

Poor Geoffrey. He had no idea the storm that was, at this very moment, gathering.

"Get something to eat," Rook grunted at me—the most perfunctory of statements that implied I was slow and soft in the head and needed to be told to eat when I was hungry.

"Are you going somewhere?" I asked, softly, in the hopes that he wouldn't hear me. The less he heard, the less chance there was of his becoming angry.

His anger frightened me.

"To check out the location," Rook replied.

I would have offered to go with him, but he had already left me behind.

The landscape was rocky and uneven here, and, as previously noted, the dirt was becoming sandier, the air drier—all these conditions pointing toward our close proximity with the desert. Here and there my fellow travelers were talking with each other, little fires glinting alongside the tents. It was a fascinating scene and I was determined to make the most of it, to receive news from like-minded, intrepid explorers . . . or something akin to that.

I was beginning to discover that fieldwork was *not* my specialty. But the man I had come here with—presumably under the conditions that we were to better understand one another—was somewhere among all these strangers, just as much of a stranger to me as all the rest.

"You look troubled," someone said at my side. "Bad news from home?"

It was startling to be addressed. At first, I assumed that the voice in question could not be referring to me, but a hand on my shoulder brought me up short.

"Oh, and it looks bad," the man—suddenly at my side—said, upon seeing my face.

In the dim light I could barely make out his descent, but his accent and the sharpness of his features were foreign to me. If I had to wager a guess on what small evidence I did have, I would have said he was three-quarters Volstovic and one-quarter Ke-Han—but just as field-work was not my specialty, neither were matters of lineage.

"What a fascinating accent you have," I said.

"Is that so?" he asked. "I could say the same for you. I must've picked mine up somewhere; I've been traveling most of my life. What's your excuse?"

"I'm from Thremedon," I said.

"My sincerest apologies," he replied. "I hope you don't take any offense, but I can't stand big cities."

"I do find it to be a polarizing topic among nonnatives," I admitted, trying to hide how shaken I was by his appearance. Something told me that Rook would never have been taken by surprise in this way, but then his upbringing had provided him with all sorts of instincts that I'd missed out on.

Funny, as always, that we were from the same place.

"Ah, but see, here I have to beg your pardon once again," my new companion said, "as I've gone and started up a conversation without introducing myself. The name's Afanasiy. Can't blame that one on traveling; I got it from my mother."

"Very traditional," I said. "Your mother must have been quite the Volstovic purist."

"Call me Fan," he countered, smiling, as though I'd said something particularly amusing. "Don't see many from Thremedon around these parts, and taking these roads. Hope you don't mind my coming up to say hello; just thought you looked like you could use some company. I know I could."

"No," I said, because even if I'd wanted to be alone with my thoughts, I couldn't find much objectionable in his actions thus far. "I don't mind at all."

There followed a slightly awkward pause in the conversation, where he waited for me to give my name, then shrugged when I didn't volunteer it. While I hadn't grown up in the Airman, I'd still managed to cultivate a certain set of my own instincts, and any Mollyrat worth his teeth knew not to give his name to a complete stranger—even when he was polite enough to offer his first.

"So, you heading into desert country?" Fan asked, scratching his neck beneath his jaw. "I only ask because if you're on this road, then that's where you're heading whether you meant to or not, and the desert isn't particularly . . . *kind* to those of us who go in unprepared."

I didn't blame him for thinking I looked unprepared. I felt unprepared, and I *was* unprepared; my only shame was how obvious it was, even to complete strangers.

"I'm meeting a friend," I said, fingering the edges of my travel journal.

"Never a better reason to go on a journey," he said. I couldn't quite make out his eyes, but his voice was filled with approval. "I'll tell you something else, since you and I are in the same boat, so to speak— being men of the road and all—but it's *my* opinion that it's never been a better time to get out of Volstov. See the world a bit, come back when things are settled. You take my meaning?"

"That was the general idea," I agreed, beginning to wonder just how long it could be taking Rook to scout the location and come back, and whether or not he was coming back at all.

To our left, a woman scurried into her tent and came out dragging a man I assumed must have been her husband. She seemed provincial, and I wondered what she was doing all the way out here. But then, it took all kinds. I was so absorbed in studying her particular style of dress that I caught—quite by accident—the tail end of her conversation.

"I'm *telling* you, it's him!" she said anxiously. "And you wanted to sleep early tonight! Teach me to marry the likes of you. Come on!"

"But what's an airman like *Rook* doing all the way out here?" her husband demanded, before they disappeared between two distant tents.

I followed them with my eyes, attention diverted from my sudden companion.

"Excuse me," I said to Fan, and started after them.

"You don't think they meant *the* Rook?" he asked, keeping step with me all of a sudden. I supposed it was another thing he'd picked up being on the road—a kind of friendliness that bordered on overbearing to people more used to the anonymity of city life. In Thremedon, his behavior would have been considered rather rude, but after some time on the road myself, I supposed I could understand the urge to strike up a conversation with a complete stranger. Hell, any more time with Rook in this temper, and I would likely be the one accosting strangers at random for a little conversation.

None of that mattered now. Rook was the center of a commotion, and I knew how he hated the sort of mindless attention that he garnered by being famous. Attention he caused was the sort he thrived on, but he had to be in control of it. The other set him snarling like a wild animal, and most people expecting a hero wouldn't be prepared for my brother's behavior when he felt cornered or trapped.

"I'm almost positive they do," I said, since if other people already knew, then there was no point in lying. "I'm traveling with him."

"Aha," Fan said.

We rounded a cluster of tents just in time to see the small crowd gathered at the outskirts of the campsite: ragtag travelers of all ages and sizes, all trying to look as though they were busy with something else but clearly surrounding Rook, as though they'd been caught up in his peculiar gravitational pull.

"I've seen your statue," one girl was telling him. She had a rosy face like an apple. "It isn't nearly so . . . so *breathtaking.*"

"That's great," Rook said, in flat tones. I could see him eyeing potential means of escape. "Real nice."

Fan whistled low, reaching his hands up to form a picture frame around the scene. "That's him, all right. You didn't tell me you were traveling with a real live airman, stranger—though I guess this might be why."

"You can call me Thom," I said, resigned. I didn't like the way he was gawking, but there was nothing I could do about that. No matter what, Rook was a hero. People responded only as they knew how. If I hadn't known him, I was sure I'd have done the same.

"There now, that wasn't so hard at all, was it?" Fan smiled again, then clapped me on the shoulder. I thought that perhaps there was something in his voice that hadn't been there before, but I chalked it up to excitement. No one much fancied talking to me when Rook was about; Fan was probably working up the courage to ask me for an introduction. "He doesn't look too happy about all this attention, does he?"

I was already cringing inwardly at the expression on Rook's face, for it was one that I'd come to recognize all too well in the time we'd known one another. In fact, I'd been the cause of it often enough.

This was certainly not going to improve his mood.

"What was it like?" asked a boy—just past puberty, I thought, and filled with wide-eyed wonderment. I had to stop him before he said it, the damning word, the ultimate offense. "Riding on a—"

I cleared my throat helplessly, trying to push my way to the forefront.

"You!" Rook said suddenly, weeding me out of the crowd as though he'd heard my thoughts. "Did you at least manage to get some dinner ready while I was gone, or've you just been wasting time writing in that damn book like always?"

"Ah," I said. "I'll go start on that now."

"Good," he snarled, and took advantage of everyone's confusion to storm toward our camp, heedless of all those around him who evidently would have been just as happy to keep him there all night.

I was all but preparing to get out of his way myself and see if I could at least make it back to our site before him when Fan made a sudden movement at my side, and I realized too late that he was heading straight for Rook.

There was being overly friendly, and then there was just plain suicide.

I made a grab for Fan's sleeve—too late again—and then could do nothing but stare in horror as events unfolded in front of me: the last remnants of the crowd scattering in Rook's wake, my strange acquaintance stepping into his path, smile like the sliver of the moon, and Rook himself halting without warning as he sensed this approach, Fan nearly plowing into him with the momentum he'd built up. It was like watching a boar cornered at a hunt—right before the boar turned wild and eviscerated its hapless pursuers out of self-defense.

"Pardon me," Fan said, offering a funny little bow. "I would never presume to delay any man's dinner, let alone one so distinguished as you."

"Then *get*," Rook grunted. "Unless you're volunteering to go into the stewpot?"

"Nothing so crude," Fan said, rummaging for something in a pouch on his belt. "We're not in the desert just yet, after all." I was still struggling with the simple human urge to get another man out of the way of the hurricane bearing down on him, but I was ashamed to admit that my curiosity was winning me over. I held my place, half a part of the crowd and half not, until Fan retrieved whatever it was he'd been searching for. I caught a glimpse of metal in the firelight, nothing more, but that was enough to make my stomach turn over.

No, I thought. *Anything but that.*

Rook's eyes sharpened. "Where'd you get that?" he demanded.

"You aren't the only one with friends in the desert," said Fan, seemingly heedless of the danger he was in simply by existing. I rose up on the balls of my feet to try to get a better look at the piece he was holding, and managed to see it over the heads of my fellow spectators. It was a talon, hooked and dangerous. It seemed to take on the colors of the firelight, a muddied red-gold that I didn't recognize; but then, the only dragon I had ever enjoyed personal contact with was my brother's.

Rook grabbed Fan up by the front of his shirt and dragged him close; it seemed all the patience in his stores had run out at last. I took a tentative step forward, though whether it was to intervene or offer my aid, I couldn't say. There was little I could do to prevent another incident like the one at the inn.

"I've had about enough of that face of yours, shit-eating grin and all," Rook said. "You have something to say to me about where you got your fucking hands on that? Think real fucking carefully about how you answer me. You feel free to take your time."

Fan coughed, looking surprised but not altogether as alarmed as I might have imagined. He had nerves of steel—or something else of steel—and I was momentarily in awe of his composure. "I apologize for coming across as ungracious," he said. "I can assure you, that wasn't my intent. Karakhum does a pretty business in the black market these days, being as it's lucky enough to border both Xi'An and Volstov. I've just come from there. I bought this because the man selling it told me it was a real piece of the action. I never thought I'd get a chance to verify that unless I somehow ran into one of the dragonmakers, hey? But here *you* are. Pretty piece of luck, isn't it? No offense meant; I just allowed my excitement to run away with me."

There was a tense moment when my brother clenched his jaw, glancing at the claw Fan held in his hand. I felt my knuckles give a preemptive throb in protest—the bruises had only just begun to heal—but I readied myself to wade into whatever fray began. We'd certainly come too far together for me to suddenly start choosing the moral high ground.

Besides, it was obvious the awestruck travelers would be on Rook's side. The odds were quite decent.

"Fine," Rook bit out, releasing Fan and shoving him backward. "You're lucky I ain't taking that piece right off you."

I privately thought that he was lucky Rook hadn't taken more than that off him, but I very wisely kept this opinion to myself.

Fan adjusted his collar, slightly pink around the ears and cheeks, but back to smiling again. He was either the most cheerful person I'd ever met, or he was slightly touched in the head.

"You've just made a stranger one *very* happy man," he said.

"Just what I always wanted," Rook snapped. He stalked over toward me, making sure to knock my shoulder with his own as he passed and lowering his voice. "I want to talk to you," he muttered.

I cast an apologetic look at Fan as I turned to follow, feeling something like the shameful beginnings of relief swelling up inside me. Being spoken to was a step up from being treated like the gravel beneath Rook's boots.

When I arrived back at our tent, he had already begun to stoke the fire. I noticed that while he'd been off checking the location, he'd seen fit to hunt down a pair of desert hares to add to the vegetable stew I'd been planning. I had no idea how he'd managed to catch them near such a populated area—doubtless he'd used his skills with a knife, or maybe he'd brought them down with a good, stiff glare. I chopped our vegetables in silence, stirring them into the pot, as Rook sat in front of the fire, poking it moodily and sending up little whispers of ash and ember.

Something—most likely sap in the wood—caused the flames to

pop and send up sudden sparks. It startled me, but I kept my hold on the cooking spoon.

"Seems we're heading in the right direction, if that sly-faced bastard's one to believe," Rook grunted into the fire circle.

"Yes," I said. "I was thinking the same thing."

"You have a lot of thoughts in that head of yours," Rook said, waving his finger in a circle near my temple. It was the most derogatory gesture he could come up with under the circumstances, and I tried not to let my expression turn sour. "You ever use 'em to think about those dragonmakers?"

"Sometimes," I admitted. "I don't have a Talent myself, and those magicians were highly specialized—it's a subject that deals in magical theory, which I have no real vocabulary to understand. I'm sorry." I added, on impulse, "that I'm not more useful when it comes to . . . them, I mean."

"Yeah," Rook said.

He was quiet for a while, still poking at the fire, sitting cross-legged with his face turned masklike by the erratic firelight. Dinner was starting to smell delicious, and I hoped that food would put him in better spirits. Now and then I openly observed him, but he was so far lost to his own private thoughts—so private I had no wager as to what they were—that there was no point in trying to be stealthy.

He wasn't looking at me. For all he knew, I wasn't even there.

"But you know *something* about 'em," he said suddenly, when my back was turned to him. I whipped around, almost knocking over the pot, and Rook had the kindness to laugh at me while he caught hold of it. "Calm the fuck down," he said. "You're pissing me off."

"You're pissing *me* off," I said. Apparently I'd lost my mind. "There. Now we're even."

"It's fair enough," Rook said—a startling moment of clarity that nearly had me gasping, like a fish, for air.

"It is?" I asked.

"I'm acting like a fucking bitch," Rook said, showing some teeth. "And you're acting like a jackrabbit. So you're pissed off, and I'm pissed off. Let's leave it at that."

"I don't really see how that *solves*—"

"Save it for when I give a shit," Rook said. "You've probably . . . *read* something about them. The magicians in charge of making the drag-ons. Were there a bunch of them? Just a couple? What was the fucking deal?"

"You want a lesson in magical history?"

Rook snorted. "Only the parts that aren't boring."

"Well, I don't know much because there isn't much written on the subject," I said finally, still of no use to him. All my knowledge wasn't anything he had any reason to respect—it bore no weight in these cir-cumstances, and it made me angry at myself. Why hadn't I studied something more practical? Still, it was all a part of the way Rook man-aged to prey on a subject's insecurities. I was very well-read. It was just that I couldn't possibly be a major in *every* subject—despite how I had once believed it would be possible if I never slept. "They are protected by th'Esar—no one knows where they are now."

"So that asshole earlier was just blowing smoke," Rook said. "There's no way to actually *talk* to one of 'em."

"You mean . . ." I trailed off. The name I had been about to utter was taboo; no one was allowed to speak it in Rook's presence. I bit my lip to hold my tongue and tried to think of a way to alter my question in time to stave off my punishment.

"Yeah. I wonder what he's like, you know? The guy who made her." Rook brought up the stick he'd been using to stoke the flames and snapped it suddenly in half, his frustration focused and released in a small burst of destruction.

"Well I'm sure someone has to know where they've gone," I said softly. "They can't have just disappeared."

"I could tell you a little something about that," a familiar voice said from the shadows. "But of course, it's all got to do with rumor."

Rook was up out of his seat in a flash and passing by me so quickly the fire in front of me flared up and scorched my fingertips. I drew back, and Rook grabbed Fan by the collar for the second time that evening, and I was certain the fool would die. My only concern was that, for a brief moment, I rather believed he deserved it.

"You been eavesdropping on us?" Rook said.

Something had kept him from killing Fan straight off, and it wasn't any keen sense of moral obligation, either. The only reason Fan was still alive was temptation—the glimmer of hope.

I had no idea how much Fan could possibly have known, or

whether or not any of it was true. But for the same reason Rook allowed me to continue traveling with him, Rook hadn't snapped Fan's neck. There was something Fan had that Rook wanted. *Knowledge.*

"It's my job to hear things other people don't," Fan said. His tone of voice held no indication that he was in terrible danger, which seemed smug to me, and offensive. He had no idea what he was toying with—one couldn't simply play my brother like a flute.

"So what've you heard?" Rook said. "Spit it out and I don't pull my knife."

"Take a step back from me and I don't pull mine," Fan replied.

"Is any of this *really* necessary?" I asked, and the tone of my own voice frightened me.

"Stay outta this," Rook said. "Just keep the fuck back."

"Oh, *we've* already met," Fan said, presumably of me, as though we were all attending a host's dinner party instead of threatening one another's lives. "Perhaps I'd rather speak with Thom, come to think of it."

"Don't even fucking look at him," Rook snarled, before I could get a word in. "He doesn't know what he's asking about; you'd be talking in damned circles until daybreak."

"Then, I suppose," Fan said, still all too calmly for my liking, "we'll have to find some way of speaking that doesn't involve such enthusiasm."

"Right," Rook breathed tightly. "Enthusiasm."

"*Do* you think you could see your way toward setting me down?" Fan asked. "It's only that I have so much trouble thinking when I'm not on my feet."

Rook grunted, which wasn't really a reply, but he dropped Fan like a sack of meal instead of setting him down, so it seemed the enthusiasm hadn't drained out of him quite yet. Immediately after that, I saw his hand move—to rest over one of his hidden knives. Though he changed their locations quite frequently, I knew the gesture, if not the coordinates.

"Dinner's gonna burn without someone watching it," he said, speaking to me even though he was still glaring at Fan. I bristled—my own stubborn, indignant nature at being told where to go and what to do as if I were a child.

I'd held a conversation quite well on my own with Fan before Rook had even known he'd existed. If anyone deserved to be shooed away for ease of communication, it was the one who'd started things off by threatening to slit Fan open bow to stern.

"I beg your pardon," I began.

"Get," Rook said, without so much as a glance over his shoulder, as though I were an unwanted dog.

"Lovely seeing you again," Fan added, waving his fingers at me.

Before, I'd felt a keen responsibility for my brother's rudeness toward our fellow travelers. And, by that token, I'd also felt a strange sort of urge to shield them from it, despite how evidently I could not discover the trick of shielding *myself*. But Fan was obviously not the sort of man who needed any kind of protection in the slightest—and after taking the pot from the fire I carefully made my way back, ducking behind the side of a nearby tent.

"Nice fellow," Fan was saying. "How'd he end up traveling with a beast like you, hey?"

"Change topics again and we might have to just see who's better with a knife after all," Rook replied. There was something in his voice I scarcely recognized. "You know what I'm asking about. Do we have to dance around the fucking point first? I don't even dance with *women*."

"I do so love the dance." Fan sighed. "But I may have heard something—one or two things that might have given me a clue. I *am* sorry for losing my temper with you just now, but every man's got a right to defend himself, and I daresay you were trampling all over *my* rights with those fine boots of yours."

"The dragonmakers," Rook said, all but cutting him off. I could have told Fan, had I been in a more charitable mood toward him, just how well flowery prose worked on my brother's mood. But as far as I was concerned now, he could very well hang himself with his own rope.

"A very interesting topic to land on, though I can of course understand why someone like you'd be interested," Fan said, clearly undaunted. "I meant it when I said I never thought I'd get to meet an airman, you know. That was *genuine* admiration."

He was stalling, I realized, recognizing the symptoms from my rhetoric classes, in which sometimes it was possible to talk oneself out of sticky situations if one simply kept talking long enough. I didn't think that sort of tactic would work on Rook as well as it did on a professor—Rook had a sixth sense about these things, could smell frightened sweat in the air and gave fear no quarter—and so I was ready to intervene if things got violent again.

There was a sound of scuffling and I poked my head out just the slightest bit from around the tent. Whatever had happened had ended just as quickly as it began, it seemed, only Rook's hands were clenched now, and Fan was clutching at his arm.

"My apologies," he muttered, for the first time looking less than pleased. "I do allow my excitement to run away with me at times; that near-fatal flaw has been pointed out to me before. I was rude enough to mention the dragonmakers to an airman and offer no further explanation; I can only hope that what little information I *do* have will suffice. You're taking this all wrong. I returned with every intention of . . . helping you."

"I'll hear it," Rook conceded. His back was to me, so that I could only guess at the expression on his face. "Start spilling."

Fan rearranged his collar and cleared his throat.

"Well, as everyone with an interest in the subject knows," he conceded, "the Esar of Volstov has kept *these* magicians locked away from the outside world. But as with everything of value—a king's tomb or a pirate's legacy—well, hidden treasures are inevitably dug up. Now that the war's over, people have more time to pay attention to these things, see what I'm saying? People are starting to make a trade in a whole new industry called *information,* and it's a hell of a way to earn a living if you're clever enough to keep your head while doing it. A fact I *almost* forgot a moment ago; luckily you were there to remind me of it. Now— and don't go losing that temper of yours—but it just so happens I know a little about you, yourself. Not a lot—not more than your average person would've learned about one of Volstov's airmen—but enough to venture a guess as to *which* dragonmaker you'd be especially interested in finding."

I sucked in a breath, crouching low to the ground and wrapping my fingers around one of the ropes securing the tent to the ground. Rook, of course, would show no similar effects of having been moved by what Fan was saying. He shifted his weight from one foot to the other and crossed his arms as though he were bored, even though I knew he was just as excited about this as I was. It was the best lead we'd had since we'd started out.

It was almost too fortuitous, I thought, but anticipation got the better of me.

"Oh yeah?" Rook asked. I saw him flick something away, probably a fingernail he'd just picked loose. But he never did allow someone else, much less a total stranger, to have the upper hand.

Fan nodded. "It's a funny story, though I doubt you'll be laughing about it, hey? Anyway, it goes that the Esar—at first, mind—had the magician exiled because of her creation's . . . shall we say *fiery* temperament. He was upset, see, having poured all this time and energy, not to mention money, into a dragon that wouldn't take a rider. It's said she took the hand clean off one man who tried to touch her, and the Esar'd had enough after that." Rook snorted; it sounded like a laugh. No wonder the dragon in question had taken a liking to Rook; their "quirks" were all too similar. "In any case, being the sort of man he is who doesn't like feeling a fool's been made of him, he sent that poor magician off to live somewhere *real* out of the way. It helped, too, once he realized the knowledge these poor geniuses had was dangerous to the crown, and the Esar got the idea to start hiding these magicians all over the place, just to protect his own interests. Once old Havemercy started being a hero instead of an embarrassment, the Esar had no real pretext for having sent her magician away in the first place, so his only real excuse was to pretend like he'd meant to have them in hiding all along. But you can bet if there's ever another war Volstov has to fight, he'll be bringing them out of the woodwork right and left, recalling them from their places of *retirement*. Doesn't seem fair, does it? But that's the simple case."

I could tell, even though Rook had his back to me, that he was having a rough time of it holding on to his temper. Fan couldn't have known that speaking so candidly of the other member in the only real relationship of Rook's life thus far was a one-way ticket to ending up as fodder for the corpse-ticklers down in Molly. The only reason he was still talking was because he was proving useful. *That* much was as plain as if Rook had stated it outright.

"So Have's . . ." Rook began, then growled, covering up something that sounded remarkably like choking, and started again. "You're gonna tell me you know where this poor son-of-a was exiled to or not?"

"As it just so happens," Fan replied, lighting up, "I *do* have that information in my possession. Normally it'd be a very valuable thing—I doubt you'd get its worth if you shook down everyone in this camp and pooled your earnings all together—but as a personal favor, seeing as how I was so rude to you and seeing as how you're fingering that pig-sticker of yours, I think I can let it pass just this once."

"That's real charitable of you," Rook said. "Glad to see you've come to your fucking senses. So spit. It. Out."

Fan cleared his throat and posed like an actor on the stage. Maybe he was the sort of man who got an illicit thrill from cheating death every chance he had. It certainly didn't thrill me. Just watching him court disaster made an icy shiver run down my spine.

"I am very pleased to tell you, firstly," Fan said, "that the direction you're headed in right now, assuming you take this road in the direction of Karakhum, just so happens to be the right one. Funny how that works, isn't it? It's almost like birds who know which way to fly south for the winter even if they were born up north. I've heard rumors—yeah, rumors, and I know you're not inclined to believe them, but I've had them from more than one trustworthy source—that your filly's illustrious creator lives just east of the Khevir dunes. Last I heard, leastways. Can't make any guarantees, but that's the information I've got, and I didn't have to come here and offer it to you, either. Free of charge."

Fan smoothed his shirt in a gesture I recognized as slightly nervous, as though he'd realized now that he'd shared what he had to offer and was no longer of much use. It was dangerous territory to be in. He'd have to hope that Rook was mollified by the offering, or trust in his skills as a very fast runner.

"So the bastard's stuck off in the desert, huh?" Rook mused.

I was not overly familiar with the geography of the desert myself, but the Khevir dunes did lie east of where my friend Geoffrey was living. I could ask him for a more detailed map than the one I was currently working with once we arrived, if I could still convince Rook it was important to stop there and not charge down into the desert this very night.

It was technically impossible to make it before morning—in fact, it would have taken three days for any *normal* man to traverse, walking solidly without stopping to eat, sleep, or even rest his legs—but then, Rook was capable of conjuring a great number of miracles.

"I have one more question," Rook said.

"I hope I have one more answer," Fan replied.

Rook fingered something at his side—and, from this angle, I could tell that was the pommel of his knife, as crude and awful an instrument as I'd ever seen, and impossibly useful as well. "Are you selling that claw?" he asked at length.

"Are you looking to buy?" Fan asked, a little too jauntily.

There was a terrible tension in the air. I held my breath.

"I know your face," Rook said. He drew each word out with painful, deliberate slowness, in a dark tone even I'd never heard him use before. "I know your name, even if it is a lie. And if you sell that to someone who isn't worth the ground they shit on, I'll find you. Doesn't matter when, does it? Doesn't even fucking matter how. Could be a few months, could be a few years, could be when you're old and fat and enjoying the spoils of war you stole when the people who won that war weren't looking. But when I'm done with you, there won't be any pieces left for bastards like you to sell. You got that?"

"Explicitly," Fan said.

I let out my breath, slowly, unsteadily. Fan cast a glance in my direction—had he heard me?—then did the bravest thing I'd ever seen in my life: He turned his back on Rook and disappeared into the night.

"You can come outta there now that the stew's cold," Rook said. "Fuck me, I should've fucking sliced him."

"I'm glad you didn't," I said.

"Don't fucking know why I didn't." Rook looked at me, then the stew I was holding, with a face that said he'd lost his appetite. "Right in front of Compassus too," he said, which I took to mean the scale.

I didn't blame him for losing his appetite. I wasn't hungry myself, either, though I thought I could still manage a few bites, despite all that.

"If he was lying," I began, trying to be helpful, "then I always have a few more contacts, channels to exploit—"

"Start writing," Rook said, and strode off, leaving me alone in the tentative firelight.

CHAPTER FOUR

MADOKA

I was being followed. Whoever was doing it wasn't being all that clever about it, either, like it wasn't his specialty.

Well, fine. Eventually he'd mess up big enough to make things come to a head, but I was gonna let him embarrass himself before I did anything. Besides which, he hadn't tried to kill me yet, and I'd given him plenty of opportunities.

This wasn't exactly *my* specialty, either.

I'd taken the south route out of the capital, with a paper that gave me permission to cross any border I came to. It might've been imperial permission, but I didn't know how to read, and frankly, I didn't even want to know who was sponsoring this. Once I got far enough south, I'd come to desert territory. And in the desert, there wasn't much that could be done about checkpoints or walls. Oases were few and far between, supplies didn't come through easy, and people wandered into the middle of a sandstorm and were never seen again. Sure, there were ways around that, but they were far from the territory the Ke-Han had sprung out of in the first place—like people made of sand, the legends said. It was a landscape that'd been our home before my great-grandmother'd been a twinkle in anybody's eye, but our illustrious heritage of conquering by horse and sword had long since made it clear that we preferred sitting in pretty castles and counting our money than braving the wind and the sand, the hot desert days and cold desert nights. I agreed with that way of thinking. I was Ke-Han, through and through.

But seeing as how it was gonna be only me and the desert soon enough, it was becoming more and more clear that whoever *was* following me wasn't doing it to kill me.

There were two choices. One: He was somebody sent to keep tabs on me by the people who'd sent me, which was the likeliest case. Or two: He was somebody acting on good information, out to make a lot of money and crazy enough to risk his life for it. I didn't like the second possibility; it was too unpredictable. I could fight and hold my own, that wasn't the problem.

But eventually I was gonna have to sleep.

Man, but this situation was fucked. *I* was fucked, and I knew it, but that preservation instinct I had—the one that outweighed my more natural instinct for laziness—had kept me going this far.

If I *could* make it—if, somehow, I could pull all this crazy shit off—then I'd be rich, and the effort now would ensure me never having to lift a finger again. It was a weird bargain to strike with fate, but fate'd dropped it in my lap and there wasn't much I could do about it.

Still, there was the whole problem of sleeping. At first I was spending my nights in small villages, with enough people around that I could pretend that company meant safety, even when it didn't. I slept then, but as the landscape started thinning and company got smaller and farther between, I started to get a little paranoid, like there was a god or some deity of vengeance breathing right down my neck.

I wouldn't have let it bother me so much if that'd been my *only* problem. I was tough for a lady, as the charmers in my old village had been fond of pointing out, and I could take a few annoyances. Hey, under normal circumstances, I probably would've been flattered that someone thought I was interesting enough to keep an eye on. Problem was, there wasn't anything even close to normal about my circumstances these days, and whatever that creep in the cellar had done to my hand was starting to tick me off. I'd found a pair of gloves in among all the other stuff I'd lifted from the capital—stuff the madman'd let me keep. The gloves helped in some ways; I didn't have to look at the metal compass, hands twitching as it sat in the corner of my palm like I was some broken clock just waiting for repairs, except when I wanted to. But there was nothing that could stop me from *feeling* how weird it was: an alien addition to a body I'd been perfectly comfortable with all my life.

Every night, when I wasn't working out a plan to deal with whoever was tailing me, I thought up all kinds of angry tirades I'd throw at the madman who'd done this to me, once I was finally out of his service. What was wrong with just holding a compass, for starters, and hadn't he ever heard of asking permission before he went and mucked around with other people's bodies? I had a lot of good one-liners, but I always forgot the best of them by morning.

The problem with men like that was, they got so used to mucking around in other people's *lives* that using their *bodies* seemed like the next logical step.

Bunch of shit-eaters.

But, much as I hated to admit it, the madman wasn't my problem right now. I'd been thinking long and careful on how to deal with my pursuer, which was new to me. Planning ahead could take all the spontaneity out of life if you weren't careful, but I figured I could start making exceptions in light of the fact that everyone around me seemed to be making plans and including me in them without my permission.

I had to do *something*. I couldn't take it anymore.

Finally, I figured the best thing for it was to stop early for the night, just outside one of the little tent villages set up by travelers on their way into the desert. Close enough for security's sake, but maybe just vulnerable enough that I could lure him out of hiding. I'd never catch him if I was surrounded by people; but if he turned out to be some kind of uncommonly skilled fighter, then I wanted to have an escape plan at the ready. Or at least some witnesses, if he was planning on murdering me. I figured at least he'd get in trouble—not that I'd be around to enjoy the retribution, what with being dead.

Maybe, if I was lucky and it was the compass and not *me* this tracker was after, they'd only take my hand.

So, yeah, I wasn't too keen on using myself as bait. It pissed me off that I was even in this cracked situation to begin with, tracking down scrap metal like a trained hound. I didn't even want to know what a man like Crazy-Eyes could do with parts of ruined fire-breathers, especially when it'd been clear to *me* that his mind was coming unglued like a badly made box. Just thinking about him made my skin prickle, and I rubbed my arms to chase the gooseflesh away. The palm of my compass-hand scraped dully against my arm and I shook it off in annoyance.

There was a scuttling sound from behind me, like an animal losing its balance on the rocks, and I whirled around.

Of course there was no one there. Just me and the dim evening light—someone's idea of a joke that they hadn't quite seen fit to let me in on.

Enough of waiting. I'd have the upper hand—barely—if I just called the sucker out. Which, worn down by impatience, annoyance, and being so damn tired, I was brave enough and crazy enough to do right there.

"Can't you find something better to do?" I called. I didn't even care if anyone from the nearby camp heard me. Maybe it was better if they did. *Nothing to look at here, folks,* I thought, *just an altered freak having a temper tantrum in the badlands.* If I'd done it earlier, called the bastard out in woodsier climes, I might've heard a telltale rustle in the bushes or the snap of a too-dry twig as he tried to disappear. Out here there wasn't much in the way of vegetation, just sandy red dirt and scrabbly rocks that meant if a man wanted to get away unnoticed, all he had to do was hold still.

"Hey!" I shouted, picking up one of the stones lying around my feet and throwing it as hard as I could into the darkness. It wouldn't hit its mark, but I wanted to make it clear that I wasn't messing around. "I'm talking to *you,* my unwanted shadow! Didn't your mother ever tell you to speak when spoken to?"

Silence met my cries, and for a minute I *did* feel as foolish as a child pitching a fit. Then I gritted my teeth and started picking up handfuls of stones, hurling them down the narrow path between rock formations—the same one I'd followed to get here. The scrabbling sound that I'd heard before started again, and I paused to get a handle on where it was coming from before I threw my next-to-last stone. It was a good one, heavy and round, and when it landed it made a *thump* instead of a *crack.*

"Fuck!" someone howled, in a voice that mingled disbelief with pain.

"Are you planning on coming out now?" I shouted, adrenaline making me a little cockier than I had any right to be. I sure as shit hoped no strangers were watching. This was top-notch crazy behavior. "I've got good aim, and in case you haven't noticed, there's an unlimited supply of rocks around these parts. Anyway, you're pretty fucking *bad* at following someone without them knowing, so you might as well give up now."

I waited, turning the last stone over in my hand.

Finally I heard footfalls on the rocky overpass above my head, hesitant at first, then growing more sure of themselves. Someone dropped to the ground next to where I'd set up camp and stood, clutching his forehead. It was hard to make him out in the shadows, but then he moved his hand and everything became clear.

"Well blow me down," I said, hand clenching around the compass stuck into one palm, the other still holding tight to my last good throwing rock.

And here he was: my friend the soldier with the ugly scar. I couldn't help feeling a little guilty, since it wasn't like his face needed any more markings on it. For now, though, anger was still outweighing my guilt. Maybe this was how he'd gotten scratched up in the first place, skulking around in the shadows and creeping people out.

"So what," I said, "you're following me now? I should've known it was you. Soldiers can't sneak around worth a damn." I didn't put the rock down and I still had my good knife hidden at the small of my back, in case things went south fast. Not that I thought I was on a level with an army man—'cause as cocky as I was, I wasn't *stupid*—but maybe I'd stunned him a little when I cast the first stone and could use his headache to my advantage. "It's 'cause you all think you have a *right* to be anywhere you're going, so you've never had to practice it. You're getting a little purple up there, by the way."

"Shocking," he said, reaching up with tentative fingers to poke at his forehead. He was going to have one hell of a goose's egg in a couple hours.

Bastard deserved it.

"That's all you have to say for yourself?" I asked. "It's not enough you shit-eating weasels made me into some kind of walking divining stick, you have to have me looking over my shoulder every other second too?" I hadn't realized just how down-in-the-gut pissed I was until I'd started yelling, and now I couldn't quite remember how to stop. What made it worse was that Goose Egg didn't seem to be getting worked up at all. He just looked like his head hurt, and like he wanted to be sleeping at home somewhere and not out on some rocks in the middle of the desert. And like the sound of my voice was a little bit annoying—but no more out of sorts than that.

"Our . . . mutual associate," he began.

"You mean that bat-shit storage cellar rat?" I corrected, just to make sure we were on the same page.

He touched his forehead and grimaced. "If you must use such language, then yes, I suppose that's who I'm referring to. He thought it prudent that I . . . ensure you don't get any funny ideas."

"Yeah?" I snorted. "How's that plan working out for you?"

"I did try to tell him that, considering your reaction when he mentioned your family, you didn't seem the type to do anything foolish," he said.

I clenched my hands so tight they ached, and the compass pressed into my fingers, making me *feel* my pulse a little too keenly. It was racing pretty fast. "Don't. You. Say. A *word* about my family."

"Yes, that's the one," he said, easing down into a sitting position. "I don't imagine he has much family himself, or else he'd have appreciated it."

I took a step toward him, then halted. Much as I hated to admit it, my anger was bleeding off into confusion real fast. We weren't trying to kill each other. He was a damn soldier, and he'd sat down instead of going for the throat. If he wanted to do away with me, then he wouldn't have been beating around the bush about it. None of it made much sense from my experience, and I didn't like it.

He lifted his head, arrogant enough to look fucking tired and not in the least bit scared.

"I don't imagine you'd have heard of me, coming from such an out-of-the-way little mudhole, but I'm known in the ranks as the Ke-Han's Wild Badger," he said.

"Can I call you Badger?" I asked, crossing my arms. I wasn't impressed.

The Wild Badger shrugged as though it didn't make much of a difference to *him* one way or another. He looked different out of his uniform—annoyed not to be wearing it, mostly, and not any smaller, unfortunately—even if it was still blazingly clear he was a fighting man through and through.

"I only thought I should introduce myself, since it seems we've landed in the same boat, so to speak," he said.

"Oh yeah?" I asked, in a tone of voice that made it perfectly clear what I thought of *that*. "How d'you figure?"

"You don't imagine I *volunteered* for this assignment," he pointed out. "Following a sow in woman's clothing while she tramps across the desert is hardly *my* idea of fulfilling."

"A sow?" I said.

"It is what it is," he replied tersely, holding tight to his head.

"A sow and a badger," I said. "Lovely image we've got there."

"I'll leave it to you to decide who's painted in a more flattering light."

I didn't much hate him in particular—I should have, because of that pig comment, but I guess I did look like a crazy farm animal at that moment. And I'd been giving him the runaround, and we *both* had the same person to blame for it.

"What's his name?" I asked finally. "You know who I mean, so don't play dumb."

"A soldier never *plays* dumb," the Badger replied. "He either is dumb, or he isn't."

I shook my head. "I don't want to stick around long enough to find out which one you are. So what's he got on you that's keeping you from answering my question?"

The Badger finally, tentatively, lifted his hand from his head, and I could see in the dim light the color his bruise was turning, as well as the dark, ugly scar twisting half of his face into a pantomime mask. "A soldier still follows orders," he pointed out. "Personal feelings about those who outrank you don't necessarily come into play."

"I guess there isn't much work in the capital for soldiers these days," I muttered, flopping down across the fire from him. After a moment of thinking things through, I took off my glove to rub at the angry skin encircling the compass. I was having some kind of weird reaction to the metal, and it felt, at times, like my whole hand was on fire. Mostly at night—so there was more than one reason lately why I hadn't been able to sleep. "Guess you're not enjoying your early retirement."

The Badger crossed his arms over his broad chest and stared at me, sitting with the same precise confidence all trained members of our illustrious army did.

"After he sent you off, his attention turned toward me," he said, in a clipped tone. "It didn't take him very long to decide that you needed an escort. I was just lucky enough to be the only bastard left standing in the room when the thought occurred to him."

I felt a thin tendril of sympathy curling up inside me and quickly snuffed it out. It was strange seeing him out of place, though. When soldiers sat like that, they were usually flanked by their brothers-in-arms, or whatever they were, looking like an army of dolls, all set up perfectly by someone who was real crazy about being precise. No hair out of order, no uniform mussed; that kind of thing.

"So this," I said, waving my hand, "isn't enough reassurance that I'm not going anywhere? Fuck, man, I want this off of me. I haven't been keeping up with the fashions in the capital, but I'm pretty sure this isn't going to become the latest craze anytime soon."

"Precautions," Badger said. At least he didn't look very happy about it, but I was really scraping the bottom of the silver lining barrel on that one.

Things got quiet the closer you got to the desert. On our left—I guess you could call it the west, though my compass didn't offer those kinds of useful directions—the Cobalt Range rose up, imposing and spooky as hell in the night. The moon just crested them, half-full and hidden by smoky clouds. Yeah, we were one hell of a pair all right.

"Guess we'd better work together, then," I said. It didn't even stick in my craw the way I'd thought it might. The way he talked, that creepy magician had *his* family under the same watch as mine. And besides, I'd seen the look on Badger's face when we'd both been down in that cellar. If he was going to double-cross me, it wouldn't be for a madman's favor. "You know how to catch fish?" As far as I knew, it'd be the last time I ate fish in a good, long while.

Unless there was some kind of desert oasis-fish I didn't have any idea about. I didn't know much about the desert, so I wasn't going to rule it out.

A couple of hours later and we were both pretty wet, but the Badger'd managed to both spear us some dinner and cook it. I couldn't risk putting my hand too close to the fire in case the metal melted or something—a fucked-up thought, but one of the ones I'd been having lately. I didn't know anything about this thing that was a part of me now, and the last thing I needed was to ruin my one clue.

"This is good," I said. "Hope it's not poisonous."

"Only time will tell," Badger said, chewing contentedly.

There wasn't much a good, solid meal couldn't solve—which was part of the reason poor people like me were so angry all the time. I was even feeling in a more charitable mood now myself, since I wasn't deep-down hungry for the first time in days. *You try catching fish with a stick when you can't move your good hand,* I thought darkly, but the crispy skin was delicious, and my dark mood had lifted. We ate in silence. He had two fish and I had three, but that was only fair, because I was the one who had the compass and I was the one who hadn't volunteered to serve my country in the first place. And also, the three fish *I* ate were smaller than his two.

"That's good stuff," I said at last, wiping something off my cheek and checking to make sure nothing had flaked off on my palm. "You're gonna make some dumb woman real happy one day."

"Intriguing assessment," Badger replied.

"Now, isn't this better than lurking around in the shadows and sleeping all cramped up?" I asked. "Don't you feel happier about yourself? A little less embarrassed?"

"Depends," Badger said, "on how often you compliment my cooking."

I laughed, near to clapping my hand on my thigh, when I realized what the action would have meant and stopped myself.

"You know, under different circumstances my situation right now would've made an old woman *very* happy," I said. There wasn't any good reason for my suddenly being in a sharing mood, but I guessed having a full stomach made more of a difference than I'd thought.

At least Badger had the decency to look surprised.

"Your mother?" he asked.

"Nah," I said, shaking my head. "She was *way* too old to be my mother. I mean, probably. Had a face like a dried-up old persimmon. Same color too, now that I think about it. Met her while we were scavenging in the capital together."

"Charming," said Badger.

"Isn't it just?" I said, enjoying the fact that I was getting in under his skin. "All *her* kids up and died in that war you're all trying to forget, so I guess she didn't have anyone to look after her. Took things into her own hands after the capital got all burned up, just like everyone else who saw an advantage to get while the getting was good. Not bad for an old broad, really. She even had a tiger-skin rug she *said* came from one of the menagerie tigers, but I wasn't buying that one."

"She sounds like a fascinating character," Badger said, which could've been something I agreed with if he hadn't had that edge in his voice.

I shrugged. I didn't have to explain anything to him. Least of all the old woman and me. "We were traveling together until *you* showed up," I said. "Made her feel good to have someone to boss around."

"I see," Badger said. "Forgive me, but I still don't understand exactly how *this* scenario in particular would be pleasing."

"Oh," I said, feeling a little stupid now that I had to come out and say it. "Well. She was always telling me I should find a nice soldier and settle down. Figure this is about as close as I'm ever going to get, so it would've been nice if she'd known. That's all."

"Sounds like my mother," Badger muttered darkly.

"Probably not," I reassured him, the fish in my belly making me bold. "*Her* kids never would've let me hit them in the head with rocks. You develop reflexes after so many beatings."

"Doubtless," Badger said, looking nonplussed.

"She really walloped me good last time," I said, miming the action and instantly regretting it when the blight in my palm flared up.

"Does it hurt?" Badger asked.

I looked down at the compass, staring glumly at the hands. They hadn't moved much in the past two days—pointing furiously in the same direction, then suddenly giving me nothing to go on at all. It was like they were trying to drive me crazy. "It does and it doesn't," I answered at length. "I mean, it's *fucking weird.* And sometimes it throbs, I guess."

"You probably can't put it in cold water, can you?" Badger said thoughtfully.

"Don't particularly want to see what'd happen if I try," I said.

After looking ugly and thoughtful in the firelight for a moment, Badger held up his hands. "Truce," he said. "For long enough to let me look at it, at least."

"Why, are you some kind of magician?" I was skeptical, but I guess I also was a little bit lonely. It wasn't nice not having anyone to talk to, even the old woman, who spoke to me only to tell me exactly what I was doing wrong. "Sure, let's make peace. You can look at it all you want, but all you'll get is nightmares."

"Probably." He came toward me with the easy movements of a trained panther and took my hand in his.

"Well, there it is," I said. "Glorious, isn't it?"

He didn't answer me—probably because he thought I was being flippant, which I was, but the reason wasn't that I was some ignorant backwater mudraker. Sure, I'd raked some mud in my time, but I had thoughts and ideas and plans for the future; I was smart and I made investments. Plans had gone a little awry, but they were still in the realm of *a little bit* fixable.

"Skin's red here," Badger said. "Has it always been like that?"

"Yeah," I told him, and then, "Well, no. Not *always*. I figured it was just angry at first, what with having a big metal compass jammed in there. But really, it's anyone's guess. Just figured the coincidence was a little too . . . coincidental."

"Understandable," Badger conceded, but he still didn't look entirely satisfied, which I took as my cue to keep talking. Or maybe I was just feeling twitchy 'cause a strange soldier was holding my hand and I still wasn't entirely convinced he wasn't gonna cut it off and run away with it.

"Afterward it even started getting itchy, like it was healing," I said. "Only it's been getting worse instead of better. Damn thing drives me nuts when I'm trying to sleep. Not that having *you* breathing down my neck helped me any with that, either."

"My apologies," said Badger, only he said it like he was talking to my hand, turning it this way and that in the firelight. I didn't know what he thought he was gonna find, or why he'd even suggested this in the first place. Maybe he was just that bored.

I was feeling a lot more charitable with cooked fish in my belly, but I'd still never been what anyone could call *patient*. The only thing that'd ever shut me up for long had been the old woman and her stick, and she was leagues away now, if not more. I let my friend the Badger carry out his examination in relative silence—since it was obvious that was what he wanted—for as long as I could before I had to start talking again. Things were getting too quiet.

"What's the verdict, doc?" I piped up. "Dragon fever? Am I a medical miracle?"

"You're certainly . . . something," Badger said. It was one of those things that sounded like a compliment only it really wasn't, and I had to give him credit for not being a big, dumb lug like I'd thought at first. He was quicker than your average grunt, even if he wasn't that talkative. "I never claimed to be a doctor, though I might have an idea as to your complaint about the itching."

"Share the wealth, then," I said, trying to hide my sudden interest.

"Wait here," he said, and released my hand. Without another word—like maybe giving me a hint as to where he was fucking going—he stood up and walked off into the rocks, back held straight like a soldier's.

I was going to have to talk to him about that. If he was meant to be traveling disguised as common folk, then I was going to have to teach him how to walk like he'd been carrying the heavy burden of poverty all his life. Soldiers worked themselves just about as hard as poor people, except they had the muscles and the instinctive self-importance to hold their bodies rigid.

We didn't.

I leaned myself back against one of the large, flat rocks littering the area. The problem with nearing desert country was that it was too hot to spit during the day and cold enough to freeze your tits off at night. I didn't like a country that couldn't make up its mind one way or another. At least the rocks held the heat well enough—they could make a pretty decent bed if you weren't soft, which I wasn't. The skin around my compass-hand was looking angry again; too much attention getting it excited, or maybe I was just thinking about it too much. I rubbed at it, gingerly, trying not to feel like I was rapidly approaching my wits' end.

The heat from the fire had only made it worse, and I wasn't feeling very good about having shown it to the Badger right off the bat like that. Something about the look on his face when he saw it had pissed me right off. It was the same way most people looked at an old man with a cane or a three-legged dog, and I wasn't either of those. Never would be. That was something I could be thankful for.

But I damned sure didn't need any pity from a man too stupid to follow the likes of me without getting nabbed. Sure enough, I could hear his footsteps coming back, like he wasn't even trying to hide them anymore. I guessed he probably wasn't, now that the jig was up.

"Take this," Badger said, kneeling on the dirt beside me. His sleeves were rolled up and the front of his shirt was covered in rock dust like he'd taken a tumble, or maybe had to squeeze through something real narrow. In his hand was some kind of plant: a bunch of green, spiky stalks that looked like they were oozing a little.

"Gee, thanks," I said. "Just what a girl always dreams of. Should I keep it in water? I don't have a vase on me, but I'm sure I could find a hollow rock—"

"Aloe," he said, breaking one of the stalks in half and squeezing out some kind of goo. If that was supposed to encourage me, then he was way off base. "It grows in hot, sandy climates. Soothes bug bites better than anything, so I assumed it would help your problem as well."

I blinked. "That plant's gonna cure my compass problem?"

"Give me your hand," Badger answered, reaching forward to take it.

I let him. I probably could've gotten one good smack in with the compass, but I figured I'd done enough damage to his head for now. And besides, we'd called a truce. He turned my palm up and squeezed the goo around where it was red, using the plant to spread it on top of the angriest spots and rub it into my skin. The crawling itch in my hand began to fade. I would've *cried* with the relief of it if I'd been alone, but I wasn't, so I pursed my lips and scowled instead.

Badger picked up another leaf and squeezed it on, being real thorough about the whole thing. I closed my eyes, luxuriating in the feeling of a hand that was a little cold and sticky but no longer driving me fucking batty.

"Guess soldiers know a thing or two after all," I murmured, more comfortable than I'd ever dared to imagine I might be.

"Well, my mother imparted more than just the occasional beating," Badger said, *almost* smiling, like maybe that'd been a joke. I was surprised he'd bothered to listen in the first place, let alone that he'd remembered long enough to refer back to it later.

"You must've been firstborn," I said. "They always miss out on the fun stuff."

"First of four," Badger said thoughtfully. "I wasn't aware I'd made it obvious."

"Only to someone from a big family," I told him, flexing my hand happily. "Don't worry. As far as I'm concerned you've done 'em proud tonight."

"I'm glad it's working," Badger replied. He threw the empty skins onto the fire, which crackled sickly in response. "You should remember what they look like so you can keep an eye out."

That was the end of talking about our families, I figured. It was about as clear as a command. That was fine. Probably for the best. No point getting too close to the enemy, and all that good sense.

"Spiky little green things," I answered. "I got it under control. When I find the motherfucker that did this to me again I'm going to show *him* what it feels like to have foreign objects jammed into uncomfortable parts of his body."

Badger snorted like maybe he was laughing, and I cracked an eye open to check.

"Didn't know they bred a sense of humor into soldiers these days," I said.

He sighed, settling back—or at least, looking as settled as he ever could. "My attitude toward our mutual acquaintance is an exception to the general rule."

"That fucking bastard," I agreed. "Whoever thought *he* was worthy of a promotion ought to be kicking themselves right about now."

Badger made a noise like there was something stuck in his throat. "Understand, it's a rather difficult time for the empire, at present," he explained, slowly, drawing each word out as though his honor depended on the enunciation. "Our great emperor has . . . and now the capital is beset by a diplomatic envoy from our conquerors. When you take into account that our magicians were all but destroyed in the final days of the war . . ."

"Leaves us at kind of a disadvantage, doesn't it?" I said. The things he was saying weren't news, by any means—enforced mourning for our great emperor aside, it was like a punch to the gut of everyone's pride that we'd lost—but it sounded different coming from the mouth of someone who got all his information through official bulletins instead of gossip and hearsay.

"It does," said Badger. "No one knows exactly how many survived the destruction of the dome. Very few, perhaps a dozen. Under normal circumstances, I believe the matter of the magicians *would* take precedence over all when it came to rebuilding. But the emperor has been distracted, I understand, with the delegation, and such things get swept under the rug. As a result, those who remain are enjoying more free-dom than they might otherwise have been given."

"Freedom?" I said. "Freedom our friends in Volstov wouldn't allow, I'd wager."

"They . . ." Badger said, trailing off again.

"Huh," I said. Why wasn't I surprised the guy was involved in some-thing shady as shit? I looked down at my hand, where the itch had faded but the skin was still red, like I couldn't fool *it* with some dumb plant. "So this guy's got a plan to track down the fire-breathers and no one thinks to ask *how* he wants to do it, so long as he gets it done."

"Favorable results are very effective in silencing those who would disagree with unfavorable methods," Badger said. There was something about the calm in his voice that made me want to clock him again. "But so long as he is successful—so long as *you* are successful—I doubt it will matter much to anyone, one way or another."

"That's a cold fucking way to look at life," I protested, surprising myself a little. I wasn't some naive kid who expected the world to be fair and just. Hell, I should've laughed at myself just for thinking about it. Still, being a part of it pissed me off—the first time I'd ever thought about general rights for the people, because it was my thumbs caught between the bamboo.

"It is what it is," said Badger, turning away from me to stare into the fire. If I hadn't seen his face before—up close and in the daylight—I would've assumed he was an old man now. There was something about the way he held himself, and the lack of passion in his voice when he spoke about things that ought to have fired up any young soldier: our country and patriotism and the like. He was a strange one. "I would keep an eye on that hand of yours, if I were you. Concern yourself with the things you do have control over."

"Yeah." I sighed, not really sure what I was supposed to do with that except agree. "I guess so."

"If we keep on this road at this pace, we'll reach the desert by to-morrow," he added, tucking back against one of the bigger rocks.

"That all depends on what my friend here tells us," I said, holding up my hand. I hadn't missed that "we," either. Privately, I was thinking it might not be so bad to have a partner that wasn't stuck in my hand and could actually talk. Not that I'd ever say it out loud.

"Of course," Badger said. "You'll be sure to keep me informed."

I didn't altogether like how sure of himself he sounded, but I guessed there wasn't much I could do about that. I faked a yawn. "If I up and leave you in the morning, you can always follow me with your great tracking skills. I'll never know you're still on my trail."

"It isn't so terrible to me," Badger said, tone measured, "that I am not adept at sneaking around in the dark."

"You wouldn't last a *day* without your titles," I told him. "Just a bit of friendly advice."

The sound of the fire dying down began to soothe me, and I wasn't planning on ignoring the aloe's help. I'd take sleep where I could get it because I was starting to get crazy with how tired I was, and that wouldn't help my case for freedom in the slightest.

"I can't help but notice," Badger said softly, "when I was looking at the compass . . . The hands aren't moving at all, are they?"

"Maybe you'd better get some shut-eye," I told him. "Don't think your eyes are working right."

I tucked in against a bundle of silks—wrapped around with some cotton fabric that'd already been damaged by the fires, just to keep them safe from all the sand and grit. It made a good pillow and it'd make some fine dresses, too, once I could get it back to my folks. My mom and my three sisters would have to drop all their regular work and start sewing, 'cause Madoka was about to bring them a gold mine.

I heard the Badger huff softly. Maybe he was laughing at the look on my face, and maybe he had every right to laugh. Or maybe he was just jealous that I had a pillow and he didn't. Either way, I didn't care much about it, because I was getting some much needed sleep, and that was something you couldn't pay for with a whole field of silk.

ROOK

I was starting to have these dreams, and I sure as shit didn't like them.

It'd been a long time since I'd had to dream about flying, since dreams were supposed to be for what you *couldn't* do. When I woke up I had a sour taste in my mouth and a dark feeling in my gut, and being around other people only made it worse.

"We're half a day from Karakhum now," Thom said. "Here's an interesting fact—did you know that *khum* is the generic name for *desert* in these parts? *Kara* just so happens to mean *capital*, as well, which makes the etymology of the name . . ."

I didn't want to know the look I was giving him right then. All I could hope was that it was enough to make him *feel* his balls start to shrivel—that is, if they were even still there, which was something I currently had to ask myself every minute of my fucking life. At least he *had* stopped talking, which was a fucking gift from the desert gods— who, by the by, shared the same mythological roots as the Ke-Han pantheology or whatever the word was—and if I'd been a praying sort of man, I would've dropped down to my knees and kissed the sand right where I was walking.

Except I wasn't a praying man, and I didn't want to waste the time.

"I've always wanted to see Karakhum," Thom said, very carefully. Good. He'd better be careful. If I had to hear one more interesting fact about something that ended in the syllables "ology," I *was* gonna hit him and we'd both fucking regret it.

"Yeah?" I snarled. "Why's that?"

He seemed shocked I'd even asked him something, then this sickening grateful look came over his face, like I'd done him a big favor just by talking to him. If he didn't start getting more faith in himself, then he really was hopeless, but it wasn't my job to teach it to him. If he acted like he was worthless, then fuck me if he wasn't. It was only once he grew a pair and stood up for himself that he'd start being worth *anybody's* time.

But apparently no amount of punching could get him to bounce right back up. He just let it roll off his back like water off a duck and kept coming back for more.

"Well," he said, stumbling over a rocky patch, "if you must know, I read a book about it a very long time ago. Not much information came out of the desert—it was too difficult, what with the war, and they trade mostly by sea with Jikji through a port city quite, quite far from Karakhum, since tensions over the mountain border were so heated. The book was a very old one, and I found it in the trash."

"Did you teach yourself to read with it or something?" I asked. The whole thing was ridiculous enough already, but when Thom didn't answer I let out a groan. "Bastion fuck," I said. "That's rich."

Thom shrugged. "I'm sure the book was somewhat incorrect factually," he admitted, like that mattered. At least it didn't have to do with his favorite topic, the *ologies* of the world. "I can't imagine—what with the trek through the desert to the port being so arduous—that things are really as luxurious as the book led its reader to believe. Still . . ."

"It's a fancy daydream," I said. "I get it. I'm glad this is *fun* for you."

"I'm trying to look on the bright side of a shit situation," Thom said, and immediately after looked horrified.

I couldn't help but grin. "That's more like it. But don't use language like that. Makes you sound uneducated."

"I *know*," Thom said miserably. "Thank you, Rook. I was aware of that."

"Guess I'm just a bad influence," I told him.

"The worst there is," he agreed.

He had me there. Bastion, I was even the first one to admit it. It was why he shouldn't've been here, talking on and on about the things he was gonna learn, when I was the one leading him through shit and muck and sand and dirt, cursing all the while and dreaming of other stuff—the stuff in my life that came between us. Life was too fucking up in the air right now, and I was too fucking down on the ground.

"Do you want to talk about anything?" Thom asked.

"We *were* talking."

He scuffed at the ground, causing himself to trip again. I could've told him that would happen, but again, there was stuff a guy had to learn by himself. How he'd lived in Molly for so long without at *least* a broken nose or a couple of missing teeth to show for it was a real miracle, but he'd done it somehow—probably by talking common thugs to sleep and giving them the slip while they were snoring. Anything was fucking possible.

"Right. We were talking . . . about something you have relatively little interest in," Thom pointed out.

"If you knew that already, then why do you keep talking to me about it in the first place?"

"Because I don't know what else to say to you," Thom said. "Isn't that obvious?"

I guessed he was right. He usually was, even if he was thick as brick most of the time. It was how much of a genius he thought he was when he could walk right into a wall because he wasn't looking where he was going that grated my fucking nerves.

"Pretty obvious," I agreed.

"Do you have any suggestions?" Thom asked, looking like he already knew the answer to *that* one. Good. He should have.

I grunted, feeling like this was a waste of time. "Half a day to Karakhum, right?" I asked.

"Yes," Thom said. He was being careful again, but I could tell he was real pleased to hear that I'd been listening to him. Someday, when I was feeling more charitable—which was liable to be never, but as they said in the Fans, a girl could always hope—I'd have to fucking teach him not to be so disgustingly *grateful* for the meager scraps of attention people threw his way. "Why do you ask?"

"When we get there, we're lookin' up that friend of yours, right?"

"Geoffrey," Thom interjected, looking at me instead of the road ahead and stumbling over some low little scrub bushes as a result. He could look where he was going; that'd help. "Geoffrey Bless."

"Whatever," I said, shaking off the annoyance like a horse shook off flies. My little brother could be a damn big fly when he wanted. "Sure. Him. How long's it gonna take to find him once we get there?"

"Hum," Thom said thoughtfully, like this'd never even fucking crossed his mind. "Well, when I last heard from him, he was still the only Volstovic man living in his city. Like it or not, visible minorities do tend to stand out."

"Sounds like a lot of fun for him," I muttered, scratching the back of my neck. "We just gonna waltz around for a while and ask for the paleface, then?"

"Rook!" Thom said, like he was a fucking woman and I'd walked in on it, scandalizing him so bad he needed a big feather fan to hide behind. "*Please.* Just—allow me to do the talking."

"Figures you'd learn sand-talk," I grumbled. I was just giving him a hard time for the hell of it now, but that was at least familiar. Felt comfortable, almost—like something we both knew how to do, and no one had to think too hard about answering or feel like an ass for too long afterward. "All that brain in your head and you choose to fill it with useless junk."

"I . . ." Thom began, wilting a little. Then his back straightened with that ridiculous, stubborn pride of his and he gave me his professor look. "The *correct* term is *Khumish;* with *khum* meaning *desert,* as I explained before. Khumish is the language of the desert—well, the most universally spoken, in any case. As Geoffrey found out, there are all sorts of offshoots in dialect that make it impossible for anyone ever to become truly *fluent*."

"Bet that broke his little heart," I said, and Thom shot me another look, this one good and mean.

"Some people find *learning* an adventure," he sniffed, following up by nearly turning his ankle on a rock.

"Some people oughta learn how to walk in a straight line before going adventuring," I said, and kicked the rock off the trail when I passed it.

"Yes," Thom said. "I take your point."

After that, I let nature and the desert take its course with the conversation, and it dried up like a prune. I was feeling too caught up in my own skin to work as hard as I had to with him, and clearly the way I was behaving was giving Thom the same thoughts about me. Whatever. Nothing I could do about it now, and maybe if we ever managed to track down my girl's magician in the Khevir dunes, then I could ask him to build me some kind of brother who could keep his footing and who ate less than a stableful of horses.

There were only two reasons I was still willing to put up with this little visit to Thom's old 'Versity pal. Number one: Apparently he was liable to have a map of the Khevir region, which I was real eager to get my hands on. Number two: Thom'd gone and written that letter to Adamo, and damned if I wasn't the least bit curious to hear his reaction to our girls being sold off, piece by piece, like they were prime parts of a cow at the butcher on Sunday morning. I was half expecting Adamo'd be there himself when we showed up to the *other* piss-pot professor's house, but Adamo wasn't bell-cracked like the rest of us, and even *he* couldn't travel that far in this amount of time. Not unless he was flying.

So that was it, everything I had to look forward to: a map and a letter. Just a heap of paper when you got right down to it, and the fact that something like that was what we were questing for really ticked me off.

We didn't even know if that dirty little snake from the campsite had been telling the truth. It made me itch at night, and when I wasn't dreaming of flying, I was dreaming of that bastion-damned claw he'd been holding. He was just lucky it'd been me and not Ghislain who'd found him, or else he might've found himself in twice as many pieces as our girls. Fuck only knew how many other parts were in greedy, grasping hands like his right at this minute, while we were wasting our time tramping through desert, desperate for whatever scraps life threw our way. It made me want to smash the whole countryside out of existence.

It was when I got into moods like that that I needed to get the hell away. Spend some time checking the path ahead just so I wouldn't knock my brother's face in just for looking at me funny. And he had kind of a funny face, sometimes—round with a snub nose that was nothing like mine—so it was hard not to. I was pretty sure he could tell too, because he stopped talking to me about *ologies* and desert wildlife and the maximum recorded heat on any given day in the dunes and was quiet, watching his feet now, just like I'd told him.

So I sure as hell wasn't the only one who was fucking relieved when we finally made it to Karakhum, cresting some dune and seeing it right away when we hadn't before, hidden neat as you please inside a dusty little sand valley. Nothing at all like Thremedon, who made damn sure everybody knew where she was.

For a capital city, it sure looked like a big dust bowl to me. First off, we passed through these high stone gates that I knew Thom was just *dying* to tell me had originated in such-and-such a place and were commandeered by Lord Obviously Compensating for Something. But he kept his mouth shut and so did I—probably because the louder we were the more attention we'd bring to ourselves. And even if we hadn't been out of place in the Volstovic countryside, we sure as shit were out of place here.

Through the gates was more fucking sand, and the sound of about a hundred different people shouting in a language I didn't understand. Merchants were holding up handfuls of cheap-looking wares like if they talked loud enough about it, it'd interest someone, *and* they had to talk louder than the guy in the stall next to them in order to snag that day's sucker. There were people milling up and down the alleys between tables—women in veils and serious-looking men—but no one seemed to notice that they were all in danger of going fucking deaf at any minute. Maybe growing up in a place like this meant they had thicker ears or something. I didn't know, and Thom probably did, but I wasn't about to ask him for the useless answer to some question that had nothing to do with my life and would only fill my brain with clutter.

Aside from all the shouting people, there were the ramshackle stands set up with all sorts of colorful silks blowing in the breeze, like someone'd taken Our Lady of a Thousand Fans and shook it upside down—keeping hold of the bitches' legs, but letting the dresses fall loose—and big crates of weird-looking fruits just sitting out in the open. *That* all looked pretty stupid to a born Mollyrat, like these people were just begging to be robbed. Too bad I was a lot bigger than I used to be and not cut out for that kinda shit anymore.

Little fingers, every Mollyrat remembered, were sticky. Big fingers'd get cut off.

Of course, with all the hustle and bustle, people still had some time to stop and stare at us. Dark eyes everywhere focused on us, probably trying to decide if we could understand enough of what they were saying to buy what they were selling. I gave a few of them warning looks so they wouldn't try anything. None of them dared to give me any warning looks back.

I scanned a few of the stalls, caught each time by glints of metal—but it was all jewelry or belt buckles or other useless shit, none of it what I was looking for, and I nearly spat on the man next to me. Would've served him right. He was getting too damn close.

"*Oh*," Thom said, like he'd seen something I hadn't. He tugged at my sleeve like a kid, and for some reason, instead of shrugging him off, I looked up at where he was pointing.

There were buildings made of white stone off in the distance, built by someone who'd clearly had a vision for that kind of thing, all thick columns and pointed turrets. They looked like bleached bones sticking out of the desert, like some giant back in the day had died here, picked clean by the desert wind. And people—just being people—had thought it was good for building. I'd never seen anything like it before. You could've dropped th'Esar's palace right into one of them and still managed to fit the Basquiat on top.

"Shit," I said, whistling. "You read about that in your book?"

"Yes," Thom murmured. He had a look on his face like he'd just seen his first dragon. Except I'd been there when he'd seen his first dragon, and he sure as hell hadn't looked anything like that.

"Well," I said, "plenty of time to look while we find your friend the professor, right? I'd ask, but I'm pretty sure you said something about wanting to do all the blabbing since that's what you're *supposed* to be good at."

"What?" Thom said, still staring off into the distance. Right when I was about to wave my hand in front of his face—and maybe smack him one, for good measure—he snapped to. "Oh. Geoffrey! You're right; I'm sorry. Yes, I'll . . . Well I suppose I'll just have to . . . Hm."

He tore his eyes away from the big white building, somehow, and started rummaging away in his bag like a squirrel looking for an acorn. What he came up with was his travel journal. I should've guessed it wouldn't be anything useful.

"You looking to get yourself sold to some desert traders?" I growled. "Don't think I'll help you out when it happens. I'll lie and tell 'em you're a cinch at heavy lifting and not as annoying as you really are, either."

Thom shot me a look, like somehow I was the fucking unreasonable one here. "It's been a while since I've spoken the language. I want to be able to write things down in case I run into a difficult patch," he explained.

"Fine," I said. "Just don't let 'em sucker you into buying anything. I don't like the look of all of 'em."

Thom was lost to the world, though, mouthing out something he was reading in his travel journal, his face red from the heat and maybe embarrassment. "Let's see," he said. "It's just that—well, that can't be right, the pronunciation is all off—"

"Let me help you out," I said, not exactly feeling like a saint but ready to get out of this place before I went crazy from the stench of incense and bought myself a copper tiara. I breathed in deep, making sure to take as much air as I could into my lungs, like they were a blacksmith's bellows. There'd never been a chance for me to bust out my Adamo impression anywhere other than the Fans. Still, I thought it'd be pretty damn impressive. I couldn't wait to see these merchants piss themselves like little boys.

"Rook, what are you—" Thom started, and I had to cut him off before he broke my damn concentration.

"Geoffrey Bless?" I hollered, loud enough to get past all the shouting going on around me; maybe loud enough for Adamo to hear it back where he was filing his nails in the 'Versity. "Geoffrey Fucking Bless?"

Everything stopped—the talking, the yelling, the exchanging of money, the jangling of trinkets. It started from right where we were and spread out like a little domino line, and everyone who'd been trying to pretend like they weren't gawkers finally owned up to their curiosity and stared at us.

"That'll probably do it," I said.

Thom was white around the lips. "You could have warned me you were doing that," he said. "I thought you were—"

"Thomas?" someone said beside us, in the sweet, ladylike tones of a 'Versity boy. "Is that you?"

"Geoffrey!" Thom said.

I looked away to avoid the reunion, whatever backslapping and hugging and reminiscing it involved. *Thomas* was the stupidest name I'd ever heard, and already I hated this asshole, who had as high an opinion of himself as anyone who did this kind of thing with their lives. I didn't buy into it. He was just a kid who never grew up; everyone here probably hated his guts more than I did.

"And this must be Rook," Geoffrey said.

I grunted. "My name's Nellie," I said, which was what I felt like at the moment.

"Ah," Thom said quickly. "We've been traveling for some time, and—"

"Of course! How awful of me," Geoffrey Fucking Bless said, "not inviting you in. I'm just back from a Khevir dig, you see, which means I've forgotten my manners completely. Won't you follow me?"

I brought myself up close to him, scowling down into his weaselley little face. It was sunburnt, but also freckled, so I could see right through his whole charade as easily as if he were a whore pretending this was his first time with a man. "Don't interrupt people," I said. "It's rude."

"*Rook,*" Thom said. "This is *my friend,* Geoffrey."

I couldn't help it, but put on my best shit-eating grin—the one that always made other people shit themselves for some reason, though I'm sure I had no fucking idea why. "So pleased to finally make your acquaintance, Geoffrey," I said. "The pleasure is all mine. Sincerely."

"Don't worry," Geoffrey said, ignoring me, though he did take my hand and shake it briefly. "The desert does this to people. I was in the worst mood for years when I first came out here. It's all the sun, you know."

He started us past a vendor, who shoved a meat skewer into my face so fast I barely had time to duck—and give his stall a good, accidental kick while I did so—and then led us off the main street and onto a narrow one, where a few scrawny kids wearing almost nothing at all were crouched, playing with a couple of stones. That, at least, was a familiar sight if ever I saw one.

One of them looked up at me as I stared down at them; I couldn't tell if it was a girl or a boy, that's how runty they were. Still, their eyes went wide when they saw me, and a grave hush fell over them and their friends, stones completely forgotten. I made a face and they winced but didn't run.

Good, I thought. They'd do okay.

"My house is, understandably, past all the regular hubbub," Geoffrey said, walking carelessly on. Thom was eating up every word he said like it was a foreign delicacy, and I supposed their friendship would last for as long as Geoffrey Fucking Bless had stupid shit to say, which might be forever, or until Thom ate him out of house and home, which might take half a day. Depended on how generous our benefactor was, and whether he'd already been shopping. "One wouldn't be able to sleep, since the market begins early and ends late," Geoffrey rambled on. "You'd wonder how they get all their wares, but this *is* a major trade route—just not inland, of course, since that would have put them at such a disadvantage during the war, considering their border with Xi'An." Thom was itching to write all this down; I could practically see his fingers twitching. And none of this mattered at all, either—geography lessons and all that 'Versity rot. We were here about something that mattered, and all this bastard could talk about was when the market opened in Kara-whatever. *Khum,* a little voice that sounded an awful lot like Thom's whispered in my head. *It means desert.*

"And here we are!" Geoffrey said finally. "I know it's not much— isn't the architecture fascinating here? Such simplicity of style, and yet indoors . . ." He swung open a door in a narrow little building with depressing windows, then stepped back to let us look inside.

I'd be the first to admit, it did look like something out of a picture book. It sure as hell didn't look like the kind of thing any student should've been able to afford. Not that I had any idea what kinda luxury students lived in one way or another; but judging by the holes in my brother's socks, 'Versity living didn't exactly strike me as cushy. As far as I knew, it wasn't like there were people in the higher-ups *pay-*

ing you to learn, but someone was sure as shit paying Geoffrey Bless to do whatever it was *he* was doing. There was a whole litter of useless-looking pillows scattered about, done up in every color of the rainbow. It was exactly the kind of ridiculous shit they had in a high-class whorehouse like Our Lady, stupid baubles scattered everywhere to distract you from where the paint on the walls might be peeling a little, or where the floorboards were cracking, or draped over the stains they didn't want you to notice or think too hard about. There were filmy curtains hanging all over the place too—those at least I could get behind, since they kept the stinging flies out, which'd been eating Thom up at night like he was a desert pastry—and low, backless couches that I was sure looked better than they felt on your ass.

Fucking students. They were real fond of a thing "in theory," and never once thought about whether or not it'd be comfortable to sit on at the end of the day.

Bless's place was quieter'n the marketplace had been, though, and he wasn't burning any of that foul-smelling incense, so at least there was that.

"Oh, my," Thom said, fingering the straps on his pack like he didn't quite have the words all of a sudden. I'd've figured him for eating up a place like this like *it* was a desert pastry, but instead he just looked like he didn't know quite what to make of it, which was fine by me. Even if it was kinda fucking eerie that we were on the same page there.

"Not exactly the style one becomes accustomed to in Thremedon," said Geoffrey Fucking Bless, proud as piss of himself for having no taste to speak of.

"Something *wrong* with Thremedon?" I asked. I was beginning to wish we hadn't run into this guy after all, 'cause he was starting to rival the stinging flies on a scale of things that annoyed the shit out of me.

"Of course not," Thom said shortly, eyes still flitting around the room in confusion. His gaze landed on a statue—a round, ugly little thing with a face like a monkey—and he all but sprang forward, picking it up in his hands. "This is—well, I'm certainly no expert, but if I'm not mistaken, this is from the Lut Period. However did you afford—Geoffrey, how *can* you afford all this?"

Leave it to a Mollyrat to ask questions about money. You never learned to tiptoe around what you didn't have, and *I* sure as hell wasn't surprised, but I could tell that Thom was, a little.

Geoffrey Bless scratched his fucking curly mop, and laughed like he was uncomfortable. Good. I was starting to get real ticked off about how he was pretending that I wasn't here. I might not've been 'Versity educated like some, but I sure as hell knew when someone was making like he didn't see me, and not because he was scared but because he thought he was too high up to notice all the people down below him.

Him and Raphael would've gotten along like houses on fire.

"Well, that's an interesting story, really," Bless began. "Oh! But I won't get into it just yet; let me get you some water, and please do sit down. Unless you'd prefer pomegranate juice? But then, so few people enjoy the real thing—it's not sweet enough for their unrefined palates . . . At any rate, take a seat and make yourselves at home; I'll get something to cool your throats." He said all this in a whirl, heading toward the kitchen and gesturing toward the furniture and all the while blabbering like a lunatic. I was half expecting him to drop in a dead faint at any minute.

No such luck.

"We'll have water, thank you," Thom said carefully, after a cursory glance in *my* direction.

I shrugged at him. Not my friend we were dealing with, now was it?

Geoffrey Bless bowed—fucking *bowed*—and disappeared into the kitchen. I was really gunning for sainthood. They'd be accepting me into the Brothers of Regina any day now and blessing me with holy water to match the goodness of my sweet, pure heart.

"Water. Guess the juice tastes like shit, huh?" I muttered, looking for a couch that wasn't about to collapse the moment I sat down on it.

"Just *sit*," Thom retorted, though for a minute there he'd looked like he'd been about to crack up. He replaced the statue carefully, then pushed aside a curtain so he could sit down. At least he had the sense to seem fucking uncomfortable while he did it, but that might've been because the couches were so low to the floor you had to crouch down way past comfort to actually sit on them.

"Didn't tell me your friend was a high-class whore," I said, picking up one of the pillows and tossing it aside.

Thom looked startled, then hissed like an angry goose. "For *goodness*' sake. He's in the next room. He'll hear you."

"Don't think my Thremedon opinions'll matter too much to him one way or another," I pointed out. "Just don't forget the reason we're here."

"I'm hardly liable to do that," Thom huffed, crossing his arms. He was sweating, rubbing his sleeve over his forehead and looking about ready to take a nap any minute. Great. That made me feel *real* optimistic about our prospects in the desert.

"Sorry to keep you waiting," Geoffrey Bless called out, stepping back in the room carrying a whole trayful of goodies. I didn't feel like telling him that wouldn't even begin to sate my brother, the fucking bottomless ravine. That could be something he found out on his own, friend to friend, with no interference from me.

"Grapes!" Thom exclaimed, looking suddenly like he could manage to go on after all.

"Indeed," said Geoffrey Bless. "And goat cheese. I think you'll find the combination simply divine."

"Is that the water?" I asked, reaching over to take one of the glasses before he could tell me it was *actually* from a nearby bastion-damned mountain *spring* and that it was just peachy fucking heaven and it went best with prunes. I drank the whole thing in one go, like a camel storing up during the dry months. At least that was good.

Geoffrey Fucking Bless didn't even blink. Whatever. He wanted to pretend like he didn't see me, that was fine. Just meant he was gonna get a real nasty shock sooner or later.

"Thank you," Thom said, looking like a chipmunk with his cheeks full of grapes and cheese and bastion only knew what else. Guess you couldn't breed some things out, even with good education and a stubborn-ass will.

"You're quite welcome," said Geoffrey Fucking Bless, like he'd been doing nothing but playing perfect host out in the desert and just waiting for someone to come by and compliment him on it. He sat on one of those impossible fucking couches without tripping over his own feet—well, he'd had all the time in the world to practice—and set the tray to one side.

"Listen," I said, patience stretched about as thin as it was gonna go, grapes or no grapes. It was pretty fucking evident—to me, if no one else—that this asshole wanted to talk to Thom and not to me, but my brother'd gone and crammed his windpipe with delectables so it was up to me to pick up the fucking slack. "We're real grateful for the fruit platter and all, but we're here on business."

"Ah, of course!" said Geoffrey Bless, taking a drink of something red and sticky in a tall glass. I didn't know what pomegranate juice was, but I hoped it still tasted like shit even to his refined palate. He turned toward Thom. "Where *are* my manners? I suppose I owe you something of an explanation."

"Mmph," said Thom, helpful as fucking always. He'd moved over to where the tray'd been set down, grapes in one hand and water in the other, eyeing the cheese like a naughty cat.

"You do," I translated, not like it was my place or nothing, but I wanted things to be moving on as quickly as possible and *not* like a 'Versity-paced lecture.

"Well," began Geoffrey Bless, scratching his enormous fucking head, "I suppose when I last spoke with you, Thomas, it was when I'd just begun to grasp the difficulty of the task I'd set myself to. Not to mention the relatively *small* stipend one receives from the 'Versity when researching abroad. As much as I hate to admit it, I was beginning to reach the end of my rope very early into my studies here."

I was pretty sure that a son-of-a like Geoffrey Bless had no fucking idea what the end of the rope looked like. I was just as sure that I'd be willing to show him, after he'd gone and helped us all polite-like.

"Go on," I told him.

He glanced at me and sighed. "I never imagined you would come to visit me, here of all places! I never imagined anyone would come, for that matter. As it happens, I might be able to offer you more aid *now* than if I'd remained in my former position, but the fact of the matter *is* . . . I currently spend the majority of my time sweating it out in the dunes. I dig up artifacts and sell them for money."

Thom's eyes bugged out, and he actually paused in trying to cram an eighth stuffed grape leaf into his mouth. "You're a grave robber?" he demanded.

"Oh, no," Geoffrey said, grimacing. "Please. I prefer . . . raider. It's not as though I'm disturbing the bodies. No money in bones, you see. But it's made me very familiar with the surrounding areas."

"You dig up dead people and sell their shit?" I didn't know whether it made me respect him more or less. At least he wasn't like most of the 'Versity kids, who respected and trusted dead things more than they paid attention to the present.

Geoffrey Bless pulled a face. "In the most common of terms," he began, sniffing, like I was the one who stank.

"You dig up dead people and sell their shit," Thom repeated, obviously not thinking about what he was saying.

I took a long drink of water. I was hell-bent on enjoying myself with some of this.

"Thomas, really," Geoffrey Bless said, but he looked a little less round and a little more dangerous. "There's theory and there's practicable action. The desert is quite unforgiving. It's why I wanted to warn you. Depending on where your search takes you, I'd warn you against traveling out into the dunes at all."

I was about to say something when Thom gulped down the last of his stuffed fig leaf and raised himself up to his full height—which wasn't too impressive, because he was short anyway, and sitting on that damn couch wasn't helping, either.

"I'll choose what I'm capable or incapable of," he said.

"Your preposition's dangling," Bless replied.

"Yours is gonna be dangling, too," I told him, "if you don't fucking get down to business."

Geoffrey Bless straightened up and tugged at his collar—he was getting hot, finally, even with all his practice in the desert. Good. "All right," he said. "If that's the way you intend to play. Thom wrote that you were looking for information on magicians banished to the nearby surroundings, are you not?"

"Not just any magicians," I said.

"Yes, I know that," Bless said, looking a little keener. "Well, I know these deserts as well as any native by now, even if it's not possible to have combed them over completely by myself. It just so happens, there *are* rumors."

"And?" I prompted.

"As you know—well, as you *might* know—the Khevir dunes are a vastly unexplored wasteland," Bless continued, clearing his throat as I leaned closer to him. Nothing like putting the pinch on a 'Versity boy, grave robber or not, to make him get to the point a little faster than he wanted to. "Not even the local nomadic peoples spend much time passing through there. It leads to nowhere; it's in the middle of nowhere. It *is* nowhere, essentially, and not many wish to test their luck against a place like that. There's almost no way to get out to it, either. The desert's too cruel for that."

"So that's the rumor?" I asked flatly. "There's a desert? How fucking unexpected."

Geoffrey Bless gave me a dark look, like I was ruining all his fun and he didn't realize that was my plan in the first place. "If your initial clue was that someone—like this magician you're seeking—lives all the way out there, I can't say that there's any corroborating evidence," he explained. "The rumor to which I was referring is actually one of legend, involving a mythical oasis from which ancient life in the desert is purported to have sprung. Fascinating stuff. But more to the point, whether or not there really *is* an oasis is all conjecture. I couldn't count on the fingers of one hand people who've seen it for themselves because, to my knowledge, no one *has*."

"So what the fuck has this load of bedtime stories got to do with us?" I asked.

Geoffrey Bless had the fucking gall to roll his eyes at that one. "Because if someone was actually living in the Khevir dunes . . . well, then, they'd be living *there,*" he said.

Thom's eyes were narrow, his tone thoughtful. "How common is the tale of this oasis?" he asked. "I mean . . . I've studied the desert to a minor extent, but outside of nomad mythology . . . Does anyone else speak of this?"

"Not particularly," Geoffrey admitted. "I was actually going to write my thesis on it . . . back when I was going to write my thesis. Unwritten mythologies and all that. But it's so difficult to sit down with these nomads—ha-ha, a bit of desert humor, hope you forgive me."

"Someone lied to us," Thom concluded, looking at me. It was like Geoffrey Fucking Bless wasn't even in the room with us, and I took the expression for a gesture of friendliness. I grinned at him, showing some teeth.

"Don't worry," I said. "I'll take care of that."

"Ahem," Bless said.

We both turned to him at once, like it was fucking choreographed or something, and gave him a look like—as he might've said—*Do please go on.* He shifted uncomfortably on his uncomfortable couch, tugging again at his collar before he took a handkerchief out of his pocket and wiped the back of his neck with it.

"Well, there is something more," Bless said, "and it's really quite fortuitous. You see . . ." He paused for a moment, then looked hopeful. "There *is* a mutually beneficial way we can *both* put this legend to rest. Aren't you the least bit curious?"

"No," I said. I didn't want to be mutually beneficial with anyone.

"Rook," said Thom.

So much for thinking we were in this together.

"Go ahead," I said, not even looking at my brother. "Just make it quick."

"There *has* been some rumor of profit to be made in that area," Bless went on, excited now. "Yet it is difficult to gather the appropriate—ah—manpower necessary to conduct an excavation. But if we were to kill two birds with one stone—that is, set out in the direction of the Khevir dunes, with me as your guide, I could translate for you the nomads' information—see if there *was* anyone to be found relating to your quest—while in the meantime . . ."

". . . you dig up dead people," I finished for him, because *somebody* had to spit it out.

"Hm," Geoffrey Bless said, but he didn't exactly deny it.

"Fortuitous. Exactly," Thom said. "Is there anywhere we might be able to stay for the night?"

"You can, of course, stay in my humble abode," Bless began.

"No thank you," Thom said. "I think we'd rather be alone."

"Suit yourself," Bless said, exhibiting a rare moment of darkness that let me know *exactly* what kind of a man he was. "I'll go see to your lodgings."

"Most fucking kind," I said.

Geoffrey Bless stood up, smoothing out his authentic clothing or whatever weird hodgepodge he was wearing, just long enough to let us know we hadn't rumpled him at all. I grinned at him a little cross-eyed to let *him* know that there was still plenty of time left for me to rumple him good. Then he left to go find us someplace to stay, all three of us in the room knowing who'd won that battle. As he left, I looked over at Thom, who was looking over at me. And for the first time in a long time I actually felt like I had a real, live, recognizable brother.

It didn't feel good and it didn't feel bad, and I couldn't look at it too long before we both looked elsewhere, just waiting for Bless to come back while we inspected the curtains.

CHAPTER FIVE

MALAHIDE

Bearing in mind the Provost's connections and his considerable success in cleaning up the three maiden districts since coming to the job, one might have expected his office to be slightly more ornate than, say, a common jail cell.

It wasn't.

"Really, Dmitri," I was saying, merely as one acquaintance concerned for another, without any intention of prying or involving myself in affairs that did not concern me. "A large painting, a nice thick rug . . . Even a desk can have personality if you choose the right one."

"Why would I want my desk to have a personality?" Dmitri asked, neither baffled nor intrigued, having missed the point entirely. He got his logical brain from his father, poor man. It was a pity his mother's imagination had fallen by the wayside. I let the topic lie for the moment, folding my hands in my lap with a sigh.

"You are the very definition of impossible," I added for good measure, just so that I could be sure he knew how deeply he'd disappointed me.

More than anything—though he was not aware of this himself—Provost Dmitri had difficulty dealing with disappointed women. It was a terrible flaw, one that was bound to get the better of him eventually. I'd point it out to him one day.

"Oh come now, Malahide," he said, tugging at his forelock in a gesture that was frustrated instead of subservient. "I've only just recovered from the shock of hearing you speak. Can't a man be given reprieve once in a while?"

"*I* am never given reprieve," I reminded him, straightening my hat. I'd come here in my Molly-guise, since Molly was where I'd been spending the vast majority of my time. It wasn't so bad, once you got used to the odor—which happened surprisingly quickly, which I supposed explained why anyone at all could live there without going completely mad—and Nor had taken quite a shine to me on top of that, as though I were the son he'd never had. One of the most important tasks in my line of work was building up esteem among the members of every group with which I came into contact. One could never tell who they were going to have to depend on in the future, and so it made sense to keep every line of communication open—just in case of trouble later on.

It took some extra work, but that was what made me so good at my job. Of course, it also led to some minor inconveniences, like the wolves outside mistaking me for common gutter trash and manhandling me most severely before the little matter was cleared up, but that was a hazard of the trade. Fortunately for everyone, I'd run into Dmitri straight after that, and he'd taken me upstairs to his office, behaving like *quite* the hero. The one flaw in all my many disguises was that the Provost could always see through them. He took after his dear father in that regard.

"I'm aware." He sighed. He was looking very tired these days, too pale and slightly saggy about the eyes, in a way I didn't like. I expected it was because he had no wife to take care of him at the end of a long day. Alone, a man could exhaust himself quite easily coming up against the unforgiving odds of Molly, without any respite. He was too stubborn for his own good, our young Provost, and far too determined to prove himself capable. I could have told him that he was wasting his efforts. Thremedon only cherished her heroes when the threat was foreign, and the hero wasn't carting off someone's husband for stealing or murder. He would never have listened, though.

He'd been this stubborn when we were younger too.

"You haven't even said whether you like it or not," I prompted, to let him know I was giving up on the idea of his office—for the time being, in any case.

"What's that?" Dmitri asked, looking suddenly puzzled.

"My *voice*," I told him. He truly was impossible sometimes, the way too many men tended to be impossible around a woman.

"Oh," Dmitri said, as though he would rather have been elsewhere at this precise moment in time. "Well, Malahide, it's a little like a cat trying to do fractions. I'm not sure whether it's a question of liking it. It's very peculiar. Unexpected?"

"You've no idea at all how to speak to a lady," I muttered darkly.

He knew enough to avoid the trap of trying to defend himself against that claim, at least. Instead he pressed his hands together, fingers steepled, and gazed at me over the top of them. He was so handsome that it made my heart hurt, and sometimes made me wish I'd thought to cut that out as well, alongside the tongue. If only it would have garnered me anything, yet there was no trade for that particular organ.

"You're here on business, I take it?" he said at last.

"Ah," I said, "and at last we arrive on the same page."

"What can I do for you?" he asked. "And please, don't make me regret asking."

"Not at all," I said, favoring him with a smile I knew to be completely unreassuring. "I simply need you to avert your eyes from a certain district in Molly for the time being. Not so long as to make you seem inept, of course; just long enough for me to seem very *ept*, indeed."

He raised his eyebrows, looking as though he had a mind to be disagreeable about things. When he didn't protest outright, however, I took my opportunity to continue.

"I need something," I explained. He liked it when I spoke with brevity and remained concise. "Information, specifically, from the black market they're running down by the piers."

Dmitri swore under his breath and let his hands fall against the desk. "I had a feeling you were going to say something like that," he said. "Judging by the looks of you when you came in here . . ."

"I just need to know where they're getting *their* supplies from," I continued. Dmitri was already on my side, I knew; he was merely looking to be convinced. "Or rather, I need to know if what they've told me is true. Once I know that, you can do whatever you'd like."

"Most of 'em brought their 'supplies' back with them, after the war," Dmitri said, tilting his chair back on two legs. "Raided what they could from Ke-Han houses and brought it back here to sell, or trade, or what-have-you. Almost everyone running the market right now is a vet from the war. Makes me feel like an ass not to be able to grant them a little peace, after everything they've been through, but the second I do that is the second I lose all damn control, and it was a bitc— It wasn't pretty trying to win it in the first place."

I shrugged. "Those who want peace don't generally conduct grossly illegal acts," I said—my womanly version of *there, there.* "In any case, Dmitri, I wasn't talking about trinkets and incense, with all the proceeds of the transactions siphoned off to fund the Ke-Han's economy at the expense of our own."

"Oh?" Dmitri asked. "I guess that makes sense, if you're on the case. And I don't suppose you're at liberty to disclose what you *are* talking about, even if you do need my help."

"Essentially that's it, yes," I said. One of my own personal rules was always to err on the side of discretion, and the fewer people who knew about the true nature of my task, the less trouble I would encounter. And the less trouble *they* would encounter, as well, on my behalf. Perhaps shockingly, I wasn't a secretive person by nature—I derived no joy from holding information back, as some might have done in my uncomfortable shoes—but it was simply one part of my duty and I preferred to be efficient above all else. Besides, to share information was to involve another party, and the nature of this assignment was too delicate for anyone but myself. "It's all terribly dull, I'm afraid. It would bore you to tears even if I decided to share it."

"You always say that," Dmitri said, as though he didn't quite believe me. He sighed like a man with the weight of Thremedon on his shoulders—and the three maidens were a heavy lot—and cast a glance around his office. I didn't know what there was to look at, only bare walls, a bare floor, and a ceiling with a crack in it shaped suspiciously like the Basquiat. Perhaps the office was like Dmitri himself: unadorned, but teeming with hidden depths. Or maybe he really did just prefer to have his office look as boring as was humanly possible. I shifted in my seat and let out a slight cough.

"Look the other way," Dmitri repeated, as though the words left a sour taste in his mouth. "That's what you want."

"Just until I can confirm I've found the market's road," I said. "I know that it's south of Thremedon, but I'd hate to waste everyone's time and money on a wild-goose chase."

"I hear wild goose is delicious, this time of year," said Dmitri. "Very fat."

"Does that mean you'll do it?" I countered. I could do this without him, of course, but it would mean risking the good opinion I'd worked so hard to build up. Contrary to what others thought of me, I did *not* enjoy spending my days in a room that smelled of mold and rot, and streets outside that smelled of worse. I hadn't been so careful all this time only to have it go to waste just because Dmitri was feeling particularly stubborn this month.

"I assume this is a job for, uh . . ." Dmitri trailed off. The words always made him uncomfortable. It was as though he couldn't decide which ones to use, and being formal smacked of being pompous, and especially in front of me, since I knew the truth.

"For the Esar," I supplied helpfully. "Yes. How else would I have gotten this?" Even though I was dressed as a common guttersnipe, I couldn't help the fluttery motion of my hand clasped to my throat.

Dmitri cleared *his* throat, staring up at the crack in the ceiling. "Yes, that," he said slowly. "I suppose that's what tipped me off."

"I think, at present, the matter with which I am struggling, and in which I require the benefit of your assistance, is more important to him than street crime," I said, pushing my advantage, though it did leave me feeling somewhat dissatisfied. It felt a little too much like rubbing his nose in the consequence of my job relative to his, which was never my intention at all. We were all necessary to the crown, but Dmitri's trouble had always been found in differentiating *that* purpose from his usefulness as a son to his father.

He wasn't a prince—he wasn't the *Esarina*'s son—and so that always had been a matter of some difficulty.

Dmitri coughed. "I can give you thirteen hours," he said finally.

"That *does* sound ominous," I replied. "Is there a particular significance to the number, or are you just being peculiar?"

"Thirteen's a good, solid number," Dmitri said. "I'll have my men look the other way, but there's only so long before they start asking questions. You're just lucky I haven't."

"You're a darling," I said, reaching forward to clasp his hands with my own. "Absolutely fantastic."

"It's absolutely crazy, that's what it is," Dmitri muttered.

"You being so helpful?"

"No," Dmitri said. "Talking to you like this."

I supposed it *had* been years since I last had any voice to speak of, and Dmitri had never approved of so many of my charades. We'd been friends since I first discovered his secret: the truth behind his parentage, and his reasons for growing up in an orphanage along with other children of a similar fortune. I'd been alone as I so often was in those days—small enough to escape the notice of most of our caretakers, and strange enough that no one bothered much to keep an eye on me in the first place—and there had been a letter upon the desk of our floor manager. She had always been a careless woman, though not ill intentioned. In the letter had been the personal details of one of our newcomers, a small, sullen boy with red hair who spoke to no one. He was, as the letter explained, the child of our Esar and Lady Antoinette. And quite candidly, in the writer's opinion, it was unfortunate that he'd inherited the Esar's looks and not his mother's darker coloring.

I'd admired him from the first for his silence, but it was only upon reading the letter that I felt I fully understood him. That was the first taste I had of the true power that a secret knowledge could give you, and I found it more intoxicating than the headiest ambrosia.

My first friendship was not perfect. He'd never quite accepted my decision to dedicate my life in service of his father, but then I'd never accepted his either. What we did agree on, however, was how important our duties were to us, and somehow through that certainty we managed to remain friends.

It was certainly very pleasant communicating with him via the post rather than in person; it gave Dmitri more time to gather his thoughts, and he had a surprisingly gentle way with composition that was extremely pleasing to an avid reader of many words.

"If I have the chance, I shall write you from the road," I promised him.

"Don't do anything that'll get you in trouble," he warned. As if I needed to be reminded of that! I could tell that he wanted to ask me, "What road?"—but he was good enough to refrain from prying, and I was good enough to offer him a smile of gratitude as I showed myself to the door.

I dropped him a stubborn little curtsy—difficult as anything to manage, wearing these awful boots—and left his office with renewed purpose.

It was easy enough to slip back from the Provost's den unseen, and I had my excuse ready even if I had been. If I so much as told Nor I'd been taken in by the wolves and managed to give them the slip—and it would be obvious I wasn't lying when no one pounded down his door in the middle of the night shouting about the jig being up—then I'd be even more the apple of his old eyes. I just preferred not to lie to him; it would so destroy him when I disappeared for good. It was simply necessary to have all my excuses in order, lest I be caught in the tangle of my own snare.

But I only had thirteen hours.

I was lucky it was nighttime.

Molly at night was pitch-dark, since there was no wasted light and the buildings were too crowded together to let in much by way of moonshine. You could hear people before you could see them, and it was best not to get involved with anyone you *did* hear.

Unfortunately, Hapenny Lane was between Provost's Den and lower Molly, which I was currently calling my home. There were ways around it, but risking a walk through them was about as dangerous as tying each limb to a different horse and cracking a whip, and I wasn't in the mood to be split open by a shanker whose own loneliness and futility had turned him to violent crime, taking the lives of other people because his life meant nothing at all.

I ran the gauntlet of Hapenny in silence, feeling young eyes on me from the corners. I didn't look like a customer, or even someone with a ha'penny to my name. No one called out to me, nor did anyone clutch at the corner of my peacoat, but the silence was more chilling than any noise could have been—only the sound of my own breaths and, matched by the child whores', my footsteps echoing loudly off the close walls.

It was one of the more hideous sights I'd been privy to—and I'd witnessed my own tongue after it had been cut out of my throat—so, noblewoman though I might have been, I was not unaccustomed to monstrosity.

Dmitri knew of it—these terrible things some men referred to as pleasures. It was one of the reasons he got so little sleep at night. To be a good man and to be aware of the way business was conducted—and to be in a position of power yet no more capable of preventing it . . . I pitied him, and would not have traded my worries for his on any day of the week.

Nor's place was just past Tuesday Street, where at least business was conducted behind closed doors—a small favor for which I could barely thank the heavens enough. One could turn a blind eye if one so wished, which was exactly what I did.

"There you are," Nor said as I stepped in, stamping mud and Regina-knew-what-else off my feet. "Been a while, hasn't it?"

"Had to give the wolves the slip," I told him neatly. "Felt like I was being followed all day. Thought it better to lie low for a while."

"Good boy," Nor said. "Well, it just meant I had to wait a while longer. But I've got a sweet little surprise for you."

My heart lit up, but I didn't let that light come all the way to my eyes. "Something good, I hope," I said instead, scuffing the heel of my boot against the floor. Nor was inspired by something—loneliness too, I would have wagered, as well as the promise I'd made to split my end of the profit halfway with him when all this was said and done—and he was working like a devil for me, just as I'd hoped. Show a man in Molly a little kindness and he'd pick any pocket you asked.

"We've got the route," he said. "Managed to get it this morning, but we couldn't find you. Some of the boys thought you were givin' us the good one-two, if you know what I mean, but I vouched for you."

"And I won't fuck you over for it, either," I swore. That much was true; I could never hand Nor in after all the kindnesses he'd shown me, whether I'd manipulated them from his weathered little heart or not. "Guess I'll be needing a new pair of boots."

"Just fished a man out of the canal," Nor said. "I took his boots off 'im for you."

What a man, I thought.

"Cheers" was all I said. It didn't do to seem overly grateful for anything in Molly. It stank of desperation, and there was nothing like sounding desperate when you needed something that made people not want to give it to you.

Nor shrugged. "Seeing as how I can't give you a personal escort and all, I figured this was the next best thing."

"Don't give me that," I said, playing along. "You'd handle the road *much* better'n I would."

"Not with these old bones, but you're a kind lad to pretend." Nor chuckled, looking pleased. "We wanted to draw up a map for you, but it was a hell of a job finding anyone who could write directions in the first place, let alone a stinkin' cartography expert."

"Any kind you found down here *would* be stinkin," I quipped, rolling up my sleeves. "Don't worry about me, I'm as good as a bloodhound once I've got some kind of direction to follow." Little did Nor know how close to the truth that actually was.

I'd started packing what meager belongings I'd brought—mostly clothes that I could layer over what I was already wearing in case it got cold on the road at night. I would have to make a stopover in my own home to get real supplies for the journey—chiefly a more universal disguise than a Molly dung-rat, since one could never tell *who* they might end up needing to impress. Outside of Molly, looking as poor as dirt closed more doors than it opened, even if it was heaps more comfortable than wearing a corset.

"You would be," Nor said, fishing around in one of his pockets for something. He came up with a grimy piece of paper, folded twice, and thrust it at me as I passed him while looking for a scarf.

"Thanks," I said, snapping it up between two fingers. On it was an almost childlike scrawl, wide-looped letters in a shaky hand that directed me straight through the lower Volstovic countryside and below the Cobalt Range. "Shit. That's farther than I thought, hey?"

"You won't be needing that," he replied, gesturing to the scarf. "They told me the road goes south for miles. You're like as not to end up in desert country, then you'll look like a right proper fool with all them scarves."

"All right, then," I said, and looped it quickly about his shoulders before he could blink. "You keep it. You could use something to cover up that turkey neck of yours anyway."

"No respect for your elders," Nor growled, in a way I'd come to understand meant he was touched. It was fascinating what emotion people could conjure simply by changing the tone and quality of their voice. I would have to work on that myself. Since it was no longer practical, I'd forgotten the natural way of it.

"'Course not," I said, securing the last of my belongings in a tatty little bag I'd brought along with me. There was one last matter to attend to, much as I hated to bring it up. If it'd been up to me, I'd have given Nor the whole pot and never looked back, but a hefty sum of money could bring just as much trouble as no money at all down in Molly. "You brought my money?"

"Sure did," Nor said, shaking a sack of coins out of a different pocket. "Was waiting for you to ask too. Gotta keep a youngster's instincts sharp. Especially with you going away and all, won't have ol' Nor around to look after you."

I took the bag, and made a show of counting it.

"You already take your share?" I asked.

"I did," said Nor.

"Good," I said, and slapped two more coins down on the table. "One's thanks for taking me to the market, one's for you to go and buy yourself a nice, stiff drink, all right? I don't wanna come back here and hear you've been *saving* them or something foolish like that. You got it?"

"Damn kids," Nor muttered, but he pocketed the coins. That much generosity, and the promise of more to drink, was acceptable for a man in Nor's position, no matter what pride he still had left.

I took a look around the little room I'd rented out for my stay in Molly. It was, to put it simply, the most god-awful wretch of a hovel I'd ever stayed in. The only way to ever make it clean again would be to burn the whole piece of shit down and start building it again from scratch. I hadn't taken leave of my senses, and so I could hardly pretend—even to myself—that I was going to miss it. Still, there had been something very enjoyable about the freedom I'd experienced during my time in Molly. Certainly, it stank to high heaven, and you didn't know what you were stepping in more often than not, but there was no one to answer to beyond yourself and no duty beyond surviving another day. It had been refreshing, and I was sorry in some respects to give it up for the life of precautions and pretenses I now faced.

"Well," I said.

"Well," Nor agreed.

"Be seeing you when I make my fortune," I finished, swinging my pack up onto my shoulders. I would be sad to leave Nor behind, but the truth of the matter was, he would soon forget about me—or assume I'd hit it big in the desert and never returned. He could imagine, with what little imagination he had, that I was sitting on a carpet and drinking wine, surrounded by camels and dancing girls and giant fans, and he'd sigh and drink to me until he found someone else to drink to. That was life.

I clasped Nor's shoulder firmly—a good manly gesture—and he clapped me on the back with one of his large hands. It made the voice box in my throat rattle; I cleared my throat to hide the sound.

"Take care of yourself out there, or you're no Mollyrat," he told me.

"I will," I promised him, and walked out the door into the night.

THOM

I woke up because Rook was shaking me. It was still dark out, and I had no idea where I was.

"Read this," Rook said, and shoved a letter in my face.

Needless to say, I was somewhat perplexed. On top of that, my entire body was aching. The beds in Karakhum were far from luxurious—or at least, the beds in the establishment Geoffrey had managed to reserve for us—and I must have slept strangely on my left arm, because I'd lost all feeling below the elbow.

It was not my most glorious moment.

"What's it?" I asked.

Luckily, Geoffrey was not there to hear me sound like an imbecile.

Rook gave me a funny look over the top of the letter, and I reached up to take it with the hand that still worked before I could embarrass myself any further. The other one was tingling back to life as I tried to remember where and who I was.

"It's a letter," Rook said, like he thought I'd taken leave of my senses at last. "You're always so keen on reading, so why don't you read *this*?"

"Ah," I said, blinking rapidly and rubbing my poor arm back to life. "Yes. I'm sorry. Just a moment."

I stared at the letter. Everything was slightly blurred, due to the fact

that, on our second week of traveling, my reading lenses had "mysteri-
ously" turned up broken. I had my suspicions, but nothing could ever
be proven one way or the other. In any case, I had no way to commission a new pair, and the light in the room was dim enough that I was
going to have a headache by the time I was through.

The writing itself was unfamiliar but plain enough.

"It's from Adamo," I informed him, after a quick scan.

"Got that," Rook said, waving his hand impatiently. "I know what it
looks like."

I cleared my throat, lifted the letter, and read out loud.

Thom—, it began.

*I'm not much in the habit of writing letters, so don't judge this
one by any standards. Things in Thremedon are the same as ever,
and the citizens being as resistant to change as they always were.
There was some talk of tearing down the old Airman and replac-
ing it with a proper monument a while back, but we straightened
them out, reminding them it was about as proper as the likes of us
deserved. You can tell Rook his statue's become something like the
patron saint for Our Lady, and you can see whores there night and
day, praying for safe childbirth and protection from diseases and
the like. Though why they think he's the man to go to for that kind
of help is beyond me. Just thought he might like to know there're
whores on their knees in front of him—so I guess that goes back to
what I was saying about things never changing.*

Rook snorted.

*As to your mention of the dragons, I can't say I'm too surprised.
Men'll do all kinds of shit in wartime, so it only stands to reason
they'd do the same kinds of shit after wartime is through. I didn't
know how much help I'd be on my own, so I consulted with a
friend of mine. Rook, of course, remembers the "Mary Margrave,"
and maybe you do too. He said that I was off my rocking groove
just asking about trying to track down the dragons, and that the
Esar himself's already put one of his spies on the case. Now, I've
gone and committed treason putting that bit in, but I'll just have*

to hope no one gets too curious about this letter before it reaches you. No one usually reads my mail, even the poor shits I send letters to. Anyway, fair warning that you aren't the only bastards from Thremedon out looking for a needle in a haystack. Roy says those spy-magicians are a nasty piece of work, and none of them welcome in the Basquiat. Sounds pretty paranoid to me too, but that's the shake. If the Esar's after what's left, then you can bet there's something to look for, so I guess one of you has as good instincts as they ever did. Bastion knows Rook can look after himself, and I daresay you can too well enough, but that doesn't mean you shouldn't be on your guard if someone's out there looking for what we went and left behind.

Sure, there might be magic-doers in the desert. Them magicians that put a little of themselves into our girls, more specifically. Roy says that these poor fools were meant to be banished better than he ever was, and I'll take his word for it, seeing as how he knows more about the creation of the dragons than I ever will. My expertise, as you know, comes in well after they were built, but that won't stop me from doing what I can. What's more, it seems like the one you'd be most interested in, the magician responsible for Havemercy, is what you might call infamous in certain circles. Banished about as far as the Esar could banish the poor fool, or so it's said. Desert seems as good a shot as any—not that it's the sort of thing his highness would let the Basquiat know about, so I've run out of leads there beyond what Roy calls a suspicion. But his hunches are usually good, and seemed like he approved when I told him your direction. You didn't hear it from me, but I think you might just be on the right track, except I'm not a snooping man, and that's all you'll get.

Not much else information I can send your way. Roy says he'll look into it all and I guess I'll pass what I can on, unless it's a matter of statewide secrecy, in which case I might or I might not. No use getting my balls strung up over a wild-goose chase, not that I wouldn't rather be out there sweating and dealing with Rook. A man feels alive when he's yelling at a stubborn bastard in ways he can't when that stubborn bastard's off and gone, so good luck filling my shoes and remember to be loud if you can.

As for the rest, the weather is fine and such. Luvander has opened a hat shop, which you may have heard from your pen pal already. Good luck as you will need it.

I didn't need to read out his signature, which was quite like the man himself—a sturdy block print of his last name with an X after it, nothing overly fancy, and yet nonetheless incredibly impressive. I folded the letter back up and let it drop into my lap.

"Well," I said, "that's good to hear about the . . . er . . . whores, anyway."

"Shut up," Rook said, but there was a weariness in his voice, and he lacked his usual venom. I was worried about him, though that was the most foolhardy emotion to experience when it came to Rook.

Perhaps he missed his friend—if Adamo could even have been called that.

Or perhaps he was offended at the idea of an airman running a haberdashery.

But, of course, it was far more than that—a deep vein of grief he could only express through anger, and even that was wearing thin. I swallowed uncertainly.

"He has been quite helpful," I offered. "Hasn't he? There's a lot to go on, here, and if Margrave Royston says that a dragonmaker—your dragonmaker, to be precise—is likely to be in the desert—"

"I ain't thinking about that right now," Rook ground out. "Read that part again, about one of th'Esar's people being on the job."

I obliged him. Rook wasn't exactly a theoretical thinker, but his critical analysis was excellent; he could immediately pick out the necessary information, when he put his mind to it, and it stood to reason that he would understand straightaway the most troubling aspect of Adamo's letter.

We were on to something. We had to be, if the Esar himself was looking into it.

"I don't like it," Rook said, folding his arms over his chest. "I don't like any of it."

"Neither do I," I admitted. Aside from how troubling it was that the Esar was capable of exiling those most useful to him because of their potential usefulness to others—an abuse of power that unsettled my very personal understanding of justice—it was difficult to address the sudden knowledge that he seemed intent on hunting down all evidence that remained of his dragons and their inventors. If Adamo's information was anything to go by, then one could only imagine what the Esar intended to do with it once he found it.

"He wants to destroy them," Rook said finally. "I *know* it."

"I'm not sure we can assume—" I began, but Rook snorted.

"Don't be an idiot," Rook said. "That's the kind of man he is. He's got power and he wants to make sure he's the only one who has it. So he's got his men going off to find everything they can. Sure, he doesn't want the Ke-Han or who the fuck ever to get their hands on 'em—the dragons or the magicians or anyone who fucking knows anything—but I bet you good fucking money that if we got in his way, he'd have us slit open just like we were the enemy too—like neither of us've ever done anything for him. He'd forget that, easy as you forget a one-night bitch. We *done* our duty. We're worth *shit* to him."

It was a sobering thought, but not entirely off the mark, either. I breathed out slowly, trying to find some logical way around it.

There was none.

Rook knew the Esar better than I did, but my own experiences with him led to the exact same conclusion. Simply put, that *was* the kind of man the Esar was. He was in a position of power that I couldn't possibly understand, so perhaps I should not have been so quick to judge him for it. Yet the point of the matter was, he would hunt us down the same as he would a Ke-Han spy if he thought we intended to get between him and his goal.

It unsettled me, not knowing exactly what that goal was. Rook's guess was as good as—if not better than—mine.

"I agree," I said finally. "Your assessment is very . . . keen."

"I been with him," Rook muttered. "I fucking *know* his kind. Wouldn't look twice at me, wouldn't care if I live now *or* die, 'cause there ain't no fucking war left for me to fight. Fair-weather friend, that son-of-a. I *always* knew it."

I scanned the relevant parts of Adamo's letter for a third time, wondering if I should commit them to memory, then burn the paper on which they were written. Surely I was being too paranoid—and yet I didn't want to involve Adamo in something that was, as they said, bigger than he was, simply because I hadn't thought of it in such dire terms when I'd begun my investigation.

"Rook," I said suddenly, realization hitting me like a sack of Molly-shit. "What if . . . What would you say if I thought that we've already run into one of the Esar's men?"

I didn't even have to say anything further. Rook whistled, then whirled to the window and spat right out of it—angry little motions that spoke of a deeper rage.

"Shit," he said when he was done. "That bastard back at the camp."

"And yet, I think we *do* have a lead," I said. Rook would like the irony in this. "He sent us all the way out to the desert, probably hoping we'd get lost or give up. But the Margrave Royston seems to believe that we're on the right track after all."

"Tch," Rook muttered, letting me know that he was as steadfast in his opinion on the Margrave as ever. Or perhaps he was still furious over letting Fan get away—just as I was, only I had to be the one who kept his mouth shut about it. "I knew I should've cut that smiling bastard up."

"Yes," I said, "but you couldn't *possibly* have known who he was at the time. Neither of us could have, and there's no point in beating yourself up over something you can't change now." I hesitated, not wanting to encourage him, yet at the same time not wanting to let him down, then added, "Revenge is a dish best served cold, as they say. I'm sure we'll—*you'll* have your chance."

Rook grunted, which I hoped meant we were on the same page.

"In any case," I went on, "as I said, it doesn't really matter, because while Fan evidently hoped to mislead us, he ended up doing the exact opposite."

"Yeah," Rook said, relishing the fact that we'd somehow managed to turn the tables. "Bet he's feeling like a real idiot right about now. He'll get his, and no mistake."

"I imagine he will if the Esar ever finds out," I said, hoping that would conjure all sorts of bloody images in Rook's mind and therefore cheer him up slightly.

"I don't like it," he said, turning sharply on his heel to pace. I wished fervently that there was no one sleeping on the floor below ours; if there was, they certainly weren't sleeping anymore. "Not one damned bright spot in this shit hole we've landed in, with th'Esar's fucking spies breathing down our necks and just when we need to be getting a fucking move on we pick up another giant waste of time."

"You're referring to Geoffrey," I said, reading the letter over once again. I couldn't help it; rereading was a nervous habit of mine I'd picked up even before school. Much as I hated to admit it, I wasn't feeling entirely comfortable with the idea of taking a friend into territory I now knew to be far more dangerous than it appeared. Terrain and hostile natives were the least of our problems if the Esar was spying on us. Geoffrey had evidently proven himself capable of looking after matters quite capably on his own—I held no illusions about how I might have fared in his place—but this was a different sort of threat altogether. One that years at the 'Versity *or* in the desert couldn't train you for.

"Who the fuck d'you think I'm talking about, Annabella the camel? Of course I'm fucking talking about that piss snake. Are you even paying attention?" Rook swung his fist into the window frame, stopping short just before it could connect. His reflexes were a constant marvel to me, someone who couldn't seem to quite get out from under his own feet most days. I put the letter down.

"I agree that the timing is not particularly ideal," I admitted, "but we can't expect to find our way through the desert on luck alone. We *will* need a guide, and we don't have the money to hire one. It's as simple as that. As long as we're useful to Geoffrey, he'll be useful to us." Not to mention we would be going back on our word if we simply left in the middle of the night, same as we'd abandoned the innkeeper to the damages we'd done to his establishment. I knew that Rook hadn't exactly taken a shine to Geoffrey, but that didn't excuse our behaving like common thieves—even if that was the turn this trip had taken in the past.

Our luck would only change once we began attempting to change it.

Rook snorted like an angry bull. "All comes down to th'Esar making things as hard as possible for anyone that ain't him," he said.

"It's going to be difficult for anyone to cross the desert," I reminded him. "Even the Esar's spies are only human. We'll have an advantage; Geoffrey knows the area better even than spies, and certainly better than we would, on our own."

"His spies're magicians," Rook corrected me, throwing himself down onto the mess of blankets and woven straw that made up our pallets for the night. He looked like he wanted to spit again, but thankfully didn't. "Magicians that even the bell-cracked fucking Basquiat won't accept, which means we don't know *what* they are, or what they're capable of. Maybe they're cold-blooded like fucking lizards and they're already halfway there while we sit here talking about Geoffrey."

"Stop," I said, and I did something ridiculously brave: I reached out and put my hand on his arm. He was tightly wound; I wasn't above thinking he might lash out at me next, just as he'd done toward the window. But nothing happened. "You aren't doing yourself any favors, thinking like that, and you have no way of knowing whether it's happened or not, either. Individual Talents are hardly my expertise, but I happen to know that it's *very* rare to have a Talent that affects your internal structure like that. Nearly impossible. So *that's* not something to worry about. We'll rouse Geoffrey first thing in the morning and tell him we intend to leave early, all right? Under the circumstances, I think that's the best we can do—and at least now we've got an idea that we're heading in the right direction."

"Yeah," Rook said, like that was a *real* comfort to him. After a moment he looked at me, and I hurriedly pulled my hand away.

"We'll just have to be on our guard," I said, as much for myself as for him. "No more talking to friendly strangers."

"You're telling me?" Rook asked, with an expression on his face like I'd just attempted to instruct him on the ancient art of sucking eggs. "I'm not the one who was all friendly with him in the first place."

That was true, I would have been the first to admit; but the reason he knew who we were was because *Rook* wasn't exactly an inconspicuous traveling companion. I didn't remind him of that, however.

"Only one of us is a chatty fucking blabberbox and it *ain't* me," Rook added, for good measure.

"I'm well aware of that," I said, my own feelings about having been either ignored or abused for the vast majority of this trip coming dangerously close to the surface. Something else occurred to me then, and I looked down at the letter on my pillow. "When did you get this?"

"Took it," Rook said, punching some life into his pillow with disturbing enthusiasm. "Saw it on one of those stupid low tables in Bless's stupid whorehouse of a sitting room and I figured it was ours. Who'd write that bastard? Not even his fucking dam."

"So you just . . . *took* it?" I asked, not even terribly surprised, which was the most frightening aspect of all. "Did you even ask if it was the right letter first? Before you robbed my friend of his mail?"

"It's *our* mail," Rook said. "And he ain't your friend, but that's not the point. Shouldn't he have given it to us, anyway? What the hell was he keeping it back for? That's what *I* wanna know."

"I'm sure he just forgot," I said, covering a yawn with my hand. "He's brilliant, but the practicalities of life tend to elude him every now and then. He was likely just excited to have company. I'm sure it slipped his mind."

"Sure," Rook said, putting his head on the pillow and rolling away from me. "Whatever you say."

With a sigh, I folded the letter up and stuck it into my pack for safe-keeping. Once woken, it was rather difficult for me to fall back asleep, and so I stared at the ceiling in silence while I waited for my brother's breathing to even out.

Eventually my worries eluded me, and I must have fallen asleep.

When I woke up next, it was morning. Rook was not only out of his bed, but he was also fully dressed. It was already starting to get hot—a most disheartening way to start the day—and I'd somehow managed to kick off all my covers in the night. From outside I could hear the shouts of the marketplace, already roaring into full swing. Geoffrey had been right; they began quite early to beat the worst of the heat.

I scrambled off the bed and to my feet, dressing and packing up what few things I'd taken out of my bag last night. I did it all in silence; it was the most efficient way.

"Good," Rook said, "you're up. I was gonna start shaking you soon."

"Let's not make that into a habit," I pleaded, achieving record time in getting ready. "May I ask what you're doing up so early?"

"I wanna go see your little friend," Rook said, looking at something out the window. I was sure it was only the market, which held enough surprises to catch even my brother's attention—but there was some-thing about the action that made me nervous too. It was too much like standing on guard, I realized, like the contents of Adamo's letter had bothered Rook more than even he was willing to let on.

If Fan was indeed an agent of the Esar, then we'd as good as told him to follow us by letting him know we were out for the dragons as well. I didn't like it, but it wouldn't do to allow myself to become car-ried away—precisely in the manner I'd warned Rook against.

Hypocrisy, I recalled, was a chink in my armor.

"I believe we were scheduled to meet Geoffrey again for lunch," I said, trying to be helpful. At the very least, it would put my mind off of being panicked, if only for the moment. "But if you'd like, we can do some sightseeing beforehand. The market's not the only thing to see in Karakhum. There are monuments and museums—not to mention the old prince's palace, which is said to be *entirely* empty these days. Did you know it's a democracy here now? Quite fascinating—"

"I ain't doing any sightseeing," Rook said, taking the opportunity to speak while I'd paused to take a breath. "We're going to see Geoffrey Fucking Bless, then we're renting some camels and we're leaving."

"I . . ." I began, momentarily at a loss. "You can't be serious."

Rook shot me a look that could have melted dragonsteel, then turned and walked out of the room. I scrambled after him, which he'd probably known I would do from the beginning, slinging my pack over one shoulder.

"Rook, we can't possibly—" I said, following him out into the street. The sunlight glared down at us from above and I had to shield my eyes. The very thought of being out in the desert, with no shade to speak of . . .

I was going to need a hat.

"Yes we can possibly," Rook said, not even looking over his shoulder as he strode off.

"No," I insisted, "I really mean it. It takes time to prepare for such expeditions—get supplies, rent . . . rent the camels, see to all the arrangements. I'm sure Geoffrey has to hire extra hands, especially since he intends to excavate. Rook, it's simply impossible!"

"Nothing's impossible," Rook said, and this time he *did* look back at me for long enough to flash a grin, "with the right motivation."

It wasn't a reassuring prospect. I skittered to one side to avoid a man carrying a giant smoked fish—it actually smelled delicious, but I had no time for thoughts of breakfast now—trying to keep up with Rook's determined pace.

There was no changing his mind once he'd decided on a course of action. There was only following desperately behind, attempting to prevent whatever physical violence was bound to occur as a result of Rook following through on his inspirations.

Rook didn't even bother to knock on the door of Geoffrey's home.

"Bless," he shouted, giving the door a good kick. "Wake the fuck up. It's time to head out!"

The door swung open more quickly than I'd expected—almost immediately, in fact, as though Geoffrey had been waiting for us.

"Ah, it's you," he said, completely unruffled by our presence. "Would you care to come in? Have a spot of breakfast?"

Well, yes, I thought miserably, not even bothering to voice my opinion on the subject.

"No thanks; we'll get our own damn breakfast," Rook said. And there it was. "You've got work to do, so get on it."

"Excuse me?" Geoffrey said, smiling broadly. "I'm not quite sure I follow you."

"We're heading out for the oasis," Rook said flatly. "Today. So get us some fucking camels and let's get cracking."

Geoffrey smiled again. This smile I recognized—the patience of a professor who'd long since lost the hope of really teaching—one who'd dealt with one too many obtuse students, and had no faith left in the system. It was a condescending smile—a smile I had always dreaded being met with whenever I stepped into a brand-new lecture hall at the start of a semester. Somewhere along the line, my friend Geoffrey had become quite jaded.

"You'd best come inside and have breakfast," he said. "After that, we'll be ready to leave."

I blinked. Sand had gotten into my eye, and obviously my ears as well. I couldn't possibly have heard that correctly. "Ready to leave?" I asked.

Even Rook had the decency to look startled.

"Don't seem so shocked, friends," Geoffrey said. "I assumed you'd want to start out as quickly as possible. I knew you'd see things my way, so I took the liberty of arranging everything last night. Didn't want to waste a moment of our precious time, eh?"

Both Rook and I were stunned into momentary silence. It didn't last as long for Rook as it did for me, because an instant later, I heard him cursing.

"Fuck you, Bless," he said. "If you lead us on a fucking chase—"

"There would be no profit in that for either of us, would there?" Geoffrey said. "No, no, no; I've lured some of the locals into offering assistance with promises of great treasure from afar. There was a little accident on our last dig that made some of them reluctant to work with me again, but they soon saw reason. Enough money *will* get you results in this world, no matter what anyone tells you."

"Accident?" Rook growled.

"A trifling matter," Geoffrey assured him, waving a hand airily. "Some natives lost, but nothing important. We got what we'd come for—achieving one's goals is the most fulfilling feeling in the world, don't you agree?"

When neither of us replied—I was too astonished to speak, and I judged Rook to be too angry—he gave a little shrug.

"You'll see how it is soon enough, I'm sure. We've got some fresh dates and the most incredible cheese. Do step in; there's no use waiting outside. We can't leave until dusk, anyway."

"Whyssat?" Rook ground out.

"Too hot," Geoffrey replied. "We travel by night. Come on in, fellows."

Rook wasn't one to make the first gesture of peace, so I did the honors, stepping past my brother and into Geoffrey's house once more. It smelled of incense and flat bread, but suddenly I was no longer hungry for breakfast.

CHAPTER SIX

MADOKA

I was having a dream, and in it, I was free from all this madness. My hand was good again, and my life simple, so I was pretty pissed when I found myself shaken out of it.

I squinted up at Badger.

"Well?" I asked. "Better be something good."

"Let's hope," Badger said. "Your hand's making noises."

I paused to listen, then I heard it, this faint whirring sound like the hands of a broken clock suddenly starting to move. I pulled my glove off and looked down at my palm. It'd been three days of walking around like lost souls with Badger by my side—three days of making awkward conversation and getting nowhere. Three days of sleeping in the shadow of the Cobalts without any compass to serve as my guide. Three days—two of which were storming pretty bad—and I was ready for something to start going right for us, or for that compass to start working again.

It had.

Not that I could make any sense of it; it was just the hands starting to whirl, round and round, without resting. They reminded me of myself—of *us*—wandering in circles with nothing to go on, and I didn't like looking at it.

"Can you figure it out?" I asked Badger. It was a long shot.

He shook his head slowly, rubbing at the bottom left corner of the scar. "Can't say that I can," he replied.

"Shit," I muttered. I suppose it'd been too much to wish that our mutual friend the madman had sent Badger down here with a manual for my new parts. "Well that's about as helpful as—"

"Please," said Badger. "Spare me the image."

"Well, fine," I said, disgruntled now that I had to watch my language on top of everything else. I was also still damp from the rain, since nothing took longer to dry than seven separate outfits all layered on top of one another. I was going to have to ditch some extra layers real soon, but I told myself to suck it up in the meantime. Most people who lived this far south were probably grateful for an *hour* of rain, let alone two whole days. Knowing that didn't make me any less sour about trying to fall asleep all clammy, but I was doing my best to find the sunshine behind the clouds—or whatever that saying was.

"I believe there's a village around here," Badger said, adjusting his sleeves where he'd folded them above the elbow. "We could stop there to get our bearings."

I looked at our surroundings: rock, sand, and more rocks. There were some sad, brown little bushes that looked like an old woman's scrub brush—the kind the old lady'd used to clean me off when I got too dirty—and a clump of those aloe plants I'd raided to soothe the itching in my hand last night. Other than that, it was just me and Badger, so I didn't see how he could possibly know there were people around here, let alone a whole village.

"You been here before, or are you just some kind of desert expert?" I asked. "Because I'll be honest, that'd be a real useful skill to whip out all of a sudden."

"I am not whipping anything out," Badger informed me. "Do you see that path through the rock? It isn't natural; there are tool marks on the stone, which means someone *cut* a path through the rock. Out here, there's very little natural protection from the elements, and I'd imagine building a village into or against the cliffs would be the wisest choice."

"So you want to go that way?" I asked, while privately wondering how in the hell he'd noticed a thing like tool marks. He was a strange one, for a soldier.

"Until your, ah, hand stops spinning," he said, looking slightly uncomfortable about having to address it at all. I understood exactly where he was coming from. We might have been nearly polar opposites in a lot of things, but where magic was concerned, we were in complete agreement. It made us both itchy. "If nothing else, I imagine the natives here will possess a greater understanding of the area than we currently have."

It was starting to dawn on me why poor Badger'd been sent after me in the first place. He didn't know the first thing about my little hand problem, but what he did know a lot about was terrain, and geography, and all this other stuff being a soldier'd taught him that I didn't know. He was life insurance.

"You mean, you think we could snag a map off of one of them?" I said, brightening just a little. I always felt better with a destination in mind. Part of what had me so bent out of shape before was all that wandering without knowing where in the seven hells I was heading. Having a plan, even a short-term one, was mighty fine by me.

"Something like that," Badger said, with another glance at my hand. I tugged the glove back on over it. He didn't need to tell me *that*.

"Let's go, then," I said, kicking sand over our fire pit from last night. "I wouldn't mind a change of scenery—no offense meant for your face, either, Badger."

"I only hope these aren't the desert-dwellers who believe in eating the flesh of foreign travelers who blunder into their villages," Badger said, looking thoughtful.

All the little hairs on the back of my neck stood up.

"*What?*" I asked, good and freaked-out now. Then I caught the look on his face. I'd never seen it before on that mug of his, so I couldn't be sure, but on any other person it would've been almost . . . amused. "Hang on a second. Was that supposed to be some kind of joke?"

"Your pardon," said Badger, a faint smile just visible over his hand. "I don't know what came over me."

"Some kind of traveling madness, more like," I said, crossly. "They say it happens when you're on the road too long. I expected better from a soldier, but *evidently* I shouldn't've."

"It won't happen again," Badger promised, shouldering my bag alongside his own. I hated it when he did that, but nothing could dissuade him—short of jumping on him like a monkey and wrestling the pack away, which, admittedly, I had yet to try. Soldiers were a whole other class when it came to dumb stubbornness, and if he wanted to make his shoulders sore, then that was fine by me. The hot desert air was making me sluggish, and I had other things to worry about.

Like how, now that I'd listened to it, I couldn't quite stop hearing the whirring sound of my hand. It made me feel self-conscious, and like it was probably the worst idea in the world to be heading into a village with other people when my own hand was ticking like a clock, but Badger's reasons for wanting to go had all made too much sense for me to ignore. I folded my fingers around the compass set into my palm, hoping to keep it quiet and not break it, and followed after him, kicking up a trail of dust in my wake.

When we got to the cliffs he'd mentioned, I paused, staring real hard to see if I could tell that these were tool marks and not just scratches on the rock. I couldn't. Hell, if I hadn't been traveling with Badger, I probably would've bypassed the village altogether and never've known it was there in the first place. I wasn't sure if I liked that or not. I was glad I had the help, I guessed, but it made me feel dependent in a way I wasn't used to. He squeezed through the path ahead of me, bags knocking into either side of the rocks. So long as he didn't bring anything down on us, I was glad to let him lead the way.

I followed after him at a distance, trying not to get hit by the showers of dust and stone the packs triggered. At one point I tripped and caught myself with my compass hand, which throbbed painfully for my efforts. It was starting to get worse. At least, it was starting to hurt more than it itched, which I didn't like.

I hadn't mentioned this to Badger for a couple of reasons. One, it was none of his business, and two, there wasn't anything he could do about it. Aloe'd helped for a while but the problem'd already changed. I'd just have to hope we made it back to our friend the magician before my whole hand rotted and fell off, or something equally pleasant.

"Watch your step," Badger called back to me, dropping about a foot in height as he did so. There was a steep slope down on the other side of the cliff wall, and I hopped down, ignoring the hand he was holding out.

There were some things a woman just had to do for herself, and risking a twisted ankle was one of them.

When I straightened up, I saw that Badger had been right about the village. At least, there'd been one here at *some* point. Little white tents huddled together, interspersed with the bigger, more solid huts, and what looked like a large well just outside the center of town. There was a rank smell on the air, though, and I noticed something else: There were no people walking around.

"Something's wrong," Badger said. His face was tight and closed off, the way it had been when I'd first met him. It was his soldier face, I guessed, and I hadn't realized it was any different from his normal face until now.

By one of the tents, something stumbled out of the shadows and fell. I was running before I knew it, pounding across the sand and toward the village like some kind of idiot.

Not my best move, but it reminded me a little too much of home, so there had to be something I could do before it was all too late for these poor bastards. That is, if it wasn't all too late already.

The smell on the air was smoke and burning things—all the little things people built up over the years, the possessions that made them people in the first place. Sure, it was stupid to get worked up over objects, but when you didn't have much, you had to think about life in those terms. The difference between a kid who had a doll and a kid who didn't was a whole world.

I should know. I'd been the kid without a doll for the longest time until I stole one for myself.

By the time I got to him, the boy had already collapsed. It was hard to tell what he was at first, because his face was covered in ash, but his hair was cut in a style I recognized—the same cut every boy got when he passed the age of eight and started toward manhood. I grabbed him in my arms, not even thinking about making him worse. His arm and chest were sticky.

"Get out of there!" Badger was yelling at me, but his voice got louder while he was shouting; he was following after me. "Whoever did this could still be close by. They could even still be here. We can't . . ."

And yet there he was, kneeling next to me, taking the boy out of my arms and checking his throat for a pulse. Typical firstborn behavior. Shout at someone for doing something dumb, then wade right in to take their place.

"He still alive?" I asked. I hated the sound of my own voice right then, but there wasn't much I could do about it.

"Yes," Badger said.

There was a sharp pain coursing through my hand—like it was going to burst into flames if I didn't do something. Now wasn't the time to worry about my own problems, I thought, but it got to the point where it was so unbearable I had to tear my glove off or faint right there. The whole compass was pulsing hot, sending bolts of heat through my blood. And the hands were going crazy.

"I'll take care of the boy," Badger told me. *His* voice was calm—he was used to giving out orders, I guessed—but it was nice to hear someone who sounded like they were in control, not just the ragged breaths the boy was sucking in through his open mouth and the sound of my own heart pounding too loud with the pain I was in. "*You*—be careful."

I stumbled to my feet. "I don't know," I said, trying to laugh. "I've gotta do what it's telling me."

That sounded crazy. More than anything, I wanted to help the boy Badger was holding in his arms; I wanted to put my hand on his forehead and tell him it was gonna be all right, while Badger put his army training to some real use and patched him up. But I couldn't. I had this thing I had to listen to, a voice that was calling me. What I wanted to do and what I had to do had never been more at odds.

I clenched my teeth and started off through the wreckage of this poor, two-ways-fucked village. Smoke was still belching out of a couple of the huts, and now that I was down in the thick of it I could see the extent of the destruction: broken bits of wood, torn cloth, the well smashed on one side, a few of the houses' roofs caved in. And there I was, picking up speed as I moved through it and past it, not even looking for survivors or people I could help—just answering to the call of the compass in my hand.

But the movements of *its* hands were starting to gain focus. Sure, two out of the four hands were still going crazy, but the other two were actually pointed in the same direction.

I stumbled past a broken-down tent with a pile of ash and cinder and a streak of blood smeared over it. The third hand, the second longest, snapped into the same direction. For the first time, I was headed the right way.

I was also almost at the edge of the village.

It was tucked into a flat place but still on the side of the mountain, for *safety's* sake—fat lot of good that'd done any of them. I rounded past a grouping of tents and the ground almost fell away from me; I was looking out over the true desert now, from a pretty good vantage point, breathing as raggedly as that kid had been and feeling pretty crazy.

The fourth compass hand locked into place, pointing out over the sand.

There, in the distance, I saw them—nomads, maybe even desert raiders, all on horseback in a cloud of desert dust, riding away. My own village was too close to Ke-Han territory to worry about that kind of thing, but it was the stuff all my childhood nightmares were about. One day, if they got cocky enough, the nomad princes would come for us, take our supplies, and be gone by morning, leaving nothing in their wake. Just like they'd done for this village.

But on top of that, they had something I needed, and they were riding farther and farther away with every second I stood there gaping after them.

My head ached; my temples were pounding. I dropped to my knees. There was nothing I could do. I didn't have a horse—certainly not one trained to outrace nomads in the desert—and I didn't have an army, so I couldn't've done anything even if I were able to ride out after them. I just had to sit down for a little while, that was all; give in to the pain in my head and my hand, and let everything take over.

I was tired. I hurt. And I was fainting.

"Shh," someone said, and a cool, feminine hand touched my brow; I was so hot that it felt like ice. I saw her for a moment; she had a funny nose and didn't look anything at all like the women I was used to. Shit, she didn't even look Ke-Han.

Then I passed the fuck out.

ROOK

Maybe, if I'd been in a better mood, I might've liked the desert. There was sand everywhere, which was far better than large groups of stupid people. And camels were bigger than horses, and the one I was riding hadn't spat on me yet. All in all, I was doing pretty good with the desert, though some people were struggling.

It was just that even watching a camel spit in Thom's face wasn't cheering me up any.

"They really do know when someone doesn't like them," Geoffrey Fucking Bless had explained, back at the beginning of our little expedition when the event in question had taken place. "That explains the spitting, do you see?"

Logical sense, I thought—something Thom'd usually eat up with a spoon—but Thom wasn't in a better mood, either, and getting spit on by the animal he was gonna be riding for the next few days didn't seem to help. Bastion, I'd even offered to trade, but he'd been stubborn as an ox, as always, and he'd stick by that camel until the day it or he died, whichever came first.

But it was nice and dark out over the dunes now, with night coming on. There weren't any sights to see, just sand and more sand, and occasionally I'd look over at Thom, nodding off over the neck of his camel, just to make sure he hadn't fallen off somewhere on the trail behind us. Him and his mount were getting along fine now. Thom just took some getting used to with everyone.

As Bless explained it, we had to do the bulk of our riding at night and sleep in tents under the sun during midday. That way, you kept from getting heatstroke. And the last thing this trip needed, on top of everything else, was Thom fainting like a lady having the vapors because of a little sunlight.

If anyone was gonna be prone to some kind of affliction I hadn't heard of, it was Thom.

For the first few days, Bless'd done his best to keep up a travel dialogue, showing off every damned fact he'd crammed into his overlarge head, but after a while it became pretty hard to ignore the fact that he was talking to himself, so I guess he gave up out of embarrassment—finally. I wasn't interested, and Thom's attention was all squared away in staying on his camel, though he did throw in the occasional "ah" and "is that so?" for Bless's benefit. I did have to give the guy credit for not ending up dead and *still* somehow managing to be the biggest idiot I'd ever clapped eyes on. They said the desert was pretty merciless with idiots, and yet here was Geoffrey Fucking Bless to prove the theory wrong, riding his camel like it was a fucking carousel horse.

We crested one of the big dunes, my camel grunting like she didn't think much about all this hill-climbing all of a sudden, but camels didn't talk, so it was harder to tell what they were thinking. Not that it mattered; it was just different. If I'd told that to Thom, he would've wanted to *open a dialogue* or some shit and I'd have had to spit on him, camel or no.

Instead, I kept my thoughts to myself and my camel did the same. It was an okay system, all things considered.

Bless'd been riding somewhere in front of Thom and me for the better part of our travels—after it became pretty apparent that neither of us gave a shit whether the old kings of the desert were buried under all that shifting sand. Thom's ass hurt too much—otherwise he'd've been eating Bless's stories right up—but I just didn't give a fuck.

On the third day, we'd passed some kind of enormous statue, buried half-underground, that Bless said was back from the days when the government had been a monarchy instead of a democracy. In the moonlight it looked like a giant being swallowed in quicksand—some king no one cared about or remembered anymore—and I got a good kick out of thinking about how th'Esar'd shit his pants if he ever saw something like that. Too close to home for comfort. Wish I could've commissioned a fucking portrait.

After we'd seen the first statue, we started to notice a lot more of them. Broken pillars, or half a head sticking out of the sand; sometimes no more than a piece of nose or a finger, but they weren't regular old rocks, and we had the faculties to recognize 'em for what they were, now. It was like we'd somehow blundered into a forgotten city—and because we were only traveling at night, it felt all the more weird to be traveling through, riding our camels between dismembered body parts as large as the camels themselves.

"Amazing what a change time can bring, isn't it?" Bless remarked, the third night, when we were setting up camp in the shadow of a wall that was mostly rubble by now, pitted and pocked like a poor bastard's dirty face. In fact, I'd known somebody who looked like that wall down in Molly a long time ago. "Not to mention a change in the government, eh?"

There was something about his attitude that rubbed me the wrong way. I guessed it was mostly the way he seemed to think everything was better out in the desert, like leaving Thremedon had suddenly made him better than everyone else in it. There was no love lost between th'Esar and me, but even an idiot could tell he'd done well enough by his country, and people who acted like they were better than everybody else while digging dead people up outta the ground and selling the pieces off to the highest bidders didn't exactly inspire feelings of affection in me.

What surprised me—I mean really fucking knocked my boots off—was that Thom seemed to have picked up on it too. At least, he'd got some sand in his britches about something or other. Maybe it was the heat, or maybe it was having to sleep during the day and ride at night. Some men just weren't made to be nocturnal; some of the boys back at the Airman'd had the same problem. I'd just have to keep an eye on my brother to make sure he didn't turn into a knife-wielding maniac like Ivory on me, and everyone'd be okay.

I didn't have a spare knife to lend him, for starters.

So it was shaping up to be one hell of a trip, each leg more tedious than the fucking last and no visible end in sight. To make my day fucking better, Bless'd slowed his camel that night to draw even with me. Sure, I'd done some bad things in my time, but nobody deserved to be saddled with this idiot.

"If we keep to this pace, we should arrive at a proper dig site tomorrow," Bless confided in me. I didn't know why he was talking to me all of a sudden and not pretending I didn't exist, like we both knew he wanted to. Maybe it had something to do with the fact that his biggest fan had cooled his enthusiasm a little, worn down by so much traveling and so little to eat.

"Huh," I said, which wasn't an answer so much as a grunt. He knew I didn't give two shits about a dig site.

"And," Bless added quickly, "the Khevir dunes are only a matter of days away. Now, I know the rate at which we're traveling has been very difficult for you, but doesn't it soothe the sting somewhat to know that we're very nearly at our goal? Of course, once we have reached the dunes, I imagine it will take us somewhat longer to comb them thoroughly for your magician, but the point remains that we are drawing very close to your destination."

"Right," I said, grinding my teeth. He didn't need to sound so fucking pleased about it. I'd already signed up for however many days in the desert it took to find that fucking magician, and I didn't need some reminder that it was gonna be difficult. "Like I said, it's not like we've got anything better to do. And if you're leading us around by the nose just because you think you can get away with it, I'll make it so you're just another statue out here. You got that, Bless?"

We were passing by a huge stone forearm as I said it, set flat against the sand, with its palm turned up. The imagery didn't escape Bless because 'Versity students were usually good with that kinda thing. He swallowed, then shook his head, still trying to pretend like I didn't get to him. We both knew how true that was, too.

"My *dear* fellow," he began, and I *would've* taken my knife out then, desert guide be damned, if Thom hadn't shouted.

I whirled around, ready to fucking flay him alive if he'd gone and done something stupid like falling off his camel again, but he hadn't. In fact, he looked pretty okay, save for the fact that he was staring at the arm like he thought it was real or something.

"Thomas?" Bless asked, in that snotty voice of his, like a mother whose child was misbehaving.

"I . . ." Thom blinked, then lifted a hand to rub at his eye. "I thought I saw someone. A man. Standing just above the wrist."

I looked, but there hadn't been anyone there a minute ago, and there sure as Molly-shit wasn't anyone there now.

"Oh, Thomas," Bless said, shaking his head. "I am *so* sorry. This change from diurnal to nocturnal's been very difficult on you, hasn't it? Perhaps you fell asleep for a moment, and dreamed it up? It's happened to better men; don't let it get you down."

"I didn't fall asleep," Thom insisted, though he didn't sound entirely sure of himself. "I wasn't even feeling tired."

"Well," I said, sliding off my camel's back, "only one way to be sure of that."

I hated to stop. It only made me feel like we were wasting time, but Bless seemed ready to write off whatever Thom'd seen as a dream, and you could bet your boots that whatever Geoffrey Fucking Bless did, I'd do the opposite.

Besides, Thom was a Mollyrat. If he was going to shout because of anything, it wasn't going to be some stupid dream. You learned quick enough not to shout in your sleep down in Molly, and even if Bless didn't know better than to call my brother a liar, *I* sure as shit did.

I stalked up to the arm, sand crunching beneath my feet. Behind me, Thom hit the ground with a thump and came racing up to follow me like he was some kind of hunting dog and I was his master.

"Get back on the fucking camel," I growled, hoisting myself up onto the broken stone thumb. "If there *is* anyone here, I don't need you slowing me down."

"I wasn't dreaming," Thom said stubbornly, scratching his arm. "These damn sand gnats . . . If I'd thought it was a mirage, I'd never have disturbed everyone like—bastion fucking *damn* it, Geoffrey!"

There was a flurry of action, and all of it happening in the fucking dark. I'd been good at seeing in the dark once, but I'd gone soft as fucking mud since then. Didn't do me any good now to think about it. All I knew was that all of a sudden we weren't alone in the desert, the night wind blowing in my face and the sand billowing up from someone *else's* movements. Thom straightened up quick—his instincts weren't bad when his thinking wasn't getting in the way—and I swung down from the hand just in time to see three men dragging Bless from his camel.

If this was a dream, it was a pretty fucking vivid one.

Thom started toward them and I could've killed him on the spot, reaching out instead to haul him back by the collar. I shoved him behind me and pulled out my knife.

But that wouldn't do any fucking good either, because we were already surrounded.

If Bless hadn't've been there—if it'd just been the two of us—maybe I'd've been able to react a little faster; maybe I wouldn't've let such a simple strategy pin us down so easy.

But there was a saying down in Molly, and it went like this: could've, would've, *should've.*

"Don't fight!" Bless was saying. "Don't fight!"

My eyes were at least getting better at seeing in the dark again after all this night traveling. The moon came out from behind a cloud and I could see everything pretty well, in fact, and I took stock of the situation as quick as I could because I didn't much trust anyone else to be able to. About fifteen men—maybe a few more—had come up on us, quiet as you like, closing me, Bless, Thom, and our other men in like we were somebody's present. There was a man holding a knife to Bless's throat and he snarled something in Bless's ear.

"What's he saying?" I demanded.

"He says that if you do not put that knife down," Bless choked out, "he intends to cut my throat."

"Tell him to go ahead," I said. "I don't give a leaping fuck what the hell he does to you."

Bless looked troubled at that. "Surely you don't mean it," he said. The man holding the knife pressed it a little closer in under his chin and Bless made the most wonderful sound, like he couldn't breathe, and also like he was shitting himself a little.

"You pass on the information yet?" I asked. "Go ahead and tell him there's no fucking deal."

"That will not be necessary," someone new said from behind us, and I whirled around, knife at the ready, to make sure they didn't think they had the drop on us.

I didn't even need the moonlight to tell me this guy was their leader. Just the way he held himself made it clear, and on closer inspection the way he was dressed sealed it. His hair was longer and his face was pretty intense, and he was looking at me the way th'Esar liked to look at me—so I knew he was probably some kind of royalty. Instinct could do a lot for you in a pinch like this one.

"You are not from these parts," my friend the desert king said. It was real convenient that he could speak Volstovic, because that meant we didn't have to use Bless as a go-between.

"Yeah, that's about right," I said.

"And this man, I think, is a robber," my friend went on, gesturing at Bless. "I do not know you, but men who consort with robbers are usually robbers themselves."

"I've picked a few pockets in my time," I told him, "not that it's any business of yours what I've done."

"Picked a few pockets?" My friend paused to contemplate this—the phrase obviously confused him—and I had to do my damnedest not to laugh. I wasn't used to being circumspect or negotiating. Maybe I should've let Thom talk—but I was the one with the knife, which meant I was the one who did the talking. At least for now, anyway.

"To *eat*," I said, making the appropriate gesture for eating with my free hand. "Money, for food. But that was a real long time ago."

"But you travel with *this*," my friend said, and spat into the sand.

I grinned. Now, that was something I could get behind. On a whim, I gathered up a mouthful and spat into the sand after him. "Me too," I explained.

My friend looked puzzled for a moment, like my actions confused

him. Good; there was still a chance we could get the element of surprise back and *not* get sliced open like lunch in the desert because of
Geoffrey Fucking Bless robbing other people's cultures blind in the
name of learning, or whatever excuse he was currently using.

"Who are you?" my friend asked finally.

"You first," I said.

"Rook, I really think—" Thom began beside me, but my friend held
up his hand.

"I am not embarrassed to give my name," he said. "I am Kalim
al'Mhed of the Khevir al'Mheds." Behind me, I heard Bless make a
choking noise; I didn't think it was from anyone slitting his throat
clean in two, which was a pity. "See?" Kalim al'Mhed of the whatever
al'Mheds confirmed my suspicions. "Your friend knows me."

"Hey," I said. "That pussyfoot isn't my friend."

"Pussyfoot?" Kalim repeated.

I gestured to my dick and then expressed, with my thumb and fore-
finger, the universal sign for *very fucking small.* Kalim took my meaning immediately. I could officially say that talks in the desert were going
pretty well.

"You travel with a common thief," Kalim told me. "We call him
rakhman. This means . . . 'pussyfoot,' in your Volstovic language?"

"Yeah, *rakhman,*" I agreed, butchering the pronunciation, but nevertheless completely getting my point across. "That's what he is, and
we're only traveling with him because we have to."

"And you are?" Kalim asked politely.

"Uh, I'm Rook," I said. "Of the Mollyrat Rooks. No titles."

"Well, Mollyrat Rook," Kalim went on, "I do not like this man behind you. Should I kill him?"

Thom made a slight noise of disapproval. I looked down at him,
wondered how many throats he'd seen slit in Molly, and sighed.

"Sure, if you have to," I said. "If he's insulted your mother or dug up
your great-grandfather or something. But don't do it in front of my
brother."

"Rook, *really,*" Bless tried to say. Then he stopped real short, on account of somebody holding a knife to his voice box. I was liking Kalim
better and better the more I got to know him.

"We will put him to trial," Kalim said finally, something struggling to show itself on his face. Emotion *I* couldn't understand, but it was obviously killing him not to order Bless put down right then and there, which at least was something I could understand *very* well.

"You've got my blessing," I said. "But we've got nothing to do with this. New to the desert and all that. We've got somebody we're looking for, so—"

"I am sorry," Kalim said, and he had the decency to actually look it. "But I cannot let you go. If you are associated with this man, then we must also take you into our custody."

Great, I thought. I knew that heading into this with Bless was gonna come back and bite me square in the ass, sure as piss after a night of drinking.

"Well, I'm sorry, Kalim," I said. "Because I can't let you do that."

"I understand," Kalim said.

"So let's settle this man to man," I told him, and indicated my knife—universal symbol for *knife fight,* I was guessing.

"Rook," Thom said quietly. He didn't sound like he was pissing himself, so he was doing all right as far as I was concerned.

"Keep the fuck back," I said, since apparently that was something he was having trouble with all of a sudden.

"This is your brother?" Kalim asked, looking over at Thom like he'd only just noticed him.

"Yeah," I said. "That's him."

"I see," Kalim nodded. "Well, I will have to be sure not to slit *your* throat in front of him, either."

Thom sucked in a breath, but I just grinned because Kalim was a man who was speaking my language—and I didn't just mean Volstovic. He said something sharply in desert talk and his men fanned out— they were pretty well fucking trained for a group of nomads—and formed a loose circle around us. I cracked my neck. This was an arena that required no translation; I'd have wagered it was the same in any country. No one left the circle until the fight was over.

I'd just have to hope I'd made enough of an impression on Kalim and the Khevir al'Mheds that they wouldn't want to play for keeps.

Kalim shed the cape and cowl he'd been wearing and drew out his knife. It was a mean-looking thing, with a curved blade and a pale handle that looked like it was made out of some kind of bone. I wasn't any kind of enthusiast when it came to blades—I'd take what got the job done, thanks—but even I could tell this thing was special. Hoped it wasn't human bone, though. That was just messy.

"If I lose," I muttered to Thom, while someone scurried forward from the circle to take Kalim's discarded overrobe, "give up on Bless, you got that? Gotta make some compromises. You take care of yourself and don't try to stick your neck out for that pisser. He's *not* worth it."

"You don't really think he intends to kill you?" Thom asked. He seemed pretty fucking calm on the outside, but I could hear his voice tightening underneath.

"Nah," I said, tossing him my best grin. It was all teeth. "Besides, I'm not gonna lose. That's some real impressive confidence you have in me."

"Rook," Thom began, and then, a lot more quietly, almost like he didn't mean to say it, "John . . ."

"Get back in the fucking circle, Thom," I snapped, like he was three fucking years old again and wouldn't listen to a damn thing I said. Then I turned away, passing my knife from one hand to the other to get a feel for the weight of it. At least *this* time what I'd said took. He walked back slowly to stand between two of Kalim's men, and not near Geoffrey, I noted, which was funny as hell. Maybe he was listening to me after all.

"Can't we just be reasonable about all this?" Bless asked, gurgling softly when the man holding him made it clear that now was the time to shut up and shut up good.

Kalim spat in the ground rather than answering him, which I thought was a pretty fair answer, all things considered. I did the same. It was good for diplomatic relations.

"Among my people, we have a tradition," Kalim said, turning to me again. "When a man is not fighting to prove his innocence, and between men who have no blood quarrel, we end the fight when first blood is drawn. It is an understanding that the man who bleeds will abide by the wishes of the victor. To attempt to do otherwise would be dishonorable."

"So even though you're not going to slit my throat and I'm not gonna beat you to a pulp, whoever lands the first scratch gets to call the shots, is that what you're saying?" I asked, just to be clear we were on the same page. I didn't trust him—it went against all my instincts as a

Mollyrat to trust a stranger in a fight, especially when I was fighting by the stranger's rules—but I was kinda *almost* inclined to *want* to trust him, which was throwing me off.

"Shots?" Kalim blinked. I could've laughed, but it would've broken my concentration.

"You get to make the rules," I clarified, and he nodded.

"Yes," he said. "The rules. I am learning a great deal of interesting language from you, Mollyrat Rook."

"You've got no idea," I said, and just like that he lunged at me.

I'd been waiting for it. Oldest trick in the book was to talk at someone until you got them to let their guard down, and what Kalim hadn't been counting on was that my guard was *always* fucking up, even when I was talking. Maybe especially when I was talking. I stepped quick to the right and he snapped back around, pivoting so the miss wouldn't leave him vulnerable. He was quicker than I'd have guessed from his size, but that didn't matter much since I was quick for my size too. Only real advantage he had on me was that he was better used to fighting in the desert, moving his feet on the sand when I was used to harder surfaces, broken-up cobblestone and the like. It was a little difference, but it was there.

Starting out, I went on the defensive, stepping back and dodging as he circled me. It was the easiest way to make out his moves, see how fast he was and which side he favored. Then, just so he didn't start to catch on that that was what I was doing, I attacked him quick, going low when he went high and catching his hip against my shoulder. I flipped him flat on his back.

"Yes!" Thom whooped loudly, probably jumping up and down like a fucking idiot. I'd've thrown my knife at him if I'd had a spare, but he caught ahold of himself real quick and piped down. Better that he didn't draw any attention to himself, or give our new desert friends reason to hold him hostage. It was one thing they were doing it to Bless, but if it'd been Thom they were ransoming, my hands really *would've* been tied.

Kalim twisted up quickly to his feet, checking his arms for a knife wound. There wasn't any. Not yet. We were both respecting each other too much to end it so quick, and I'd done him some kind of honor by prolonging the fight. He grinned like the crescent moon and dove at me again, his hand a blur as I hopped back, doing my best to dodge the sudden flurry of knife strokes as they sliced the air in front of me. I lost my balance in the sand for a second and one came dangerously close to my eye.

Dangerously close, but not close enough. Best kind of close there was.

"Tell me," said Kalim, sounding out of breath enough for me to feel satisfied about my performance. "What is it you are doing in the desert, if your business is not with the *rakhman*?"

"Looking for something," I grunted, knocking his arm back when it swept forward.

"I hope it is something that—belongs to you," Kalim said, rolling to one side to dodge a kick I'd thrown at him.

"She is," I snarled, taking a lunge at him again. "It's *other* people tryna take her from me."

"Ah," huffed Kalim. "*Woman trouble.*"

"You could say that," I told him. I'd been marking which side he dodged to more often—everybody had one, and there was no reasoning to it beyond simple human wiring—so I could make the next one count. The next time I dove at him, I kept my knife to the left, so that when he did that neat trick of his, darting to one side with only a sliver of space between us, he caught the edge of my knife on his shoulder.

It wouldn't have worked if he'd been wearing sleeves—the difference was that fucking tiny—but he wasn't. For a minute neither of us was sure if we had to stop. I was holding my knife up to defend in case he threw himself at me, and he'd assumed a similar pose, both of us waiting to know, one way or another, whether the fight was done.

Most people got nervous in that moment. I didn't. It was exactly like being up in the air and I fucking loved it.

Then a bead of bright red formed, on his shoulder, sliding dark and liquid down his arm. A murmur went up from the circle around us—not a peep from Thom this time—and Kalim held up his knife. The crowd shut up instantly.

"What happened?" Geoffrey was asking. He was starting to sound real fucking unhinged. "Did we win?"

"This is for you," Kalim said, holding the knife to me, handle out. He looked almost pleased with himself, which was a real funny way to look at losing, no two ways about it.

I held up my hands. "That's not necessary," I said. Trophies weren't my style. "Really. All I want is for me and my brother to get going. That's all."

"Tradition," Kalim insisted.

I was still coming down from the fight. It'd been a good one, the first good one in a while, and maybe this Kalim wasn't half-bad to begin with, so at least I had a reason for what I did next. I took his knife, but then before he could retract his hand I slapped mine into his palm.

"It's a trade," I said, tucking his away. It was about the same weight, and a little longer than mine'd been, but I'd manage. I still fucking hoped it wasn't made out of somebody's arm or leg bone, but that was personal preference.

Kalim held on to my knife a little longer. He had to have known that it was a cheap fucking piece of work—it'd served me pretty good but it wasn't anything fancy, not like his. The trade wasn't fair, and it shouldn't've been, either. I was the winner, so I deserved the real prize. But the way Kalim was looking at my knife, it was like I'd gone and made things even between us, and now he owed me one since I'd kicked his ass good and proper.

"Something wrong with the knife?" I asked.

"It is a good blade," Kalim told me. "You use it often?"

"Only when I need to," I said, grinning again. The cold air from the desert at night was blowing over my skin and cooling me down; I'd broken a sweat while fighting Kalim, but my blood wasn't up anymore and I was even a little chilly, which was nice. Perfect weather for fighting, nice and cold and dry.

Two of Kalim's people had broken the circle, coming forward to check out his arm no doubt, but he waved them away.

And then, just like that, life suddenly got interesting.

"This woman you are seeking," Kalim said. "I think that I know where she is."

CHAPTER SEVEN

MALAHIDE

It was lonely on the road, and I did prefer things that way. I had been traveling south for a week, and still I hadn't tired of watching the Cobalt Mountains, which changed shades of blue depending on how they were lit.

It seemed strange to me that I could count myself among the few men and women who were truly happy with their station in life. Most people seemed to find the idea of a life like mine ghastly, or even laughable. As a consequence I had very few acquaintances, aside from those I used for work, but that too suited me. Some were simply born with a restlessness in their blood, a calling that urged them to travel over oceans and mountains. I myself was incredibly fortunate in that I could earn my keep while doing so.

It had been too long since my last job promised to take me out of Volstov. After nearly losing us—his own precious magicians—in the plague that had come over the Cobalts, the Esar had kept all his old guard close at hand, almost like a concerned father. It would have been sweet had I not already known exactly what kind of father the Esar could be. When I thought of Dmitri, I wrote him, though they were frivolous letters by necessity, speaking nothing of the task at hand. I had no return address to which he might reciprocate, and so I received none in return, though in strictest honesty the freedom that silence granted allowed me to be much more candid in my writing than usual.

Lovely scenery, only my thoughts to occupy me, and the occasional illegal deal taking place right before my eyes. My idea of perfection—or at least, as close to it as something as imperfect as me was liable to get. No one ever knew that I was watching; that was the entire point. My duty was to be neither seen nor heard, and I fulfilled it well enough even now that I had a voice.

Yet there was still no sign of my bounty.

A hunter was only worth as much as his or her quarry, but if that quarry was no more than a theory, the hunt was only *in theory*, as well. I would have readily admitted—were there anyone to whom I might have offered my admissions—that I was feeling much like a ghost as I made my way along the Black Steppe. That was what they called it, and I appreciated its tonal qualities, but there were points at which I found my self-definitions slipping away, now that they had nothing to operate against. A dangerous, tricky business indeed, this loneliness.

It had been different when I'd worked with my partner. More difficult, in many ways, since it was harder to ignore two people than one, and you always needed a better excuse for why the *both* of you were hanging around. He'd been a strange fellow—a combination of his predilections and his quiet Talent had made him so—but good enough company in the mountains when the days grew long and the air grew still in my sails.

I was not sad when I thought of him, but I did miss his presence.

Fortunately, it was in the steppe that I encountered my first real piece of luck: the man I was now following, who moved with such speed and such purpose that I knew he was either carrying something of great value or racing toward it. I could also smell dragonmetal on him, so my hunch was not entirely unfounded. I did not know his name, nor did I know his face, but since I first caught wind of his scent and, subsequently, his trail, I was drawing ever closer to him.

Now the chase was on.

I first smelled the dragonmetal in a dream; I was still in Volstovic territory, on Thremedon's side of the Cobalt Range, only five days into my travels. It woke me instantly and I covered all traces of my camp better than he was currently covering his. After that, I was on my feet and back on the road in no time at all, ready to begin my hunt in earnest. He was deviating from the steppe. In point of fact, he was leading me straight *through* the mountains.

Neither of us slept for days, and the knowledge thrilled me to the core. It was the rare man who could lose more than one day of sleep without his brain turning funny on him. *This* man was not only holding to his pace, but he was keeping sharp while doing so. It was still impossible for him to hide his trail from me, but he was getting better at it, not worse. It was quite possible he sensed my presence; he had no evidence that I was there save for a shadow of paranoia in his own mind, but he was picking up speed, moving with preternatural grace and purpose along a very narrow pass through the mountains. But so long as there was wind and air, I had my advantage. He was not yet suspicious enough to cover the scent of his own skin, and I doubted anything would cover the odor of the dragonmetal. And so long as I had my scents, I had my prey. I kept well enough away from him so that he would never have cause to hear the echo of my footsteps across the rocks above and realize that this shadow of fear had taken shape and was coming for him wearing *my* features.

I could not wait to meet him. Our skills were very nearly evenly matched, and though he was traveling somewhat carelessly in his haste, he was clearly quite the extraordinary gentleman.

A woman could wait years, even a lifetime, before she met her match.

I was very nearly face-to-face with mine; I was exceedingly lucky that he just so happened to be carrying something of use to me. I intended to have it in my possession before we left the mountains, but he was taking the most twisted route through them possible, and I had to be careful not to press my advantage too quickly and have him turn the element of surprise against me. Suppose he were to have superior strength, or a Talent I could not sniff out from such a distance?

No; I would have to wait and see where he led me.

I hadn't been born with the skills necessary to follow a man as I now did. It was my Talent that made me preternaturally suited to it—a strength of mind and body that made it possible for me to subsist on very little sleep and food. If I'd been of a stronger build, I might have made an excellent soldier. As things stood, at the time of my birth, the Esar had been in greater need of spies. There were precious few magicians who did not count themselves among the members of the

Basquiat. My hard-won Talent made it such that I quickly surpassed those others being trained for the same purposes. I simply had an edge—one that separated me from even the small, distinctive group that lived in the Esar's employ. Even that hadn't been enough for my satisfaction, however, and on the occasion of my sixteenth birthday I gave up my speech for an extraordinary sense of smell.

There were those who argued I had given up a great deal more than that, but my stubbornness matched their own quite easily. It had taken the Esar weeks to set up the ceremony in secret and far longer than that to find someone willing to perform it. Trading one sense for the magnification of another was clumsy magic, from another time entirely, and strictly outlawed for the mischief it could cause. Of course, the Esar was a man given to circumventing his own laws for the greater good, and he'd never hesitated after I'd made my decision. Of my own volition—that was the phrase he himself employed.

I'd never been given cause to regret my decision. Speech could be clumsy, it could delay or mislead, but my nose had never lied to me. I was an instrument well suited to my position, and that was all I needed to be satisfied with my life.

Although I would most certainly have been cheered by some further prospect of my quarry, as well.

After three days in the mountains—three hungry, weary days, drinking only enough water to keep my energy up, and sleeping in hourlong fits and bursts whenever he paused in his breakneck pace—I could tell by the sand and the grit and the heat on the air that we were coming close to the desert. How curious.

This was not the Black Steppe any longer. He was traveling via his own peculiar route, and not one that had been forged by any travelers ahead of him. It made the going difficult, but my innermost self was elated at the challenge he presented. It had been ages since I was tested so. There had been none among the Esar's ranks who could challenge me *before* I'd traded in my tongue. Afterward, none had dared.

I was, admittedly, delighted to come to a change in scenery. The mountains all around me had made me feel somewhat claustrophobic, and I was ready to see some open air. I was also ready to see my quarry's face at last. I could hardly wait to meet him, though I could not allow my eagerness to overtake my plans. Patience was the most difficult virtue to cultivate, since it went against my every instinct as a human being. I imagined myself instead as a spider, a veteran hunter, craftily spinning a web as I waited for my prey to fall into it.

As I spun, I formulated my next move. There was no time to send letters anymore, and no post to send them by, either. From here on out, it was strictly business—between my quarry and me—and no other thoughts would invade my mind.

The next time he rested, I would not allow myself to sleep. Instead, I would come upon him in the darkness and pin him down. Then we would discuss a great number of topics, such as how he had the dragon piece in his possession and where he was heading with it so excitedly. If he refused to tell me, then I would be forced to persuade him—which was often a time-consuming process, but one that always prevailed in the end.

Unfortunately, I never got my chance.

It was on the dawn of the fourth day in the mountains that I at last crested the trail at a plateau and found myself looking out over the desert. Sand stretched out before me like some foreign, amber ocean. Indeed, it was an impressive sight—so much sand for a Volstovic native was quite exotic, and I was breathless as an observer, as well as a great lover of natural beauty. It spanned as far as the human eye could see, the smell of sun on sand positively overwhelming, and its size even dwarfed the Cobalts—themselves an awesome sight.

However, I could also see quite clearly that a raiding party of nomads stood between me and my man. As dark spots against the tan hide of the desert, they stood out quite easily. If I'd had a horse—or no, a camel—I might have stood a real chance in overtaking them. But then the proverbial game would be up, and I wasn't yet willing to concede what few advantages I had on my side.

Over such open ground, I would have to divine a new way of following my elusive friend.

The stench of burning and killing wormed its way into my senses, and as the wind changed course, I found myself doused in the stink. The scent of dragonmetal had disappeared completely; only the faintest hint remained, overwhelmed by the fiery air. That would be the nomads, and he couldn't have chosen a better screen to cloak his tracks if he'd tried. Blood and fire were two of the likeliest things to confuse a nose like mine, and the nomads here had been responsible for both all too recently. For the moment, my man had the upper hand. Too much stood between me and my trail.

He had, I realized, excited and furious, given me the proverbial slip.

Whether he'd done it on purpose or not was immaterial. I had no doubts that I'd covered my presence completely, but there was always the possibility that he too was possessed of some extraordinary Talent that had alerted him to the chase. The other option to consider was that he was simply *monstrously* lucky, and that fate was not on my side in this endeavor. That at least I didn't mind, since I'd found myself on the wrong side of fate many a time since I'd been born and had not let it hinder my proceedings as of yet.

I began my descent down the path toward the desert, warm wind swirling angrily around my hair and face. It was as though the very air around me was as agitated as I. As I surveyed the horizon once more, I realized that fate hadn't entirely consigned itself to my quarry. The sun would be setting soon, which meant that I could keep going without fear of how I'd hold up under the unforgiving heat of the desert. I had no idea whether my Talent extended to protect me from something like this—a climate of the severest nature—and in my current mood, I was in no hurry to find out.

As I reached the level of the desert, I saw that there was a little village set into the foothills of the mountains. That was the source of the burning smell *and* the blood; one did not require a nose like mine to suss that one out. I'd just made up my mind to bypass the place entirely—my business had nothing to do with desert villages and their troubles—when the wind blew something strange and wonderful to my nose.

It was the unmistakable tang of dragonmetal once more. Different, I thought, from the dragonmetal I'd been chasing all this time; there was a wilder, fleshier spice to it, like blood and Talent. The combination was a perfume whose peculiarity I could not resist. I had to discover the source.

The man I'd been following was still beyond my reach, but this smell was instantly recognizable. I didn't have time to wonder whether he'd led me here on purpose. More likely was the explanation that he'd had some dealings here, possibly either to sell or buy, which meant that whoever he'd been dealing with was now in the village. A beautiful combination of events.

Fate *was* on my side after all.

Without a second thought, I switched my course, making for the village at once. I already knew that the nomads had ridden off with whatever their quarry was; with them gone, the village was safer, if still in turmoil. My heart all but skipped a beat as I picked up the pace, drawing closer to the smell of burned things, death and injury and fear alike. I pulled a handkerchief from my sleeve and tied it firmly over my nose. There were *some* disadvantages to the gift I'd received, the main one being that I smelled even the things I didn't need nor particularly wished to. Still, it was worth it. It had always been worth it to me to have a purpose in life that I could call my own.

As I came up to the village outskirts, I noticed a man crouching by the tent nearest to me. He held something in his arms, but neither man nor object smelled of the dragonmetal I sought. I was about to ignore them so that they might ignore *me* and delve farther into the village in pursuit of what my nose dangled tantalizingly in front of me when the man called out. His senses were keener than a simple villager's ought to have been; I had missed my mark on that account.

"Hey!" he said, in a soldier's unmistakable bark. "You, over there. Give me a hand with this!"

I made a cursory effort in looking around, but I was already quite certain that it was me to whom he was speaking. No one else native to this wreckage remained in sight. It was also uncertain whether or not they remained at all. Reluctantly, I strode over to him, determined to at least see what it was he needed before I made my way along. As I came closer, I noticed two things: one, that the soldier was clearly of Ke-Han descent; and two, what he was holding was not an object at all but a very small boy.

"I just need someone to hold his arm while I set it," the soldier explained, not giving me a second look. Trained as I was for the Esar's current purposes, I spoke his language fluently; it took me a moment to realize I needed to translate, but this had as much to do with the time I'd spent alone, away from language of any sort, as it had to do with the differences in our native tongues. With my handkerchief covering my face, it was also possible that he thought I was local to these parts; my hair was black, like his, and the confusion might serve me well. "Can you do that?"

The boy made a pitiful sound, more like a wounded dog than a human child, and I crouched in the sand beside him. I supposed I could do as he asked.

"Thanks," the soldier said. He reached over to show me where I was to hold, and I caught the faintest trace of a familiar scent on his hands. My pulse quickened. It couldn't possibly be. And yet my nose had never led me astray.

My interest was suddenly renewed in this man—though the scent was not as strong here, it nonetheless lingered on his hands, strong enough that I could smell it as he reached across to me.

I held the boy's arm; the sight of pain and injury did not perturb me as it did some, though I felt a distant pity for the mewling creature. The soldier was staring at me, and I supposed I should do something to help the child; with one gloved hand, I patted him faintly on the head. The other I kept to the soldier's instructions.

Together, we reset the bone. The boy lost consciousness some way through, which I supposed was for the best; whatever dreams he was host to now could not possibly be worse than the pain he would have experienced were he conscious.

The soldier sat back, sweat damp on his face. It only heightened the scent of the metal on his hands, however, and I glanced at them, allowing a moment of contemplation to overtake me.

His eyes narrowed as he observed me, and I knew the moment he realized I was *not* a local occupant.

Of course, it was only natural for him to wonder what I was doing here, my face hidden from view, my clothes foreign, and my eyes very green. But I had been friendly from the first, and that initial kindness would go a long way toward helping the informal peace talks that were about to take place between us.

"I mean no harm at all," I told him, holding up my hands.

"Who are you?" he asked. "What're you doing here?"

The truth, or a complicated lie? Both had their benefits; both, their drawbacks. He had a keen kind of face, marred only by one nasty scar, and though he was young, it was obvious he was a soldier of some experience. Ash made my eyes water and I looked away—a wile that might influence his inclinations somewhat. If he thought that I was troubled by the destruction wrought around us, he might just soften.

After all, he'd paused to look after a little child in the midst of what was, essentially, a battlefield. He had a streak of human gentleness that I could manipulate to my needs.

"I'm a mapmaker," I said finally. When in doubt, giving away truths was never the best plan. "Part of Volstov's plan to chart these mountains, now that they are peaceful. Yet it seems they are not as peaceful as all that."

"You're not alone," the soldier said. He doubted my lie.

"No," I said, and turned to him with a frightened expression on my face like a mask. "My company—I was separated from them. Do you think that they have been taken by the madmen who did this?"

My fear seemed to assuage *his* fears, though he was still wary of me. "Too many people here that shouldn't be," he said, and then, as if that reminded him of something he'd forgotten, his eyes widened. "Madoka—"

That was a word I did not recognize. After a moment's consideration, I knew it must be a name.

You're not alone either, I thought. And whoever he and his companion were I knew they were relevant to my search.

The wind picked up; though it blew more burning my way, I also caught the tantalizing scent of dragonmetal—that distinctive burst of blood pulsing against steel, making the magic more immediate than I'd ever sensed it before. This was something special.

I rose to my feet. I couldn't allow some fire, some unhappy accident, to take away my lead.

"Where are you—" the soldier asked, but I was already following it. Past houses, burning, and the smell of death all around me, I picked up my pace—running now, and lucky there was no one here from my old life to mark me. Such excitement was not an emotion I often exhibited. But I was among wild things now, and that was the element that had been added to the dragonmetal: wildness. Blood, foreign Talents, brutal flesh.

The scent led me to a woman on the verge of collapse. I caught her as she fell, and so cradled her to my chest, waiting for the soldier to come and find us both.

THOM

Though we'd started out on our travels presumably to learn more of the world, and I had already seen a great deal—sights unimaginable to any common Mollyrat—I was now confronted with a sight I'd never expected to see, watching my brother fight blade to blade with, as Geoffrey came to tell me later, a nomad prince.

I wasn't much inclined to listen to what Geoffrey had to say, but that piece of information, at least, was useful to me. The contempt that the native peoples of the desert showed for my old friend confirmed my suspicions; he was a cad and something of a monster, not at all the shy studying companion I had remembered, and my decision to involve him in Rook's and my life was exceedingly ill-advised. Whatever scolding I received from Rook afterward would be one I thoroughly deserved; I was prepared to take it like a man, unflinching and stolid.

I never got the chance, as Kalim al'Mhed of the Khevir al'Mheds had offered my brother something even I couldn't.

"You know where *who* is?" Rook demanded—he was going to ruin the uncommon truce he'd managed to form in a matter of seconds if he wasn't careful. Risking his anger, I stepped forward to lay my hand on his arm.

Kalim took note of me for the second time; I tried to explain to him with my eyes that my brother was, in some senses, very mad, but there were too many cultural differences between my expressions and his. He looked away from me, the point not taken, and back to Rook.

"You speak of a troublesome woman; you have come looking for her here," Kalim explained. "I know of one woman in the Khevir dunes who lives by herself. She is the only woman I can imagine who might give *you* troubles."

"This woman," I interceded, on all of our behalf. "Is she a native to this place?"

"Under heaven! No," Kalim replied. "She came some years ago— four now by my count. Like a storm she came too." He shuddered for a moment, lost in some memory, then laughed out loud while slapping his thigh, once more in good humor. "She has . . . a similar look about the face as Mollyrat Rook. He is like a storm, himself."

Very apt, I thought. I looked to Rook, whose face was a dangerously unreadable mask, like one of the beheaded statues we'd passed on our travels. I shuddered, but did him the honor of refusing to turn away from him.

"One of the magicians," I said. "It's possible—"

"All right," Rook said in a hard voice. "I'm calling in the favor you owe me, right now."

Kalim's eyes glinted. "What do you ask?"

"Take me to her," Rook said. "I'm going to the Khevir dunes."

"Aha," said Kalim, and he got a hesitant sort of look on his face. I could have told him it was the sort of thing Rook would pounce on instantly—he had an impossibly keen sense for hesitance in others—and indeed, Rook took a step forward, fists bunched, bracing for a confrontation.

"There a problem?" he asked, like things hadn't just calmed down by the grace of the desert gods, and we weren't all trying *very* hard to keep matters from erupting once again.

The men behind us, Kalim's men, had begun to whisper in their language—a soft, fleeting speech that sounded like wind moving over the sand. Geoffrey, in the first sensible act he'd taken since our capture, had lost consciousness; his captor now carried him over one shoulder like a sack of grain except worth considerably less.

"My men will not follow me there," Kalim explained, face suddenly absent of the good humor it had worn a moment ago. "They believe, perhaps not without reason, that the woman carries a curse with her."

"*I'm* gonna do a lot worse than curse 'em if we don't get moving," Rook said.

Kalim shook his head. "I cannot ask them to come with us. It would be . . . What is the word?"

"Reckless?" I asked, unable to help myself when someone was struggling for a word. "Or possibly negligent?"

"Bad," Kalim agreed.

"Come with *us*?" Rook asked, already having taken the most valuable part of the sentence to heart. "Does that mean you're sticking around for the ride?"

"It is the duty of a ruler to honor his people as he would honor himself," Kalim explained. "To ignore their fear of the desert woman would be a great dishonor. But as for myself, I am not afraid."

Rook snorted. "You should talk to th'Esar sometime." He looked around for a moment, taking stock of matters, and I noticed him touch the handle of his new knife consciously, rubbing it with his thumb as though he could feel the difference. "We leaving now? Still plenty of hours of night left ahead of us."

"There is the matter of your . . . Not your friend. The *rakhman,*" Kalim explained. "If you would not protest, I will have him sent back to camp with my men."

I felt a small but insistent anxiety rise in me. I was not feeling particularly kindly disposed toward Geoffrey, and I was fairly certain I would no longer call him friend after the trouble he'd gotten us into, but I still didn't feel entirely comfortable abandoning him to a host of men who wanted nothing more than his death. Kalim had proclaimed himself a man of honor, but none of his host had done the same.

"Fine by me," Rook said. "Tell them they can cut his throat if he tries to escape."

I winced and made up my mind to say something, but before I could do it Kalim was laughing.

"They will not kill him before I return," he said, sounding quite sure of himself. "Knowing I travel alone, with two men of Volstov, one of whom has proven himself in combat, they will not do anything to provoke you. For fear of my safety, do you see?"

"Wouldn't put *me* out any." Rook shrugged, with a glance back in my direction. He made a face, as though this was somehow all my fault *and* I was ruining his fun by trying to keep someone I'd once known and liked from being murdered in front of me. I'd had more than one such experience during my childhood, though that—alongside everything else I'd picked up in Molly—was something I'd done everything in my power to forget. Simply put, I was not in the mood to see the experience repeated, when Molly was so far behind me.

"He will be safe," Kalim promised, looking at me this time. I knew then I must have been doing a very poor job of keeping my feelings to myself for even a stranger to pick up on them. He turned to give a sharp command to one of his men, and there was a flurry of activity as they moved like trained soldiers changing formation. They were wonderfully organized, I thought privately. They clearly knew the desert intimately. It was no wonder they'd been able to sneak up on us so easily.

The man Kalim had spoken to came forward with our camels, alongside another one that must have belonged to the nomad prince himself.

Rook looked up sharply, a hunting dog scenting something he liked in the air.

"This mean we're traveling tonight after all?" he asked.

"Tonight, and the next night," Kalim said, checking the bags strapped to the camel. We were all well provisioned, at least. "You are closer perhaps than you thought, but we cannot cover the distance in what remains of this night. Tomorrow night . . . Perhaps. It depends upon how well you Volstovs ride."

Rook swore, and swung up onto his camel in a practiced motion that made me ache just looking at it. I was none so graceful, and being conscious of my own awkwardness didn't make it any less evident. Kalim no doubt was laughing at me as I scrambled onto my mount's lumpy, ungraceful back, losing my footing more than once as I did so, nearly falling squarely upon my backside in the sand. At least I managed it without taking a full tumble. That would have been shame of the highest order, and I might never have been able to recover Kalim's esteem after that.

Privately, I was not at all looking forward to getting back on a camel, especially at this hour of the night. I didn't know how Rook had managed to adjust so quickly to a schedule of sleeping during the day and riding all night, but as always it seemed to me to speak of some discrepancy between us. We shared the same blood, and yet Rook was able to accomplish all manner of feats I could not. I had my education, yes, but that was an earned skill, not something I'd been born with at all.

Perhaps, if Rook had gone to the 'Versity, he would have had no need for me at all. It was a question I held deeply hidden in my heart, so I could examine it only when I was feeling particularly disheartened.

It was merely difficult being so useless when all I wanted to do was help.

"You are sure that this is the path you wish to take?" Kalim asked, so that for a minute I thought he was asking us about directions. "The Volstov woman has a fearsome temper, they say, and I have never known her to accept a visitor."

"I'm sure," Rook said, his face set as stone. It was clear to anyone with eyes what he was thinking: *She'll damn well accept me.*

Anyone who didn't know Rook might have thought this was born of hubris, but his arrogance was always based on some truth. If anyone could convince her, it would be he.

Kalim shrugged, as if to say it was our funeral, then turned atop his mount to address his men. With some difficulty I adjusted my perch upon my own camel, hoping that since everyone was currently listening to Kalim speak, there would be no one left to notice me. From somewhere to my left, Rook sniggered, and I felt at once both ashamed and resigned. It was a strange mingling of emotions, with neither battling the other for dominance, and I wondered if it meant I was finally reaching some level of comfort with my brother. At the very least, now that we seemed to be closer than ever to our goal, he'd forgotten to be as cantankerous as possible to me at every interval.

At least Geoffrey had been good for taking the brunt of Rook's scorn for a short while. I had to grant him that.

Rook tutted at his camel, twitching the reins and bringing her up next to mine. I still didn't understand how he could be so violent with his fellow man and so easy when it came to dealing with four-legged creatures. It was a fascinating inconsistency, and one I was quite keen to study when all this was over. For now, however, I had more important tasks to put my mind to—like trying to get *my* camel to turn at all.

"You gonna stay on that thing, or do I have to tie you on?" Rook asked.

"I," I began, pausing to smother an inconveniently timed yawn. "I'll manage."

"Uh-huh," Rook said, not looking at all convinced. "Just keep your wrist looped into that bridle and maybe you won't fall off this time."

I did as I was told, hoping that I wouldn't break my wrist—probably better than breaking my neck, in the long run.

"We'll travel faster without all that shit weighing us down too," Rook said, and for a minute I honestly couldn't tell whether he meant Geoffrey or all the supplies and workers he'd needed for the dig.

"I agree," I said softly. I wasn't as worried for my former friend now that it appeared we were taking a nomad prince with us as collateral. It seemed a highly inequitable trade to me, but I wasn't about to spoil things by commenting. Kalim was clearly a man of honor; if he said Geoffrey would not be harmed in his absence, then I believed him.

A shout rose from the crowd, and Kalim raised a hand to silence them. I thought for a moment that we were in trouble again, but as no one moved to attack anyone, I realized it was no more than a very enthusiastic farewell from Kalim's people. Rook seemed to like it, in any case, since he pumped his fist into the air too.

Then, with a look over his shoulder just to make sure we were paying attention, Kalim took off across the desert. His camel moved like nothing I'd ever seen before, like it was an entirely different breed of animal, which it might well have been. It made sense for a nomadic people to breed their animals for speed more so than for anything else, as covering a great deal of space in a short amount of time would be vital to their success and survival.

Unfortunately, while I was thinking about this, my brother had already taken off, kicking up clouds of sand and dust in his wake. I was left in the undesirable position of bringing up the rear. As always.

It hadn't been as difficult before, because back when we had been on foot, I hadn't been staring into a camel's ass the entire time. Now that was the only view I had; we were riding too quickly, and my attention was too focused on not falling off to observe the other desert sights.

I was also sore everywhere, and the uncomfortable pace the animal kept was magnified only by the unshapely angles of its ridiculous body. We were not friends. We would never be friends. Riding more quickly meant we would reach the end of this torment sooner, but it also heightened the pain I felt with each jolt and jostle. On top of that, my nerves were frayed to bastion and back, as the beast preferred to test my attention at random intervals.

The damn thing was *trying* to buck me.

It was a contest of wills, and I did not intend to lose against a camel—no matter how damned this particular creature was. I could be stubborn, too, I thought, and I refused to let Rook down again.

We rode this way for the rest of the night, without pause or rest, until at last the camel was too tired to try his games and I was too tired to hate him. We were both in the same boat—and by the time we stopped when the sun rose, cresting the far-off dunes, we'd made an uneasy peace with each other. Neither I nor the camel appreciated our current lots in life. Both miserable creatures, we could agree not to make each other's lives worse. We would just have to accept our differences for the sake of our similarities and try to get along.

"Here!" Kalim said, drawing his mount up short and leaping from its back with such exquisite grace that I was, momentarily, breathless. "We rest!"

"There's still an hour before the sun's too hot," Rook pointed out, but he dismounted too. It wasn't with the same fluidity as Kalim, but it was with its own steely grace. Meanwhile, I clambered down from my camel like an old painter off his rickety ladder.

"That is not how you do it," Kalim said.

"I am aware of that," I agreed.

"Don't be rude to our guide, Thom," Rook said.

I hadn't been trying to be, but I was ashamed nonetheless. "I *am* sorry," I said. "Please, Kalim; I hope you will forgive me."

"I have no room for more grudge-bearing in my heart," Kalim said, and clapped me on the shoulder. "Do not worry, Mollyrat Thom. You are given my forgiveness."

Relieved, I fumbled around in my pack for my tent while Rook finished setting his up against the side of his compliant camel.

"If you would like, I will teach you how to mount when we next ride," Kalim offered. "And how to dismount. You would not last moments here with such technique."

"My brother has more aptitude than I," I explained wearily. The exact technique of tent-building was also eluding me, and Kalim did me the great honor of pretending he didn't see me fumble. I was grateful for that.

Rook had already disappeared inside his tent; knowing him, he was also probably already asleep. I rubbed sand out of my nose—this happened when the wind was up, and it was one of the most disgusting facts of desert life I had yet to accept—and managed to get the tent up at least enough to keep the sun, if not the sand, out of my eyes. Kalim shook his head, very clearly pitying me, and gave me one last shoulder clap before he created, with impossible speed, a tent out of his riding stick and cape, disappearing underneath it at once.

At least, I told myself as I crawled into the dark space, which smelled of sunlight on camel, Rook might be able to find the answers he thought he was looking for, somewhere in the Khevir dunes.

I only hoped they'd make him happy.

MADOKA

When I woke up there was somebody holding something cold and wet against my head. It made me cranky as shit from the beginning, because what I'd really wanted was to wake up and be dead.

"Hey," I said, my voice cracking with disuse. I sounded like an angry frog. "That you, Badger?"

I didn't know who else I thought it could possibly be, but a creaking female voice answered me instead.

"Your Badger has taken a short rest," it said. "He needed it, and I was finally able to convince him of the practicality. Once I am assured you will be all right on your own, I will go get him."

"Okay," I agreed. "Sounds good. Who are you?"

As I looked at her, her face resolved itself in the darkness. It was nighttime, and we were outside, and the air was cold against the wet spots at my temple. I shifted uncomfortably, but at least the dizziness and the headache that'd overtaken me were gone.

The woman who was sitting next to me looked strange as anything, like a ghost out of one of the stories the old lady used to tell late at night to scare the kids into bed. Never scared me; I was too practical for that. But seeing her here, in this desert town, with all my memories slowly starting to come back to me . . . I definitely felt a chill. For a moment, anyway. Then it was gone.

Her nose was too sharp for the rest of her delicate face, and her skin was very pale—the kind of white that all the court ladies *wished* they had. No wonder she looked like a ghost. If I squinted, I could see that her eyes were green, so all that meant she had to be foreign. Her lips twitched when she saw I was watching her and she looked away, but I knew she was just playing at being shy. I'd lived with a lot of people, and I always knew when someone was being truthful or when they were playacting.

"Any guesses?" she asked softly. There was something *wrong* about her voice; my hand started throbbing all at once, and I closed my eyes with a groan, curling up around it.

She said nothing at that—maybe, if she'd been looking after me, she was used to this. I didn't know. She moved the compress to the side of my throat, easing the racing pulse there, and it *did* make things feel better after a little while.

"My name," she said, like a peace offering I guessed, "is Malahide."

"Strange name," I said. "You raised around here? How do you know Ke-Han?"

"Hm," she murmured. "You're very sharp. I've had to learn a great many things that are not natural to me."

"Your voice sounds off," I told her.

She blinked down at me, her green eyes going wide, but I *still* wasn't fooled by the show. "Does it?" she asked, and pressed one dainty little gloved hand against her throat.

"Yeah," I said. I was still kind of out of it, and feeling pretty woozy to boot, so I wasn't too sure what I was saying. "Like wind chimes, or a music box, or something. Tinny. Pretty, though."

"Oh, dear," Malahide said, putting her gloved hand against my forehead. I wanted to tell her that it was a good way to lose a glove, since my face was smeared with soot and sweat and who knew what else, but I couldn't quite get the words out of my mouth. "I see you're still a little disoriented."

"That's a good word for it," I muttered. Didn't get the chance to see many foreigners where I came from. Xi'An kept to itself, for the most part, and the people did the same in some kind of twisted show of patriotism. Nobody from other lands bothered to try our borders anymore, and I'd gotten out before the Volstovic diplomats arrived. So I was more than a little interested in this woman, with her skin like parchment and her strange green eyes.

I wanted to ask Badger what *he* thought of her, but according to Malahide, he was taking a little snooze. He sure had great timing. I guess I felt a little guilty, since I hadn't been able to tell that he needed to stop and rest, but then it was his own damn fault for not speaking up in the first place. I wasn't his mother, and I sure as hell wasn't going to start acting like it. Where I came from, people always told you when they needed something. You sure as hell couldn't trust anyone else to look after you.

Malahide, I repeated to myself. It was still a weird name, no two ways about it, but then again she *was* a foreigner. Maybe everyone where she came from had a name like that, and mine was the weird one. She took her neat little hand off my forehead, and *my* hand gave a sudden, insistent throb just to remind me it was still in business. I flinched, curling my fingers around my palm. Never thought there'd be a day when I'd miss it itching like fire all through my skin, but now I kind of did. This pain was definitely worse.

If Malahide noticed what I was doing, she pretended not to see. Instead, she busied herself with something just out of my line of sight.

"Hey," I said, rasping just like the old woman.

"Water?" she asked, holding a canteen up to my lips.

Without any kind of modesty whatsoever, I took it right out of her hands, and she helped me to sit up while I did my best impression of a dying woman. Maybe I had been dying. I had to slow down when the water started dribbling out of my mouth and running across my cheeks, though, since I didn't want to waste it. Especially not in a place like the desert; it was disrespectful to the gods. When I'd finished, I handed the canteen back to Malahide, who looked a little surprised, but she didn't call me a desert pig the way Badger might have, so at least there was that. Maybe her kind was too dainty for it, but something about her face made me doubt that.

"I'll refill it at the well," Malahide said thoughtfully, screwing the top back on.

My hand pulsed again, hot and sharp, and I traced the lines of the compass's hands with one finger, keeping the whole spectacle out of Malahide's sight. The hands were still in alignment, pointed straight out over the desert on whatever path those nomads had taken. I knew I had to follow them, but right now my bones felt about as sturdy as mud in a rice paddy, and it was doing a wood-heeled clog dance on my morale.

"Were you here when the village was attacked?" Malahide asked, her queer voice trembling like a bowstring. The nervous show didn't quite reach her eyes, though. She was a lot tougher than she was letting on, for whatever reason. But if she was as noble as she looked, then toughness was considered right up there with the big sins, so it was probably a lot less trouble to go around fainting at spiders and whatnot than to let people see what she was really made of. I didn't envy her *that* kind of playacting one bit.

"No," I said, starting to sound halfway back to human after drinking all that water. "Just caught the aftermath."

In a flash, I remembered the boy I'd tried to help, before Badger had taken over. Was he all right? Maybe it was stupid for me to get so attached to someone I hardly knew, but the kid's situation and mine'd been more similar than I liked to think about. In fact, his whole village was making me itchy, like I'd somehow made a wrong turn and ended up back home again. *Snap out of it, Madoka,* I told myself, sternly. The old woman would never've allowed wallowing like this, and for a minute I imagined I could feel her stick across my knuckles. The memory of the sting was still fresh in my mind, and it did pull me out of it. For the moment, anyway.

Malahide turned around, and I snuck a look at my hand, peering close because of how dark it'd gotten. I didn't particularly like what I was seeing. My skin definitely wasn't any less red than it'd been at the height of the burning stage, and slowly but surely there were little red lines filtering their way out from the center, like little green sprouts growing up in the ground. If my compass was a big, fat spider in the center of my palm, then it'd started growing legs. I was gonna *kill* the magician when I saw him next.

I was too busy seething to hear Malahide when she came up behind me, which was probably why I nearly jumped straight up to the moon when she took hold of my bad hand.

"Yow," I said, startled as I'd ever been. "Don't sneak up on me like that."

"My apologies," Malahide said, but she was staring intently at my hand with something pretty close to reverence. She glanced up at me, and this time her eyes betrayed nothing. "Your hand is troubled."

No shit, I thought, but didn't say. "Yeah, that's one way of putting it, I guess."

Before I could stop her, she was touching the hands of the compass, little white gloves tracing the direction they indicated. The added pressure was small, but it was enough to send a dull pain through my palm and all the way down my wrist. I gritted my teeth, more frustrated than actually upset. I was sick of this whole stupid thing. I wanted the compass out of my hand, I wanted someone else to do the job—Badger, maybe, 'cause he seemed like a responsible kind of guy—or maybe I could give it to this woman, if she wanted it. I didn't care. All I knew was that I hadn't signed up for this of my own free will, and now more than ever, I wanted out.

But all I had to do was conjure up my family's faces to know that getting out was impossible.

"It doesn't agree with you," Malahide said at last.

Well, even I could've told her that.

I was feeling better now, at least. Less light-headed, and more like my bones were real bones again, which was always a comfort. Maybe

I'd been going too many days on too little water, but it wasn't like I'd known I'd be ending up in desert country, of all places. Just one more thing I'd have to thank the magician for when we met again.

"Not much I can do about it," I told her, wanting my hand back. It was making me uncomfortable the way she looked at it, but I didn't quite know how to tell her to stop without being rude. For all I knew, she'd saved my life. It wasn't something you just spat on—that, too, would piss the gods right off.

"It's broken," she said, sounding concerned. "The direction it's pointing isn't north at all." A weird thing to focus on, I thought; it didn't faze her one bit that I had a compass in my actual fucking hand, but it did freak her out that the direction wasn't right. They came in all shapes and sizes, crazy people.

"It's not supposed to," I told her, to cover up for my one second of panic when she'd called it broken.

"No?" Malahide asked, her voice drenched in curiosity. "What do you follow, then, if not true north?"

"Just . . . something I'm looking to get my hands on," I said, being evasive. I'd never been trained in espionage, so I wasn't the best liar or anything; I just didn't feel like getting into what'd happened in that storage cellar, with that madman of a magician. Even to me, it sounded a little nuts. There was the added matter of Malahide being a foreigner, for all I knew even from Volstov, and the last thing I wanted was to bring up the fire-breathers to a Volstovic. "For now, it's those shit-eating cowards that hit this village," I added, which was the truth, if only a part of it.

Malahide nodded as if she understood. "You'll have to make preparations before attempting to cross the desert," she said then, like she was some experienced traveler herself. I guessed it was possible; she just really didn't have the complexion for it, not even so much as a single freckle.

"I know," I told her. I'd already resigned myself to scrabbling through whatever these poor people had to see if there was something I could use in getting across all that sand. It made my heart hurt worse than the throbbing in my hand, to steal from dead people who couldn't defend themselves, but I wasn't about to go killing myself in the desert out of sentimentality. When you were dead, you had no use for the stuff left over from living.

"Are you feeling better?" she asked me. I nodded. "Then I'll go and wake your soldier friend."

"It's okay," I said. "It's dark out. Should probably let him sleep."

"You might prefer to have this conversation with all three of us," Malahide said. "Unless, of course, he doesn't know about your hand."

I snorted. The compass in my palm was as plain as the eyes in my face. I couldn't keep it covered up with a glove anymore; it hurt too bad for that. And now I'd just gone and shown it to a total stranger— someone who by all rights had been an enemy up until a few months ago. I wasn't ready for this mission; the magician'd made a real big mistake. He could've chosen anyone, a soldier, a seasoned tracker, somebody who knew what he was doing. But he'd chosen me, I guess to absolve him and the emperor of having anything to do with it if I was caught. They trusted me not to turn myself in to the emperor's men, to remain beholden to the people who'd put this foreign object inside of me because I needed them to take it out. And if I died, I was expendable. Badger'd just chop my hand off and it'd be given to someone else, maybe better'n I was.

"What about it?" I said lightly. "Common practice here in the Ke-Han. It's in fashion; women wander around with compass hands all the time."

"That," Malahide said, pointing gracefully at the item in question, "is no simple compass. You said so yourself." Her nostrils flared; it wasn't a dainty expression at all, maybe the first true face I'd seen her make. Suddenly, I felt afraid, and would've scrambled away from her if she hadn't reached out to clasp me by the wrist.

"You looking to fight?" I asked.

"Who sent you on this mission?" she asked. Her voice had gentled, and she wasn't hurting me, either; the way she held my wrist was tender, and her thumb rested on a pressure point that eased the pounding fire in my blood. She was trying to help me—even if I couldn't trust her motives, I could trust the result. I was so pain-crazy by that point I was willing to accept help, even if I didn't have much faith in the source.

"Don't know . . ." I said. *What you're talking about,* I meant, but the lie was flimsy and she leveled a look at me.

"Let me be honest with you, little woman," she said. I resented the nickname, but her voice was commanding; and there was that strange, tinny quality, like it was coming to me across the blade of a sword. She expected me to listen, and I *did,* if only because I couldn't resist the strength of her grasp and the color of her eyes. "I am here because I seek the same prize you do. My methods are different—I was not so lucky to lay my hands on a compass like this one, though 'luck' in this matter is a purely relative state of being. You do not consider yourself lucky to have it, and I do not blame you. Yet I consider myself *very* lucky to have found you here."

So she knew, I realized. Somehow, she knew about everything. She knew why I was here, and she wanted the same thing I did.

"You gonna chop it off?" I asked, breathless. "I'll fight you. Might be little, but I'm strong, and you don't look so good at one-on-one yourself. I'll scream for him too; he'll take you out—"

"Stop babbling," Malahide said. She eased her grip slightly, letting her soft hair fall over her brow as she looked away from me. It was seductive. I didn't trust it for a second, didn't understand what the hell she was trying to do to me. "I did contemplate removing your hand from your body while you and the soldier slept, but it would have been messy. All that blood would have obscured the scent of my quarry— *our* quarry—and I prefer not to leave such . . . blatant statements behind me when I work. Surely, I thought to myself, whoever charged you with this task would be as ruthless as the man who charged me with mine. I would not want to complicate matters more than necessary."

"Oh," I said. "That's great." I'd never known someone who could be so rational about whether or not to slice off a complete stranger's hand, and now that I did, I was pretty sure I wished I didn't.

"I suppose, since you are the possessor of this new clue," Malahide continued, "we can talk without your companion present. Woman to woman."

"Okay," I managed to choke out. I wished Badger was around, if only because I needed someone else to confirm for me: This lady was crazy. But she was the kind of rational-thinking crazy that was more dangerous than all the bell-cracked loonies wandering around blathering gibberish.

"This piece," Malahide explained, "this compass. Does it point to dragonmetal?"

"As far as I figure it, yeah," I said. I was too tired to argue, too tired to lie, too tired even to start shouting my head off for the Badger. I didn't owe that fucking magician any loyalty, and if he'd clapped this thing into my hand and figured sending Badger after me would be enough to keep me in line, then he was dead wrong. "You can take it," I said suddenly. "I don't even fucking want it anymore. It's brought me nothing but trouble; this whole thing's crazy. Just rip it the hell out, right now, you can have it. I hope you find what you're looking for, 'cause I sure as hell don't want it."

"Come now," Malahide said. "You must know you're lying."

I thought about it, just like she said. And maybe I was lying—but only halfway. I did want to be free of it; I just didn't want to suffer the consequences.

"I'm not offering you nothing," Malahide said, coming close to whisper the terrible words in my ear. "There are ways I could help you, should you choose to work with me. I know of magicians in the city of Thremedon who could remove that with less pain, I think, than it was given to you. You are a woman; this is your body. You are beholden to no one, Ke-Han or Volstovic. Right now you are working for someone whose motives you do not trust, whose methods you despise."

"So you're on this quest for yourself, then?" I asked. It was a pretty speech. I just didn't know if I could really believe it.

Malahide's pretty mouth quirked into a wry smile. "Very astute," she said. "In a manner of speaking, I am on 'this quest' for my commissioner. In another manner of speaking, I do what I do for myself and myself alone. We are in the same position, and because of that, I believe we should work together. You assisting me, and I assisting you."

"And if I say no?" I asked, more than a little afraid to hear what she'd answer.

"Then I will hunt you down and kill you," she said simply. "Both you and your friend. I will dispose of your bodies so that no one, not even this employer whom you fear so greatly, will ever have any hope of finding you. I will take the compass for myself and I will be the sole proprietor of the bounty. Despite how unpleasant it will be to traverse the desert on my own, to come up against whatever raiders and whatever sandstorms the desert tosses my way, I will nonetheless use the advantage now buried in you to win this hunt."

"Oh," I said again. My voice croaked, but not because I was thirsty.

"If we follow my proposal," Malahide promised, "we will find the bounty more quickly than if we were working alone, and at cross-purposes. Once we have our hands upon the prize, we can settle our disputes properly."

"You mean, decide who gets to take what back to her master?" I said, feeling bile rise in my throat.

Malahide's soft smile turned into a sharp grin. "Why yes," she said. "That is what I mean exactly."

I wondered if I'd be able to face this woman and take her down when we came to the end of the trail—that is, if she didn't stab me in the night.

But I had Badger, I told myself, and we could take turns keeping an eye on her. As much as we didn't *exactly* get along, I knew he'd take my side over hers. We were countrymen, if nothing else. We had the advantage of numbers; we had teamwork. She was all on her own.

It was cold comfort, but I'd take it any day over knowing she was creeping up on me in the night.

"I promise I will contribute equally to the cause," she said, holding out her dainty little hand.

"I'd shake on it," I said, "but I'm missing the hand to do it with."

"Never mind all that," Malahide said. "We shall just pretend it happened."

CHAPTER EIGHT

ROOK

As we rode across the desert, it became pretty obvious that my new friend the desert prince was a talented guy, who was used to things going his own way. Sand gnats never bit him, his mount never stumbled, and I never caught him rubbing at his eyes on account of a sudden strong wind blowing half the desert up into our faces.

But when it came time for him to try to teach my brother how to ride a damn camel, all his luck seemed to dry up like a spot of piss in the sand.

Suited me just fine, since I could've told him that trying to get Thom to do anything coordinated was pretty much a waste of time. He was all right once he got on, so long as he remembered not to think too much, but the in-between stuff was pretty fucking hilarious to watch.

"It must be one swift motion," Kalim explained, demonstrating on his own camel, which was clearly some kind of hybrid camel-horse beast and not a camel at all from how fast and delicate she was. I wanted one for myself, and Kalim was clearly the guy to get one for me, but there'd be time to discuss that later.

"I *am* trying," Thom insisted, and even I couldn't argue with that. But for him, one swift motion became about seven awkward, scrabbling motions instead. I had to hand it to him—he didn't give up, no matter how high the odds were stacked against him, but that was a Mollyrat for you. You grew up stubborn or not at all.

There must've been some kind of rat-crazy stubbornness in our desert prince too, because he kept at it, late at night and early in the morning before Thom could start struggling with his damn tent. After a while, though, the whole thing started to make me sick to watch, all balled up and impatient inside, even though it'd never really slowed us up any—he probably knew I'd leave him behind if it came to that. It'd be better once we finally got to wherever we were going and I could stop feeling like there were bugs crawling in my skin. I *knew* I was acting like a real prick, but I also knew that once I reached the Khevir dunes, things'd ease up a little bit.

The way Kalim rode made me think we probably *could've* gone on through the day, and that he was just stopping out of pity on us "Volstovs," but I couldn't ask him without Thom hearing too, and he was already looking about as miserable as that camel he rode. Just about as mulish too. So I clammed up good, and the time passed like fucking grains of sand, one minute after another until they all blurred into the same mess in my head. At least we were traveling faster now that we'd left that Nellie Bless behind, and Kalim didn't seem to feel the same urge to stop and talk about the *historical significance* of this and that as we passed it by. A statue in the sand was a statue in the sand, and I could appreciate it just fine without having to hear about who it was and why it'd ended up buried.

In the morning, Kalim told us we'd reach the magician's house sometime during the next night.

"First bit of good news I've had all day," Thom muttered, throwing his tent around like a laundrywoman. It curled up and tangled around his arm like a snake and he stumbled backward into his camel, who gave him a look of such piss-poor disdain that I wondered how both the rider and the mount managed to sleep at night.

I couldn't look anymore. It was like watching a dog tart itself up for th'Esar's next ball, all wrong and fucking awkward, and I didn't know where to start making sense of it. It was a lot easier just to set up *my* tent and disappear into it; both Kalim and I knew, no matter what we did, we'd still wake up the next morning to find the damned thing wrapped around Thom like a body bag. How he'd managed to survive long enough to get to the 'Versity was beyond me.

The next night, I woke up early. It was still pretty light out, the sun going down and staining everything an eerie red color. It was my time, or *had been,* once, back before shit had stopped making sense and I'd gotten my brother back. Part of why I was having less trouble than Thom adjusting to desert living was probably because I'd spent half my damn life sleeping through the day and doing my real work at night. Your body just adjusted to it, after a while, and your mind could catch up after that pretty damn quick.

I squinted into the horizon, like I'd done about a hundred times before, and thought about things I sure as hell didn't need to be thinking about right now.

Things looked different on the ground, that was all. It took some fine-tuning, just like sleeping all day and riding all night did. One thing I had in common with my bell-cracked brother: getting *used* to anything we weren't already used to made us crankier'n th'Esar during th'Esarina's time of the month.

Something made a sound to my left, pained and half-asleep like a pissed-off camel. I thought it *was* a bastion-damned camel until the canvas mess that'd buried my brother last night started to stir, and his head popped out like a jack-in-the-box.

"Is it time to go?" he asked, looking like he'd spent the night in some animal's mouth instead of inside his own tent. Good, I thought. Served him right for being so damned cheerful in the mornings all the time back when we used to have beds. Let him see what it was like to have the boot on the other foot; he'd come around.

"Go back to sleep," I told him, looking away. "Kalim's not up yet, either."

He made a snuffling, sleepy sorta noise and rubbed his nose. He'd been complaining about getting sand up there lately, but I wasn't having any trouble. "I don't think I'll have time to make it back to sleep," he said, sitting up like a grub in a cocoon. "Best to put my energies toward waking up fully; I'll have a better chance at foiling that beast."

"You mean Bessie?" I asked, tearing my eyes away from the sun when they started to burn.

Thom paused, halfway to wrestling himself out of his tent, and stared at me like I'd just told him I was gonna marry his camel.

"You *named* it?" he asked.

"What's wrong with that? Can't curse her if she doesn't have a name," I told him. It was a reasonable enough argument. Especially for me.

"I'm fairly certain it's a *him*, for starters," Thom said. "Although if there was ever a male I wished to embarrass by calling him a female name . . . *Not* that I condone such practices, you know I don't, but it's a camel, and . . ."

"Sure you don't," I said, grinning. The desert was making my brother into a real cindy shitkicker, just like the boys back home, and if I'd been in the sort of mood to appreciate it, I'd have been loving every second.

Thom cursed at me, which just proved my theory, and set to balling up his tent. It was never going to come out right if *that* was the way he folded it up, and after trying not to crack a rib laughing, I couldn't take it anymore. I went over there and took the stupid thing out of his stupid hands, folding it up neat and proper in a matter of minutes. They weren't *meant* to be complicated. It was just cloth and a riding stick; how hard could it be?

"Real fine education you paid for," I needled him, handing it back.

"Technically," he said, looking decently ashamed of himself, "I didn't pay for it at all. I was a scholarship student."

"Guess it's all right to waste other people's money, then," I said, and I meant it. "Taxpayers' money, come to think of it. The whole of Volstov, paying for this." Thom flinched.

"There wasn't a class on pitching a tent," Thom said, then quickly added, "I *don't* want to hear it."

"Only 'Versity boys'd need a class in pitching tents," I said, just to show him I didn't care what he thought. "Hell, they could have a guest speaker in from Our Lady just to drive the point home."

"You're disgusting," Thom said, but he didn't even look like *he* believed that anymore. He was just saying it because it was easy, because he was too tired to come up with anything new. And also, more than probably, because he had sand up his nose.

Well, it was his own bastion-damned stubborn-ox fault, wasn't it? I'd told him not to come, but he'd insisted, and here we were, Thom wiping sand from his upper lip and wishing he'd taken a few classes in how to be useful rather than how to name every speck of sand from here until they reached the ocean.

The sun disappeared below the horizon like a candle winking out, and just like that, the sky was gray. Pretty soon the winds'd be kicking up, and the air would get real cold, so it was important to start moving soon. I broke down my tent like a fever, almost slipping up a hundred times because my mind wasn't on the job. *Tonight,* said a little voice in my head—the only woman whose tones I'd bothered to memorize, the only girl that'd ever mattered one shit to me. Tonight I was going to meet the magician. I didn't know what came after that, and I didn't much care. I only knew that meeting her was gonna help me get back what was rightfully mine in the first place.

There was a flurry of motion from my side that meant Kalim was awake, collapsing his tent by touching it with his index finger and all those little things he did that made me think he wasn't quite human, just a trick of the sand.

"Good evening, Mollyrats of the Volstov," he said, no trace of sleep in his voice. "Tonight will be an auspicious night, but we must be on our guard. Do not let the nearness of our goal allow you to become overexcited."

"No danger of that," I assured him. Thom looked like one good shot of excitement'd probably kill him, and what *I* was feeling definitely didn't fall under the banner of excitement.

Kalim gave me a look, like he wasn't quite sure I was telling the truth, and I stared back at him until he looked away. Surveying his land, he might've said if I asked him, but every now and then I liked to win a contest of wills with somebody, and even a desert prince'd do in a pinch.

"I mean only to remind you of my previous warning," he said. "The lady of Volstov is not the sort to welcome a visitor."

"So long as we aren't flying th'Esar's flag, I think we'll be more welcome than some," I said, and he looked puzzled.

"Our Esar," Thom piped up, looking at least like he might make it through the night now. "Our ruler; he banished her to the desert in order to keep her powers from being exploited."

"Aha," said Kalim, nodding like he understood. "I see. This Esar, too, had woman troubles."

"Kalim, you've got no idea," I said, and I swung up onto my camel's back.

For a little while, I waited for Kalim as he tried once more with Thom—neither of them giving up, and neither of them getting anywhere, either. Kalim allowed about ten minutes to be wasted on his lessons in the morning when we made camp and at night before we set off. Then, exactly ten minutes into it, he let Thom climb onto the camel like a kid just out of his diapers while he mounted up like a bolt of lightning, and our night really began.

We rode over the uneven dune terrain at a swift enough pace that I could feel the wind in my hair, the sand tossed from Kalim's camel in front of me swirling around my face. The Khevir dunes were dangerous country, Kalim had explained, because of the high winds and the complete fucking lack of anything to use as cover. Even *he* wouldn't cross 'em during the day, he'd said, making a mark over his chest to protect against evil spirits getting the wrong idea, or whatever it was the desert people believed in. The high winds were what built up the dunes, and it could make the crossing painfully slow if you didn't know the right paths to take. Somehow, we'd as good as stumbled onto a guide who knew the area like the fortune lines on his palm—and who wasn't a grave-robbing shit-eating pussyfoot, to boot—and the dunes didn't much get in our way. Another difference was that the sand here was looser, less packed in, so you had to be careful your camel didn't up and turn an ankle in the softer stuff. This last part was more for Thom than either of us, but to my everlasting shock and fucking awe, he managed to keep himself *and* Bessie intact.

Miracles could happen, I guess. Even here, where the gods didn't know my name.

There was something different about the ride today, something that got my blood pumping the way it had in the old days. It was like I could smell something on the air, something an awful lot like metal, and old, smoky memories that wouldn't get out of my head no matter what I did to try to shake 'em off. It was like the magician somehow knew we were coming for her, and this was her way of letting us know we were on the right track. Whatever it was, I breathed in deep, and on my left Thom let out an explosive sneeze.

"Someone is walking over your future grave," Kalim said, smiling slyly in the dark in a way I was sure Thom didn't much appreciate.

"I hope we locate it soon," he muttered, rubbing his nose while he kept his wrist twisted into the reins like I'd shown him. Just in case. "I'd like to lie down in it and take a good long nap."

"Race you to the next dune," I said, in no mood for his morbid, drippy crap. The moon'd come out now, a cold white sickle overhead that seemed impossibly far away from the ground. It was hanging around up there just to piss me off—it was in the sky, and I wasn't—so I needed something to distract me from having a staring match with it.

Kalim heard me, and slowed the pace of his camel to match mine. "We have nearly reached the place the desert woman calls her home," he said. "If it is a race you are interested in, I will take up the challenge, Mollyrat Rook."

"All right," I said, already feeling the familiar, gut-wrenching mix of blood and adrenaline kick into my veins. "You're on."

"I am on?" Kalim asked, dark eyes clouded with confusion.

"Means *go!*" I called, giving my camel a good dig with my heel. We took off, almost like flying only not so smooth, and kicking up sand every which way so I couldn't see what the hell I was doing. Just the outline of my target, the dune, no more than a big slumping outline against the dark sky. Kalim came pounding up behind me and I leaned forward, urging my camel on. It wouldn't take him long, with his mount, to draw even with me, and once that happened it was all over. Still, I wasn't about to let a man win a race with me just because he happened to have something like years of experience and a better-bred mount under his belt. This was a matter of *pride*.

I steered suddenly to one side, cutting him off so that he'd have to slow down or risk introducing his mount's head to my camel's ass. It wouldn't be a pretty crash, in any case, and maybe it was kind of a dirty tactic to use, but I was representing Mollyrats everywhere, and damned if it wasn't what every one of them would have done. From somewhere behind us, Thom let out another whoop, and I put on a brilliant burst of speed just as the dune loomed up ahead of us.

Kalim's camel was coming up fast behind us, but it was too late for him, and I took both hands off the reins right as we crashed into the dune in an explosion of sand flying everywhere. My girl grunted, like this wasn't at all her idea of a good time, and I laughed like I'd forgotten how to do it in the first place, somewhere low and deep in my chest.

Kalim rode up seconds later, before I'd even had the time to stop laughing. He didn't look all that pissed about my dirty trick though. In fact, when I calmed down enough to look at him, I was pretty sure he was smiling.

"I will remember that trick for next time, Mollyrat Rook," he said.

"You'd better," I answered. "Hey, you can even use it, pretend it's yours."

"You're both insane," said Thom, after we'd waited for him to catch up with us. But I knew my brother, and I was pretty sure he was smiling. "Completely and utterly."

"Perhaps next time you will join the race, Mollyrat Thom," Kalim said innocently, starting the slow climb up the hill, sand scrabbling down behind him.

Thom snorted, then followed after him, which left me bringing up the rear. My girl was still tossing her head around, like she wanted me to know she was better than what I'd put her through, and I took a hand off the reins to pat her head. She'd done an okay job, beating a real nomad-bred camel. It'd be something for her to gossip about, back in the pens at Karakhum. And everyone needed a little bit of flying just once in their lifetime.

We crested the dune and came to a shallow valley, glittering gray and empty in the night. Kalim pulled up short, and Thom gasped, and I stopped telling my girl just what a good girl she was long enough to take a look.

In the middle of the valley was a dark little house, bigger than the tent Bless'd used to store all his supplies, but still not much more than a shack. It was next to a stretch of water; there was some vegetation, too, not looking too pretty but still managing to be alive. The whole thing looked like a painting, but definitely not real at all, shining ghostly under all that moonlight.

"That is where she lives," Kalim said, speaking softly like he thought she might be able to hear us from all the way up here. "If you wish to turn back, now is your opportunity."

"Hell with that," I said.

"I share my brother's opinion, if not his eloquence," Thom agreed in a roundabout sort of way.

"I did not see you as the sort of man to change his mind," Kalim confessed, and he chirped at his camel to start her forward down the sandy slope.

I'd be a rotten fucking liar if I'd said my heart wasn't pounding—partly from the adrenaline of the race, but partly from what I was riding to. I didn't want to come out this way, on the back of some ordinary beast; whether the camel'd been brave or not had no bearing on what I'd known, once upon a time, like a legend from one of Thom's pieces of research. No less important and more fucking real.

There was no telling what this magician'd think of three strangers riding down on her in the middle of the night, either.

I wondered, idly, what she looked like. Pretty, maybe. Probably a little scary too. But she'd been a part of my girl and I knew she'd be beautiful; I could feel it, and my blood was hot as the sand at noon.

Kalim pulled up short before we even got halfway there.

"This is as far as I go," he said. "This business is not mine."

"You're just gonna wait here?" I asked. "You come all this way to hang around outside?"

"I do not entirely understand this phrase *hang around*," Kalim said. "But I will be here when you have concluded your business; I will guide you back, as I have promised."

I felt Thom's eyes on me and I looked over to him, not even having to ask him what the fuck he wanted from me. "Well," Thom stammered. "I just . . . Do you want to go alone?"

"You turning pussy on me?" I asked.

Thom shook his head quickly. "That's not it at all," he said. "But this isn't about me, Rook. I just wanted to be sure—"

I didn't wait for any more of his out-loud thinking, just nudged my camel back into a trot. If he followed, he followed. If he stayed behind, then maybe Kalim could teach him how to ride a camel in all that extra time they had alone together. It said a lot about my esteem for the nomad prince that I'd leave him alone with my brother, but to be honest, Thom could probably do more damage to himself alone in the desert than someone who was actually trying to fuck him up, so I was glad Kalim was around to look after him.

Except then I heard the sound of Bessie snorting, and I realized Thom was coming with me after all.

It wasn't what I'd been expecting, but count on my brother to pull an unpredictable move out of nowhere. He did what he wanted to when he wanted to do it, even if he tried to pretend that wasn't what he was doing at all. We *were* a lot alike; it was just that he didn't want to be compared to a bastard like me, and I guessed I didn't exactly blame him for it. Just got on my nerves sometimes to see him pretending to be somebody he wasn't, that's all.

"Are you nervous?" he asked, then laughed quietly to himself. "Of course you're not."

"Are you kidding?" I said. "I'm practically shitting myself."

We came up on the house, trying to be quiet, but not *too* quiet; no use making anyone think this was some kind of ambush. Thom even had the decency to dismount with less comedy than usual, and I squared my shoulders.

It wasn't *like* heading to meet my maker, because that's *exactly* what it was.

"I guess we gotta knock," I said. It burned my balls that Kalim was up there at the top of the dune watching us shuffle around down here like frightened goats who'd got lost on the way to the watering hole, but I wasn't going to pussy out, either.

Instead of wasting any more time with second-guessing my actions—the moment I started to do that, I didn't have anything left—I strode up to the door and knocked on it, loud. I wasn't just anybody. I was here and I was gonna get some of the answers I deserved.

"It's open," a voice came from inside.

I looked at my brother. He was looking at me. We had a moment—one that made all the sand sticking to my skin start to prickle. Then I stepped forward and took control, shoving the door open with my shoulder.

I had to duck a little just to get inside.

It was quiet in the room, but it wasn't lonely. Smelled good, like home cooking might've smelled; some herbs and spices that burned in my throat going down. There was a chair and a table and a curtain separating the room in two; I couldn't see what was beyond all that, and I didn't care to try. Sitting in the chair at the table, holding a cup in both hands, was the shortest old bag I'd ever seen, and monumentally fucking fat, wearing a pair of too-large spectacles on her big nose that made her look half-witted and cross-eyed.

The first thought that ran through my head was that I was too late. The magician was dead and we'd come out here for nothing. Anger sparked hot in my chest and my belly and I turned to leave, but Thom put both hands on my back and forced me—with strength even I didn't know he had—all the way inside. He closed the door behind us, too, and that left us just standing there, me and Thom and the old bag.

She had sharp dark eyes that looked familiar to me, like I knew her from somewhere.

"Pardon me for interrupting your deep fucking thoughts," she said, "but I think I have the right to know who you are, boys."

If I hadn't known her just by looking into her eyes, then the voice was a dead giveaway. I heard it every night in my dreams; before I'd needed to dream about it, I'd heard it every night while my life was still *like* a fucking dream, or at least the life I'd always dreamed of living. Me and Havemercy, together, just like that.

For the first time in a long time, I was floored. Needless to say, I couldn't open my mouth for anything.

Thom took control in all the ways he didn't know how when he climbed up on a camel's back. "My name is Thom," he said, "and this is my . . . brother, Rook."

"Okay," the magician said. "I'm Sarah Fleet. Names mean nothing when I haven't heard 'em before."

Thom looked at me again, realized I'd lost all my faculties, and, like a brave little soldier, pushed on. "Rook was a member of the Esar's Dragon Corps," he explained. "Back when the war was still . . . Have you heard about the war?"

"Son, I'm living in the desert," Sarah Fleet, the dragonmaker, said. "Not down a fucking well or anything. We won. Hooray."

"Right," Thom said, somehow undaunted, though I guessed he'd at least had a lot of practice trying to talk to people who couldn't give two shits about what he had to say—it was called "Thom's Fucking Life," and I was currently experiencing it myself. "Then you must also have heard about the role, ah, that the Dragon Corps performed in securing our victory?"

"I might have," Sarah Fleet said, adjusting her giant specs to look up at me. She was the one with bug eyes, and yet I was the one who felt fucking pinned down *like* a bug. It was un-bastion-damned-fair, and I was just opening my mouth to tell her so when Thom stepped down hard on my foot.

It hurt. He was heavier than he looked.

I was gonna kill him.

"That's good," he said quickly, voice cracking there for a minute like he could feel the end of the world sneaking up on him. "You . . . You

ought to be very proud of yourself, for your contribution to the na-
tion's victory."

"Oh, *yeah*," said Sarah Fleet, contempt practically dripping from
her jaws. A dragon in an old bag's skin, that was her. "I'm real proud of
myself. Can't begin to tell you. Got myself a one-way ticket out to the
middle of nowhere on account of how clever I was, just because I went
and made something a little too fiery for th'Esar's tastes. You come to
bring me my medal of honor or get up my hoo-ha like a lot of sand?"

I spat on the ground when she mentioned th'Esar's name—I'd gotten into the habit of spitting, thanks to Kalim—and Thom looked horrified that I was spitting on somebody's floor, but Sarah Fleet didn't
even blink a buggy eye. I was starting to get the feeling back in my
hands, but slowly, like a dying man coming back to life just after seeing
what was waiting for him in the great beyond. I didn't know what the
hell'd come over me—I'd never felt like this before—but it sure felt like
some kind of magician's trick to me.

"Your pardon," Thom said, pressing on bravely like he didn't know
he was walking straight through a battlefield. He even gave a little bow,
like he thought that'd make it any better, and wouldn't you know it?
The old bag cackled and looked pleased. "I shouldn't have brought up
such a sensitive topic."

"What's sensitive is leaving an old woman in peace, not barging
into her only sanctuary in the middle of the night," Sarah Fleet corrected. She peered at him with her creepy, unblinking eyes. "What *you*
are is rude, young man. I ought to send you back to your mother for a
good wallop and a change of diapers."

"My mother's dead," Thom said evenly. He'd learned a little from his
time in the Airman, even if it'd take a dentist's pliers to yank the truth of
it out of him. "And I *do* apologize for the interruption. It's just that we've
been traveling a dreadfully long time, and I'm afraid there's no excuse
for the toll the desert's taken on my manners. We certainly didn't intend
to barge in on you in the middle of the night. However . . ."

She looked at me again, Sarah Fleet, with Havemercy's eyes—only
magnified to about five times their usual size, and looking all wrong inside some old lady's head. "This bed wetter for real?" she asked me.

Just like that, the ice melted. I let out a real whoop of a laugh, while
Thom stared at me like he wasn't sure I hadn't finally up and lost my
mind on top of everything else.

"He's for real," I told her, breathing deep to ease the tightness in my chest. "And I'm the one who rode your fucking dragon."

"Watch that mouth," Sarah Fleet snapped. I could've kissed her, toad face and all, but something told me she'd've snapped my dick off for trying. In her eyes, I wasn't anything special, just some rat from the worst part of Molly, but it was the exact same look I'd always gotten from Have, and it comforted me, like a babe at his mama's breast.

"He can't," Thom said wearily, and I knew he really *had* given up on all his fancy etiquette rules, at least for the time being. "This is what he's like. All the time."

"Well no wonder your mother left you," said Sarah Fleet, "since one of you's a brute and the other one's a damn Cindy. I'd've had you drowned at birth, myself, but then the only child I gave birth to got me bounced from the capital, so how's that for gratitude?"

It was the weirdest fucking experience of my life. For the first time, I wanted to shut up just so I could hear someone else talk. Thom looked at me, then shook his head, clearly reading whatever he needed to off of whatever expression I was wearing. I didn't know, and I couldn't be bothered to guess. Without warning, Sarah Fleet stood up. She was just about as tall standing as she had been sitting, which was a feat in itself, and she moved like her bones ached, if there even were bones buried under all that jelly. I couldn't exactly be sure.

Anyway, she was real slow moving, but I could wait.

"You're the one who flew my girl, then?" she asked, looking me up and down. I wanted to correct her—*my* girl—but whatever magic she was working kept my tongue in my head.

"That's me," I said instead, tossing a loose braid over one shoulder. "She wouldn't look twice at *no one* before me. Heard she even bit some poor fucker's hand clean off."

"Wouldn't look twice at *anyone* before you," Sarah Fleet said sharply. "That's the correct way to say it. I can see you were raised in a gutter, but don't let's drag everyone else through the same muck."

Yes ma'am, I thought, but I kept that one all to myself.

"You must be wondering why we've bothered to come all this way," Thom interjected, either because he felt left out or because it was killing him to go so long without talking.

"Boy," said Sarah Fleet, "you *are* a clever one. 'Versity-educated, no doubt, with a stick like that up your ass. 'Course in the *'Versity,* you'll find more and willing things besides sticks, but I'm betting you know all about that."

Thom turned red all over and started to sputter, face looking kind of like a squashed tomato, and that was all it took. I was laughing my damn fool head off again.

I felt better than I had in weeks, maybe even months. It was the kind of good feeling that settled in real deep down and got its hooks into you. If Thom hadn't been here, I probably would've just sat there all night and let the old bag hurl insults at me. But as much as I wanted to do just that, I couldn't. Outside of Sarah Fleet's little pisshole-in-the-sand shack, there was a whole world that wouldn't slow down for nothing—anything—and somewhere out there someone was still selling parts of my girl to strangers who didn't know her and didn't deserve her either. I couldn't ignore that. Not even when I'd found the one who'd breathed the life into her in the first place.

That thought sobered me up pretty quick, but at least the sour-bastard mood I'd been in this whole time didn't come back.

Sarah Fleet sniffed and gave us another once-over, which made it a twice-over, all things considered.

"Havemercy," she said then, and Thom put a hand on my shoulder just as my knees damn well turned to water. I needed to sit my ass down in a chair, all right. "I never thought she'd have such rotten taste, but there's no accounting for what the magic does when it gets loose of you."

"She was a bat-crazy piece of work," I said, more sure than I felt. "Should've known there'd be a crazy bat behind her."

"You watch your mouth," Fleet said, brandishing a fist that looked like bird suet in a flesh-colored sack. Then she turned to my brother, who seemed to have recovered from his bout of embarrassment or whatever-the-fuck he'd been suffering from. "And I've got some idea why you're here too. I'm old, boys, not deaf, dumb, and blind."

"Really?" Thom asked, and the hope in his voice was pretty hard to listen to. I guess I'd been making his life all kinds of miserable these days, and what I hadn't managed to crush out of him, the desert'd gone and finished for me.

Of course, I could probably blame that camel just as much as I could blame myself, but we were equally at fault. A sobering thought.

"Sure," said Sarah. "You're here because you can't move past your own damn stunted adolescence and you don't wanna let go of any chance you have to recapture it."

That wasn't it at all, I thought. Fleet might've had Have's eyes and her sense of humor, but only one thin slice of her insight.

"Someone's *sellin'* her," I broke in. I didn't even want to think about what my voice sounded like just then, too earnest and fucking sincere. I didn't know how in the hell someone who looked like cooked pudding was going to help us, but I knew that if anyone *could* help us, it was this bizarre old loony holding my heart in the middle of the desert. "Havemercy. We crashed in the Ke-Han capital, morning of the last battle we ever fought, and now there's carrion birds breaking her up and selling her off piece by piece, like a fucking animal you buy for dinner. It ain't right."

Sarah Fleet stared at me, past my eyes and right down deep into my fucking soul, like Thom was always talking about when he got into a poetic mood, only this didn't make me want to punch anyone's lights out. Hell, I let her do it; I even stared back. I didn't have a damn thing I was ashamed of anymore, and Have herself'd picked me when I was little better than one of the muck-boys cleaning out stalls. If that was what Sarah Fleet was looking for—some quality that made me stand out better'n the rest—then she'd probably be looking a long damn time. She was and wasn't the same as my girl, I realized. She had the same attitude, the same whip-smart tongue, and I bet she knew all the dirty words to the drinking songs, but that was only *almost* enough. We hadn't been through the wars together.

"All right," she said finally, throwing up her big hands in surrender. "I'll help you track her down. But only because you spat on my floor when I was talking about that motherfucker."

"Esar's looking for her too," I pointed out, while next to me Thom tried not to have a stroke.

"Oh, honey," said Sarah Fleet. "I know."

CHAPTER NINE

MALAHIDE

Neither of my new companions trusted me.

I hardly blamed them for their paranoia. The big soldier—whose name, I'd since discovered, was the same as the Ke-Han word for *badger*—never once took his eyes off me, no matter where I was, or what I was doing. Even if I told him I needed to freshen up and would require some privacy for the task, he was always there, lurking in the shadows and making a true nuisance of himself. Luckily for him, he'd been given an excellent chance to recuperate before he'd learned a little something more about me from the Ke-Han girl Madoka.

Unfortunately for me, because of his prying eyes, I had yet to bathe the soot and mud from my body.

A lady needed to keep some parts of her body secret.

I was unclean, and that always irked me. I truly loathed the prospect of setting out with them into the desert unwashed, and I needed to be able to smell our quarry over the stench of my own body.

"Really, Badger," I said, watching him from the corner of my eye, "I am in need of a bath."

"Fine by me," Badger replied, his face unmoving as the mountain rock rising up around us.

We were at a stalemate. I had no idea what Madoka had told him, but surely I wasn't as dangerous-looking as all that. My Volstovic charms worked no wonders at all on him; I'd already played the strongest part of my hand, which meant that I had no further tricks just yet up my sleeve. Those would require more finesse, some study of my friends. Once I knew them better, I would better be able to play upon their senses with a show of my own emotions—or rather, I hoped that I would be able to do this. The only trouble was that Madoka herself saw directly through me; even under Dmitri's disapproving stare, I had never before felt so transparent.

"It's not as though I'm going to run away," I tried to reason. Badger crossed his arms over his chest and said nothing. "After all, as I'm sure Madoka has told you, I intend to set out with you."

"You a magician?" Madoka asked. She'd been relatively quiet all day, after we'd come to our little agreement; she was recuperating, and it was understandable. The compass buried in her skin had been placed there with such miserable clumsiness that it was difficult to look at it for too long, and the stench of rotting flesh had been overwhelming me since I'd started tending to her. A friendly enough gesture, I thought, though it seemed to make Badger extra wary of me.

It taught me one thing, however: The girl was essentially expendable, at least to the mastermind behind all this.

The Esar had incredible instincts—he was paranoid himself, sometimes to a fault, but he always knew when someone was plotting against him. His plan had been to strike first, and there was his only error. He hadn't struck first, just simultaneously, with the half-imagined, half-real enemy that rose constantly like a specter, reaching for him over the ridge of the Cobalt Mountains.

Honesty, I thought, would be the sweetest trick of all. Perhaps I could assuage their fear of me somewhat if I showed them I was harmless as a little fly.

"I am," I told her.

Madoka spat. "Hate 'em," she said.

"You must have had a bad experience," I replied benignly. "I can tell that the man behind that blight on your palm was a careless individual, and selfish on top of that. If I were in his shoes, and capable of such power, I would be much more precise in my actions, so no one would suffer needlessly."

"Yeah?" Madoka demanded. She was fiery; I appreciated that in a conversationalist, and was happy to talk to her for as long as it took to get myself some time alone with a washcloth and a bucket of water. We'd decided to leave the following morning—whether or not Madoka still had her fever.

Foolish of her to agree to that, but commendable, in any case.

"Indeed," I replied, trying to indicate to her how a proper lady would speak.

"What *is* in your power, then?" Madoka asked.

I let out a delicate sigh, adjusting my collar around my throat. "Scent," I replied. "I'm a tracker."

"Like a dog, you mean?" Madoka asked.

This time, when I smiled, I made sure she saw my beautiful, pearl-white teeth. "Like a wolf is the comparison I prefer," I told her.

That might not have helped my attempts at innocence, but at least it gave her a lesson in thinking a bit before she spoke. Ironically, I had become quite fond of her—less so of her overly large, relatively brutish bodyguard, but he was a simple man, and simple men were not my point of interest. If he had a single perceivable complication beyond the physical presence of that unfortunate scar, I might have appreciated his sullenness more.

"I *do* need a bath," I said. "And I intend to have one."

One thing I knew of the Ke-Han was that they were far less prudish about nudity than Volstovics; it was physical intimacy that bothered them, whereas holding hands or even offering a public kiss in Threme-don would not cause any passersby to so much as bat an eye.

I lifted my hand to my collar, then gave up the pretense that I could bluff them in this matter.

"I am a private woman," I said. "I do not enjoy bouts of exhibition-ism like the one you both seem so intent on forcing me to display."

"We'll look away," Madoka offered. "But if you bathe anywhere, you're doing it right here."

They had forced my hand. At least, in the little house we'd chosen to take up as our quarters for the time being, there was the remnant of a standing screen—once operating, I assumed, as a makeshift wall for the tiny hovel. I stepped behind it, where it was dark and shadowy, and there was no chance for my silhouette to be cast clear against the surface.

"Do keep your promise," I murmured gently, and began to undo the buttons at my throat, lace tickling my chin.

"Can't imagine anyone going to such great lengths to spy on a skinny thing like you anyway," Madoka said, and the echo of her voice told me she had indeed turned to face the wall.

"Not everyone was blessed with such a full figure as you, dear," I trilled in sharp retort. That particular topic had always been a sensitive issue with me, and it was the most common observation thrown at me by other women with the express intention of wounding the image I held of myself. I'd grown used to such jabs long ago, but as I'd said: Going so long without a bath was taking its toll on my normally equable nature. I stepped eagerly into the little basin—hardly a proper bath, but it would have to suit my needs for the time being—and crouched low to soak my washcloth.

The Badger man huffed, a noise that made him sound like a badger indeed, and I was reminded to be as quick about my actions as possible. The standing screen would serve its purpose, but as someone who normally bathed with at *least* two locked doors between herself and the outside world, it was safe to say that I was feeling ever so slightly vulnerable.

"Don't suppose you're going to tell us what's got *you* tramping through the desert like a camel in a dress?" Madoka called. "I mean, what's so special about this dragonmetal anyway? What was good about it is all torn up and destroyed now, isn't it?"

"Well, I can't speak for myself," I said, wringing out the washcloth before resubmersing it. "You may not believe this, but I am at heart a rather simple girl."

Madoka snorted, and I liked her even more.

"Just seems to me like trying to gather up stones after the castle's been blown apart," she said, and I somehow knew that she was examining the compass in her hand. Cursing it, no doubt, and I didn't entirely blame her. "Doesn't make any damn sense to me."

"You have to think further along than that," I said gently. It was a bit like leading a horse by the nose, but I wanted to give her some feeling of control in this matter. I could detect the beginnings of defeat in her voice—the fever talking, and doubtless the constant pain in her hand—and it would do her some good to sort out a problem or two with my guidance now rather than let it all overwhelm her a second time.

I'd told her that I could just as easily carry on without her, and that remained the truth. My personal preference, however, was to carry on *with* her, and that I kept to myself.

"You're going to have to give me more to go on than that, Malahide," Madoka said. "I'm no visionary, just a Seon sow with incredibly bad luck."

"Indeed," I said, enjoying some private amusement at the colorful language she chose to employ. It distracted me from the chill of the water, which was refreshing but somehow didn't leave me feeling as satisfactorily clean as a good, hot bath would have managed. "Here, then. What is the likeliest thing someone would build with old castle stones?"

"'Nother castle?" Madoka asked, after she'd taken some time to think about it. She didn't sound entirely certain of the answer, which was darling. I bent myself practically in two in order to submerse my hair under the water, taking care that every inch of me remained behind the shadowy protection of the screen.

"Quite so," I replied, and Badger huffed again. "Did you suspect that yourself, my soldier friend? How clever you are."

"War's over," said Badger, simply. "Man'd have to be a fool to try to build himself a dragon now. They're outlawed. Part of the treaty. Was there when it got signed."

I wondered how much of that he believed.

"And yet the race carries on," I said, twisting my wet hair over one shoulder, wringing it out. One couldn't be too rough during this process—that would split the ends—but I wished for my hair to dry quickly, and so these precautions were necessary. "I imagine there are some among your ranks for whom creating a replica of Volstov's dragons became something of an obsession. Understandable, since they were such a visible force in the war, not to mention the considerable damage they were able to accomplish, visited upon your very capital. I myself, were I to see such things firsthand, might fall prey to the same obsession. You mentioned that only a fool would take it into his head to reconstruct a dragon. Have you considered a madman?"

"Watch it," Badger said, and I heard him moving to take up his guard post by the door. He was constantly on the alert, a quality I admired deeply. "Remember who you're talking to."

"My apologies," I offered, stepping carefully out of the basin. The towel I'd brought for traveling was a small and scratchy piece of work, but it did the trick well enough, even if it did leave my skin redder than usual and splotchy with the cold. "I spoke impartially, without any particular bias toward one side or the other. I did not fight in the war per se—as you can see, I am *no* soldier—so it is not a matter of any real meaning to me, one way or the other."

"Sure," said Badger, but I could tell that it bothered him. The only consolation I could award myself was that he already didn't like me very much; nothing I did now would lower me too drastically in his esteem. "Don't worry about it."

I dressed myself quickly, in the spare set of clothes I carried with me for just these emergencies, then bundled my dress away for washing later. My hair would dry quickly in the hot desert air, and that was as much as I could wish for, at the moment. Already I felt better, if not completely presentable, and my senses were clearer and sharper than they'd been in days.

I knew exactly what path we would take to follow those nomads, and in following them, we would find my man once more. Now I had an extra weapon on my side; he stood no chance of evading me a second time.

When I emerged from behind the screen, Madoka was holding her hand above her face like she was staring into the sun. The hands on the compass had remained locked into place ever since she'd fainted, which was for the best. It meant that the nomads were keeping to a straight course for the time being, which would make following them considerably easier. And as long as they did not pull too far away from us, the mechanism should still continue to prove beneficial to our team.

I was no expert on the desert, and I highly doubted my Ke-Han companions were, either. We would simply have to be cautious, and pace ourselves according to the whims of the sun and sand.

When I sat down next to Madoka on the bed, she was too tired even to pull away.

"I'm helping this bastard," she said instead, staring up at her hand. "I think he's totally insane. What's he going to do after he's built a dragon? Send it on a rampage? Try and attack Volstov? Best thing I can think of is he gets caught and the emperor makes him take his life for treason, but then everyone involved with him'd have to go down too.

And that includes me and Badger. Doubt Volstov'd really appreciate the excuses, would it? 'I'm innocent, but I did all this shit anyway . . .' Don't think it'll really fly, will it?"

"You have a fever," I told her, laying my cool hand over her forehead. "And you're babbling. It's my fault for bringing up such a polarizing topic in the first place; I merely thought it might do you some good to have something else to think about."

"I've got too much to think about in the first place," Madoka said.

"We'll leave at nightfall tomorrow," I told her, smoothing the sweaty hair back from her forehead. I had no reason for being so kind, only that people responded to it better than anything else. "Then you'll have to concentrate on keeping your body upright, and you won't have the time to think at all."

Madoka laughed like a barking dog. "You're a real comfort, Malahide. Anyone ever tell you that?"

"Rarely," I confessed, which was the complete truth, for once. "Get some rest."

Truth be told, I was having some difficulty at present with following my own advice. I could not coax myself, however hard I tried, to sleep while the sun was up, and it seemed that the Badger man couldn't either—though whether or not that was because of his natural predilections or his refusal to take his eyes off me was unclear. He would regret it later, though conversely *my* Talent would shield me from feeling the effects of missing a good night's sleep. We sat on opposite ends of the small room, Madoka stretched out and snoring on the bed between us and Badger with his back to the door. He was evidently a vigilant soldier, and a man of some honor, since when first I'd met him he'd been using his skills to help that boy. If only, he might have been thinking, he could stay and help the child further. But now we had our own mission, and we would leave him to the hands of fate rather than the hands of soldiers. Whatever happened would happen. It was none of our concern.

Neither of Badger's traits, unfortunately, was one I could use to my advantage. Men of honor disliked a spy on principle, and that he was having difficulty in pinning me down clearly made him anxious.

These were not ideal traveling companions. As fascinating as Madoka was, she had no Talent to speak of; all her importance rested in the palm of her hand, and keeping her alive would be more difficult than anything else. Likewise, Badger would be good for brute strength, but as he was no magician and no mastermind, I needed to hope that he would serve as an arm of strength and justice . . . and serve *me,* while we were at it.

By the time true night fell, I'd been pretending to sleep for hours, and it was only when Badger himself began to stir that I felt safe enough to do the same. Still, I held my position a moment longer, eyes slit open in the dark to watch him as he bent to wake Madoka. He was gentle with her in the same way he'd been with the boy, which could easily have had to do with her injury—or it might not; in which case, it was something I could use to my advantage.

He cared for her, at least to the point where he felt she was his responsibility.

I held still until Madoka began to stir, then I sat up myself, rubbing the arm I'd been lying on. It was stiff, the elbow sore.

"Time to go already?" Madoka muttered, though to her credit, she didn't complain any further than that.

We were all up and outside in a matter of minutes, and I drew in a grateful breath of the desert air. The wind was picking up again, and it blew the scent of our quarry into my nostrils. Interesting. His scent had changed since I'd last picked it up. Or rather, someone had joined him.

It was a small detail—one that I didn't find necessary to share with my companions just yet—but I resolved to watch it closely. If my man was really one of a pair, that was all the more reason to be extravigilant.

Madoka studied her hand with an air of disgust, then shook out her shoulders and stood up straight. "This way," she said, and strode off with a purpose in her step, leaving Badger and me in her wake.

"I was just about to say that," I informed him, and hurried along after her.

THOM

Months of traveling with my brother, chipping away at him like a sculptor using a mere toothpick to carve a solid block of marble, had done nothing for Rook in comparison to what half an hour with the magician Sarah Fleet had managed. He was like a different person, like a child coming home to his mother, and had I not felt utterly different about her, I would have said she *was* his mother.

It was just that she was not *mine.*

I was wary of her, and, truth be told, a little jealous, though at least she had warmed to me somewhat. The verbal abuse with which she gifted me, I had come to understand, was of the same tonal quality as that which my brother employed. It was affectionate teasing—I hoped, or at last had learned to assume—and it didn't mean I was as loathed as it first appeared.

Still, it was difficult to abide.

"Stay put," Sarah Fleet told us, shuffling into the back of the house. From beyond the dividing screen, I could see a very homey kitchen. "I'll get you boys some coffee and we can talk."

Rook took that opportunity to flop down on her lone settee, which groaned in agony at the sudden, violent application of weight. It was moments away from collapsing, and I didn't want to be the straw that broke the camel's back, as it were. I pulled up a chair and watched my brother's face keenly.

He had changed—he was relaxed now, easy, a little eager. Like a child, I thought, with the same pleasurable giddiness I'd seen him exhibit only once—the first and last time I'd accompanied him in the air.

My knowledge of the dragons was limited; my knowledge of Havemercy herself fleeting and very personal. I'd been terrified to death at the time, and so the trouble was I couldn't remember her nearly as well as Rook did. Still, I thought, this woman was quite reminiscent of the dragon in question—or, I supposed, the dragon in question was reminiscent of this woman.

Magic could be as personal as a memory. The dragons had exhibited their individual quirks and flaws, inspired by their creators. This was only to be expected, but Rook, I realized, searching to replace what had been lost, was far too close at present to putting Sarah Fleet on his camel and eloping with her.

All physical logistics aside, it simply couldn't be done.

"Here you are, boys," Sarah Fleet said, shuffling slowly back into the room and offering each of us wooden cups filled with a brew so strong just the smell of it made me jittery. I let it warm my hands but didn't drink yet, not wanting to burn my tongue. Besides—though I would never mention this for fear of being murdered by Rook—I preferred my coffee somewhat sweeter than this.

Conversely, Rook took a gulp and sighed deeply while Sarah Fleet levered herself down on the other end of the settee from him.

"Well," she said. "Where were we?"

"Looking for Havemercy," Rook said. The word came easier to his lips, but I saw him hesitate just after he said it; he looked around, then took another deep swig of his coffee. I blew gently on mine, wishing I was not so far removed from the center of the conversation. I couldn't ignore the imagery present in the very way we were sitting: Sarah Fleet and Rook upon the settee, while I was perched opposite them. I might just as well have been on the other side of the world for all I was necessary to proceedings.

"Never thought she'd go down that way," Sarah Fleet said, with a sigh. "Guess it always stood to reason. Wouldn't want her dusting up in a museum somewhere. Better to go this way, when you think about it." She turned to level a fearsome gaze on my brother, and I was grateful not to be between them at this moment, much less on the receiving end of an expression as ferocious as that. One of her eyes was slightly lazy, but she managed an intensity that was only magnified by the fact that the crossed eye made her seem marginally unhinged. "So," she said flatly. "What're you looking to gain by getting her? You just wanna stop someone else from rebuilding her, right?"

"And rebuilding her wrong," Rook snarled, almost spilling his coffee. "She wouldn't want that."

"Guess not," Sarah Fleet agreed. "So you're going to make sure no one else rebuilds her, is that it?"

"She isn't anybody's," Rook said darkly.

"Son, she's not yours, either," Sarah Fleet said.

The tension in the air became immediately palpable, and I swallowed nervously. It was one thing to keep Rook in line; it was quite another to tell him that the one thing that had even remotely made him happy hadn't actually been his in the first place. I wanted to explain that Rook loved that dragon—loved her as he was incapable of loving anything else—when I realized how sad it would have sounded, and how little it was my place to put into words what my brother himself was feeling.

I had been rash in judging all his unkindnesses. I had never been as close to anyone as Rook had been to Havemercy.

"Don't give me that look, baby," Sarah Fleet said, leaning back and folding her hands across her mammoth, dunelike bosom. She drew in a deep breath and expelled it slowly. "Made me feel sad to give her up too, but I'm glad to know somebody loved her. Everybody needs to be loved."

"You don't know," Rook began, then trailed off. Sarah Fleet *did* know, and Rook knew it. The usual excuses wouldn't fly. He looked at me, and I stood quickly, setting my coffee down and moving to stand beside him. I didn't know how I'd suddenly met the requirements necessary for aiding my brother, but I was grateful to have a place, any place, in this conversation.

My brother needed me to take charge, and I was more than happy to oblige him.

"In any case," I said, stumbling over my words, "we feel as though she is currently being mistreated. You said you could help us find her. Is that really possible?"

"Oh, I'll do it," Sarah Fleet said. "But I'm not doing it for any other reason than to give his royal pain in the highness what he gave me. You probably understand that."

"So you don't think," Rook said slowly, each word twisted and dark, "that *you* could rebuild her or something?"

"Could," Sarah Fleet said. "Probably. But I'm not gonna."

Suddenly, I wondered what Rook's plan had been all along. It stood to reason that the idea of Havemercy being chopped up, the magical technology behind her being used for ill purposes, would make him raw with anger. But had he been fooling himself, all this time, into thinking he would be capable of resurrecting her?

By the expression on his face now—one of such sheer, mottled disappointment it was difficult to look at for too long—I realized that, whether he'd known it or not, he had been expecting just that.

"Rook," I said carefully. He might turn on either of us, searching for someone to blame.

"I think he needs to take a walk," Sarah Fleet said. "Get out there, get some fresh air, and come back when you're ready to talk about what we're *going* to do. How's that? I've got some rice pudding that won't last; you boys can help me eat it."

"Thank you," I said, "but I don't think—"

" 'Scuse me," Rook said, standing quickly, and heading out the door with a bang.

"That went well," Sarah Fleet said.

"It did, actually," I said, because no one had been hurt, no limbs were missing; there hadn't even been any shouting. It was all the more dangerous for that reaction, though, and I excused myself quickly to follow my brother out into the night.

He was already halfway across the desert basin that cradled Sarah Fleet's strange little house, and walking on foot. His camel stood forgotten. I ran after him, not calling out, but catching up. He was in no mood for company, I knew, but I couldn't just let him wander out into the desert alone. Kalim was waiting for us on the other side of the basin, and Sarah Fleet didn't exactly seem the patient type. She *had* agreed to help us, which was more than I'd allowed myself to dare hope for during our expedition, and we hadn't yet heard all she had to say. Further proof that my brother was not operating upon principles of logic but rather those of emotion.

Rook didn't slow down when I caught up with him, but he didn't speed up either. "Don't," he bit out, without a glance toward me. "Whatever you're about to say, whatever cracked *aphorism* you've got cooked up in there for this occasion—just *don't.*"

"Aphorism?" I asked, unable to help myself. I stumbled in a pocket of sand, but managed to keep my balance. The ground was beginning to rise.

"Whatever-the-fuck," Rook said, sharply, storming up the hill. "You know what I mean."

"No, *aphorism* is correct," I told him, feeling foolish and helpless that all I could do for my brother when he was miserable was talk about *language,* of all things. "I was merely . . . taken aback that you'd know it—much less use it properly . . ."

"Yeah, well." Rook shrugged like he was trying to throw something off his shoulder. "Can't help soaking up some of that 'Versity shit you're always spewing, I guess. Just soaked into me like I'm a sponge."

We crested the dune and he collapsed in an effortlessly graceful act of rage against the sand, which billowed delicately out around him and danced against a sudden gust of wind. After a moment of uncertainty, I seated myself nearby him, drawing my knees up to my chest. It was an uncharacteristically lovely night for the desert, for which I had come to have no lovely feelings whatsoever. The winds were gentle, the sky was littered with the sorts of constellations one needed an observatory telescope to pick out in Thremedon, and there was only a minimal amount of sand in my nose. All in all, conditions were perfect, but neither of us was in the mood to appreciate anything.

Rook grunted.

"We've some time until morning, it looks like," I said foolishly, tracing idle shapes in the sand at my feet.

"Guess so," Rook said. He tossed his head back to stare up at the moon, and not for the first time I was reminded of everything my brother had lost in the war. There was a phenomenon among certain soldiers who'd been away fighting for too long: that upon returning home, they found themselves lost, without a proper place in the world, nor even a sense that their "homes" were still their own. Reacclimatizing to civilian life after years spent on the battlefield was difficult for any ordinary man, and my brother was far from ordinary. The Esar had specialized the Dragon Corps so utterly that it nearly made it impossible for them to imagine doing anything else with their lives. It was even difficult for *me* to imagine it: Adamo as a professor, Luvander's hat shop, and Balfour in training to be a foreign diplomat. Some were better suited to repurposing than others, but it seemed all wrong somehow, like suddenly explaining to a boot that it was now a lady's dancing slipper.

I didn't envy my brother his position.

I only wished I understood it better.

"You must have known that . . . There would be no way of keeping it a secret, were she to be rebuilt," I said, as gently as I knew how. I hated myself for saying it, but as Sarah Fleet had demonstrated, there were certain things my brother needed to hear.

Rook snorted. "I ain't some cindy head-in-the-clouds piss-in-my-boots dreamer," he said. He certainly had a way with words—almost a poet's grasp of rhythm and cadence. "Anyway, I *know* what's what."

And yet, he'd still hoped. That, I knew instinctively, was what was bothering him. He was angry with himself on top of being angry with the situation, and it had crystallized the sentiment into something with which he could no longer avoid coming to terms. Even now I could see it in the rigid line of his back, the unforgiving set of his mouth, the muscles in his jaw hard at work and tightly clenched. He'd done his best to make his posture relaxed, but it wasn't enough to fool me. I saw right through him and realized he was empty tonight—had been empty, and I had my suspicions for how long.

"I really think that," I began, unsure of my words. Words were all I was really good at; I felt entirely useless without them. "Jo—"

"Not now," Rook growled, and though he didn't look at me I felt the shift in his attention as keenly as if he'd grabbed me by the collar. "Can't deal with that right now."

"Rook, then," I amended, not leaving the time for my feelings to be hurt. This wasn't about me, at the moment. It was about my brother, and the only something—someone—he'd ever loved. "I'm sorry."

"Not looking for pity," Rook said, the terrible flat anger returning to his voice.

"I *know* that," I said quickly. "I didn't mean to imply otherwise. I merely meant . . . I wish the situation had turned out differently."

"You know what they say about wishing in one hand and shitting in the other," Rook said, citing a proverb that had always made my stomach turn.

"Be that as it may," I acknowledged, trying desperately to remember what my original point had been. This was his technique, throwing my game by interjecting off-topic stings into the conversation and sitting back as I fended them off, my original thrust completely lost. He neatly turned my offense into defense on any given day, but I couldn't allow him to do it this time. He needed me. "I think we should take up, ah, Miss Fleet's offer. She said she could help us find Havemercy, which means no more wandering around with no idea whether we're on the right trail or not. That will give us an immediate purpose. I mean, I don't pretend to have any idea of how it would work, but if we had some way of *knowing* where the pieces were, her vital parts, at least, then we could have some sense of closure." I hesitated, lifting my head and turning in the sand toward him. "We . . . I mean *you* could give her a proper burial. I think that would be very fitting, under the circumstances. It's the decent thing to do."

"Yeah," Rook said, leaning back on his elbows in the sand. I wondered if it felt strange for him, to have to look up at the sky instead of being an integrated part of it. I'd only been up on Havemercy once, and I still felt sometimes as though my perspective had been entirely changed. It wasn't that often that a Mollyrat was able to rise above palaces and mountains. And Rook had done that—all on his own—for himself, then lost it as suddenly as it had become his in the first place. His world was still reeling from the aftershock. "Not really used to it being up to me to do the decent thing," he added.

"I'm aware," I said coolly, and before I could react he'd cuffed me on the back of the head. "Ouch."

"You were askin' for it," Rook informed me, his posture more relaxed than it had been only moments ago. He tore his gaze away from the sky, finally, and settled it squarely on me.

I stopped rubbing the back of my head. "Just consider the alternatives," I said. He hadn't meant to hurt me—I would have known if he had—and that was the kind of gift Rook was in the habit of giving me. Backhanded, yes; hitting below the belt, certainly; but kind in its own peculiar way. I smiled privately to myself, if a little sadly.

"Yeah?" Rook asked. "What're those?"

"She'd have no purpose in a world like this one," I explained. "Not now. Even if we did rebuild her—and if I thought we could, if I thought that would make you both happy . . ." I shook my head. "In any case, with all that being beside the point, she'd be too big for how things stand in Thremedon now. So the only other alternative would be to make her smaller—take that same spark she had, reduce her to something tiny enough to fit in your pocket, or the palm of your hand. And that's all wrong too, isn't it? She wouldn't be the same. What you might have thought you could do—return to a time and a place when the war was still being fought, when the Corps was still trying to *win*—it would require a different sort of magician. I don't think there's ever been one that powerful."

"Stories," Rook said, snorting. "S'all stories."

"And you're far too practical for them," I agreed.

"I wouldn't make her like that," he said, suddenly fierce again. But he wasn't angry at me, and he wasn't looking at me, either—just staring up at the sky, probably remembering.

"I know you wouldn't," I told him. "That's exactly my point."

For a moment, things were almost companionable. I, with my arms wrapped around my knees; Rook, leaning back in the sand and staring at the sky. We were as different as different could be, yet we *didn't* dislike one another. I was relatively sure of it.

"Anyway," I concluded, always incapable of letting any silence last for too long—a weakness in my conversational skills that Rook never failed to point out to me, "those were merely my thoughts as I had them. I didn't mean to pontificate; I only hoped to reassure you somehow."

"Nah," Rook said. "You were probably right."

It was the first time he'd ever said that to me, and once again I had to remind myself that my victories could be savored later, once we had time for them. "Thank you," I said, feeling pleased.

"Don't get too happy," Rook said. "It's a rare enough occurrence that you should be thinking about all the times you *aren't*, instead."

"Believe me," I told him, in no uncertain terms, "I often do."

"So you think we should let that old bag give us a hand?" Rook asked, as though he really wanted to know.

I nodded. "I do. I think it's the best lead—the best *chance*—we have at . . . at putting Havemercy to rest." It was something Rook needed as much as his dragon did, though I would never tell that to him outright.

"And I think you want that rice pudding she mentioned," Rook said shrewdly.

My stomach chose that instant to let out an untimely growl.

"Always were hungry," Rook told me, as we stood up and headed back to the house. "Especially when you were little. Fat as fucking hell as a baby—don't know how, since there wasn't much to feed you—but ever since then all you did was eat, eat, eat."

Sarah Fleet was waiting for us in the doorway. She nodded upward, and I followed her gaze to see Kalim's silhouette stamped out against the moonlit sky.

"Who's that handsome devil?" she asked.

"I'm offended," Rook said, sounding something like his old self, "that you would ever look at another man when you've got me."

"Baby, I've got *two* eyes," Sarah Fleet said. "And if you hadn't noticed, one of 'em points in a different direction. Don't worry, I can handle it." She let out a soft little laugh, and Rook ducked in past her, leaving me to follow behind. Whatever Sarah Fleet had to tell us now, we were ready for it.

I only hoped it would require much less time in the desert.

CHAPTER TEN

MADOKA

We stopped by the stream feeding the ruined village to stock up on water.

"Hey, Malahide," I said.

She turned to look at me like she wasn't expecting me to talk to her, and I didn't know *what* to make of the smile she gave me. We weren't friends, and I didn't exactly beam at her like that when she tried to talk to me, but she was a magician and my impression of magicians so far was that they were all crazy as piss. So maybe that was a good enough explanation for it.

"You called?" she asked, while Badger looked on like he disapproved. Not for the first time, I was actually glad to have him with us. We weren't having any more fireside heart-to-hearts like we'd done that first night, since we didn't want to talk around Malahide any more than we absolutely had to, and I had to admit, I kind of missed it.

If it'd been just me and Malahide out here, I definitely wouldn't've made it.

"Can I put this thing in water, do you think?" I asked, and then, because she'd probably want an explanation and I was too tired to keep hiding things from her when she was the only one of us who might actually know something, "It's hurting."

"How badly?" she asked. Her hands were gloved, and she took mine in both of them so delicately I felt uncomfortable just watching her. Nothing was that delicate where I was concerned, I thought, but I guessed she must've wanted to keep that compass pretty safe. And I guessed I didn't blame her for that, either.

I didn't really much want to look at my own hand anymore. Every time I did, it just got worse; if I knew that was the general pattern, then I didn't have any reason to check it anymore. I had nightmares about it too, and I knew it was giving me this fever. Sometimes I imagined what'd happen if I just ripped it out—might make things worse, for a time, but after that it could've solved all my problems.

"It's getting worse," Malahide said.

"Tell me something I *don't* know," I replied.

Badger, who had finished filling up our skins with water, came over to join us; it was a good thing he had such keen eyesight and didn't trust Malahide for a second, though I wanted to tell him he could relax just a little bit, save all his worrying for later when it'd really start to count. She wasn't going to try anything out on us *yet*, and what good would all this vigilance do if it wore him out before she chose to strike?

Soldiers, I thought. They were all the same.

"We've been treating it with aloe," I said, while Malahide continued inspecting the site of all my woes, like it was a code she was trying to break or a foreign language she was trying to decipher.

"Well that's all wrong," Malahide said. "It might get into the mechanisms, and stop the compass from working." She looked at my face after a moment, rolling my sleeve back up around my wrist.

"Can't have that," I said, with just a touch of sarcasm.

"Use your wit all you like, if it makes you feel better," Malahide said. "But what it won't do is help you much in the long run. Instant gratification is all well and good, but you should think ahead. To your future."

I looked out over the desert. *That* was my future, I thought, and it must've shown some on my face, because Badger moved to stand next to me. He looked like he was starting to pity me, and if that much was showing on his face, then I really was fucked.

"Whoa, boys and girls," I said. "I'm not dying or anything. Let's get moving or we're gonna be late."

"Our target has traveled far, on horseback," Malahide told us—a cheerful prospect, indeed, and I'd've thanked her if her words before hadn't hit home just a little bit. "We haven't much chance to catch up with him on foot; we can only hope he stops to rest somewhere in the desert."

"Oh yeah?" I asked. "And why's that?"

"Because my impression is that he is traveling to the sea," Malahide said. "And I do not believe you have much time to waste."

"I ain't getting on no boat," I said, almost like a reflex. I'd never spent much time thinking about the sea, and as far as I was concerned, I'd be real happy if things stayed like that for the rest of my life. The desert was one thing. The ocean was just out of the question.

"I didn't imagine you would," said Malahide, as though the idea'd been right out of the question from the beginning. "But my own interest in this matter is . . . sadly, quite tenacious. And *if* it were to come to that, I myself would have little choice in the matter but to continue my pursuit."

Not for the first time, I wondered who Malahide could possibly be working for. Or what kind of person would *hire* someone like Malahide, who looked more like a ghost from the hills than a real person: a distant spirit, with no particular ties to the real world. She looked part fox—and for all I knew, she was. I'd grown up with the idea that you couldn't trust people who lived without ties. Meant they were free to do whatever came into their heads, whenever it occurred to them, with no caution and no caring. My mother'd always told me people like that were dangerous, and now I was beginning to see why.

"We must leave quickly, in that case," Badger said, and for a minute I thought he was going to put a hand on my shoulder, but he changed direction midstream and scratched his chin instead. "So that the sea will not become an issue."

Just like a soldier to think he could get around something as big as all that water.

"That's fine," I said, squaring my shoulders. "And I'm fine, for that matter. Ready to go when you are."

That turned out to be a lie, but I was damned if I was going to admit it to anyone but myself.

The problem with my fever wasn't that it was particularly intense, or painful, or causing deliriums left and right, or knocking me off my feet, or anything like that. Those kinds of fevers burned hot, then went out, whatever was causing it seared from your body with the heat of the disease itself, or whatever. But this was low-grade, like shackles around my wrists and ankles. I could move, but it was slower going than usual. And among the members of our makeshift party, I was definitely the slowest. That pretty little snake Malahide was crossing the sand like she had camel blood in her, and Badger moved like a soldier, which meant he'd march at exactly the same pace until the clockwork in his back ran out and he had to stop for the night. Or the day, I guess, out here. By comparison, I was lagging, and I wasn't used to being the weak link in anybody's chain. I'd won every footrace in my village hands down, boys *and* girls.

It was all due to this damned hand, and I was too tired even to be really angry with it anymore. It was what it was. And now it was a part of me.

Every so often, Malahide would stop to smell the air, like a trained dog hunting down its prey. I'd thought she'd been pulling my leg about that whole smell-magic thing, but either she was really dedicated to the act or she'd been telling the truth after all. Now and then she'd switch course, and I'd check the compass to find she was going the right way. It was a damn good show.

"Do you know what sand smells like?" she asked one time when she caught me watching her.

Badger raised his eyebrows but didn't comment, which was a real big help. I had no idea what sand smelled like and wasn't about to stick my nose in and take a big whiff.

"The sun?" I guessed. Baked things, the way the hot stones in the old woman's oven had smelled when she didn't have anything cooking. It was the smell *I* associated with heat, and though it might not have been the same—I didn't know shit about the desert—I thought it was a pretty okay guess, all things considered.

"It smells like the most boring thing you could possibly imagine," Malahide informed me. "All flat, dry, and utterly colorless. There's no flavor to it at all. Now, the sand by the seaside is a completely different tale, but that has moisture to give it flavor. Not to mention countless delightful little organisms living and breathing and expiring on the beach. But yes," she added. "There is the occasional hint of sunlight, I suppose. And it is unbearably pedestrian."

"Aha," I said, because what the hell did anyone say to something like that? She was smiling, sure, and she hadn't stuck anything into my hand yet, so she had one up on the *other* magician I'd had the privilege of meeting, but she still wasn't doing much to discourage me from my theory.

"It's the most wonderful thing for tracking in," she elaborated, picking up the pace. Badger moved when she did, and I was forced to scramble after them. "Like a blank slate. It holds the scent of our quarry because it has nothing of its own to retain. See, just here, the nomad group paused for rest. It positively *stinks* of sweat—both camel and human. And, underneath that, metal. They must've been feeling very pleased with themselves, attacking an impoverished village. And they certainly do not expect anyone to follow them now. Who from that village would be strong enough to demand revenge? No; they were not expecting *us*."

I saw a flash of something like anger in her eyes, and at least that was something I could get behind.

I was glad, anyway, that we didn't have to use my hand any more than was strictly necessary—just anytime Malahide wanted to double-check her directions, mostly—because that meant I didn't have to look at it as often as I used to. I couldn't exactly ignore it, since it hurt too much for that, but I could put it out of my mind, at least for a few hours at a time. Take a backseat while someone else held the reins for a while. I was no follower, but I knew when I was in over my head.

We stopped for a rest so that Malahide could scent out whether the man she'd been following was still caught up with the nomads, since that was something my compass *couldn't* tell her. I was almost hoping we wouldn't catch up to him, since apparently whatever he was carrying was what that rat-crazy magician wanted so bad for himself. Hell, for all I knew we were following *him* straight into some kind of trap.

I'd thought he needed me for tracking the dragon part. Now I wasn't so sure.

"Thirty minutes," she'd said, before springing off like a mountain goat to taste the air and sigh and mutter to herself. I was pretty sure I was starting to like her—or at least she was starting to be real entertaining, and making me feel better about myself to boot—but that didn't mean I could trust her any further than I could throw Badger, which was an image that made me snicker.

"Something funny?" he asked, settling down in the sand. It was different, not having anything to build a fire with. I'd always heard that the desert was hotter than my grandmother's oven on the emperor's birthday, but it was actually kind of chilly at night. It was the kind of thing you didn't notice while you were struggling to put one foot in front of the other, but now that we'd stopped, I was almost a little cold. The quick wind didn't do anything to help that either. All it did was cool the sweat on my body and make me shiver.

"Nah," I told him. "I'm probably just going delirious."

Almost at once he got up, coming over to me and putting his hand on my forehead before I could tell him it was just a joke. That was the problem with Badger; he had no sense of humor to speak of. Unless it was about cannibalism, which I guess was a soldiering kind of humor I didn't understand and didn't care to.

"Your fever is troubling you?" he asked.

"I'm fine," I muttered, sorry I'd said anything to begin with. Me and my big mouth—story of my life, though, and not much anybody could do about it.

He kept his hand on my forehead for a moment longer, then dug around for his waterskin and handed it to me. I still had enough left in my own to get me by, but I was too tired to reach for it right now, and I didn't want to offend him by refusing the help.

Plus, I was thirsty.

"I think," he said, once I'd stopped guzzling, "that perhaps once this *Malahide* has tracked down what you both seek, we should question her further about what she spoke of: the magicians with the skill to break the spell in your hand."

"What, you mean you don't think our friend'll keep his word?" I cracked.

"It is my opinion now that he assumed you would either bring him what he needed or that you would die trying," Badger said, like he was talking about the weather and not about how I was as good as garbage. *Dead* garbage. "If that was all that he required of you, that is. I have come to wonder if perhaps our initial—my initial assumption may have been wrong."

I thought about that for a minute. "So . . . You're saying that even if I find this thing, he might not be finished with me then? That there might be even *more* crazy exciting experiments for me to be a part of?" I asked finally. I felt slow, but there were those chains again, as heavy as if they were really shuffling along behind me in the sand.

"It is merely an assumption," Badger admitted stiffly. "I don't pretend to know the innermost workings of a man like that. I've just been thinking. About our situation, as it stands. And you."

"You sure know how to comfort a girl," I told him, suddenly feeling the night chill a lot more than I had a minute ago. Another little desert breeze kicked up, and I wrapped my arms around my body, trying not to shiver too bad.

"My apologies," Badger said. "I didn't intend to be so blunt. I only thought to tell you, *should* that be the case, then your best chance might very well be this . . . Malahide."

We looked after her together: There she was, on the top of the hill, her skinny little body like a wraith in the wind. She had her skirts pinned up with one hand, arms akimbo, and she was stretching forward, scenting the air. Pretty fucking outlandish if you asked me, and totally insane that she had to be what I now considered my last real hope.

"I don't trust her either," I told him. But I was pretty sure I understood what he'd been trying to say. Couldn't help being a soldier. And kind of an ox, on top of that. "Hey, Badger—"

"Well, don't *you* two paint a lovely little picture," Malahide trilled, tramping back toward us over the dune's face and kicking up sand behind her with her sharp little boots.

Badger scowled, and I was pretty sure my own expression wasn't that far off. I handed him back his waterskin and he sat down in the sand, returning it to its rightful place.

"You're in a chipper mood," I noted. "I was beginning to think you'd fallen asleep out there."

"Hardly, my dear," Malahide said, tapping the side of her strong nose. "In fact, it's quite the opposite. I've detected something in the midst of all this sand at last—a change in the geography, if you will— and I'd be willing to stake my life that it's where our quarry will stop for the daylight hours."

"An oasis?" Badger asked.

"Precisely," Malahide said, with a frightening glimmer in her eyes.

"So we're catching up?" I asked. Didn't make sense. They had to be traveling too slowly, because they had a head start on us if you *didn't* count the fact that they were riding and we were on foot.

"Somehow," Malahide said, "they don't sense us as well as we sense them. Something is not right."

We all stayed still for a while, trying to think about it, and I would've been the first to admit that, just the same as my body was lagging behind theirs, so was my mind. Being sick all the time, not being in control of your own body—it'd do that to you, faster than you'd like, and then you were worse'n some dumb pack animal, because you couldn't even carry your *own* weight, much less someone else's. I was beginning to hate myself, and the only thing keeping me from getting too mired in it was knowing I had other people to blame for my current situation. Whenever things got so bad I couldn't stand it anymore, I just pictured that magician's lean, ratty little face, and I was good to go again, if only for a little while.

"They're not expecting to be tracked," Badger offered sensibly, breaking me out of all my slow-paced thinking. Easy to get distracted too, my thoughts running every which way like wind furrowing the sand.

"Still, they aren't headed toward the seaside at all," Malahide said. She folded her legs gracefully to inspect a bit of a tear in the hem of her skirt. I envied the knowledge that, no matter how cracked up she was, she was still in a better state than I was—mentally *and* physically.

"Maybe they've gotta meet up with somebody first," I said. "How the hell should I know?"

"There's more to this," Malahide began, then trailed off, huffing as the wind picked up, this time from a new direction. "Press on," she said sharply.

She stood at once, and Badger followed her; he offered a hand down to me and I took it with my left one, letting him haul my ass up. Pride was one thing; being practical was another.

"I'm fine, I'm fine," I grumbled, when he looked too closely at me. "Let's keep moving. Can't let the scent go dry or whatever it does."

"Don't push yourself too hard," Badger warned.

"Don't have a choice," I told him, and I guessed he knew I was right, 'cause he didn't say anything else after that.

The days were all starting to blend together, and even worse than that were my dreams. Flashes of light, the sound of water, voices I didn't remember. Everything smelling like metal, the hot sun beating down on me, only a few of my silks left to shield me from the sky. I didn't know what the hell I was doing anymore or why I was doing it; I could remember the faces from my dreams better than I could remember my own mother's. And when I woke up it'd be dark out, dunes rising and falling around me, like a sea of sand I was drowning in.

"Madoka," a female voice said.

I snapped awake to find Malahide kneeling beside me. She even managed to make that look delicate; if there was sand getting everywhere on *her*, she sure as shit didn't look too bothered by it. Her hair was perfect, her skin still the same milky white court ladies kill for, and I had no idea how she did it.

"It isn't your fault, my dear," she said gently, and wrapped her arms around me, pulling me against her chest. I could hear her heart beating and I wanted to throw up, but eventually the rhythm soothed me enough so I could pull away and breathe easier. "We're close now," Malahide went on, gently taking my arm once more. I felt her roll back the sleeve and I winced. "I wager an hour is all we need. They slept there all day, and I do not believe they are getting an early start, like we are. Think of the water, and the trees; the *shade* at last. But most important, think of our prize."

Since when is it "our" prize, I thought, but there was something about her voice that was soothing.

Malahide held up my hand in front of my own face without any warning, and I was forced to look at it. The places that'd been red before were laced with green; the skin directly in contact with the metal had turned a sickly shade of black.

"Concentrate on this," she said. "Do not avoid it. There is someone in this world who turned your own body against you. I know it is difficult, but you must continue to fight in the hopes that one day you will be able to turn his own body against him."

Sounded pretty good, I thought. With new strength in my legs and arms, I hauled my own self to my feet this time.

"An hour away, huh?" I asked. Badger was already raring to go, and I was getting used to walking on empty promises and feet that felt like deadweights.

Malahide nodded.

"Well, that's not so bad," I said, and started on my way, not looking to see if my two new friends had my back.

ROOK

Of all the things I'd been expecting, milking a little practical under-standing out of Professor Mollyrat Thom wasn't one of them.

But I didn't want to think about all that. I'd wasted enough of our precious fucking time already nancing around the desert and crying about my horseshit feelings, and now it was time to wake up and get a little practical. Because the last thing I wanted to do was show the mastermind behind my girl that I was some wishy-washy weepy-whiny shitbag who couldn't handle the truth when he saw it with his own two eyes.

"Just needed some fresh air," I said, stepping back inside.

"That's my excuse for coming out here too," Sarah Fleet replied. "Have some pudding and let's talk."

So there we were, eating bowls of pudding that had rice in it, trying to get around the weird feeling that part of it might've been burned, or maybe we just didn't understand the delicacy, being Mollyrats and all. I looked over at Thom and saw him wolfing it down, and I slid him my own portion. Whether he took it or not didn't matter. I was too fucking excited to be hungry.

"So," I said. "What's the plan?"

"You don't like it?" Sarah Fleet asked.

"It's delicious," Thom reassured her, snagging my bowl after setting his down.

"Grows on you, this one," Sarah Fleet said. "All right, you're anxious to get started. I'm assuming you've brought me something I can work with? All I need's a memory to start with; you leave the rest to me."

More magician mumbo jumbo, I thought. Even Sarah Fleet, who was different from the rest, couldn't help it. I shook my head.

"Don't speak in riddles," I told her. It was more polite than I usually had reason to be, but this woman was special. She licked her spoon and shook her head, like for whatever reason she was disappointed in me. I didn't like the feeling.

"And here I thought I was being straight as an arrow with you boys," she said. "Guess that doesn't help us any if you're slow as mud."

"We don't have that much experience with magicians," Thom clarified, his mouth full of rice pudding. Just like a real diplomat.

"Well I don't mean a real memory," Sarah Fleet elaborated. "I'm not one of those creepers with a quiet Talent who'll go mucking around in your head quicker than you can say boo! No offense, boys, I'm sure you've got a lot of those hanging around, but what good's a memory for helping you to find something, anyway? Memories are in the past, and what *you* want is decidedly from the now." She shook her head slowly, punching the air with her spoon. "Now, what I meant is a physical memory—like a remembrance token. If my little girl was your lover, you'd have kept a lock of her hair in a ribbon, wear it next to your heart, that kind of bullcrap. You get me? Or is that still too much of a riddle for you?"

"Oh," said Thom, blinking. "You mean . . ." He trailed off and turned to me, clearly not wanting to say anything without my rogering it first, which I guess was loyal, if misguided, of him. Wasn't anything like working with Havemercy—doing first, asking later—but what was like working with Havemercy?

Answer to that was: Nothing.

"Yeah," I said. Only problem was we didn't have anything like that on us. I had a scale from Chastity and a claw from Compassus, and nothing at all from my own girl. Just more proof that the world wouldn't pass up a chance to shit on a Mollyrat. I had a feeling Sarah Fleet knew it too, or at least she could tell by the look on my face.

I didn't go in for wearing my heart on my sleeve like *some* idiots, but people always knew when I was upset.

"What's the matter, boys?" Sarah Fleet asked, looking from side to side, even though she didn't really need to, her eyes being the way they were. "You look like I caught you with your pants down."

"Nothing like that," Thom said, sounding horrified at the very idea. "I'm merely afraid that we don't have what you're looking for. Of the parts we *have* been able to locate, neither of them has come from Havemercy herself."

Sarah Fleet sat back in her chair and grunted. There was a glimmer of something in her eye—the lazy one—that I was pretty damned sure I recognized. "Lucky for all three of us that I wasn't asking, then, isn't it?" she said, before getting up from the chair and disappearing into one of the rooms farther back in her house.

Something inside of me did a flip, just like Niall messing around on Erdeni before we flew out. Luckily I had better control over my outsides than my insides, and Thom had no clue.

She hustled back pretty quick for someone with her build, which was just as well, since if she'd taken any longer, I'd've probably lost my cool and gone back there to haul her in. There was something in her hands, largish, with a bit of a curve to it.

Sarah Fleet put the scale down on the table, and it was almost like she'd torn a hunk out of *me* and plonked it down in the dining room.

I'd have known one of my girl's scales anywhere, even if this one was in way better condition than all the rest of 'em put together. It was what she'd looked like brand-new, and I had to swallow quick because otherwise I was gonna hurl all over the place. She was just sitting there, resting smack-dab in the middle of the dining-room table like no more than a potholder or one of those round things you put under mugs of coffee to keep the table from staining. Somehow it looked right at home among the bowls of rice pudding. I snorted, because there wasn't much I could say.

"Don't start blubbering," Sarah Fleet warned. "And I don't want to hear any lectures about stealing, either, because you can't steal something that came from you in the first place." *She* didn't seem that impressed by the scale, but then I wasn't really surprised. That was my girl all over. She *did* reach out and touch the metal, her finger against the arc of white steel, and she sighed, like coming home. "All right," she said. "I only have one rule, and that's never mix food with magic. You get all kinds of unwanted mess that way, and it *always* spoils the taste."

Thom slowly lowered his spoon. There was rice in the corner of his mouth, but I wasn't about to tell him that. At least he'd had time to finish, though he'd eaten two portions in the time it'd taken Sarah Fleet to eat one. If we'd been alone, I'd have told him to take a good look at the magician, because that was where he was heading with an appetite like that; but the magician in question had sharp fucking ears and might've been able to use a spoon as a weapon.

We weren't alone, and I needed Sarah Fleet's help, and even someone like *me* knew when to keep my mouth shut about a woman's weight—when it worked to my benefit, of course.

"I'll clear the table," Thom said, with an eye between Sarah Fleet and me like he knew his place among the three of us. *Someone* had taught him real manners somewhere along the line, on top of all that horseshit he'd picked up at the 'Versity. Before Sarah Fleet could say otherwise, he'd scooped up the bowls carefully and scuttled out to the kitchen like an unwanted roach.

"Not bad, that one," Sarah Fleet said, with an approving eye that made me jealous for no good reason. "He's got *lovely* manners, for example. Unlike some no-account brawlers I could name."

"You want me to clear the table, or you want to get this done quick?" I replied.

"Guess you can't take a hint," Sarah Fleet said, rolling up her loose sleeves to reveal her soft white arms. She looked a little like the pudding she'd made, which nearly made me laugh, but I was getting real good at this whole controlling-myself thing. "All right, have it your way. Bring that thing over here now and be quick about it. My boyfriend won't stand out there waiting all night."

"If you're talking about Kalim—" I said, with a warning in my voice. But I picked up the scale and brought it around to her side of the table. It was hot in my hand—maybe it held the heat from the desert or something—but to me it felt like the blood pumping underneath skin and not like a part of a dead thing at all.

Sarah Fleet, the dotty old bag, winked at me with her wonky eye and pulled out a tatty old magician's pouch. She rifled through it for a moment, and then came up with what looked to me like an ordinary old sewing bodkin.

"Ha!" she said.

"We gonna do some needlepoint for Havemercy?" I asked, unable to help myself. From the back of the kitchen, I could hear water being pumped and the clink of dishes being washed. It was just like Thom to pick up a skill like that out of all the things he could've learned. Probably did an ace load of laundry too. And considering how he was in charge of washing things, and how we didn't go around smelling like cows, I guess he did. "Sew a few doilies and that'll lead the way?"

Fleet smacked my arm with her free hand, scooting her chair closer. "Watch that smart mouth," she said. "I'm the one holding the needle here, so don't get cocky. Now give me your hand."

"Why?" I asked, instantly suspicious of anyone who pointed out that they were wielding a weapon, then asked for my hand. It sure as shit wasn't because she wanted to shake.

"Oh, my mistake," said Fleet. "I was under the impression that I was speaking to Airman Rook of the Esar's famous Dragon Corps, not Sissy-man Sal of Miss Petunia's Flower-Farting School for Pansies. You got a problem with that?"

I slammed my hand down on the table, then turned it over, palm up. In the kitchen, the water stopped running. Bastion only knew what Thom thought we were doing in here, I told myself, and grinned.

Fleet pricked my finger with the needle before I could blink—she moved fast for an old sack—and before I could tell her *exactly* where to stick that needle next, she'd pricked herself too.

"Hate doing it this way," she muttered, pulling the scale closer and turning it over, so it made a shallow metal bowl. After that, she squeezed a few drops of her blood into the scale, then lifted my hand to do the same to me. "It's messy as anything, but it works. Well, sometimes. Try not to faint, now; it'll all be over soon. Besides, I just washed these floors last month."

I wasn't complaining. Pain wasn't something that bothered me much. I'd been pretty well versed in it since I was a sapling, and I was too eager to get going to even feel it, really. Adrenaline always worked the same, whether you were in the air or in some grandmother's kitchen. Nothing in the moment mattered; you were already somewhere else, in front of yourself in time.

Fleet picked up the scale real carefully, turning it slowly one direction, then the next. Mixing our blood together, I guess. Then she picked up the needle and dropped it into the center of our little puddle of combined blood. All at once, I felt a deep kind of tingling in my skin, like something in the air had changed, or the wind was picking up quick—except we weren't outside anymore.

There weren't any sounds of dishwashing coming from the kitchen now. I could feel Thom watching us, but I couldn't look away from the dragonscale.

"So when's the magic start happening?" I asked, like I couldn't feel a thing. Fleet probably knew better than to let me make shit up.

"Shut it," said Fleet, all her attention on the scale. "If you distract me, I could always mess up and have a compass that leads to Shirley-Sue the milk cow instead of your girl."

I buttoned my lip.

But nothing happened.

That was usually the case with magicians. They talked big, set things up with a lot of bluster and bravado, then you sat around while the clock ticked, waiting to be impressed. Some of them had little magic shows to make idiots like me, common people without any Talent to speak of save the ones that *weren't* blessed with capitalization, understand something was happening at all. But Fleet wasn't like that, and I was glad she wasn't like that, and this wasn't some Hapenny Lane stage but an old lady's house. All I felt was uncomfortable between my skin and my muscle, like I was getting a fever.

Then the needle started moving.

"Bastion," I said.

"Shut the fuck up," Fleet replied, standing. I did the same.

She wouldn't have to tell me a third time. Why the hell was I acting like a wide-eyed penny-parlor boy in the first place? Guess my girl always had one over on me, even from the grave.

I smiled thin and watched the needle gain momentum, spinning round in its little bowl like a clock gone crazy, a compass with no due center. Our blood—Fleet's and mine—together, had done this. Kinda special when you thought about it. Never seen anything like that before, and I'd seen a fuck-ton of all kinds of strange things in my time.

"Patience," Fleet said, more like she was talking to herself. I was on the edge of my seat and feeling weak in the knees like a lady from the Fans who'd just found out she was in the family way, but I kept myself up anyway. Didn't want to embarrass myself in front of anyone.

"Ah!" Thom said from the kitchen.

The needle stopped turning, righted itself, vibrated a couple of times, complete with a low whining noise. Then it fell flat into the bowl, pointing, as far as I could tell, just a hair shy of due north.

"Huh," Fleet said, sitting down hard. The chair beneath her groaned. I pretended like I didn't *need* to sit and was just *choosing* to 'cause the chair was there and all, and let my knees give up.

"Huh what?" I asked.

"Seems like someone else got the same piss-poor idea into their head as you," Fleet said. She had a thoughtful look on her face. "Direction's pretty precise, too."

"Okay," I said, like that actually meant something to me. It didn't, but maybe I'd get lucky and the old girl would elaborate.

"Don't humor me," Fleet snapped. "You know what this means?"

"Nope," I told her flatly.

"That's right, and don't you forget it," Fleet replied, wagging her finger. She looked tired, though, and I wondered if Thom and I were gonna have to haul her to bed after this was all over. "Means you're not the only one who can't let little darlin' go, apparently. Someone in the desert's having a go at putting her together," Fleet explained finally, letting out a deep breath. "They've got the soul too, or they're close to it, which means at least one of 'em knows their top from their tail. Just look at that needle."

I directed my attention back to the dragonscale. Had to have something to focus on, or else I was gonna tear down this house over the idea that anyone'd try and remake my girl. It'd been my stupid idea, but I had a right to it. No one else had that right, except maybe the mad bag sitting in front of me. The needle was starting to move, not so much that you'd catch it if you weren't looking at it, but by a hairbreadth; it clocked over to north, then stopped, then slid a little bit west after a few more seconds of me watching it.

"She's on the move," Fleet added. "Don't think she's flying herself just yet, boy, so somebody who can travel real quick through the desert's probably transporting her. You know of anyone who can travel quick through the desert, or do we need to have a few lessons before I get you out of my hair? It's short for a reason, you know," she added, then looked cross-eyed at me.

"Nomads," I said.

"Bull's-eye," Fleet replied.

There was only one nomad I knew, and he was standing just outside on top of a sand dune.

"Rook," Thom called after me, but I was already out of my chair. I'd been led in so many circles by now, crossing my own bastion-damned path more than once and allowing myself to be tomfooled into all kinds of half-wit fuckery. I was taking this camel by the reins and I wasn't letting go until someone gave me a solid answer. I'd beaten Kalim once before man-to-man, and, if necessary, I'd do it again.

The wind had picked up pretty fast since I'd last been outside, and

I sure as shit didn't like the way the air smelled. There was something nasty and dark blowing in from not too far away, but I wasn't a master of the desert. All I had were my instincts.

"Ah, Mollyrat Rook!" Kalim said, like butter wouldn't melt if I shoved a whole pat into his mouth. "Did you find what you're—"

"Listen to me," I said, grabbing him by the front of his robes; probably a killing offense where he was from, but I didn't care anymore. "You got something you're hiding from me?"

Kalim didn't blink, but I *had* taken him by surprise. "Do you seek to offend me?" he asked.

"Do I?" I asked. "Doesn't matter right now, Kalim. Are you *keeping* something from me?"

So, maybe it wasn't one of my finest moments. I probably was babbling like a madman who thought he could talk to someone special up in the heavens. Something told me I wasn't going to be able to explain myself, either, so I dragged him down off that dune as fast as I could, yanking him back toward Fleet's house and shoving him through the doorway. He was going along with all this, but at any moment I knew he could respond to the assault on his pride and turn on me. That didn't matter. I was gearing for a fight. Bring it on, Prince Kalim, and all that fuckery.

"Hey, boys," Fleet said, calm as punch.

Kalim made a sign I didn't understand in the air in front of him, like warding off the evil eye.

"That," I said, pointing at the scale on the table. "You seen something like that before? One of your men have it? *Are you fucking trading in shit like this?*"

Kalim's mouth was tight. "I have seen something similar to this before," he said at last. "It was in my possession until three nights before I met with you, your brother, and the *rakhman,* when it was stolen from me."

"Plot always thickens, doesn't it," Fleet said.

CHAPTER ELEVEN

MALAHIDE

Our quarry had made a fatal error, which always thrilled and disappointed me.

My worries about the relative potency of my Talent in the desert had turned out to be unfounded. So long as we stuck to traveling at night—and we did, for the sake of our good health and sanity—I was as spry as a country girl and as fit as a good musician's fiddle. The dune sands made for the most wonderful backdrop I could have asked for—all potential, lively smells burned clean out of the landscape by the midday sun. There was nothing to distract me from my prey—a group of men who stank at once of blood and dragonmetal. It was wondrous, and better than if I'd planned it myself. I would doubtless be home in no time with the Esar's gratitude jingling in my pockets, yet I found myself somewhat unsatisfied.

If I were to be perfectly honest—as I could only be with myself—I had to admit I was missing the ecstasy of the hunt as I'd felt it when I was still in the mountains. Chasing the man whose skills so matched my own had left me nearly breathless with delight, my head spinning from the rush of blood, combined with a lack of food or sleep. But ever since the burning village, I hadn't been able to detect the familiar tang of dragonmetal from anywhere but here: among the quarry we now pursued. Such disappointment came with not being a free agent. I was not at liberty to choose which trails to follow and which to leave cold. What the Esar had sent me to look for was my *only* concern, and whatever had intrigued me about my chase through the mountains had been completely obliterated by what the nomads held. Chasing them was dull, unfulfilling work, but the prize they held was nearly enough to make up for that. I had never smelled the soul of a dragon before, but all my instincts were telling me that my work was going to be accomplished sooner, rather than later.

They'd stopped to rest, and very shortly my pursuit would be over as a consequence of their carelessness.

The girl Madoka called me strange, and I supposed I was, if it came to that. Everyone had their peculiarities. In truth, it was she who seemed strange to me, carrying on with that thing festering in her hand as though it wasn't about to cause irreparable damage. As an agent of the Esar, I'd been trained to withstand certain methods that the enemy might use to extract information, but I knew instinctively that what Madoka was suffering now was something I would have never been able to tolerate. Pain unimaginable; even I was impressed.

I tried to keep her downwind as best I could, so that the scent of rot did not overcome my sensitive nose. After all, the smell of the nomad raiding party was bad enough already, but I could allow no further distractions than the ones with which I had already willingly burdened myself.

Why they'd chosen to take refuge in the oasis at such a time was unfathomable to me. Perhaps it was as simple as Badger had so eloquently stated, and they didn't even know that they were being followed. It smelled distractingly of green things, of water bubbling up from the rock, and smooth, wet stone. The nomads had tainted it with their presence, of course, but it was easy for me to pick their stench apart from the rest, now that I knew it so well. In among the rest of these exotic little odors was the most alluring perfume, twined around the others like a complacent cat welcoming her master home and waiting for him to pour the cream.

That was the dragonmetal, and it was going to be *mine*.

Of course, I *had* promised Madoka certain things, and I had no intention of going back on my word. The Esar had sent me on my mission because he'd sensed trickery afoot, and his instincts had proven themselves to be correct. He expected me to bring back what he'd sent me for, of course, but how much more *highly* would I be held in his esteem if I managed to capture not only the soul but the Esar's enemy as well?

Madoka had no uses for the dragonmetal herself. She'd as good as told me so by the look on her face whenever it was mentioned. I had my own private concerns about the true nature of her mission, which were in part due to the man I'd followed over the mountains. There was no reason for me to be so suspicious of course, but I'd made my life's work out of seeing connections where others did not. It didn't entirely make sense to me, that Madoka's magician would require her simply for retrieval and nothing else.

There was a piece missing to the puzzle. I couldn't allow myself to become so distracted by the proximity of my goal that I forgot it.

I hadn't yet broached this subject with Madoka herself, of course, or her stolid companion. Her moods varied with the fever, and I feared that she would not rightly be able to understand the intricacies of what I was planning. Her mistrust of magicians did me no favors, and I couldn't be certain that what small kindnesses I'd offered up until now would be enough to tilt the scales in my favor if I shared my concerns with her. She might simply suspect I was trying to trick her in some way, and the careful trust I'd been working hard to establish between us would be as good as destroyed. This was a job that required the utmost circumspection. Fortunately, that was a trait I had in spades.

"How far along to the oasis?" Badger asked me, coming up at my side while I'd been thinking. He moved with curious silence for a soldier, though the wind and the sand did a great deal to hide everyone's footsteps, and my particular senses had always been stronger elsewhere. I was not entirely surprised.

I pointed to the next dune, obscuring our view of the horizon as we strode across the little valley. It obscured what might have been a clear view of the oasis grove, but I didn't need to see it to know it was there.

"I see," he said, judging the distance and perhaps calculating how long it would take us to reach it by the speed of our current pace. I glanced over my shoulder and, sure as anything, Madoka was still tramping along behind us. She was a good girl, and remarkably sturdy—certainly more hardy than some Volstovic stock. Badger seemed to follow my gaze, and he lowered his voice before speaking again. "I believe the fever is getting worse," he confided.

How wonderful at last to become a confidant. If I had worked trust on Badger, then I could do anything at all.

"Oh?" I said, trying not to betray my surprise at this sudden confidence. It was unlike him to speak to me at all, let alone of Madoka. Perhaps he'd come to realize that my concern for her was genuine—or at least as genuine as a person like myself could maintain.

"She tosses in her sleep," he continued. "And the hand grows worse."

"Now, *that* I *have* noticed. I can't say as to her sleeping patterns," I added, a little too slyly. If it hadn't been dark, or if his coloring had been fairer, I might have squeezed a blush out of him like water from a stone. But being a soldier on top of being Ke-Han meant there wasn't much success to be found in squeezing. Badger frowned and turned away, which was as good as any cue to continue. "Whoever did that to her clearly didn't have a handle on what he was doing," I told him frankly. "It seems desperate, like an experiment as much as anything else. Decidedly *not* the work of someone who's an expert in the field— but then, this is highly experimental magic to begin with. Dealing in prosthetic limbs is one thing, but inserting something once enchanted into a working body part is . . . well, opportunistic at best. Monstrous at worst. You see for yourself the consequences; I myself would never engage in such beastly hack-and-slash."

"I would agree with the second of those two choices, I think," Badger said, neither agreeing nor disagreeing with my own self-assessment.

"The quicker we work, the more likely it is that whatever has been done to her will be able to be undone. If my hunch about your magician is right, then I will simply have to take her to Volstov," I said, with a confidence I didn't necessarily feel. I wasn't on good terms with the magicians of the Basquiat—wasn't on *any* terms, if it came to that— but the simple fact of the matter was that some of the greatest minds for research, magical or otherwise, resided there. If anyone could reverse the damage done to Madoka by an inexpert magician, it would be one of them. And I did have ties to the Esar: Whether or not the Basquiat was feeling friendly or wary of him, they were his for better or worse, and he could be very convincing. Some magicians, leaving the matter of the Esar aside, would leap at the chance to experiment in such a specialized way; I knew a few who would rise to the challenge without even needing to be convinced. So I was confident about that much.

Badger glanced back toward the topic of our conversation as we crested the dune, and I pulled him hurriedly just past the hilltop. Having the element of surprise would do us no good if we were to pause at the highest point nearest the oasis and stand there like bull's-eyes. Better just to broadcast our presence to the skies with electric lights and a marching band, if it came to that, and at least give ourselves away with a little bit of personal flair.

Madoka scurried up behind us, and had the blessed sense to drop low on my other side. She had wonderfully fine instincts, and I felt quite warmly toward her because of them.

"You two trying to ditch me?" she asked.

"Not at all, my dear," I said lightly. "Badger and I were just attempting to survey the area for your safety, that sort of thing. You are, after all, our little treasure." A quick wind picked up, and the scent emanating from the suffering flesh around the compass nearly overwhelmed me. I covered my nose with one hand as discreetly as I could. I did not wish to offend her.

"Any sign of 'em?" she wanted to know, arching her neck to peer down into the valley basin.

"None yet," Badger said. "We should be on guard. Don't know how many of them are down there, but it was enough to hit that village, so we can't be too careful."

"Don't remind me," Madoka muttered.

"Well," I murmured, lowering my voice as I rose to my feet, "no sense in waiting to find out."

"I'll come with you," Badger said at once, though I knew better than to be touched by this sudden display of concern for my safety. "Madoka, stay here," he added, confirming my suspicions.

"What? All of a sudden I don't get to play with the big kids?" she said, clearly affronted. In this as in all things, she was endearingly quaint.

"You *are* our most valuable asset," I told her, with what I hoped was an apologetic tone. Badger had already started down the dune's slope in the direction of the oasis, keeping low against the sand, and I turned to follow after him. "Don't worry; we'll be sure to come back and collect you once all the kicking and screaming has finished."

"Yeah, well," Madoka muttered.

I reached out to clasp her warmly upon the shoulder. "Stay low," I suggested, "keep your head down, and remember this: Even if I were to abandon you, our mutual acquaintance, the Badger, would never. He'll be back for you, even if I am not."

"That's great," Madoka said, but she did seem somewhat comforted by my assessment. Then we left her behind us, scurrying down the dune in a flurry of sand, hoping the wind would cover us.

It was neither of our areas of expertise; we were both better accustomed to different terrains on our individual battlefields, and there was sand up my skirts and inside my boots in no time. I kept a kerchief held against my nose and mouth, which seemed thus far to be the best way to keep the tools of my trade safe. At least Badger was quick, quiet, and efficient. A very solid man, if not the most quick-witted.

"We'll split up and survey the perimeter," Badger mouthed, blocking out our path with his hands. "And don't make any sound."

"Silent as death," I promised, my own voice barely above a whisper. For whatever reason the phrase seemed to give him the chills, then we parted, keeping shadows between us and the main camp.

Close up, the stink of dragonmetal was drowned out by the stench of flesh, sweat, and human blood. Fire was also thrown into the pot, and whatever spices were being included in dinner. I breathed shallowly through my mouth, using trees and low-level scrub brush for cover. Silence was one of my specialties, and the nomads in question—tall, bluff men, most of them stripped down and bathing in the fading daylight—were drinking and laughing, completely oblivious. Naturally, this was their terrain. They had every confidence it would never betray them.

So, I told myself, it was obvious that they did not know anything about the chase that was currently being waged. If they had any idea of it, then I would never have been able to get so close. That was interesting to note; my first prey had been running from or to something, but these men were not a part of it at all.

And yet I could smell dragonmetal on them.

I crept closer, the sound of their laughter and stories in the language of the desert—one I'd only just begun to study and did not have nearly so much fluency in as the many Ke-Han dialects—obscuring all possible noise that either the Badger or I would make. They were gathered around a single man, half-dressed, who appeared to be their leader; at least, they treated him differently than they treated the rest, with a sort of awed deference. And, I noted as I drew closer to the scene, nestled behind a tree and with a very good view of the proceedings, he was holding something in both hands. He lifted it high, and his men let out a loud cheer.

What was it? It was *vital* that I manage to get closer. It was about the size of an infant, though the way the nomad was holding it was *vastly* inappropriate for that to be the case. Also, it positively stank of dragonmetal, and when it caught the light it shone like liquid.

It was like nothing I'd ever seen. When I got closer I could see that there *was* liquid inside of it—clear, and very alike to something I had seen before in my lifetime. Water from Volstov's Well, from which all magicians could trace their powers, though slightly less translucent. And it smelled of fire.

After spending so long on the hunt, one grew to nurture certain instincts. I knew without having to breathe in any deeper that the heady, giddy scent it gave me was because it was something more powerful than even I could fully comprehend. This was a prize to end all prizes. My man from the mountains seemed dwarfed by comparison.

I could have gazed at that strange piece all day.

Unfortunately, I was not given the time.

A shout went up from the far end of the camp, and at first I could only assume that Badger had done something careless, like getting himself caught. Perhaps he too had been lured like a fish by the sight of that beautiful little vial—for those not accustomed to magic, the very sight of it was singing like a siren. It had even caused me to draw a little closer than I might have otherwise. Temptation and Talent were too alike at times, and I cursed all soldiers. But I cursed too soon.

The leader quickly passed the beautiful thing—it must've been the soul, I could imagine nothing so fitting—to a lackey, who tucked it under his shirt and spirited it out of my sight. All members of the camp, who'd been as transfixed as I was, jumped to attention.

From somewhere deep in the bushes, a guard appeared, dragging someone behind him. We *were* found out, I realized, but it was not Badger who'd been caught. It was Madoka.

I drew back from the trees at once—it would do none of us any good if I was caught as well. Badger and I had planned to meet where we'd left her, and I could only hope he was soldier enough to stick to the plan rather than barge into the middle of a very tense situation and try to rescue her right away. The soul momentarily unimportant, but not altogether forgotten, I hurried back to meet him, hoping I would find him waiting for me where last we'd all been together.

He was, face mottled with anger, hands braced in fists.

"Calm down," I told him, first and foremost. "Your anger will do her no good."

"She's been captured by those . . ." he said, searching for a word. Apparently he was unable to find it, and he spat into the sand, looking startled by his own vehemence. "You saw what they have done—"

"I have seen it," I told him, and grasped one of his large hands in both of mine. "Don't worry. We *will* save her."

I wished I'd had a plan to back up my words, but one would come soon enough. With Madoka as our distraction, we would take my prize from their leader, as well. We had our trump card. Now we needed only to play it.

THOM

In the end, it was Sarah Fleet who kept Rook from attacking Kalim.

"Look," she said, standing and speaking in a voice far louder than I ever would have expected from such a short, stout woman. "You kill that desert rider, you feel good for a little while, sure, but you don't learn anything. Get your hands off his throat and let him say something. Just might turn out to be interesting."

I would have been the first to admit that I was worried—I did not want Rook to continue manhandling our guide, of course, but neither did I want him to release him and be attacked himself. It was an awkward situation, no other way of looking at it, and I was feeling somewhat trapped by everything when Rook unclenched his hands from where they were holding on to Kalim's cowl and whirled away.

My brother, of course, was ready to be attacked. When Kalim made no move to go after him, he straightened halfway, still poised like an alley cat ready to jump.

"I have not misled you, as you seem to believe," Kalim explained. "Some time ago—perhaps three weeks, it was not so far back as all that—a new magic came to our people. I was the one who found it: carried into the desert by a man who did not know the ways of the sand. He was dead, and I buried him, and thus the gods gifted this magic to me. As I am prince of my people, it was a sign. I was to inherit the tribes. Even my enemies agreed."

"Got a regal air about you," Sarah Fleet conceded, just to be difficult, which was a behavioral trait she seemed to *greatly* enjoy exhibiting. By my calculations, according to Kalim, Havemercy's parts had been traveling since the crash, while Rook had been in captivity—tortured—and then recovering in Thremedon with me. She had a considerable head start on us, then.

"I thank you," Kalim said, though he still looked a little bit uncomfortable to be addressing her directly.

"You're gonna have to be a hell of a lot clearer than *that*," my brother said, his tone no less dangerous. He still mistrusted words more than anything else, and especially when it seemed as though someone was employing them to keep him from the information he needed most.

"It was stolen from me," Kalim continued, the look on his face growing dark. "By rights, any leader may challenge another if he feels it is his place to do so, but none had come forth to challenge me in the custom of our people. Thus, I was convinced that all supported me; but I was wrong. One of my enemies—a leader of a lesser tribe and one of my half brothers—crept in at night like a filthy *rat* to take what was not his. When I woke in the morning, my symbol of inheritance was gone, and with it my right to unite the tribes under my rule."

"That's a real sad tale, Kalim. You're breakin' my heart," Rook said, in a tone that I knew all too well. I could easily predict what would come next too, and I stepped closer to the center of the conflict in case it became necessary to prevent another fight from breaking out. "But I'm not all that interested in who gets to plant their ass in a throne of sand, you got me?"

"I . . . do not follow," Kalim confessed. Seeing the set of my brother's shoulders, and Kalim's basic inability to grasp the facts from Rook's more colorful language, I knew what I had to do. I sent up a prayer to whatever foreign deities might currently have their ears open over the desert and waded in.

"What we'd like to know, Kalim," I clarified, "is if you could be a bit more specific about this *magic* you found. It was a physical object with a form to it, yes?"

Kalim nodded, stretching his hands apart to indicate dimensions. "Form, yes," he said. "About the size of a nursling just born, and clear like blown glass, though not nearly so fragile. There were bands of gold wrapped about its body, one about the top, and one about the bottom, so as not to obscure the wonders within. *Inside* the glass were the movements of a machinery I did not understand—a part of the magic, no doubt, beyond my understanding—but it had gears and workings in bright gold, the likes of which I had never seen. Traders have brought all manner of . . . what is the word? Mechanical, yes? They bring these mechanicals to our people, but I had never seen the equal of that magic which I myself, with these hands, took away from the dead man."

I was privately fascinated by the tale, and the description of the mysterious object thrilled me, though I couldn't even begin to guess at its nature. Kalim had a way of speaking that was truly rare, persuasive and absorbing both in one. It was a skill I wished more of my professors in the 'Versity had exhibited, but there was no point in thinking about that now.

I could tell by my brother's face that Kalim's story had not illuminated *him* in any of the ways he'd been hoping for, and I frantically raced to try to think of something—anything—to keep the tension from boiling over.

"Well, slap my ass and call me Nellie," Sarah Fleet said, breaking my concentration. I'd all but forgotten she was there, which seemed downright impossible considering how much trouble she went to in order to make her presence known at all times. There was a queer look on her face all of a sudden, and for a brief moment both her eyes were fixed on the same target: Kalim.

"I do not understand your request," Kalim said.

"It's a saying, dear," Sarah Fleet told him. "Just me reacting to what you found out there. But I never thought it'd end up in a place like that, no sir. Not that I'd *mind* if you took me up on it—just in passing, and just thought I'd mention. I'll explain it to you sometime. You're a hand-some one, but unfortunately I'm all business tonight." She let out a sharp, unexpected whistle. "And too bad, 'cause I'm betting I could teach you a thing or two about slapping and Nellies."

"Woman," Rook began, as Kalim blanched a full shade paler. "Get down to the point."

"Don't you hustle *me*, airman," Sarah Fleet said. She huffed, rub-bing her hands together and adjusting her glasses. She seemed reluc-tant to part with her information, for whatever reason, and it occurred to me that this was in all likelihood the most company she'd seen since her exile. Perhaps she wished for us to stay a while longer, keep her company somewhat in all this expansive, sandy darkness.

It didn't seem particularly fair to me. Especially when she made such excellently seasoned rice pudding—just the barest hint of cinna-mon dusting the top.

"Do you recognize Kalim's description?" I prompted her, as gently as I could. I was still wary of her—as wary as I'd ever been of Have-mercy herself, in fact—but she wasn't a dragon. She was just a lonely old woman whose skills had gotten the better of her.

"Any one of us who worked on the dragons back in the day would recognize something like *that*," she said finally, giving Kalim a sharp look. Her eyes passed over to Rook, and I saw him shoot a glance at the compass they'd made on the table, Rook's blood mixed with Sarah Fleet's, puddled together in Havemercy's scale. "It just so happens that this here desert rider found a dragonsoul."

"Beg pardon?" I asked.

"A what?" Rook demanded.

"Dra . . . gon . . . soul," Sarah Fleet repeated slowly. "You idiots got sand in your ears? It's the guts of what makes a dragon *your* dragon. Weren't you listening before? Magicians aren't mechanics. We get some say in what goes where, but it's not like we all had the skills to build those pretties from the ground up. 'Course, old Alan—he worked on a real beauty, named her Proudmouth—built that thing with his own two hands and made the rest of us look bad, but he was the exception. There's one in every bunch. What *we* worked on was the heart and soul of th'Esar's little pet project: how to make our babies live and breathe—without them doing any *actual* living and breathing, mind. Dragon-souls're what kept them alive, say, and fuel's what kept them in the air.

All the rest was just a home to what we came up with, like putting a soul inside of a body, so that's what we called it. Wasn't a heart; those were made out of cogs. And it wasn't a brain, 'cause those were made out of cogs too. So we played Regina a little bit, got fancy. Sounded good at the time. You catch my meaning?"

"So," I began slowly, to give Rook a moment to collect himself, "their relative . . . personalities . . ."

"Never supposed to happen that way," Sarah Fleet said. "By the time I got brought in, they said th'Esar was already boiling mad about what he thought was our little trick, sneaking bits of ourselves into the dragons to keep them from being *his*. They were just supposed to be flying machines, I guess, but the men and women who put their blood and sweat into the project had different ideas. Guess you could say we were all pretty attached, after spending years trying to craft 'em. Some of us didn't have families or children; those of us who did spent all their time working on the dragons rather than visiting with the families they did have. Why, there was one woman who treated hers like it was a baby. I'd catch her cradling that thing in its work blanket when she thought no one was around. Yeah, we were real special all right. Bat-shit bell-cracked you might say, but everyone who creates something's always a little bit off in the head region. Otherwise you don't have any imagination."

"So that's what Kalim had," Rook said, for confirmation more than anything else. He looked a little calmer, though his anger was still lurking just beneath the surface, waiting for a chance to reveal itself. "Had it, then lost it."

Kalim scowled darkly.

"Sounds like." Sarah Fleet shrugged. "Judging by the way that needle went, too, I'd say the dragonsoul he picked up belongs to our girl. Just in case you were curious. Call it a hunch. And if I'm right about someone wanting to put her back together, well. They'd need the soul, that's all I'm saying. It's kind of a key ingredient. Like cinnamon. "

Rook whirled back around like the crack of a whip, and Kalim immediately tensed, clearly expecting my brother to start another fight. When he didn't, Kalim lowered his hands and looked at him curiously.

"I did not understand a great many things about the witch's speech," Kalim confessed. "Nor do I understand the sudden nature of your assault, Mollyrat Rook."

"I need to find the guy who stole your magical inheriting-whatever," Rook told him, calmly. "And then I need to kill him."

"Easy there, tiger," said Sarah Fleet. "Is that any way to convince someone to do you a favor?"

Kalim was frowning, clearly thinking something over before he replied next. "I believe that I can take you to him," he said at last. "It is his men that we were pursuing, before we came upon you and the *rakhman*. They are not difficult men to track, as their leader is a proud man, and like all proud men he leaves his mark wherever he goes, not mindful of any dangers the desert might hold for him. I can lead you to him, but I must be the one to kill him, Mollyrat Rook. It is a matter of honor."

One look at my brother's face told me all I needed to know regarding what he thought about *that*.

"Guess we can fight over that honor when the time comes," Rook offered. "That's if we're not fighting over the dragonsoul first."

"If I choose to give it as a gift," Kalim said, "that is different than it being taken from me. For a king, or even a prince, it is a desirable thing to be generous. But I must first dispose of the man who took it, and my men will follow me for the chance to restore our honor."

"But when the dust settles, I take the soul home with me," Rook said, just to confirm.

"What you do with your soul is your own business," Kalim said, eyebrows raised. "But if you speak of the magic, then I may be able to make this gift to you, yes."

"That would indeed be *incredibly* generous of you," I said quickly, believing it almost too good to be true and not willing to let Rook's temper interfere with the deal.

"Then we shake upon it," Kalim exclaimed, offering his large, callused hand. Rook took it, and they looked for a moment or so as though they were going to arm-wrestle. Then, abruptly, Rook released him, and Kalim smiled very subtly, just like the slight shifting of the sands against the touch of the wind. "This is good," Kalim went on. "Now we are allies."

"Never needed allies," Rook muttered.

"Now, Rook," Sarah Fleet warned. "Play nice with the other boys."

"When we go back in time and you give me your tit to suck," Rook replied flatly, "then we'll talk about what I can and can't do."

"Fair enough," Sarah Fleet said. "You've got a mouth on you like nothing I've ever heard."

"And you're ugly as a brick shithouse," Rook countered.

"They do not like each other?" Kalim asked me privately. "Because you have come all this way, through dangerous territory, to see her—and this is how they speak?"

I watched them, standing next to one another, Rook tall and hard and lean, Sarah Fleet short and soft and round. They both turned on me the moment I let my gaze linger, and I looked away hurriedly, trying to pretend I'd been studying the design of one of Sarah Fleet's dining chairs.

"Boy's gonna catch flies in that mouth of his," Sarah Fleet said.

"I'm working on it," Rook replied, "but he's even more fucking stubborn than I am."

"Serves you right, then," Sarah Fleet said. "Now go on and get the fuck out of here."

Rook was stalling, I realized suddenly. He hadn't enjoyed this kind of easy banter since he'd been able to ride—and Sarah Fleet had said nothing about this dragonsoul having a voice. It was just a piece of the "mechanicals," as Kalim would have said; its form and vision were gone, and only the theory remained.

In any case, all contemplation aside, Rook was clearly reluctant to depart. If only we could have taken Sarah Fleet with us, I thought, then banished the very idea from my mind. As difficult as it was to travel with Rook, it would be unimaginable to travel with someone like Fleet.

"Thank you for your assistance," I said tentatively, finally allowing myself to return my attention to Sarah Fleet.

She tilted her head to the side and scratched her neck. "Work that stick out of your ass," she said, by way of *you're welcome.*

Rook snorted, and I tried my best not to feel *too* humiliated. Perhaps I was doomed—no one like Rook would ever find reason to respect me—but Rook elbowed me in the side, a little too hard, I thought, and I stumbled forward.

"I'll . . . consider the advice," I mumbled, then, somewhat more forcefully, "in the spirit it was given."

"Attaboy, Thomas," Sarah Fleet said. "You boys want to come back this way when all this hoopla's over, I'll be more than willing to tell you

some stories about Havemercy when she wasn't any more than a fat little baby."

Rook's jaw hardened, and I saw him stiffen. "Maybe," he said.

Just maybe.

Then we turned and filed out into the night, me to face the camel,
Rook obscured by darkness. The moon was high, the stars so bright I
could count each and every one of them and recognize a few constellations from my textbooks, but I was too distracted to remember their
official names properly.

"This is what matters," Rook said to me suddenly.

"I know," I told him. "We'll find it."

"Damn right we will," Rook replied, "even if I have to fight every
last one of these bastards single-handed."

"Well," I said, "not quite . . . *single*-handed."

"You'd just get in the way," Rook said, but I thought I could hear
him grinning, and he didn't even laugh when I dragged myself up bodily onto Bessie, which was an olive branch if ever I'd seen one. Heart-
ened by his good mood and the promise of some conclusion ahead of
us, I hushed Bessie as she snorted at my weight atop her. If I could last
this one out, then so could she, the cruel, spiteful animal.

"You coming, Thom?" Rook asked. Like I was a person, a friend,
someone to counsel.

I wiped the fresh sand from out of my nose. "I am," I said.

"Excellent," Kalim told us. "Now we ride hard."

CHAPTER TWELVE

MADOKA

People had this saying: Don't ask *how can things get worse* when you don't want to find out the answer. It was a wise saying. I hadn't stuck to it, and now here I was, being talked at by people in a language I didn't understand, with everyone shouting at once and my hand hurting so bad I thought my arm was going to fall off.

I'd stopped trying to explain myself or even plead innocent when the sound of my voice'd earned me a boot to the face. They didn't appreciate my words. I didn't appreciate theirs, either, but the thing was, I wasn't the one holding all the dice so I wasn't the one who got to call the shots, and it was shut up fast or get kicked to the sand again, so I chose the first option, thanks very much, and hoped that'd earn me a short reprieve.

Wherever Badger and Malahide were now, it certainly wasn't helping me. I hoped they hadn't gotten their asses snagged up too—if I was lucky, they wouldn't abandon me completely, but I had a dark feeling about my luck lately.

Leave it to me to get snagged by a scout while I wasn't paying attention. So here I was, held back by my hair, while some desert rider shouted in my face. He was probably asking me something, but I didn't know what the hell he wanted from me; maybe he'd wise up and see nothing was getting through. Limply, I held up my hand, the universal symbol for *wait just a fucking second.*

Wrong hand, I thought a moment later.

Everyone gasped and pulled back.

"That good, huh?" I asked, not actually thinking for long enough to stop myself from being stupid.

The man in charge's eyes narrowed, and he pointed at my hand.

"Oh, *this* bad boy," I said, holding it up; the guy yanking on my hair dropped me like I was on fire, which sometimes I felt like I was, and scurried quickly away from me. Suddenly, I realized something pretty sweet.

I wasn't the only one who was afraid of this thing.

I looked at it like I was thinking about something real hard, and then I held it up again, just to see what would happen. The men all shrank back like I was a witch or something. And hey, if that was what I needed to be to get the hell out of here, then so be it.

It explained why they hadn't nabbed Malahide yet, anyway. If *any-one* ever looked like a witch who'd cut out your eyes and use 'em for marbles, it was her.

"What can I say?" I asked, getting to my feet, brushing the sand off of me with my good hand while still brandishing the bad one like it was a weapon. "Sometimes a girl just gets a little bored, likes to conduct a few experiments on herself. Nothing you guys'd understand, of course. Really powerful magic. That kind of thing. Not the sort of mess you'd want to get caught up in, if you catch my drift," I added, punctuating my warning with a hand gesture I'd made up on the spot.

The man who'd been holding me by the hair crossed over to talk to the one who'd been shouting at me, giving me a wide berth while he did so. They murmured to one another in desert-speak, taking the time to glance over at me every so often just so I could be sure to understand their topic. Remarkable what you could still overcome with a language barrier between you. Well, at this rate, they'd be giving me a real big head.

Just like that, Shouty started shouting again, gesturing wildly all around like a playactor miming a part, then jabbing his finger in my di-rection. The hair-yanker shook his head, holding firm to whatever line he'd drawn, and I took a curious step forward. I didn't want to get *too* cocky, of course, but my hand was throbbing like fire. If they were planning on letting me go because they thought I was going to curse them with my evil-witch presence, I wanted to know sooner rather than later. And if they weren't about to let me go, then I figured it couldn't hurt me at all to stall a little, give Malahide and the Badger time to come to my rescue while my new desert-rider friends argued among themselves about what the hell to do with me, if anything.

Shouty and Hair-Yanker both looked at me like scared rabbits, and I was the slavering hunting dog coming to bring them home.

"It's rude to talk about someone when she's sitting here right in front of you," I told them, not that it mattered, since they couldn't understand whatever was coming out of my mouth anyway. "I assume that's what you're talking about, anyway. Guess it could be all about how I've ruined your dinner plans because I'm spoiled meat now."

"*Meat,*" Shouty repeated slowly, though the word sounded all wrong in his mouth, like he had something stuck in his teeth. Next to him, Hair-Yanker had his eyes on me like a hawk—or more specifically, he had his eyes on my hand.

"Hey, that's not half-bad," I told him, and took a chance on getting a little closer.

You'd have thought I'd dropped a bomb into the middle of camp, the way everyone jumped up, frantically scurrying every which way like mice caught in the granary.

Shouty yelled something—I was getting *really* sick of not understanding anything that was going on around me—and the desert riders all froze in place like he'd turned them to stone. Then he turned back to me, and I could still see the fear in his eyes, but there was something below it, like pure, hard determination, which scared me just a little.

Luckily, I was still carrying that trump card of mine. Not like I could let it go.

"Look," I said, holding out both hands this time. Everybody flinched back—it reminded me of the old woman, when she said I hadn't bathed in a while and that I'd be driving off any prospective husband who could get over my looks—but I tried not to let it get to me too much. Hell, after spending so long as someone else's helpless lapdog, it felt nice to have some power for a change.

"*Look,*" Shouty repeated carefully, but he got his tongue hooked around the beginning of the word and it came out sounding garbled and wrong. He took a step toward me, and I didn't bolt. *I* wasn't some scaredy-cat desert rider. I was a bona fide Ke-Han witch. He looked like he was afraid I'd rip his tongue out, which I guess was a fair enough assessment. It'd be a fair exchange, since his man had made my scalp pretty sore, and probably had a handful of hair for his pains.

"Yeah, that's it," I said, just to be encouraging. It made me a little sick to be this close to them—voluntarily, since I wasn't exactly being held captive any longer. Shouty had sand stuck in the grizzle on his cheeks, and his cloak was streaked with dried blood. I tried my best not to think about where it might've come from, like that poor fucking boy Badger'd bandaged up before we left. "You think you boys could find your way toward letting me go, seeing as I'm a menace and all?"

Shouty tilted his head to one side and shook it, the international symbol for *do-not-understand.*

I hated motherfucking bandits. I'd seen what they'd done to the desert village, and probably dozens of other villages before that. And for what? Probably just because they'd been bored. Just knowing I couldn't reach up and choke the life out of them was killing me a little. I wasn't exactly the most self-righteous person when it came to fancy morals, and I *definitely* didn't count myself among those idiots who followed all the rules of society without really understanding why, but what these men did for profit was downright unforgivable. No judgment from the emperor, no jail sentence, nothing. In the court of Madoka, people who preyed on and stole from the poor and helpless deserved to be buried from the neck down and left to die in the desert while the birds pecked out their eyes.

Just like that, Shouty turned away from me and hollered something for the rest of his tribe to hear. The gang looked between me and him, like even *they* didn't quite understand, then—like they'd come to some kind of mutual agreement all of a sudden—they let out a real hoot-and-holler of a cheer.

It was the kind of sound that sent shivers down my spine since it was pretty obvious that if something made the nomads cheer, it spelled bad news for me.

Shouty fixed his gaze on me, and this time there was no fear at all, just the set jaw and hard look of a man about to do something in spite of the fact that deep down it still scared him shitless.

He started toward me, and I threw up my hand like a warning. This made him hesitate, but not for very long. He was evidently the leader of the tribe—the one man who *didn't* have a free pass to cower back from the girl with the compass rotting in her hand. Bad news for me again, because it looked like he was calling my bluff. And before I could do anything he'd seized me tight around the wrist, throwing me off-balance.

The damned fever'd really messed with my reflexes. If I'd been at the top of my game, I'd never have let a throat-cutter like him put his hands on me, *and* he'd have had a nice pain between his legs for trying it too.

"Get off me!" I grunted, tugging hard and feeling only a dull throb in my hand for the effort. He was a strong guy, though, and he had a pretty good grip on me. I stamped hard on his foot—not caring that I was pretty much surrounded—and we went over and into the sand, with me falling hard on my back. Shouty landed next to me, and I realized we'd tripped over something, half-covered by someone's stinking shirt. It rolled free into the sand and I stared, unable to do anything but gawp like an addlepated brat. It glittered on the sand like fish scales but smooth, about the size of a fat marmot, if marmots were silver instead of furry. It rolled a short distance along the ground, away from us both, then stopped. I'd never seen anything like it—I couldn't even *start* to guess at what it was—but I still couldn't take my eyes off of it. Without thinking, I reached for it and all of a sudden my hand pulsed hard like something'd slammed straight into it. All I could do was curl up in a ball, gasping from the sudden pain.

Shouty made a grab for the thing, kicking up the sand around us as he scrambled after it. It was only after he managed to get hold of it that he noticed me, writhing on the ground and shaking my hand like that'd set me free once and for all. He stared down at me like he'd just seen a dog get run over by a merchant's cart—that same mixture of horror and disgust. Then he grabbed me by the arm once more, prying my fingers back to stare at the compass.

The hands were on the move again, spinning around and around like a clock gone out of its mind, which must have been what'd set the flesh to burning. Not that I was exactly in a rational frame of mind to appreciate that kind of thing.

Shouty's prize started to vibrate softly in his hand, like a broken piece of machinery that didn't know quite how to function anymore, and I stared at it, completely transfixed. I was scared he was going to drop it, but I guess he needed the other hand for holding me. For a few moments, I felt nothing. Just the sight of it washed over me, cool and calm, and there was nothing else in the world but it and me.

Then the pain in my hand started up again, so bad and so hot I couldn't help but scream at it.

Seeing my reaction, Shouty held it up to the light of their campfire, and closer to me. He'd turned the tables on us right quick, and no mistake. Fire raced through my palm, shooting through my veins and down my wrist, throbbing all the way up into my chest, and I tugged like hell to get away from him and that *thing*. I was too crazy with the pain to worry about getting kicked anywhere now. Distantly, through the red fog in my brain, I heard something come crashing through the foliage, and someone yelled in Badger's voice. It sounded like he was saying my name.

All at once, the nomads who'd shrunk back from my hand crowded forward again at the sudden invasion of their campsite, all of them on the alert and probably drawing out their weapons. I was about to open my mouth and tell Badger he was a real damn fool when all of a sudden Malahide sprang in front of him looking like a sprite from an old myth—the kind that stole babies away from their mothers and replaced them with lumps of coal or stone. She shouted something in the desert language the riders had been using—it figured she'd know that, on top of all the rest—and they all halted, staring at me fearfully.

Shouty got to his feet at once, not bothering to drag me up along with him, which was fine by me since I wasn't all that sure I could get my legs to work right now. My knees felt like they were made out of water and my blood felt like it was made out of fire, and put those two together and you got something that didn't know what the hell it was anymore: me. He said something to Malahide, who answered in turn, and whatever magic she'd been trying to work on me and the Badger seemed to work *really* nicely on desert riders, since he nodded, then gestured toward me.

"Hello, my dear," said Malahide, crouching down at my side while Badger stood over the both of us like a papa bear. "I've just explained that you were having a fit, so do feel free to continue lying on the ground foaming at the mouth."

"You're a little late," I hissed through my teeth, the pain in my hand flaring up all over again with every movement Shouty made.

"Well, you can thank your stalwart protector for our timely arrival," Malahide informed me, carefully taking my bad hand in both of hers. "I would've been much more comfortable with a chance to observe the situation further."

From above us, Shouty said something that didn't sound *entirely* rude.

"He says that you are working a magic on his prize," Malahide informed me. "Or . . . that your prize is affecting the magic. I'm not entirely sure," she confessed. "There are so many different dialects for the different nomad tribes, and I admit I only studied the main four branches . . . which leaves me at a loss presently, although I am able to communicate on a very basic level."

"I don't *want* to affect it," I told her, swallowing against the suspicion that I was about to lose the battle waging in my stomach. Whatever feelings I'd had for that beautiful thing in Shouty's hand, however much it'd entranced me before, I didn't want anything to do with it now. I could barely look at it without wanting to throw up. "I don't mean to. See what it's doing to my hand? I'm not *doing* it on purpose. If I could control it . . . If I could just *control* it . . . !"

"I can see very well," Malahide told me, hushing me kindly before I made an even bigger ass of myself. "But—well—perhaps the pain has dulled your instincts somewhat." She leaned her face very close to my own, dropping her voice to a whisper. "The perfume of dragonmetal here is unmistakable. The device in your hand has led us to an unimaginable prize."

I wished she wouldn't say crazy things like that while my hand felt like it was about to fall off. Then it hit me all at once: It was possible that this thing the desert rider was holding in his hand could very well be my key to freedom. It was what I'd been sent questing for in the first place, set free like a rat in a maze, only now I'd found my way right to the hunk of cheese at the end. So long as no one changed the rules on me in the middle of the game, I could be a free woman.

"You sure?" I asked her.

Malahide barked something in the desert tongue. Shouty hesitated, clearly not wanting to let go of his prize, and she grabbed my wrist, holding my hand up to Shouty's merry band like a proclamation to onlookers, a general holding up his enemy's head so his army would feel real good after battle.

Slowly, Shouty lowered himself to the ground, kneeling next to my pathetic body and across from Malahide. He spoke a few short sentences, and Malahide replied in her effortlessly levelheaded tones, though I could tell she was having a bit more trouble with *this* language than she had with mine and Badger's. At least there was something in this world she *wasn't* perfect at.

Shouty, clearly satisfied with whatever she'd told him, held out his prize, but it didn't look like he was about to let go of it, either. He clearly didn't trust us enough to even let us hold the thing for a minute, but I guess I couldn't really blame him.

Above our heads, Badger let out a soft *tsk,* but his sour mood seemed to have more to do with the desert rider than with our situation, or with Malahide and her method of operating.

Malahide didn't seem to mind—about whether Badger approved or not *or* Shouty's lack of trust. She reached over to examine what he was holding—what she'd called *dragonmetal,* though it was a cobbling of words I'd never heard before, and led me to believe something was being lost in translation—but it didn't look like any kind of metal I'd ever seen before.

It was *almost* like a ship in a bottle. At least, that was the only comparison my fevered mind could come up with at the minute, distracted as I was by the throbbing in my hand. My problems got worse whenever it came near, and it wasn't like I could begin to explain why. The object in question was made out of what looked like glass, with two bands around its body like the hoops around a barrel to hold it all together. When Malahide held it up to the firelight, I could see its insides—all sorts of finicky gold pieces that didn't quite look like jewelry. I could've priced it based on its materials, but something told me I wouldn't've come too close to the *actual* price. The insides were what was vibrating, I realized, and they weren't shaking but dancing, very weakly, like they'd been at the dance for a long time and were starting to slow down.

By contrast, the compass in my hand whirred like crazy and I was starting to feel like I might bite through my lip if the pain didn't get any better soon. I could be as tough as the next girl who'd grown up on the Seon border, but I wasn't too proud to pass out in front of my enemies if it came to that.

A body knew what it could and couldn't take. Too much more of this, and I'd go mad.

Shouty began muttering some further information, and Malahide looked up quickly, her entire attention on him while he spoke. When he'd finished, she chirped something that sounded like a question, and he shook his head, gesturing toward the capsule.

Malahide made a soft *tut* in her throat and shifted her grip on this dragonmetal thing so that Shouty would have to do the same. It was when he moved his hand that I saw it, a concave groove set into the topside of the whole contraption, like someone'd taken a loose part clean off of it. The imprint was about the size of a woman's palm, only shaped in a perfect circle, and just looking at it gave me a bad feeling.

"Aha," said Malahide, with triumph in her eyes.

"Uh-uh," I said, not caring that Shouty was staring at my hand with something that was more like desire than fear, but nevertheless a pretty good approximation of both. "I don't know what you're thinking, but I don't want anything to do with it. I'm not . . . I can't get any closer, Malahide. I can't do it."

"Nonsense," Malahide chided me. "Don't be so suspicious! I was merely feeling *extremely* gratified that my hunch turned out to be correct."

"What hunch?" I asked, not paying one bit of attention to that horseshit about not feeling suspicious. I'd stop feeling suspicious when she stopped giving me reason to. We both knew that much.

"Oh, merely my instinct that traveling with you would prove incredibly profitable," she said, batting her eyelashes at me, then shooting the same treatment in Shouty's direction, probably just for the hell of it. She added something in desert-speak that sounded like a solicitation if I'd ever heard one—I'd heard plenty in my time—and for the first time since I'd been taken captive, Shouty broke into a sharp smile.

Too many teeth for my taste, but Malahide didn't seem to have a problem with it.

Badger cleared his throat, and I drew in a deep breath, trying to ignore the twisting feeling I was getting in my hand, like the entire compass was set to start turning on its own axis, also known as my palm. In fact, it felt like it was about to wrench out of my skin, and as much as I'd wanted exactly that to happen countless times before, now that I was faced with the physical prospect of it, I was pretty afraid of what it'd leave behind.

"What'd you say?" I demanded.

"Just that it seems as if we might be useful to one another for longer than I'd anticipated," Malahide said innocently. "Do you know he told me—back when I'd just convinced him to show us the thing, of course—that this little beauty is already quite notorious among the desert tribes? Quite a lot to accomplish in such a short time, isn't it? He seems to feel it's quite important."

"Guess he's not just going to hand it over, then," I said, gritting my teeth as Shouty drew the dragonmetal back, tucking it carefully away in some hidden pocket in his robes.

"No," said Malahide, looking forlorn. She brightened almost immediately though, the force of it nearly knocking me over. "But I *did* manage to convince him that you were an expert in such magic, which is why you carry that piece with you at all times. I told him that if you got a better look at the device, you might be able to teach him how to unleash its secrets and aid him and his sons and his grandsons and so forth in ruling the deserts for a thousand years hence."

"Oh," I said, tentatively flexing my hand out. The pain was still bad, but not as severe as it'd been a few moments ago. I was glad Shorty'd put the damned thing away. As far as I was concerned, I didn't ever need to see it again, not as long as I lived. "So," I asked shakily, trying to ease the pounding in my chest somewhat, "what happens when he realizes I'm *not* an expert, and he cuts all our throats and leaves our bodies for the vultures to pick at?"

"I do wish you used a little bit more of that imagination toward *constructive* purposes," Malahide lamented, smoothing the hair back from my face like a sister might. "We're going to steal it long before that becomes a problem."

"Oh," I said. "I see."

I didn't—but even if I didn't have faith in Malahide, I did have faith in her methods. Shouty stared at me, and I lifted my hand—half as a promise, half as a salute.

"Good," Malahide said, and nodded once. "Let us get ready."

ROOK

Maybe Sarah Fleet had worked some of her old-bag magic on Thom's camel, or maybe up until now he'd just been too damn stubborn to get better at riding, but for whatever reason, when Kalim had told us to ride like the wind, my brother actually did.

We *all* did, of course, but it was Thom's sudden change that took me by surprise. It was almost like the desert gods had decided to stop punishing him for bringing a piss-pants like Bless over their borders, which would've gotten my goat like nothing else if it'd been me.

I'd've flown back to Kalim's camp if I could, especially now that we had only half the night left for riding. I knew I wouldn't be able to sleep through anything until we were heading after this enemy of his who had the dragonsoul in his possession—but if I'd spoken to Thom about it, I knew what he'd say. *Better to rest and get ready* or *Don't be too hasty* or *Do these petunias go with my tulips or not,* and I didn't have the time or the energy to consider any of that.

Except when I looked over my shoulder at him his face was about as determined as I felt—and it wasn't the same angry determination you could usually pick out on him, trying his best to keep his legs tight around the saddle and not get dislodged by the camel's hump. I'd have to ask him sometime if he'd *ever* rode a woman before—because if so, and she'd said she was satisfied at the end of it, then I could tell already by his technique that it was an outright lie, and he needed more pointers than Kalim *or* I could ever give him.

Guess he didn't have much time, what with all that studying, to get some real, hands-on experience.

"I'm fine," he called up to me breathlessly, the words jostled with the camel's ungainly ride. "Ride . . . like the wind . . . Kalim said . . . riding very fast . . . I'll manage!"

"Save your breath," I snapped back at him, like I would've told my girl if she started chatting during a fight, and I whipped my mount harder to catch up with Kalim.

At least we were covering a lot more ground. I'd refrain from being the pussy who kept asking "Are we there yet"—and uncharacteristically Thom hadn't volunteered to be the pussy, either—so it was anybody's guess. 'Cept for Kalim, who probably knew already when we'd meet up with his men.

I'd never staged some kind of combative strategy on ground level before, but there was a first time for everything. Maybe I'd turn out to be good at it. I could live in the desert—maybe—if it didn't mean I'd have to live with Thom's whining the whole time.

And, I guessed, I was kind of saddled with him now. I didn't trust him to be able to take care of himself, not while he was making friends with people like *Geoffrey Fucking Bighead Bless.* That just went to show you how poor Thom's decision-making actually was. He needed somebody like me, who could see right through people and all their horseshit and tell him when to say yes and when to say no.

At least until he learned how to say it himself.

I was filling my head with all kinds of thoughts about Thom because I couldn't let myself think about my girl anymore, and I didn't know any word puzzles or the things Thom explained that he used to help him get to bed, like listing ancient methods of agricultural farming from one hundred years ago until the present. Just the thought of doing that put me to sleep, so I guessed it was a good way to go about things, but describing it wasn't doing him any real favors.

Don't know what our mother'd done while she was carrying him, but *that* hadn't done him any real favors, either.

The problem with riding like this was that it didn't require any thinking. It was mindless, just staring at the camel's ass in front of you and making sure you didn't fall asleep and fall off your ride. And you'd be okay, riding until the sun rose, which eventually it did, all pale and blushing, with the dunes in front of us peeking out like a lady's behind.

"You know what that looks like?" I told Thom, when Kalim slowed his pace.

"I think I have some idea, yes," Thom replied. He looked tired but he looked like he wasn't gonna let that bother him, either, and I was pretty grateful he'd finally decided to grow a pair. And all it took was one fast slap between the eyes by Sarah Fleet's hand, bastion bless the woman. She was just like Havemercy in that respect too—'cause I'd always thought, kinda privately, that a few more flights with Have and Thom'd be fixed like new, or at least like somebody who could be of use to the world instead of a beauty mark on a high-end whore's rear end.

"I think I'll tell Kalim my little comparison," I said, seeing if it'd get a rise out of him.

"Oh please, you've already tried to kill him," Thom replied. "Now you're just adding insult to injury."

I grinned and clucked my camel into a faster trot, sending her forward over the sand. "So, Kalim," I said, feeling Thom staring at the back of my head. What'd he think he could do, I wondered, if we really did start fighting again? He'd better stand back if it came to that. I wasn't letting him get himself between two people who knew how to use a blade when their blood was up like ours could get.

"We will ride through the morning," Kalim told me curtly. There was a light in his eyes I recognized, and it was an emotion I could pretty well get behind. "If we do this, we will come to my camp."

"That kinda like your home?" I asked, just trying to be friendly-like.

"We are already at my home," Kalim replied. "You are already in it."

"Oh, well, thanks for the hospitality," I replied, just to show Thom I knew how to be polite after all. "You've done wonders with the place."

It wasn't exactly my style, but it was a sight better than being cooped up in Thremedon. Even without sticking around to wait for it to get small I could feel it shrinking; with every letter Thom got from Balfour or whatever, letting us know what everything was "becoming" or what everyone was "doing" I felt the dread chill of people going back to being too fucking tiny to look in the eye, and I was glad I'd hauled ass outta there before people started offering *me* guest-lecturing positions or places in their hat shops. But then, I'd never been one of the boys who talked about "after" the war. "After the war's over" was a favorite game they'd all played and it was one I'd always laughed at. Personally, for most of us, I didn't think there was gonna be an after. Sure, we all wanted to win, and sure, we had the means to do so. I chalked it up to being a little bit smarter than the rest and let it go at that; they'd all found out eventually, hadn't they? And the few of them that did get a word in after were happy enough with sticking to their plans, 'cept for me, since I hadn't made any.

The desert looked real nice in the very early morning, just like a lady before she woke up. It wasn't so hot I was pissing boiled water yet, and the sunlight was even glittering or whatever—you know, a right nice scene. Kalim was proud of it, and I had to admit it was more real than anything you could get back Volstov-way. Up ahead of us we were drawing back into the thick of buried statues and monuments, so it kinda looked like we were about to start knocking on some giant's door. But if there was ever a place to stop, this was probably it; you could use somebody's big toe for shade, cool skeins of water underneath the palm of a giant stone hand, that kinda thing. And on top of that, it'd hide everybody's camping gear pretty well, if not all the camels. We'd also passed a few nearby watering holes, so the situation, as they liked to say, was fucking ideal.

And I was starting to think like an honest-to-bastion desert rider.

But like I'd said before, that shit wasn't going to pull it for me, at least not for the rest of my life, anyway. I still wanted to see those Hanging Gardens, whether or not we'd suddenly gone off trail. We could still make it before summer ended. And maybe in Eklesias there wouldn't be any camels or sand or things Thom could complain about; I'd seen some of Compagnon's collection, *Ladies of the East,* and some of *them* came from Eklesias. A few prints had naked ladies doing all kinds of things to grapes that were also emotions I could get behind, just a different kind of getting behind was required. I was also willing to bet they could teach anyone, including my own brother, which end was up—if he was a willing student himself, of course—some things that Kalim and I *coulda* taught him, except it just wouldn't've been natural.

At that moment Kalim cupped his hands over his mouth and called out into a valley created by a lopsided foot with a stone bangle 'round its severed ankle, and somebody's long-lost wrist. Out of the shadows a scout scrambled to his feet, saluted, then shot off quick as a rat deeper ahead of us, on foot. I guess Kalim expected a hero's welcome.

I personally could've done just fine with some water and maybe some desert women to fan me while I took a nap.

I'd seen *those* in Compagnon's collection too. They were real good.

"You have to wonder at a civilization," Thom whispered to me, showing he was back to his old self through some mean trick of fate, "that could create such incredible monuments literally in the middle of nowhere."

"Well, it ain't nowhere," I reasoned.

"Yes, but natural resources are slim," Thom explained, "and the stones for such endeavors must have come from all over the world. It's simply not indigenous."

"You got me there," I told him, because I didn't want a lecture on what *indigenous* meant. "If you ask me, the whole thing's more funny than anything."

Thom stared at me. "Funny?" he repeated.

Some people had to have it all spelled out for them. "Yeah, funny," I said. "Bet when whoever built all this was building it they were thinking about how great they were. Wanted everyone to come and look at their big statues and think they had a big—yeah, I know you know what I mean. Well, here we are. Looking. Just not how they wanted things to turn out at all, right?"

"Oh," Thom said, and I saw him shiver even though it was getting pretty warm. "I suppose you're right."

At least he recognized *that* straight off, so maybe we were gonna be all right, after all.

Kalim'd slowed his camel down to an easy trot, so I did the same, patting my girl on the neck and telling her she'd been real good today. If she'd had a little more brainpower, she might've wondered what the fuck we thought we were doing, putting on that kind of speed and riding through the day. Couldn't explain to a camel why all of a sudden she needed to ride faster, so I guess my brother had one up on them now.

Thom drew even with me as we passed deeper into the valley of broken things, Kalim up ahead just so we knew who was boss. The statues actually made for some real good shade, though I got this feeling like it wouldn't make much of a difference once the temperature really kicked it up a notch.

"Excellent location for a camp," Thom murmured to me, and I saw someone moving in the distance, just a little ways off. Probably getting set to roll out the welcome mat, or whatever customs of their own the nomads had. The professor probably could've told me, but I wasn't about to ask. More fun to wait and see.

"Guess it's not so bad for the guys who built it, if it's still being useful to someone," I added, and I could tell that wasn't the kind of answer he'd been expecting.

"Rook," he began, then stopped himself, because that was how they did things in the 'Versity: taught you how to start things you didn't have the balls to finish.

"Spit it out," I told him. "Soon as we get to Kalim's camp I'm taking a nap and letting some beautiful women feed me dates. With any luck, they'll have traded Bless for some faster camels, and we can ride them to wherever the dragonsoul is without deadweight holding us back."

"That isn't funny," Thom told me, but I could tell even *he* was sort of hoping to get a new camel. "I was just going to ask you whether we were really about to involve ourselves in a conflict between warring tribes, but then I realized the question was probably irrelevant."

"Probably indigenous," I agreed, pretty sure I was using that word wrong, and even more sure it'd rile Thom up. He made a choking noise, and we passed into the shadow of a giant stone hand, this one held palm down, like it'd been waving at someone. Truth was, it got me to wondering what'd happen to the statues built of the airmen, a couple hundred years down the line. Thremedon wasn't the desert, but that didn't mean that someday, some poor bastard might not be walking through some ruins when he came across *my* giant bronzed head, half-buried in the dirt. Maybe only my eyeballs'd be left or something. He'd probably shit his pants. "Anyway, it's not about the tribes, it's about what the tribes *got.*"

"Have," Thom said, like he couldn't quite help himself.

"That's right," I said, grinning like a real jerk. "They've got Have."

He made a face like he'd stepped in it, and I wanted to ask him how it was that a 'Versity genius like him kept falling for the traps I set. Up ahead of us was a crooked stone forearm with a crooked stone bangle around it, and it was here that Kalim stopped.

He let out another shout, hands cupped around his mouth, and *this* time a whole mess of other voices answered his call.

We rode on, passing under the archway made by the arm. Now I could see the white tents, same style as Kalim rode with, tucked into the shadier pockets of the makeshift valley. There was a fire pit in the center for when night fell and the air got real cold again, and Kalim's men were all gathered in front of it, smack in the center of their camp. That scout'd probably told everyone to get their asses up and welcome their prince home; I could tell when a man'd been woken from good dreams, and these men had that look about them.

Still, not too bad of a system Kalim had here, all things considered.

"Welcome to my summer camp," Kalim said, dismounting like a desert breeze. Two of his men rushed up, one of them taking off the camel's extra bags and one of them leading the animal herself off somewhere to cool her down. "No man from the north has ever set foot here."

I knew what that meant, easy enough. *This is a big fucking honor, so don't fuck it up, Mollyrat Rook.* I got off my own camel easy enough, though no one rushed up to *me* to ask me what I wanted, guest of honor or not. The dulcet scrabbling of my brother making an ass of himself followed, and Thom landed with the dull thump of his feet against the sand. At least he'd landed on his feet. It was good progress; he wasn't shaming me in front of anybody, or shaming himself.

Kalim barked something in desert tongue and his men hopped to, springing forward to take our camels like the sand they'd been standing on had turned into red-hot coals.

"The animals must drink and rest," Kalim explained. "They have done good work, but soon we will have to ask more of them."

"Sounds good to me," I said, stretching my arms out. I was used to riding. It didn't bother me the way it bothered some people, but even *I* was glad to get a minute to spend some time on my own two feet. "Nice setup you've got yourself here, Kalim."

Someone in the crowd made a noise like a camel right before it spits, and a scuffle broke out in the crowd. Kalim's attention whipped around at once, and I took a step in front of Thom, putting a hand on Kalim's knife in my belt.

"Is that—is that Rook?" someone asked in a weedy little voice that was all too familiar to me by now. "I say, this is highly inappropriate. I've already *told* you I don't plan to escape. Where would I go? I haven't the slightest idea where we *are*! I merely wished to investigate whether— *Oof.*"

The scuffling died down, and I could only hope it was because someone'd seen fit to wind that little weasel with an elbow to the gut.

"Geoffrey," Thom said, though he didn't sound particularly happy to see him.

Kalim's face darkened like he'd passed under one of the shadows from the statue. "*Rakhman,*" he said, spitting into the sand. "Your trial will have to wait a little longer. For now, we have men's business to discuss." Kalim raised his voice and started yelling at his other men, all of whom straightened up quick and stopped picking their ears or muttering to each other.

It was the same trick Adamo'd had. Raise your voice loud enough, and even the meanest sons of bitches couldn't pretend to have cloth ears.

"I wish I understood what he was saying," Thom confessed, standing at my elbow.

"Probably just getting 'em all pumped up to go and take back what's rightfully theirs, all that good stuff," I reasoned. "You hear one speech like that, you've heard 'em all. 'Sides, you majored in enough useless shit for one person. Gotta leave some for the rest of the idiots."

"Well," Thom said, with a look on his face like he knew something I didn't. "It wasn't *entirely* useless."

I didn't have time to ask him what he meant by that, since the desert riders were cheering again. Same as in Volstov—same as everywhere— that meant the proclamation was over and it was time to get to work.

Kalim turned back to us with a sheen of sweat covering his face. He was grinning like a mad dog.

"We will take the day to formulate a plan," he told us. "Then, when night falls, we will hunt down the man who has stolen my right to succession. We will fight like honest men, even though he has forsaken that right, and there I will win. Then we will take from him this ... what the witch named *dragonsoul.*"

"Sounds like a good plan to me," I told him. "You got any ideas of where to start looking?"

Kalim nodded, the smile slipping from his face. "The leader of this tribe does not live off the desert, as we do. He finds it too taxing, per- haps, or the rewards too small. Much *easier* to take from those who are weaker than he, I believe is the philosophy he's undertaken. He has be- come a lazy man who steals what he needs from others instead of earn- ing it for himself. Therefore, he spends much of his time on our land's borders, near the mountains, where the terrain is not so rough and there are many little villages."

"Bandits, huh?" I asked, rubbing at the handle of my new knife again. Thremedon was too well protected to ever have a problem with bandits, but there were always men *like* that. Their attitudes were the same, no matter what you called them.

"That is not a word I recognize," Kalim admitted, scratching his chin in thought. "But I can tell by the look on your face that it is a just perception."

The other nomads had started to clear out of the center of camp— probably because it was in an area less protected from the sun. One of them had been charged with the responsibility of keeping Bless trussed up like a holiday goose, I saw, and I felt nothing but sympathy for that poor son-of-a. They could've at *least* taped Bless's giant gob shut for him. Though maybe it was easier to tune that noise out when you didn't understand what the fuck he was saying. Bless had a peeling sunburn on his nose and sand stuck to his cheeks. He looked worse than Thom *ever* had, and the desert was supposed to be his thing. Fucking rat bastard didn't know what he was doing, and it was a good thing Thom and I hadn't let him fuck us two ways the way he'd fucked himself.

"Come," said Kalim, starting off toward one of the tents and clearly expecting us to follow. "Men cannot strategize on an empty stomach."

"You've got an excellent point there," Thom agreed, practically mowing me down in his sudden eagerness to pick up the pace. I was starting to think he had a hollow leg—either that, or he was sweating the pounds out just as quickly as he packed them on—but either way, it was mind-boggling to watch him go at it. Made sense that a Mollyrat'd still be hungry, all these years later, even after getting the hell out of Molly in the first place.

One of the desert riders held a tent flap open for Kalim, and he ducked inside, followed by Thom, with me bringing up the rear.

It was real posh inside, even better than a room at Our Lady, because it didn't have any pretenses. Instead, it stank of camel and leather and sweat and sweet incense on top of that, a few cushions thrown here and there, some soft skins tossed around. No chairs or tables or anything like that, but at least it wasn't flopping down on hard ground. This was more than just a makeshift tent in the middle of nowhere to keep the sun off your face. This was Kalim's version of a palace and we were living like kings now—or at least like princes.

"What is mine is yours," Kalim said. And then, with a wink, "At least, for now."

"Yeah, we'll see about the rest," I promised him, and took a seat when he gestured we should make ourselves comfortable. I took a big pillow next to a group of smaller ones, which Thom gratefully sat down at, and then a few young boys brought in trays of dried-up fruits and milk that smelled a little too much like goat for me to get too comfortable after all.

"Drink, eat," Kalim offered. "My strategists will join us."

Thom didn't have to be told twice, and I had to start eating just so there would be something I could get my hands on—there wouldn't be anything left over if I let Thom at it first. I guessed it was only polite to

be all *Mm, delicious* when a man like Kalim was giving you the delica-
cies of his homeland, so we tucked in real good.

While we were eating, the men in question joined us: only three of
them, one old and one a little too young and the third one dark and
scarred and grinning like it was his birthday. I liked the third one the
best, but only because he reminded me a little of Ghislain. They didn't
look alike, mind, but they had the same happy attitude in the face of
danger, and it felt good to work in a group again, instead of just a team.

"This is Bakr," Kalim said, indicating the old guy, "and Jabr," meaning the one who was barely out of his diapers. "And this is Abbas; he is
our enemy's brother."

"Hello!" Abbas said proudly.

"That is the only word he knows," Kalim confided, "but he is ruthless as a lion, from which he draws his namesake."

"Hello," Thom replied helpfully, around a mouthful of wrinkly nuts.
"Can we . . . you know, I mean, if we intend to fight his brother . . ."

"He swore a blood oath to me," Kalim explained. "The penalty for
betrayal is death, and besides! Our enemy is my brother as well, but this
does not slow my hand!"

I snorted—guessed there was some guy out there hoarding all the
women, but that was okay. I was all bluster right now; hadn't been with
one since I started traveling. Just wasn't in the mood, and I was glad
there was nobody around to notice it, save for Thom—who wouldn't've
noticed it unless it danced up to him dressed like a sweet prune with a
side of cool yogurt. Sometimes you had to mourn somebody more important than all that, and I guessed this was probably less embarrassing
than wearing a black band around my arm and a dark shawl over my
head sobbing at funeral pyres and praying for forgiveness, or whatever
it was rich wives did for their dead husbands.

Man, but Have'd be laughing at me if she could've known what I
was thinking.

"So," I said, "any specific plans, or is it just kick 'em where it counts
and take what we came for?"

This wasn't the technical talk Kalim could understand. He struggled over *where it counts* for a moment, then turned to consult, in his
own language, with his advisors. No matter where you went, even in
the desert, there was still all this discussing to trip up any man in power.
Sure, three men, one who was clearly bell-cracked lion-wrestling crazy,

wasn't exactly the same as having to talk to everyone in the bastion and the Basquiat before you could put a rule through, but in principle it was totally the same concept. I felt bad for everybody, except not for th'Esar, who was number one right now in my shit-book—the only book I'd ever write or read, 'cause I kept it all up inside my head where no one could touch it.

"Shall we consult among ourselves?" Thom asked.

"You got yogurt on your face," I told him.

"How embarrassing," he replied, hurrying to wipe it off.

I wished he was a kid or an adult, not this in-between monster I had to take care of but who kept insisting he could take care of himself. I'd never been like this, and if I couldn't understand it, I sure as hell couldn't explain it.

Then again, there were a lot of things John'd been through that Hilary hadn't—I could only assume based on the way Thom was acting—and it wasn't like I wanted him to know the things I knew. Better for everyone that he didn't. I guessed I couldn't help it, being angry, and one day it'd stop, if we were lucky.

"We don't know anything about the desert or how to fight on camelback," I said, snorting at myself. "So I think we'd better leave this one up to the professionals."

"I've studied a few major desert campaigns, actually," Thom said slyly. "Remind me to tell you about them sometime."

"Now if only we could put that knowledge toward something useful," I said.

"It's possible," Thom sniffed. "Once we see what their plan is, in any case."

"You're bad at bluffing," I told him.

"Don't be a bitch," he replied.

We were really getting something going—a kind of rhythm that I didn't actually hate—when Kalim cleared his throat and we both turned our attention back to him, probably wearing about the same face, like *excuse you* and *what the hell do you want* and a little bit of *we were fucking talking*.

"I do not mean to interrupt," Kalim said, crouching down to enjoy some of his own food, "but my friends wonder about your ability to participate in this fight."

"Don't worry about me," I said. "I can take care of myself."

"I understand that," Kalim replied. "It is not you about whom they are concerned."

We both turned to look at Thom this time, who colored and wiped at his cheek. All the yogurt was gone, but I wasn't gonna tell him that *now* or anything. Wasn't the time for it.

"I see," Thom said.

"He's right," I added flatly. "You can't even stay on that thing, much less do it while people're fighting. You're not ready for it."

"I don't want to be left behind either, Rook," Thom began.

I shook my head. "No way," I said. "I'm not letting you."

"Aha, this is a matter for personal discussion," Kalim noted, scooping some yogurt up with a piece of flat bread and chewing thoughtfully. I wished that Abbas guy would stop staring at me, but I wasn't going to start anything with our allies; I was put out but not fucking stupid. Save all the fight for when it counts, Adamo used to say, and I was finally starting to understand the strategy. "I will let you two discuss this matter, brother to brother. I merely wished to explain that we would not be able to account for someone who is not trained in battle."

"We don't do that in Volstov either," I told him. "Don't worry, he's not coming, and that's that."

Thom's face was mottled and mulish, and I knew I'd catch hell about it later, but for the time being the matter was settled. Thom'd only hold us back when we were fighting, and I knew I'd lose sight of the real prize if I had to keep my eye on him while trying to learn this new way of warfare. Not a war exactly as I knew it, but a battle nonetheless, and I wasn't going to flake out on it or do it half-assed just because it wasn't my usual.

Just hoped my camel was up to it.

She had a lot to live up to.

CHAPTER THIRTEEN

MALAHIDE

The circumstances were not ideal. Nonetheless I had to come up with the bare bones of a ceremony, trading in a magic I did not entirely understand, to impress a group of bandits with whom I could not entirely communicate. The site of this battle was Madoka herself, and Badger was leveling looks my way that were extremely distracting. For example, it was clear that if I did something to harm her, he was going to kill me—or at least try.

Little did he know that the last thing I wanted right now was for Madoka to be harmed.

I was not the magician who had done this terrible thing to her in the first place, nor was I some new mongrel who desired to further her troubles to benefit my purposes. She was useful to me, yes, and never more useful than she was now, but I was not about to employ her very body to her own detriment.

I had a great deal at stake at the moment as well. Because of my own twisted sense of compassion, I had bartered my life with the nomad leader, whose name, I had come to understand, was something that sounded like *Abbud*. He thought it quaint that I referred to him as "leader" in his own language, and requested that I continue to call him that. Embarrassing as it was, I acquiesced and deigned to flatter his rampant ego, for he held all the cards at present in our little game, and a bit of flattery never hurt anyone, when used with discretion and care.

In any case, on the chance that this little plan of mine did not go as I was hoping, then it would be my life on the line alongside Madoka's. That should cheer Badger up somewhat; at least he would be able to see me held accountable for my own actions.

However, I did not intend to allow things to progress in this fashion.

I would have assured Badger that matters were less dire than they appeared, but I could not afford to be seen as consorting with my allies to put one over on Abbud. The only person with whom I could consult was Madoka, and I was grateful for the language barrier between us and our captors.

"So you've got a plan?" Madoka asked.

She was looking, as Nor would have said, quite shitty indeed. Her skin was pale, her eyes rimmed with bruises, and I was reluctant even to look at her arm, since there was nothing more I could do for her, and to see the extent of her condition would have sobered me beyond the point of inspiration. It was best if someone was allowed to keep their wits about them.

"There, there," I told her, trying to be helpful. It was not within my nature to be gentle unless it was completely necessary—and even then, a sense of urgency destroyed all true gentleness. Madoka saw through me—not completely through, I hoped; there were still some secrets I wished to keep as mine and mine alone—and she scowled at me. If only she and Badger would just accept my assistance and come to hate me later on, when my actions actually warranted it! "I do have a plan," I continued. "I intend to stage some manner of ceremony."

"Great," Madoka said. "That's great."

"And, as you may have suspected, you are the guest of honor," I concluded. "It is a pity that I don't yet know myself what this ceremony is."

"Oh," Madoka said. "This is getting better and better."

"Don't be cross," I told her, and then, for further reassurance, "I *am* working on it as we speak."

That, in any case, was entirely the truth. I was still in the process of cobbling together something appropriately bizarre that would at once be believable while working to our advantage. These men wanted to see a witch draw out the full potential of the magic they had so clearly stolen, and I needed them to be dazzled enough—not to mention cowed enough—by our little show that we were able to sneak the prize in question entirely away.

"I've told them I need to prepare you," I explained. "Or that I need to reverse you—I'm really not certain either way. But any confusion of language might work to our benefit. It lends to the air of mystery, don't you agree?"

"Don't know what to say," Madoka said. And then, a little quieter, "I have to go near that thing again, don't I?"

"Most likely you do," I admitted. "I can make no promises, either. You saw the place where that compass of yours fits, did you not?"

"Guess I did," Madoka said, and I was impressed once again by her resolve. There were not many women—or even men, I'd wager—who would've overcome their own pain in order to notice a small detail like that.

"So you admit that the best course of action is to use that as our 'magic'?"

"And just hope for the best?" Madoka asked. She wasn't exactly impressed by the clumsiness of the plot, and I couldn't entirely blame her for that. I was asking a great deal of her; everyone was. And even if she was as strong as a bull, even a bull would have stomped his hooves and protested a burden of this weight. Any lesser woman would have given up days ago, sat down in the sand, crossed her arms over her chest, and refused to travel any farther.

"And just hope that your hand isn't torn off, that these bandits do not cut it off, that something significantly magical happens to assuage their desire for showmanship, and that we are able to run away with that thing—Badger will have to carry it, of course—before we ever come to cope with this issue of a ceremony in the first place," I concluded. "We shall have to convince our friend out there that you must be alone with this piece in order for the magic to work. So the act you must put on while I attempt to translate for you . . . It must be consummate."

"Oh," Madoka said, looking startled. "So I don't have to go through with the whole hoopla?"

"Hopefully not," I said. "We must find a good piece of wood and knock upon it for luck."

"Well," Madoka said, "at least you're being honest with me."

"Come now," I told her, "I am *always* honest. Let us make a few ridiculous demands from this man. That should lend to our air of absolute authenticity."

"What, you mean like the blood of a virgin and six hares collected by the light of the full moon? That kind of thing?" Madoka asked.

"Oh, no," I told her, shaking my head gravely. "The full moon won't occur for weeks yet, and I *don't* think we want to spend that long in the company of these bandits, however hospitable they have been toward us thus far."

"Yeah, real hospitable," Madoka muttered, glowering. "I feel just like the emperor making his rounds."

"Ah, but I imagine you're far more handsome than he is," I confided with a wink.

"Thanks," said Madoka, not at all amused by my antics. She was so terribly sober that it stung me to the core. Between her and Badger, I was liable to develop a complex about my wiles and charms.

"A lady always appreciates a good compliment," I told her, a gross hint on my part, but a gift as well, since Madoka seemed to enjoy rolling her eyes at me. Anything that would distract her from the growing problem in her hand—which was now spreading to her arm.

I swished my skirts in a businesslike fashion and set off to have a conversation with my new acquaintance Abbud. Madoka trailed reluctantly in my wake, clearly not at all enjoying her part in this endeavor. I was sorry to put such a burden on her when she was already so beleaguered, but she was my trump card and the ace up my sleeve. *She* was the witch they were all so afraid of, where by contrast I was simply a foreign woman, and not a terribly imposing one at that.

Without her, I wasn't very impressive. That was all it came down to. It was a change of circumstances that I wasn't yet accustomed to, but I was certain I'd see the humor in it soon enough.

True to what I already knew of the leader of the bandits, he was sitting near the extinguished fire pit and sharpening a good blade. Perhaps he'd sensed something on the wind, or perhaps he was merely honing a stolen item to bring out the best of its potential. I *did* hope it didn't have anything to do with our own little party, but there was only one way for me to be sure of that. I settled myself down next to him, arranging myself as daintily as I could when the seat beneath me was little more than a tatty blanket spread over the sand. There was less shade here, since the pit had been built near the center of the camp, but it didn't seem to bother Abbud any. He was better accustomed to such climes, whereas I was going to be in need of a good parasol if I wished to keep my complexion.

Madoka hung back behind me, practically looming over the both of us, though Abbud was not a small man. Her reluctance could very well work to our advantage in this situation, though. To those who did not know what made her hesitate, Madoka portrayed the expert witch—one who was too good to sit down in the sand with the rest of us commoners. It was an unspoken show of superiority, whether she meant for it to be taken that way or not. She was practically a natural at this.

Abbud neither spoke nor looked up when I sat down next to him, which was a sign of just how unimportant I was in the tribal hierarchy, I supposed.

"She needs some things for the ceremony," I said, keeping to my role as the servant of a great witch. I didn't like to brag, but it was something I was exceedingly good at, as well. *Keep your eyes down* and *don't speak unless you're spoken to* were the only two rules a servant had to follow, and those just so happened also to be the basics of espionage.

It was rare that I ever played a role so suited to my natural personality.

Abbud paused in sharpening his knife, but when he looked up, it was at Madoka, and not me. I wasn't exactly his "type"—a fact for which I was exceedingly grateful. He grinned at her—Madoka evidently satisfying some requirements I myself lacked—and then turned his attentions back to the knife.

"What things?" he asked, only he used a different word for *things* than I had, which was a very small thing to be embarrassed over, yet I was kicking myself all the same. There were so many strange little variations in the desert dialects that I hadn't yet managed to get a solid grasp on all of them. In fact, I was rather ashamed to admit that I'd let them go neglected in my studies, simply because I hadn't ever needed them before today. Now I was paying for my hubris.

"Freshwater," I said at once, "but it must be collected under the light of the moon. She told me the ritual cannot be performed until nightfall," I emphasized, on a sudden inspiration. Under cover of darkness, we could escape much more easily—not to mention that we wouldn't have to concern ourselves with making our way through the desert under the full sun. Madoka and I hadn't discussed beforehand the nature of the items I'd be asking for, but somehow I knew she would approve of this extra detail. "She will also need fire. And something made of copper," I added. "It must be pure to counteract the gold workings in your magic, she says."

"What're you telling him?" Madoka asked, whispering at me sharply.

"*And* she requires the pelt of some great predator of the desert," I told him, taking her words for instructions. "Your camels won't do at all."

"That . . . may prove difficult to find," said Abbud, his tone of voice not remorseful in the slightest. *Convince me,* it said. "Fire is simple enough. That we have much of. But the other items—the water we may take readily enough from the oasis, but it is more precious to us than gold or simple copper, another thing you have requested. As for the animal, it would take a campaign of at least a few days to stalk down a suitable beast, not to mention the difficulty in killing it."

"He's being coy," I told Madoka in her native tongue. "Testing you, I think."

"What?" Madoka asked, looking tense. Underneath that, she was angry—the very picture of the weapon of a violent god. "What kind of test? Can't I just hold my hand up and threaten to blight him and his ancestors with it? Because you just say the word, and I'm on it."

"I don't think that will be necessary," I told her, working very hard to keep the smile from my lips. "We're looking to cement his trust in us now. Intimidation is all well and good for convincing a man to open up negotiations, but it can also breed suspicion. I want everyone to be well away from wherever you are to begin our little ceremony, not creeping at the sides of the tents."

"Well, great," Madoka said, kicking the sand in an idle gesture of frustration. "How am I supposed to pass a test when I can't even understand the questions?"

"*That* is what you have me for, Madoka," I told her smoothly, figuring that was enough conversation to suitably convince Abbud that what I was about to say had come from Madoka and not myself.

She made an irritated noise when I turned away from her again, and I silently made a vow that I would somehow make it up to her.

"She says that she has seen a trinket of copper on one of your men," I told him, which was almost the truth. The man who'd taken Madoka so roughly by the hair that night had been wearing a locket, badly tarnished. The sort of thing a young girl kept as a memento of her lover, though it didn't surprise me that a bandit would allow it to fall into such a state. Copper *was* copper, however, even if I'd pulled the idea straight out of my ladylike rear end. "The fur does not have to come from a live animal—she never said as much, that was simply your assumption—and she points out that many of the rugs and blankets in your own tent are the skins of once-powerful beasts."

He nodded, looking not at all put out by my arguments, which he seemed to accept came from Madoka herself. My hunch had been right, then, and he was simply testing the keenness of her mind as it related to her supposed expertise in the field of magic. We were asking Abbud to trust us with the most valuable object in his camp; it was my job to ensure that we seemed worthy of that trust.

"As for the water," I continued, when it seemed he had nothing to interject, "she understands what a precious commodity water is, to someone whose home is the desert."

"My home," Abbud agreed, releasing the knife to stretch out his arms and fingers as wide as they would go. I got the feeling he wasn't just speaking of the camp.

"Precisely," I agreed, as Madoka shifted her weight behind me, clearly bored but unwilling to show it. "You value water above all else, and that makes you clever, but in order to obtain the power of her magic for your own, you must put your desire for that power above everything else. Do you truly wish to hold the land in your hands? To secure your rule not only for yourself, but for your future sons and *their* sons, as well? Such power takes a sacrifice. If you are unwilling to make it, then you do not deserve to wield this magic. Perhaps it is too great for you," I added, bowing my head as if in apology. I did hope I hadn't gone overboard with the threats, or implied he was *too* much like a Charlotte-born chicken. Goading a man's pride was a dangerous game, and it required the ultimate finesse. I would have managed it without question if I were speaking in my own language, but there was always the chance I would not wrangle his words properly, and one or two of them may have gotten away from me. These were delicate negotiations, wherein the slightest awkwardness could sour everything.

I could feel Abbud staring at the top of my head, while I kept my eyes firmly averted from his face. I'd told Madoka that now was not the time for intimidation—and it most certainly wasn't—but I was fairly certain that the only thing guaranteeing my safety right now was the fear Abbud had of my companion. I was, and not for the first time, exceedingly grateful for her presence. Rotting arm and fevered mulishness aside, she was utter perfection.

"It will be done," Abbud said at last, after a few long moments of breathing like a wildebeest. "The items will be brought to *my* tent. The witch can perform her ritual in there."

"She must be alone," I cautioned him, just in case he was getting any ideas about taking himself a witch-bride. "And left *uninterrupted.*"

"In my tent," Abbud assured me, "no one will disturb her."

I supposed I'd have to be satisfied with that, and pray to whoever was listening that he included himself in that account.

In the hours we had before nightfall, Madoka and I took the time to carefully hash out our plan, such as it was—if it could even be ranked as a plan at all.

Madoka was the only one who could pass along information to our third ally—to make sure Badger knew his duties—since of everyone, Abbud's men were least suspicious of her. Or most suspicious, but watching for other cues than a simple human betrayal.

During all this ruckus, when the members of the camp were focused on their leader's tent and the actions within, Badger would cut loose a pair of camels and make his way to the back of Abbud's tent. It would be difficult to miss, since it was the largest. Madoka would then pass the dragonmetal out beneath the tent to him, and afterward escape herself. That took care of the pair of them, and I could concern myself with my *own* getaway when the time came.

It was merely fortunate for everyone that I didn't require a camel of my own. I could ride with Madoka for the initial burst of speed, but since I didn't tire, it would prove unnecessary later on. I didn't intend to burden Badger unduly—any more than I had to, of course—and stealing three camels when only two were needed definitely qualified as such a burden.

Besides, if the distraction I was planning worked out the way I'd hoped, no one would be looking in my direction when the time came for me to slip away.

In my personal luggage, I carried with me certain things that a woman in my position must necessarily have about her at all times. Among them was a small ration of gunpowder, suitable enough to create a flash explosion, though the methodology was clumsier than that with which I normally preferred to work. The fire I'd requested would be more than enough to set it off, and the *copper* I'd requested would turn the flames to an unnatural blue color—one I was willing to bet these men of the desert had never seen in their lifetimes, nor knew of from their grandfathers, et cetera. The fur and the water were for Madoka herself, in case things sprang out of control too quickly, or the pain in her hand made her clumsy. I planned to have her soak the skin and wrap it around her own body as protection—though she would still need to be swift in order to avoid any risk of danger.

"You *must* light the compound only after you've passed the dragon-metal out to Badger," I told her. "And *only* when you've got one foot out the door yourself, do you understand?"

"I'm starting to think it might've been easier just to stick my hand in the damn thing," Madoka said gruffly.

I patted her on the back. A very sisterly gesture, I thought, though her body stiffened when I touched her—as always. "If you change your mind, you can always try that instead," I assured her, "and see what happens next. I have no idea what would occur, but of course it is all up to you in the end."

Madoka snorted, an eloquent noise that let me know all too well what she thought about *that* as a backup plan.

Then we waited.

I enjoyed my position, almost invisible—though every now and then I did feel the weight of some bandit's eyes upon me, measuring my movements. It was a lucky fact indeed that they were far more caught up in the promise of some great spectacle, and for the time being, that spectacle had become—in their minds—manifest in Madoka herself. She could look after herself even in this state; I fully trusted her. And this distraction gave me ample time to pass all the stages of our plan over to Badger, who was currently enjoying life as a prisoner, tied efficiently to a palm tree.

At least he was in the shade. Besides that, I'd already slipped him one of my own knives, and he'd be out of bondage easy as a prostitute sleeping with a rich man, as they said back in Thremedon.

After that, I was left to my own devices. I pretended to be very interested in a local tree in order to avoid the advances of a lonely young bandit who was apparently desperate enough to try anything and less interested in more archaic forms of magic than the mundane sort two bodies could achieve when they rested together. I was flattered, I wished to tell him, as it had been a long time since I found myself on the receiving end of such attentions, but now was hardly the time. In any case, I gave him the slip, attended to the camels, assessed all possible cogs in the gears that might potentially arise, and prepared myself for everything I considered a viable threat to our well-being and, even more important, our success.

I was ready by nightfall.

All too quickly, it was evening, and I found to my surprise that my own pulse had quickened with the excitement of it all. Tonight we were going to make off with a prize more valuable than I had ever before brought back to the Esar. I would be rewarded, certainly, but it was not the prospect of riches or esteem that fueled my excitement. Rather, it was the promise of another job well accomplished, the most difficult mission my liege had ever sent me on, succeeded and surpassed. There was nothing so satisfying as meeting the Esar's expectations. He gave me the tasks he would not or *could* not trust to anyone else, and I continually delivered. This mission would be no exception.

If I hadn't been surrounded by bandits and murderers, I might well have kicked up my heels to express my delight.

Then again, I couldn't afford to rest on my laurels just yet. No need to count the chickens when the eggs had only just been laid.

"Derga will bring your witch her ingredients," said Abbud, slipping up to me like a shadow in the night. "I will bring her the magic."

"Very good," I said, trying to sound as though everything was going according to plan. For all intents and purposes, it seemed to be.

The rest relied upon Madoka. They were leading her inside already and I was now no more than the playwright who must be content to sit in the audience and wait until the curtain fell to learn just how it had been received by the masses. I drew closer to Abbud's tent.

Good luck, I thought. And with all luck, she'd perform very well, and wouldn't need it.

THOM

Needless to say, I had not been deemed fit by either my brother or Kalim to ride with the rest of the party into battle.

Admittedly, I did not believe that I was the best suited for such a job, nor did I particularly wish to learn the skills of such a trade so quickly before I would be called upon to use them. I was not, nor would I ever be, a desert rider. They were right not to trust me or encourage me, and I should have been grateful that—at the very least— Rook cared enough about my well-being to stop me from doing something quite hazardous. Sensibility and good common sense told . me all these things, and there was no reason to ignore such principles now, when they'd aided me my whole life.

And yet I was incapable of feeling anything other than left out.

I spent the rest of the day sulking and attempting to enjoy the views; my ink had run out, but I still had my graphite pencils, and here and there I attempted a few notes upon the statues, the garb, the camp life itself. Everyone operated efficiently, like the gears in a well-made machine. Everyone clearly had a designated place, or duty, and they saw to it without any confusion among the ranks. No one seemed to be speaking, and yet they worked with a synchronization that I had only ever imagined coming from a great deal of communication. At any given point there was no one who was not seeing to some matter of business—but then, I was observing the tribe under extreme duress. This was an observation of how a foreign tribe prepared for battle, and hardly a slice of normal life. And yet it reminded me of something— another time I had sat to one side and diligently attempted to parse the working mechanism of fourteen men who appeared to have as little as possible to do with one another outside the sphere of their work.

Every man here had a purpose, except of course for *me*.

Come now, Thom, I told myself, *it is important to record history as it happens.* And when were theories useless? I was a thinker, not a fighter, and the world was always in need of thoughts.

It was simply that those hadn't exactly proven themselves useful, either. The basic "theory" at hand was that I needed to stay out from underfoot, and so there I was, perched upon the giant thumb of a forgotten civilization, their last memory in the entire world, watching things happen in the present without actually being a part of them.

That was the kind of man I was.

It was extremely disheartening.

Once again, I reminded myself, I did not want to be a man like Rook. There were a thousand flaws in that way of living, not the least of which a dark venom that hurt even those he presumably cared about. That had never once appealed to me. Nor did I wish to be the sort of man who, like Rook, could easily take another human life—and would, tonight, when all went well. That was what disturbed me most of all: I wasn't even nervous, or afraid that my brother would be hurt by all this. I knew he wouldn't. All that harmed him physically rolled off his back like water off a duck; he was naturally suited to violence, and violence was naturally suited to him. Again, it was not the sort of ideal I personally strove toward.

But there was that terrible feeling again—the one that told me I was exactly like Geoffrey, except with even less of a practical bent. To what had I actually managed to apply myself? I had survived this far, but never once had I stuck my neck out. I was always there, in the background, observing and recording, but all that was starting to wear thin. My thoughts were selfish, messy and tangled. I hated considering them. That which had once been my strong suit—or so I thought—was now like chains around my ankles. I kicked my feet sullenly against the wind, feeling and acting like I was a child again, hiding from Georgie Pluck, who spent far too much time around a brothel for a child of thirteen, and who enjoyed giving me at least one bloody nose per performance hour during the ladies' shows.

"You look like you ate something that didn't agree with you," Rook said, leaning up against the wrist at my side.

"Mm," I replied. Not my cleverest comeback, but I was hot and I was glum, I was sticky, I smelled of camel, and even the smallest of my triumphs was truly nothing in the face of all that greater men than I had managed to accomplish in a shorter amount of time, and with less self-doubt.

"You don't honestly fucking think I'd let you fight, do you?" Rook added. "I mean . . . you're not exactly Molly's finest."

"I am aware of my shortcomings, thank you."

"Whatever," Rook said. He folded his arms over his chest and didn't pull away. At least I could tell myself that he hadn't completely acclimatized to the desert just yet. There was some chance left for me that he wouldn't join with Kalim to rule the sand, leaving me to become his biographer or something else that required very little of my actual presence.

"Whatever," I agreed.

"So stop sulking," Rook snapped. "It just doesn't make any sense. 'Sides, it's up to me to fight on Have's behalf. You don't have to be a part of it."

"But I would like to be," I said, with more candor than I usually exhibited. "I *want* to be a part of it."

Rook didn't say anything at first, and I wondered briefly if I'd managed to surprise him. Little did he know I actually wished to be of some use to someone—to anyone, though to *him* at this point in time would have been preferable. Maybe, judging by my behavior and failure to perform even the most basic of duties, he *hadn't* known, and this had come as a shock to him. But when I looked over at his face to try to read his reaction he was just staring out into the lowering sunlight, his mouth a tight line and the muscles in his jaw hard as twine.

"Never mind," I said. "Just be careful, I suppose. Don't get hurt."

"Can't promise that," Rook said, because he never pulled any punches, nor did he ever lie—unless it was to suit him. "You know. Fighting's dangerous."

"I'm aware," I told him.

"And you're a jumped-up little 'Versity boy," he added, looking at me sideways.

"Stop that," I warned.

"Probably couldn't punch your way out of a fight with a kitten," Rook continued, looking thoughtful. "One little scratch and the fuzzball'd have you cornered."

"That's not fair," I said, the blood starting to pound between my ears.

"In fact, I should probably tell Kalim I think we should leave you back with the pregnant women and children," Rook concluded, a little *too* smug. "I mean, if something bad happened to the camp while we were all gone, they'd end up having to defend you from the enemy."

"Enough!" I shouted and, in a moment of extreme insanity, I threw myself at him.

He'd been nothing but awful to me throughout our travels. I'd been abused, mistreated, put down, insulted. He'd threatened to leave me behind, feed me to the camels, and it was all nothing in comparison to what I could expect from him in the future. We were supposed to be brothers; we were *supposed* to be good to one another.

This was not any definition of *good* that I could understand.

However, I honestly had no plan for how I'd beat him man-to-man, and he had me pinned in the sand after I got one pathetic little blow in, clipping his chin with my fist and hurting my hand, I suspected, more than I'd managed to hurt him.

"Feel better?" he asked me, while I tried to catch my breath.

"How could I possibly?" I demanded.

"Wanna have another swing at me?" he offered. "Makes you feel good though, doesn't it—just punching someone."

"Bastion damn it, Rook," I said, but he was right. I was acting as I always blamed him for acting. It wasn't very pretty. Also, there was sand in my mouth now, not just my nose, and I inhaled too quickly, choking on it.

Rook clapped me—a little too hard—on the back, finally letting up, and I used that moment of weakness to tackle him again. This time I did hit him, soundly and solidly, a full three times before he overpowered me. My hand was throbbing now, as if to ask why on earth I'd insisted on putting it through such abuses, but I supposed I could be grateful it wasn't my head. This time, as I tried to regain my breath with my face pushed firmly into the sand beneath me, I heard Rook laughing.

"You dirty fucking bastard," he said. "Guess I've got less to teach you than I thought."

It was almost—*almost*—like being complimented.

"Peace," I said, the word muffled, and he pulled back just slightly. Nonetheless, I knew that the same underhanded tactic wouldn't work a second time; it was lucky I had no intentions of continuing the fight as it was.

"Nasty," Rook said appreciatively, and I pretended the blush on my cheeks was the hot flush of battle rage inside of me.

It might seem plausible.

"At least tell me there's something I can do," I said.

"Yeah, actually there is," Rook replied, taking me completely by surprise. "Kalim doesn't want to leave the, uh, *rakhman* with the women and kids, so he's gotta take him with us. But he'd just be a liability, so you're gonna look after Bless."

"Oh," I said.

"Think of it like this," Rook offered. "He's a low-down dirty prisoner and you're the jail warden. It's an important fucking job. If he says anything, we all give you full permission to rough him up a little. Just gotta follow through with your punches. Don't be such a Cindy about 'em."

It appeared that I was being given brawling advice by my brother. At last, a true moment of bonding, and it was over fisticuffs.

"Oh," I said once more.

"Get real angry again, just like that," Rook said. "Take it all out on Bless if you wanna; I sure as shit wouldn't mind, and nobody *here*'d give a fuck, either. Probably cheer you up." He paused to laugh, then sighed. "We're riding out a little before sunset, so think about how much you hate me and that camel and sand and the sun and daytime and nighttime and sleeping outside and moving and everything that doesn't involve sitting on your bony ass and reading about other people doing things, and Bless'll shit himself with how scary you look, trust me. He won't try a thing."

"Is that official advice?" I asked wryly.

"Are you kidding?" Rook asked, pushing off the statue's remnant and heading off through the sand. "Out here, I'm the fucking Esar."

I supposed, for all intents and purposes, that he might as well have been. Since leaving Thremedon, I had never seen my brother so loquacious about anything. If I'd been making a study of it—as I suppose I was, in my own, unofficial way—I'd have said the desert was the cure for whatever melancholy he'd been experiencing. Of course he *would* take to such a beastly place, the landscape as wild and unforgiving as he himself was. I wanted to love it, however misguided my reasons, but there was altogether too much sun and *sand* for that ever to be a real possibility. Yet I still couldn't begrudge the place, if only for what it'd done for my brother.

Experimentally, I made a fist. It looked all wrong for some reason— or at least rather knobbly and ineffectual as compared to when Rook did it. Then I imagined slamming my fist into Geoffrey Bless's face, and though it was a terribly violent image, I found myself not particularly averse to it. I was quite sure that I had never been as angry with *anyone* as I'd been with Geoffrey—not even that little Pluck rat—the night the nomads had come upon us and my brother had challenged their leader to a duel. I was not often given cause to worry after Rook's safety, but the uncertainty of the circumstances coupled with the unfamiliar territory had created just enough room for the shadow of doubt in my mind. If I hadn't been so concerned with not disrupting the fragile peace we'd made with these desert men, that night I *would* have struck Geoffrey. How *dare* he lead us into such trouble—and it didn't seem to matter much now that inadvertently he'd also led us into Sarah Fleet's lap. He was clearly not our ally. We were only lucky that Kalim had gotten to him before *he* was able to get to us.

As the sun began to set, I gathered up the few notes I'd made. There weren't many, since I'd been so distracted by Rook's impromptu lesson, but they would have to suffice for the time being. It was rare that a man was given the opportunity to observe a nomad camp in the state it was now; apparently all it had taken to change my attitude was being thrown down to the sand a few times. Or perhaps it was just the possibility of having my revenge on Geoffrey, although either option said rather unsavory things about me. Best not to dwell too closely on such thoughts, I decided at last. After all, Rook hardly ever did, and though he was decidedly *not* the kind of person I wanted to be taking life lessons from, his way of doing things seemed to work enviably well out here.

After I'd packed my notes, I made my way back into the camp proper, taking care not to get in anyone's way as they went about their business, some towing camels while others sharpened their weapons. I could only hope that my *own* camel would somehow get lost in the shuffle, so that I might be able to trade it in for a slightly more equable model, but that didn't seem too likely. Kalim's men were too organized ever to let such an error take place.

I was doomed by the very efficiency I had previously been admiring in my notes. Truly, irony at its best.

Kalim's men had been holding Geoffrey captive in a tent somewhat nearer to the center of camp—so that they might more easily keep an eye on him, I suspected. None of Kalim's men spoke Volstovic, aside from the one with the frightening face, Abbas, who seemed to take great pleasure in creeping up behind me and proclaiming "Hello!" as loudly as possible whenever he had a spare moment. Afterward, he'd clap me on the back and wander off until the next round, which I was never quite able to anticipate.

Nevertheless, it seemed Kalim had fully explained the situation to them, for when they saw me, Geoffrey's captors all began to move at once. Two of them rose, pulling Geoffrey to his feet while another pushed past me, making his way toward the camel enclosure.

"Thomas?" Geoffrey inquired, his voice thin and parched like he hadn't been using it—which seemed terribly unlikely, considering the source. "That *is* you. Hurrah! Have you any idea what's happening? Are we leaving tonight?"

"Kalim has a score to settle with a rival tribe leader," I explained, hustling to follow as Geoffrey's guards dragged him out of the tent and secured him on the newly arrived camel. I was deeply grateful that mounting the prisoner on the camel had not been a part of my duties, but then I realized that most of these men had seen my own efforts where camels were concerned, and doubtless had decided to compensate for them.

I neglected to inform Geoffrey that, in reality, we were heading out after a better prize than anything tribal warfare might have to offer. I didn't trust him—especially after hearing how lightly he held the lives of the natives in his esteem.

"Oh," said Geoffrey, his eyes following a man with a long, cruel-tipped spear as he passed us by. "I had a feeling it was something like that. You can tell by the way they wear their cowls, did you know that?"

"Indeed," I told him sternly. "And they refuse to leave you here with the women and children, so you've earned the lucky position of accompanying us."

It was hardly *us,* if I was being entirely truthful, but Geoffrey didn't have to know that.

Once the sun began to set in the desert, it went down very quickly. Already the sky overhead was growing dark, and I realized that many of the men were already mounted in preparation for the ride. There were women too, gathered into groups for solidarity, or bidding their men a last farewell. As someone who'd very nearly been left behind, I felt nothing but sympathy for their position. It was difficult being the one left behind while someone you cared about rode off to commit great deeds of heroism.

In the distance, I could even see Kalim making his final preparations alongside his strategists, but I didn't see Rook with them.

"Are you riding with *me*, Thomas?" Geoffrey asked, apparently feeling in much better spirits now that he'd been tied to his camel. "Truly, I appreciate the show of support. I must admit, I'd half expected you to go riding with that beast of a character Rook, but I see now that all my worries were unfounded."

"And here I'd have thought you had more important things to worry about than little old me. I'm real flattered," Rook said, appearing out of nowhere in that disconcerting way he had. Somehow, I managed to keep from jumping clean out of my boots. "Here," he added, slapping a knife handle first into my palm, which I'd held out on instinct. "If, and that's *if*, mind, you get into some kind of trouble, use this. Might have to use it on him if he pulls anything; you never fucking know with weasels." Rook nodded toward Geoffrey, who gulped rather showily, and I quickly tucked the knife away.

"I see we've graduated from fisticuffs rather speedily," I said foolishly, because I didn't know what else to say.

"Can't intimidate a prisoner with something like that," Rook explained, with a look toward Geoffrey in case he'd forgotten we were still speaking of him.

"Really now," said Geoffrey, in a huff. "I hardly think *that's* necessary. Thomas and I have known each other for years! Why, we're practically brothers. Of the mind, I mean, but still! It's a very close bond. It's one ruffians couldn't *possibly*—"

"That's enough," I said coldly. Geoffrey fell silent at once, which at least meant that he hadn't taken leave of *all* of his senses. Once Rook was gone—to play with the big boys, as it were, leaving us at our children's table—he might not find me quite so intimidating, but for the time being he did fall silent.

"Better mount up soon," Rook said, clapping me on the shoulder for the second time that day. "We're leaving pretty quick, and I know how long it takes you."

"Very funny," I muttered, and he strode off to his place at the front of the lines, up ahead with Kalim himself.

I mounted my own camel with a certain grim determination that served me well—I didn't fall off the animal, in any case, which would have made Kalim doubt even the small responsibilities he'd granted me, nor did I shame myself in front of Geoffrey—no longer a friend and certainly no longer a colleague. A shout went up from the ranks ahead, and I saw the few remaining women and children scurrying to either side of the crowd of mounted warriors. I gave Geoffrey a sharp look, just to let him know I was keeping my eye on him, then we were off.

Never before had I been privy to such a sight—men and camels moving together like the waves of a desert ocean, purposeful and momentous. They moved silently, strange as shadows, in a single rush. It lacked the overwhelming majesty of a dragon midflight, but it offered the same immediate danger as dragonflight did—the mechanisms different, the basic principles the same. To suddenly become part of such a group was something I'd never once dared to imagine for myself. For the first time, I had no desire at all to take notes or record what was happening in any way. If I were to take my eyes off anything for even a second, I would miss a vital moment of the action, and that was an unbearable thought.

"You aren't *really* going to use that knife on me," Geoffrey said, over the thudding of camel's hooves.

"So long as you don't do anything to warrant it," I told him, knowing perfectly well what sort of comfort he could derive from *that*. I was becoming more and more like Rook with each passing day. It wasn't what I wanted, but neither did it seem to signal the end of the world, as it might once have done.

Geoffrey fell silent again, and as we rode on I found it rather preferable to fumbling for awkward methods of conversation about topics on which we assuredly did not see eye to eye.

I had no knowledge of how long it would take us to search out our enemy. I'd been privy to the strategy talks, and Bakr had named the place in the desert he thought it most likely for the enemy to be sequestered at this season, but my knowledge of the desert was not extensive enough that I could recognize it—and the scales of measuring distance on their maps were unfathomable to me. In essence, I was riding blind into the wind, and even though I knew I would not be joining the others "in the thick of it," as it were, I was still a man of their number. Humbling, sobering, and exciting all at once. Somehow, I *did* like it.

Time passed, and the sky overhead changed into true night, a dark inky blue above our heads. The troops—I had no other word for them save for a Volstovic approximation—had become precisely spread out along the sand, so that no rider was crowding up on another, and I could barely make out the twin dots that were Kalim riding alongside my brother. For all I knew, they were using this opportunity to race again. I felt a little left out, perhaps missing the days when it had simply been the three of us riding toward Sarah Fleet's ramshackle little house in the middle of nowhere—or even just Rook and me traipsing through the Volstov countryside—but there was nothing to be done about that now. I studied the constellations without knowing their names, and kept a sharp eye on Geoffrey as my duties dictated. I didn't think there was much he could do with his hands tied to the camel, but he'd always been a mean kind of resourceful in school, avoiding bullies with methods I could never quite divine. At the time, I'd found his willingness to bend the rules in the name of learning rather admirable, but needless to say, my attitude since then had found reason to change considerably.

I settled into the rhythm of riding after a time, accepting the fact that we would reach our destination whenever we came to it, and nothing I could do would speed things along, one way or another, nor ease the aching in my rear end as the saddle jostled against it. In fact, I'd accepted it so completely that it startled me when Geoffrey began to speak, and I privately cursed myself for not paying better attention.

". . . coming up on an oasis," he was in the midst of saying, voice bouncing along with his mount. "Do you see it, just up there? Well, it's partially obscured by the dune, but it's tucked all neat into the basin, a little pocket of greenery. Do you think that's where they've made their camp, Thomas? It seems the likeliest place, to me."

"You're the expert," I said, in a tone not at all meant to flatter his ego.

The riders around us quickened their pace. I quickly switched my attention to keeping up with them, and even reached a hand across to speed Geoffrey's mount along as well. We bounced violently alongside one another, and I prayed to the unnamed gods of the desert that I wouldn't fall off and shame my name any further than I'd already done. I wound my hand more tightly in the reins, as Rook had taught me, and I allowed the others to draw ahead of us somewhat.

"Guess it doesn't make sense for us to stick our necks out, now does it?" Geoffrey murmured, a little bit slyly, as he followed suit. "Let them ride in. They can take the sweat and blood alongside the glory if that makes them happy, then afterward, we come along and take all the rest."

"A very tidy outlook on life," I told him, horrified.

"You've always been such a prude," Geoffrey replied.

I didn't have much time to be offended. The first riders had crested the hill and sound erupted from within the oasis valley.

If we hadn't found our targets, then we'd found *someone,* and I didn't much envy their current position.

Kalim's riders had already encircled the camp, camels cresting the dunes and disappearing just beyond them. There were no smoky blasts, only individual battle cries rising up together on the air in a single uncoordinated chorus. It chilled my bones. I couldn't see how the men down below would have any hopes of defending against such a swift and unexpected attack; the advantage was strictly on Kalim's side—*our* side rather—and if he'd managed to catch the other tribe off guard as it seemed he had, then there was no hope for them whatsoever. The best they could wish for, if their honor provided for it, was a swift surrender.

I was so caught up in the sounds and the sights of the battle—my camel now close enough to the dune's edge to witness the carnage down below—that when I next glanced to my riding companion, perhaps to make some manner of commentary on the scene, Geoffrey and his camel were no longer beside me.

My heart plummeted from my chest to my gut as swiftly as an anchor tossed off a ship.

"Geoffrey," I said, as though *that* would do any good. The sound of my own voice, small and childishly begging, offended even me.

It had been my job to see to it that the prisoner didn't escape, and I had fucked it up most royally.

I turned all around to scan the horizon, but Geoffrey had at least not ridden off in any of those directions. I couldn't have hoped to chase him down if he'd had a head start; he was far more accustomed to riding than I was, and begging my camel to work for me rather than against me had never worked before. Why should it start now? The camels, unlike their riders, had no reason to hate Geoffrey.

But if he had not ridden off, hoping to escape the punishment of the *rakhman* with his life, then he must have gone straight into the midst of battle.

I peered down into the oasis valley—so much fighting was enough to turn my stomach, and I wished there *had* been call for a surrender to avoid such unnecessary bloodshed. *And all over an item that wasn't theirs to begin with,* I thought, honestly saddened by the events.

Then I saw him—the only man avoiding the skirmish—no longer on his mount, but sneaking through the trees toward what appeared to be the largest central tent. Somehow he'd slipped free of his bonds.

I was off my camel at once, and I only almost fell. Scuffling desperately through the sand, I stumbled after him. This was incredibly foolish, but looking away from him in the first place had been foolish, and now I had to risk my own life in order to remedy what my own carelessness had done. I had to hope no one saw me creeping after Geoffrey—both of us hopping like shadows from one rock to the next, through the tents, as real men fought all around us, blade against blade.

I was so busy focusing on not losing sight of Geoffrey while still maintaining my cover that, in the end, I wasn't paying attention to much else. I lost sight of Geoffrey all at once as he disappeared behind the large tent, which appeared now to be his goal all along. A camel charged past, without a rider, and I was just standing to head after Geoffrey into the tent when someone barreled straight into me.

I heard a cry of outrage—a woman's voice—right in my ear, and we both went down, her on top of me, hitting the sand hard. There went my cover, I thought dizzily, and also, there went Geoffrey.

Then someone grabbed me one-handed by the collar and I made a move for my knife, only to discover it was gone. I'd lost it somewhere, maybe when I was creeping like a thief through the brush after Geoffrey. I was probably going to die here, I thought, as my captor demanded something of me in a language that wasn't Volstovic.

Neither was it Kalim's language, I realized a moment after that.

In fact—from my studies back in the 'Versity—I actually recognized this one. The person shaking me by the throat was speaking to me in the Ke-Han tongue—words that I could even translate from my elementary studies.

I lifted my eyes to a woman's face. It was strong-boned and dirty; there was ash streaked over her nose and a cut on her cheek, and in the moonlight she was as pale as a ghost, her lips cracked and white. She looked ill—but beyond that, I could only wonder what in bastion's name a Ke-Han woman was doing all the way out here.

"What have you done with it?" she shouted. "What have you done with it?"

I could understand the words, if not the question. I was about to formulate my reply—a resounding *Please repeat*—when I felt the point of a knife against the small of my back.

"You smell of dragonmetal," another woman's voice said, this one curiously tinny. "I *do* wonder how you're going to account for that."

CHAPTER FOURTEEN

MADOKA

Everything was going fine. Well, as fine as could be, given the circumstances. So everything was going to shit but I wasn't dead, just on my way toward dying—captive and presumed to be some kind of witch, currently standing inside some bandit's tent, all the while staring straight at the very thing that was giving me all this trouble in the first place, about to light some explosives and duck for cover.

Everything was going fine. That was what I would've written home to Mother, if I'd known anyone who could write and if there had been anyone who could read it.

The thing in front of me sure was a beautiful piece of work. Too incredible to price, probably worth ten times my weight in gold—the sort of piece master thieves fell in love with and dreamed about the rest of their lives, and never got up the nerve to steal. And here I was, about to steal it.

But stealing it required touching it—something I really didn't have the nerve to do. Even as I stood there next to it, watching the weird white liquid inside of it swirl, my whole arm was throbbing—and I was keeping a good, safe distance.

I took a deep breath and inched myself closer.

Fuck all, but it hurt like devils gnawing on my arm. I kinda wished

I could just lose all feeling in it so I could get this over and done with. Pass the piece out under the tent to Badger, who was waiting outside, then strike the flint Malahide'd given me, run like hell, and hope these nomads feared magic more than they trusted their instincts. We just needed some time.

But man, I really didn't know if we were gonna pull ourselves out of this in one piece.

Outside, there was a whole lot of shouting. Figured, I guess, since this was an important ceremony and all. Big magic. Praise the gods. Maybe Malahide was whooping them up into a fine frenzy so, when the explosion did go off, they'd all pass out from excitement and buy us some more much-needed time.

Meanwhile, I was sweating like a beast and stinking the whole place up, and with every step I took, the blood in my arm twisted and pounded and burned, and the murky liquid inside the glass case twirled like a summer storm.

Part of me—the bad part, the crazy part, but weirdly enough *not* the part wracked by the fever—wanted to put my palm flat against the space made for that compass. It was the perfect fit, but I had no idea what'd happen if I did it, and the *smart* part of me didn't ever want to know.

Malahide had friends back in Volstov. She was gonna have them look at me. She hadn't stuck a knife in anyone's back yet and that was a start. Maybe I didn't trust her as much as I trusted Badger, but at the same time she was doing all this so she could get the *three* of us out of the shit we'd stepped in. In other words, she still had good use for me, and she was keeping me alive—definitely not to slit my throat in the desert.

Honestly, I didn't know anymore. And knowing whatever was going on in her brain on top of having to know everything that was going on in mine would've been the final nail in my coffin.

I edged closer to the glass and the liquid and the swirling and the dull light glinting off the metal. Looked like gold, and I *knew* gold. There were also some metals I didn't recognize—they sure as hell weren't local—laced all up the side, as delicate as the patterns on a butterfly.

Then I got too close.

White pain flashed behind my eyelids, not quite so delicate. I made a sound I really wasn't proud of, grateful as hell to be alone while making it, and dropped down to my knees, putting my back between myself and the liquid. The pain died down, slowly, ebbing like the tide.

If I couldn't even get close enough to touch it, how the hell was I supposed to hand it over to Badger? I was gonna fuck us over on this one. I could feel it.

The shouting outside was getting louder. Sounded like it was coming from all sides now. Either I was hallucinating or some kind of fight had broken out—maybe it was all part of Malahide's plan.

I couldn't be the broken wheel on this caravan, I told myself. I was gonna do this if it was the last thing I did, which it damn well was shaping up toward being. See it through to the end, do something important for a change, and even if no one else was around to see it or know about it, Badger would remember. It was more than some people got in their lives: just somebody to talk about them for long enough to make a difference.

I turned around to face the piece, determined to finish what I'd started. Even if it had been by accident, a foul bit of luck.

But the piece was gone, and the tent flap was waving in the wind like someone'd just run through it.

Well, I thought. *Fuck me.*

At least the pain was less now that I could actually hear the sound of my own brain and the thoughts bottled up inside. I scrambled to my feet and started after the culprit—it was the only thing I could think of doing. I couldn't let my only ticket to freedom run out on me like that. The ceremony was fucked—but everyone else would probably know that when they saw a thief making off with their treasure.

Outside, it was cold, the way all nighttimes were in the desert. And things definitely weren't the way I'd been expecting them. Not even a little bit.

Where were my fawning admirers, hanging tight like Malahide'd told them to, concentrating on making the magic work, all wills turned to one and all that? It'd sounded good even to me, and they'd definitely bought it hook, line, *and* sinker, so what the hell'd happened here?

A second later, I had my answer. It was a common enough scene for any country girl.

Raid.

Sure was a neat piece of luck they'd pick now, of all times, to make the hit. Since everybody'd been gathered around the tent for the cere-mony, it'd probably been like stabbing fish in a barrel. That explained all the shouting. Now things were a little too quiet at the center of camp, meaning all the fighting had fanned off, people chasing their en-emies down while others just plain tried to escape. I was alone here—I wondered briefly where Malahide and Badger were, before telling my-self they could both take care of themselves and I was the one they were probably worried about—and then I saw him, a thief if I'd ever laid eyes on one. And I had. A whole bunch of them, as a matter of fact. He was skulking through the mangy scrub brushes that speckled the place and I wasn't gonna let him get away with stealing what I'd been plan-ning on stealing before he'd ever clapped eyes on it.

Hell, he didn't even see me coming, and I definitely wasn't at my best that day. He ran straight fucking into me, on top of all that, and we both went down.

It took me less time to get myself together after falling like that. Maybe he was a little slow—even more reason why I shouldn't let him put one over on me. When I grabbed him by the collar I half expected him to fight back, but he just stared up at me with these big green eyes, full of total confusion, like I was doing him a wrong and not the other way around.

"What have you done with it?" I shouted, more than a few times, probably more than was strictly necessary. I could've asked him a few other choice questions too, but right now this was what my brain seemed to have focused on. I wasn't doing too well. It was a miracle I'd managed to get one up on him at all.

Still, he just stared back at me like he didn't know what the fuck I was saying—and then maybe he started to get it, but didn't know how to reply.

His face was too pale for him to be desert people, I realized, but it wasn't pale enough for him to be Ke-Han. He wasn't from around these parts; the green eyes were what cinched it for me. Maybe he didn't look exactly like Malahide, but there were enough similarities for me to fig-ure this guy was probably from Volstov.

I just hoped he wasn't as nuts as the other person from Volstov I knew.

And then, like I'd conjured her up just by thinking about her, Malahide appeared over the Volstov thief's shoulder.

He went stiff, and I realized Malahide'd pulled a real nice number in thinking to pick up a knife somewhere.

She said something to him in Volstovic, looking pretty pleased with herself, like a cat in the fisherman's house when he was off cheating on his wife. The thief stiffened, then replied to her.

"What're you talking about?" I demanded. The last thing I needed was to listen to a conversation I couldn't understand and waste more time not knowing what was going on.

"He says he is not the culprit we seek," Malahide translated. "I suppose you know something about that?"

"Someone took it," I said. "I must've blacked out for a moment— it hurt too bad to see when I got too close to it—and the next thing I knew, the tent was flapping and the piece was gone." I glanced at my captive. No dragon-thing on him, and we would've seen it. "He was the only one out here," I added, angry and sheepish at the same time. "Fuck this, where the hell'd it go?"

"What's happened?" Badger asked, coming up on my side and nearly getting himself a punch square in the jaw for his troubles. I pulled back just in time, and I'd've apologized, except it was already clear I was a little on edge. Badger'd forgive me. "I waited, but the sounds of fighting . . ."

"It's a raid," I said, my jaw tight. "And someone stole the thing right out from under me. Guess we aren't the only ones who wanted it, after all."

"Let's not lose our heads," Malahide said, still holding on to the Volstovic with one hand, the knife pressed against his side with the other. She was looking around in the dark with her sharp eyes, like maybe she had a mind toward hunting the real culprit down and frying him for her supper. If I weren't so furious with whoever'd gone and stolen the dragon piece from me, I'd have almost felt sorry for him. Having Malahide as an enemy was probably a fate worse than death.

Distantly, I could hear the clash of weapons, and the bandits shouting to defend their camp. *Good,* I found myself thinking. Let them see what it was like to be totally defenseless against an attack. They might not learn anything from it, but at least it was well deserved.

The Volstovic piped up with something that sounded like a question, and Malahide shook him like a mama dog shaking one of her puppies.

"What is *that*?" Badger asked, apparently noticing him for the first time.

"Thought he was the one with the sticky fingers, but he doesn't have anything on him," I explained. "That kind of thing's pretty hard to hide. Plus, I'd know if it was here." I glanced down at my hand, just to check.

As I'd thought, it wasn't close by. Not anymore.

"He'll *escape*," the Volstovic finally said, in desperation, speaking with words I could actually understand. It startled the hell out of me, since I'd just assumed he had no idea what I was saying, same as I had no idea what *he* was saying, and both of us were even. Apparently we weren't.

"Well, fancy that," said Malahide, looking at him with sudden interest. "A man with a brain in his head." She added something in the Volstovic tongue. "Perhaps he knows something about our thief after all," she translated, for our benefit.

"You know him?" I asked the Volstovic. They'd shown up at around the same time, after all. They might even be partners, for all I knew, and he'd just passed the dragon-thing off to his buddy before running straight into me.

It took him a minute to think about how to reply, biting his lip and squinting his eyes and looking about seven different kinds of constipated, before he finally gave up. Looking deeply frustrated, and more than a little bit sorry, he nodded.

Obviously, he understood more than he could speak. That was just swell as far as I was concerned since I didn't plan on letting him do a lot of the talking anyway.

"That settles it, then," said Malahide, continuing before I had time to ask what exactly was settled. "He can't have gone far. Not without becoming caught up in the fighting itself, and I doubt that he would risk such a prize amidst all this chaos."

"So you think he's just hiding somewhere, waiting for it to die down?" I demanded, with a sharp look at the Volstovic, just to see what he thought about *that*.

"I think that's a distinct possibility, but our chances of finding him grow slimmer the longer we stand around talking about it," Malahide said, suddenly sharp. It wasn't just me who needed that dragon-thing bad. "Split up," she added. "Madoka and I will take the north, Badger can take the south. The size of the dragon piece in question *should* hamper the thief's movements slightly, but we should still be on our guard."

"Understood," Badger said, and he touched my shoulder before striding off into the night. I hoped he wouldn't do anything stupid. There was no telling with soldiers.

"You, my dear little captive, will come with us," Malahide said, and the Volstovic blanched. "Ah, you really *do* comprehend! How marvelous. You mustn't think I begrudge you giving me the opportunity to relish my native tongue once more, but my companion here would feel *extremely* left out. Do you understand?"

". . . Little," the Volstovic said hesitantly. His accent wasn't bad, but he looked like he was about to piss his pants. He eyed me nervously. "*A* little bit?"

"Let's get a move on, yeah?" I said, not particularly interested in bridging the gap between our two distinct and beautiful cultures right now, or whatever the hell Malahide was trying to do.

"Of course, my dear," said Malahide, springing forward and dragging our captive along behind her. "Now the hunt begins in earnest."

I followed her swift footsteps as we cut through the main camp, passing the place where the tents for sleeping had been cloistered together. Here, farther from the center than the chief's tent had been, the sounds of battle were much louder. The dull, dry thud of camel hooves beating the sand filled the air, and my ears rang with the clash of metal on metal. Someone howled like he'd been stabbed straight in the gut, and I caught the Volstovic flinching at the sound. Of course he'd shown up at around the same time as the raiders; it made sense that he'd have friends among their ranks. What *didn't* make sense, as far as I was concerned, was what a Volstov was doing running around in the desert in the first place. It wasn't exactly my first choice for a vacation spot, and he didn't really seem to be the rugged adventurer type.

Then again, he was probably asking himself the exact same question about me.

I checked the compass hands, which were useless anyway, pointing all over. Then I headed in the direction of the tents. Good place to hide; made sense. Good place to start.

We tore into the first one like wild animals, knocking aside a makeshift hammock strung up between two of the oasis trees. Fortunately, the lifestyle of the bandits made it pretty easy to search their tents—they were small and necessarily left uncluttered, easy to pack up and pack out as quick as you liked. That left no room for a sneaky thief to hide himself, and if he'd ducked inside hoping to wait it out until the battle'd ended, he was about to get himself a real nasty surprise. I figured I'd pretty much lucked into the better team, since Malahide had that whole trick of following her nose to get to the prize, but in close quarters like this, I guessed it must've been harder to tell where the smell was coming from. And considering all the shit that was flying around us . . . We'd have to rely more on my hand than her nose, anyway.

After the fourth tent, though, she pulled up sharp, and the Volstovic went stiff like he thought he was about to get a knife in the back.

The compass hands were whirling now, like they didn't know which direction to point.

I stared at Malahide, hoping she had some better clue.

"West. Toward the water?" she mused, in her strange little voice. Then she picked up the pace, and I threw myself after her, ignoring every signal in my body that begged me to just lie down and sleep for the next fourteen years or so. "He can't *possibly* be thinking of swimming out, can he? He'd get it wet . . . though perhaps it doesn't rust . . . ?"

"He was crazy enough to steal the thing right from under my nose," I pointed out, which only made her pick up the pace. Meanwhile, our hostage followed, tripping now and then over his own feet, his mouth set in an unhappy little line. I didn't blame him one bit, except of course he'd gone and gotten himself involved in the first place, so maybe he'd think twice next time before he pushed himself into other people's crazy business.

We came to a rockier area, where little scrubby bushes were sprouting up between the cracks, and the path narrowed, like the one Badger and I'd followed to find the desert village. Now we'd come to the end of the road as far as the oasis was concerned, and my hand was starting to pulse. I didn't even have to check the compass to know we were getting closer.

"You first," Malahide said to the Volstovic, adding something in his language. I could only assume it was just in case they were in league together; she must've wanted the thief to see a friendly face and let his guard drop before we all came swooping down on him.

Reluctantly, with the hunched shoulders of someone well used to being bossed within an inch of his life, our captive took the lead. *Not exactly a vision of bravery*, I thought. Malahide plowed right in after him, ducking and weaving around the shaggy palms like some kind of expert, while I followed clumsily behind. The Volstovic stumbled against the wet stone, and she yanked on his arm, pulling him back neatly to his feet.

He muttered something that might have been his thanks, then fell silent once again.

I scraped my leg against the rough bark of one of the trees, and privately cursed up a storm. I wasn't normally such an ox when it came to navigating on my own two feet, but this pain in my hand was throwing me for a real loop. The fever hadn't gotten any worse, but it wasn't getting any better, either. I had to find the little rat-turd who'd stolen what I needed to get back to my old self. My brain was cooking inside my head—it had to be, with how hot I was all the time now—and there was still some chance I could save it. Getting that dragon stuff back was the only way I knew how to do it, and I was damned if I was going to let a common *thief* get in my way.

There was something different about the air over by the oasis pool—a strangeness I couldn't quite put my finger on. Maybe it was how distant the sounds of the battle suddenly seemed—as though we'd moved far enough down the camp so as to be removed from the danger completely—but I knew in my gut that it wasn't just that. The old woman had always told me that your gut sense was the only one worth paying even a smidge of attention to, since it only spoke up when it had something important to say.

I had no idea what my gut was trying to tell me as I followed Malahide farther down the path toward the oasis pool; but whatever it was, I had a feeling I wasn't going to like it very much.

Then the Volstovic let out a shout.

He broke into a run, and Malahide took off after him, leaving me— as always—to bring up the perpetual rear. There was something near the lip of the pool that I couldn't quite make out—it was too dark for that—but it was definitely a big something. Too big to be the dragon-thing, too. The Volstovic was the first to reach it, and he pulled up short, like all of a sudden he wasn't so sure he wanted to be this close to whatever it was. His back was rigid, and his hands shook at his sides. Malahide reached him a short few seconds later and she immediately dropped to her knees, turning the thing over with her delicate white hands.

I saw two eyes, glazed and fixed in a staring face, before I had to look away. It was a body, lying suspiciously far from the battle currently raging around the camp.

I wasn't exactly new to a sight like this. Hell, it'd been home for a while there; the capital'd been full of death the days following the war.

This was a personal death, though; a man whose throat had been slit. I couldn't tell whether he'd been our hostage's friend or not, but they definitely knew each other, because as soon as the hostage took one look at the dead body he turned away and threw up. Malahide let him have his moment, checking the guy's pulse, but I could've told her that wasn't necessary. I knew a dead body when I saw one.

"Did you know him?" Malahide finally asked.

The hostage nodded. "Y-yes," he managed, wiping his mouth with the back of his hand.

"Who was he?" Malahide pressed.

The hostage struggled, obviously at a loss for words, then said something to Malahide in a language I didn't understand, with an apologetic look at me.

"Spare it for someone who needs it," I told him, a little too harsh. He winced and I felt bad, but not bad enough to do anything about it. Then I turned to Malahide. "What's he saying?"

"He says that this man was once a friend of his," Malahide replied. "He was a researcher in the desert."

"Yeah, well," I said, feeling uncomfortable. "If he doesn't have the goods, who does?"

The pain in my hand was receding. Whoever had the dragon piece now was already moving farther away, far enough away that I could start thinking, in fits and bursts, for myself. Malahide's mouth tightened.

"He had it once," she explained. "I can smell it on him."

"Not anymore," I said grimly, and looked out into the darkness to see nothing but the sand. He was getting away from us, but we had two up on him: my hand, and Malahide's nose.

We were gonna track him down, no two ways about it.

We were gonna find him.

ROOK

It'd been a hell of a long time since I'd been in the middle of a real fight. That shit back at the inn on the other side of the mountains didn't count, barely even got my blood up, though it relieved the itch at the time. But it couldn't get me going like a real fight could, and this was a real fight.

Some of the principles were the same, and some were totally different. Keep your legs tight so nothing and no one could come up and knock you off your mount—that one was basic. But I wasn't used to having a mount that spooked in battle, and maybe Kalim's camels were used to being caught right in the thick of it, but the one I'd got in Karakhum sure as shit wasn't. That was fine, just meant I had to be a little more forceful with the reins, dig my heels in a little harder, that kind of action. If *anything*, I knew how to be persuasive no matter what—or who—I was riding.

'Course, it wasn't the same as how things used to be. I guessed things'd never be that way again, and there wasn't anything I could do about it. No one to talk to while I fought, no one to tell me what I was doing wrong and—more likely—what I was doing right. A couple of times I found myself coming up next to Kalim, but he was in his own world and I was in mine; the two of us might as well've been completely alone for all we weren't paying fuck-all attention to one another.

He was a good fighter, Kalim, serious and down to business, with no unnecessary flourishes. I'd had a good time fighting him one-on-one, so it stood to reason I'd have a good time fighting *with* him, both of us on the same side. There were some guys who just understood the rules: how to cover someone's back and how to lead a real charge, and you didn't have to worry about covering their asses because they knew what they were doing as well as you did. *That* was what I'd really missed. Working in a group that knew its head from its ass.

One of the bandits came shouting toward me and I pushed a sudden burst of speed onto my camel, getting up a good momentum to knock him over. I guess we'd really surprised them, since a lot of them had just run out screaming over the desert like ants, without even taking the time to mount up proper. Bad luck for them, but it made picking 'em off real easy. I caught his sword against my blade—all sorts of jokes you could make about bringing a knife to a sword fight, but I figured there were *more* jokes you could make about bringing the weapon you didn't know shit about using to any fight at all. I'd never had to use a damn sword before, and I wasn't about to test out learning one in the middle of the desert. Besides, I was quicker with a knife, and on my camel I could keep the advantage easy enough.

On my right side, I could see Kalim giving ground against two enemies. To anyone else, it might have looked like he was struggling, but I'd come to know a little something about the look on his face right before he pulled a tricky maneuver. Sure enough, he twisted his mount around in a neat, swift movement that I'd have to get him to teach me someday, dodging one enemy's rush and skewering the other ferociously. One side of his face was covered in blood, and he was grinning like some little baby's idea of a bogeyman in a nightmare. My own opponent came at me again and I caught him in the chest with my boot, sending him sprawling over backward into Bakr or Jabr or whichever brother it was who looked about one week away from the eternal dirt nap himself. Whoever he was, he finished the job for me, and gave me a funny little wave with his sword before he went plunging back into the heart of battle. He'd lost his camel and I hadn't. I was doing real good.

Even though it hadn't been long ago that we'd started, I could already smell the end of the fight coming up soon. But it'd been one of those scrapes from the beginning: over before it really started, and every man worth his blade knew it. They hadn't been expecting us, and I was cutthroat. We'd come riding down on them like hellfire and worse, and we didn't leave much in our wake.

I had half a mind to throw myself off the camel just to even up the odds a little bit, prolong the fight as much as I could, but I wasn't that stupid. Getting cocky was one thing, but giving up your advantage because of it was just plain suicidal. Besides, I wasn't the kind of guy to yield high ground to anyone.

The one rule we had to follow was to spare the leader—probably so Kalim could do the honors with his own hand—and I could respect that. Didn't know how I was going to recognize the guy if or when I saw him, but I stuck to Kalim and I cut down anyone who got in my way, and yeah, it made me feel pretty good about myself. Probably lucky that Thom was somewhere else and didn't see me get into the thick of it—not because he didn't know what I was capable of already, since he did, but because he would've given me hell if he saw it with his own two eyes, and I didn't need to be lectured.

I grabbed one of the ones who'd had time enough to mount up and cut his throat while I was dragging him off the camel. Sure, it probably did say something piss-poor about me as a person—that I could feel more alive while other people were dying—but there wasn't much I could do about it, let alone anyone else. It was what it was. No arguments there, and no amount of talking about it would make anyone feel better. In fact, it'd probably make everyone feel worse, and it was my job to make sure we didn't come to that. Contrary to popular bastion-damned belief, I thought about that kind of thing; you could do it *and* be particularly good at cutting up your fellow man, which was something some people had a real hard time understanding.

There was blood all the way up to my elbows and spattering the front of my shirt when we finally found him, Kalim's enemy, the leader of the rival tribe. Kalim grabbed him by the hair and held him up and everybody started cheering, myself included, despite me not knowing what the fuck I was actually cheering for. Kalim might've had what he wanted, but I didn't. And I wasn't about to sit through a cross-examination in a language I didn't even know. That wasn't why I was here.

"Do not worry," Kalim said to me; it clearly made his captive piss his pants that a stranger was here and that Kalim was talking to him in a strange language, so the kindness for me was probably a tactical maneuver. It was a good one. "Go find your brother. I will take care of this—I will get the information that I need."

"That we need, you mean," I said.

"Hm," Kalim said, a little wickedly. We both had that same dead man's humor—not when we were dying ourselves, mind, but when we were looking straight at somebody we'd have no problem killing—so I let him have his moment and I headed off to look for Thom.

First thing was first: He wasn't where I left him.

This wasn't a new feeling for me.

There were plenty of things that could happen to Thom in between me leaving him and me coming back to him; he'd started doing that a whole lot of years ago, probably kept on doing it to somebody else when I wasn't there to be a part of it, and once we'd started traveling together he'd picked it right back up with me again. *Wait right here by this bush* would always mean you'd never come back to find him waiting by that bush; there was always an excuse for why he hadn't waited— always a long speech about what'd made him wind up standing next to a tree in the next glade over or lying in a ditch a few feet away, or ass deep in some spring staring at all the little fishies wondering if they were flesh-eating or not. Yeah, flesh-eating fish, in a stream in Volstov. That made fucking sense. Made sense to get into the water too, if that's what you thought they might be.

He was a real piece of work, my brother.

But that wasn't the point, anyway. The point was, Thom wasn't where I'd told him to stay, and this time it was a place where it actually counted. Sure, in the barren wasteland that was the Volstovic countryside it might've been a little dangerous. Might've been wolves or a bear or something, and trust Thom to get into an argument with a cub about honey when the mama bear was right nearby.

This wasn't "might've been dangerous." This *was* dangerous. And Thom'd pranced off somewhere with his camel he didn't know how to ride and his friend I didn't trust and a whole resting hole full of angry fucking desert riders who'd probably kill first and find out who they'd killed later. Just like me.

When I found him I was gonna clap a collar and a leash on him. That way, he couldn't ever wander off, and if he found it offensive to his pride or whatever, then he might as well complain to the dogs, 'cause they were all that was gonna listen to him after this.

Yeah, I guess I was a little angrier than I should've been. But Thom wasn't anywhere in sight, and since I'd told him to stay out of the fighting, I could guess that he'd gone and done the one thing he always did: He hadn't fucking listened. I got off my camel, since I wasn't about to go charging into an enemy base *looking* like I was charging into an enemy base. Kalim had their attention, we'd all but wiped out their forces, and I stalked straight into the heart of the rival camp, listening with both ears for anything that sounded like someone trying to kill my brother before I got the chance to.

It was quieter in the center of camp—a real deceptive kind of quiet that made it seem like the fight hadn't only died down, but like it'd never happened in the first place. And I hated that sound—silence like nothing'd ever happened. Like no matter where you were, dirt or sand or wind or time or *whatever* was gonna come and bury everything sooner or later, everything I'd done and everything Thom'd said buried along with it. Kalim's men'd already rounded up the survivors, and I stepped neatly over a body without batting an eye, the kind of thing Thom'd never be able to do.

"Thom!" I shouted, not giving a fuck who heard me. I could handle myself. Bastion, I was mad enough to *want* someone to have a go at me. "Hilary, you little shit! If you make me track you down instead of coming out on your own, you'll think everything that happened up until now was just a real pleasant dream, you hear me?"

I heard a scuffling sound from behind and I whirled around quick, putting my knife up even if—and maybe especially if—it was my dimwitted brother.

It wasn't him, though, and it wasn't even a desert rider. It was a fucking *Ke-Han* bastard, and of all the things I needed to see right now, a face like that definitely wasn't one of them. He said something angry in that language of theirs that sounded like river murmurs, and all of a sudden I was remembering all kinds of things I didn't particularly want or need to. The scars on my back itched like fire, and I did my best to remember what was important—because I was pretty sure it wasn't starting up another hundred years' war in the middle of the fucking desert.

"Go fuck yourself," I told him. He had a long, ugly scar down half his face, the kind you got from real mean fighting, war battles and not sitting up on your horse for most of them, either, and I was pretty sure he wanted to talk to me about as much as I wanted to talk to him. I could just count myself lucky that he didn't know what I really was: not just your typical Volstovic to hate but probably one of the people he had reason to hate most. And I had my reasons to hate him. So everything was fair and square.

He shouted something again—the same thing, I was pretty sure, even without good 'Versity learning—and I snapped a little this time, making damn sure my knife was visible. Maybe the idiot hadn't seen it before. Maybe he was looking for a fight. Maybe I was gonna have to kill him.

"I don't know what the fuck you're saying," I told him, calm as I could when I felt like all my nerve endings were going off like homemade firecrackers. "But I'm pretty fucking sure it's got nothing to do with me though, so *like I said:* Go fuck yourself. Have a great fucking day."

He stared at me like I was speaking a completely crazy fucking language—which I guess I was. I was about to pop him one for getting in my way while I was already pissed off when someone came crashing through the bushes behind us, followed by a couple of other someones, all making as much noise as they could. Just like that, my Ke-Han barrier up and melted away, avoiding me to move sharply across the sand and toward the intrusion. I had more than half a mind to just continue where I'd left off, but a relieved, strained little voice pulled me up short.

"Rook?" it said, all happy and terrified at once.

I stormed right after that Ke-Han bastard and straight up to my brother, who'd—judging by the looks of things—apparently gotten himself taken prisoner by two women. Sure, one of them was kind of beefy and the other one looked suspiciously like a skinny man in a big dress, but it was still a pretty fucking embarrassing situation. I grabbed Thom up by his collar and dragged him forward, spitting mad twice over now, if such a thing was even possible.

"What in bastion's fucking name is wrong with that head of yours?" I demanded, one fist inches away from his face, so he knew I meant business. He cringed. "You can tell me all about Kara-fucking-khum and whether or not the rainfall this year's been up to snuff or what the national flower is, but when it comes to staying in *one damn place,* that's too hard for you? Common sense just too much to process on top of all those cindy lessons of yours?"

"Geoffrey's dead," Thom choked out, which wasn't a fucking apology, but it *did* bring me up short.

"Dead?" I repeated. Not my finest fucking moment, but I was surrounded by a bunch of strangers in the desert; two of 'em were Ke-Han and one of 'em, the boyish-looking woman, might've been Volstovic. Nothing was making sense, so as far as I was concerned, I was holding my own pretty nicely.

"Indeed," mused one of the women—the smaller one, whose face just wasn't quite right. I didn't like it. She looked like the kind of woman who'd have a few surprises waiting if you took her to the mattress, but fortunately, taking anybody anywhere was the last thing on my mind. "He stole something of mine, then quite unfortunately turned up with his throat slit. I'm terribly sorry for your loss."

"I'm not," I said, and meant it. "He was a thief. Got him into trouble out here more than once, and if that wasn't enough to stop him, then he got what he deserved. Pity I didn't do it myself."

I was half expecting to get myself chastised for that one, but I guess even my brother knew how to keep his trap shut once in a while.

"I take it this one belongs to you?" the woman went on, not looking at all fazed by what I'd said.

"Yeah," I told her. "Something like that. Unfortunately."

"I think he stole . . . what we were looking for," Thom said uneasily, as I lowered him back to the ground. He leaned closer to me, and dropped his voice to a whisper. "The Ke-Han woman has a compass embedded in her hand. I've seen it. And . . . I heard them use the Ke-Han word for *dragon* more than once. Its etymology is different from that of the creature in their myths; the word even sounds like ours. And it's not entirely out of the question that they would be here for the same reasons we are. Otherwise, how do you explain their presence? They clearly aren't native to the desert."

"Huh," I said, looking at them again.

Thom was pretty close to pretty fucking right. Even I had to admit it. What in bastion's name were these three freaks doing working together? A Ke-Han soldier, a Ke-Han woman—who would've been real pretty, not my type but still good to look at, if she hadn't been drenched in sweat and sand—and then this Volstovic bitch who made me fucking uncomfortable and no mistake, staring at me with her big eyes and smiling at me with her thin little mouth.

"Whisper, whisper," she said, tilting her head. "I recognize you."

"Who doesn't?" I muttered, not in the mood. "I don't sign autographs and I don't tell stories, so don't even try it."

"I'd never dream of insulting you so," she replied. "My name is Malahide. I believe we've both worked for the same man."

Everything was starting to click. Not that I wanted to stand around and contemplate or theorize or even put two and two together to make four, but sometimes I guessed I had to do the bare amount of thinking in order to get shit done—and the problem was, what we'd come here for was still missing.

If this bitch was telling me we'd worked for the same person, then I could wager a good solid guess as to who it was, and it probably wasn't Charlie the Grinder down on Hapenny, because she wouldn't've turned enough coin and he wouldn't've bothered with her. It was th'Esar she was talking about, and anyone who worked for him and was going after my prize wasn't on my side at all.

I fingered my knife—Kalim's knife—and the Ke-Han soldier stiffened.

"Don't work for him anymore," I said. I didn't want things to get too real too fast, but I didn't want to be the last one to draw my knife out, either. And the nice thing was, of these three idiots, I was the only one armed. Even the soldier wasn't carrying a sword, or at least he wasn't wielding a weapon big enough for me to see from where I was. He was a mean-looking bastard but I wasn't being delusional when I thought, just looking at him, that I could take him. "So what's this I hear about a compass?"

The bitch's face changed; I could practically see her thinking. She was a Mollyrat at heart if ever I saw one, with one of those mean narrow faces you couldn't trust long enough to let them look at you, and I stared her down while the cogs in her head were turning. She was trying to figure out a way to get one up on us, but she sure as bastion wasn't going to on my watch.

"Whatever you're planning, don't fucking bother," I said. "I'll know when you're lying too, so don't fucking try it."

"You have me there, Rook," she replied, holding up her hands. It was a typical tactic—pretend to surrender when you still had all your weapons—and I took my knife out, real slow, just to examine it. The soldier stepped in front of the bigger woman and the Volstovic "lady" didn't do anything except for rearranging some of the lace at her collar. Thom swallowed, too loud, beside me.

"Rook, I really think . . ." he said, then shook his head. "No, never mind. They're dangerous. I don't like it."

"My name is Malahide," the bitch said, when she saw we were done conferencing. "These . . . friends of mine are named Badger and Madoka, respectively. We are, it would seem, after the same treasure."

"Imagine that," I said. "Small fucking world."

"Hmm, eloquent as one might expect," Malahide said. "That does put us in a bit of a pickle, doesn't it?"

"Not really," I told her. "Way I see it is, I've got an army of desert men on my side. All I gotta do is say the magic words and they'll be on your tail, so . . . Not really a pickle for me. You guys, maybe. Us? Nah." Maybe it wasn't the whole truth—I was embellishing a little—but it was kinda close to the way things were. If I told Kalim these three idiots were *rakhmans* or whatever, no doubt he'd come down on them the same way he'd come down on the rival tribe. Especially if I pointed out these knuckleheads were after the dragonsoul. Sure as hell didn't jibe with Kalim's plans—not mine, either, but a good way to convince Kalim he didn't like somebody was to give him a reason why that somebody didn't like him.

I just had to hope none of them had any power that was useful. Didn't think so. If they did, they'd probably have called it out on us already.

Malahide turned to talk to her friends, and of course they were speaking in Ke-Han. It was quiet but I could still hear them, a foreign word here and there, so I looked at Thom—maybe, for once, he'd have something to say that was actually useful.

"She's trying to convince the other—Madoka, her name is Madoka—to show you her hand," Thom said tensely. "The soldier doesn't want her to. Maybe you should put your knife away."

"Here," I said, shoving the knife into my belt before stepping forward. "See?" I said, holding up my hands for everyone to get a real good look and know for themselves that I was disarmed. "Nothing up my sleeves, no trick weapons, not even a pocketknife. I'm clean and you can pat me down if you want. Show me that bitch's hand."

"Really, Rook," Malahide said, *tsk*ing and trying too hard to be a sweet little buttercup—but I saw right through that act and, personally, it made me sick. "Your reputation is something of a bother to every-one—his highness included, as I'm sure you already know—but that kind of language is uncalled for. I doubt sincerely you would be able to do the things 'this bitch' has proven herself capable of."

"In other words, hold my fucking tongue and show the fairer sex some well-deserved respect?" I offered, parroting some words that Thom probably recognized well enough.

"Somehow it sounds so dirty when you say it," Malahide said.

"Show me the fucking compass," I replied.

Malahide turned to the Ke-Han woman—Madoka—and put a hand on her shoulder. In response, Madoka flinched, and I thought, *Attagirl.* Badger, the soldier, wasn't having any of it; he gave me a look like he wanted to tear my throat out, and I grinned back at him until he looked away, back to his friend.

Her face was nice and strong, and she was clenching her jaw real tight, like something somewhere was hurting her. There wasn't much I could do to *not* look threatening, so I just stood there, waiting for them to make up their minds. They could do this easy or they could do this hard, but it looked like everyone was gonna forgo pride and go for option number one, which was a real nice change from the way things usually shook down.

Then Madoka stepped forward, holding her hand out.

It looked bad. I'd seen wounds festering in my time—mostly while I was still in Molly, actually, since if a man got hurt in the corps he kept it between him and the meds—but this was one of the worst. Even the smell was bad, and when I made a face like I was gonna puke, Madoka laughed. Not at me, but at herself. I liked that. Of our three new acquaintances she was the only one I didn't want to punch in the face. It reminded me a little of how the boys acted when they'd been injured, back in the old days at the Airman. This was a woman who knew how to take a hit and go on standing. I could respect that, if nothing else.

"What is it?" I asked Malahide.

"A part of a dragon," Malahide replied. "It was placed in her hand by a third party—someone it has not yet been my *pleasure* to meet—for reasons that are becoming increasingly murky."

My jaw clenched, and I looked Madoka in the eye. "That hurt?" I asked.

Malahide translated, and Madoka laughed again, then nodded.

"So let me work this out," I said, turning my focus to Malahide. I'd rather have spoken to Madoka, but we didn't exactly speak the same language, so I'd have to go through a go-between or not talk it through at all. "You're here 'cause th'Esar sent you after *my* dragon, since he's under some big fucking delusion that she belongs to him. And *she's* here 'cause someone—probably to do with the Ke-Han—is under some big fucking delusion that they can make her belong to them."

"And you're here because you're under some big fucking delusion that you can turn back the hands of time," Malahide concluded, smoothing her hair back from her face and looking proud of herself for getting a good one in, past all my armor.

Behind me, Thom stiffened, but I ignored the words for the bullshit they were. Only thing you could do to prove a liar right was start arguing with 'em. "So what the fuck's he doing here?" I asked, nodding at the soldier. He scowled.

Malahide shrugged. "Backup, I suppose," she answered. "As you can see, he's very protective of her."

I shrugged too, but it was because I was done talking with her. My attention back to Madoka, I held out my hand, palm up. "Show it to me," I said, hoping she could understand that much.

She hesitated, giving me a look, and I tried to explain with my fucking eyes that I wasn't gonna pull a fast one on her. In her hand was a piece of my girl—I just knew it—and even if it wasn't the dragonsoul I'd come here for, it was something.

It was also the biggest clue we had for where the dragonsoul'd gone, and I needed it to tell me where I was heading next.

Slowly, Madoka put her hand palm up on top of my own palm. It was kind of like I was holding hands with my girl, and I swallowed, staring down at it. Sunken into all the peeling, miserable flesh, I could see it, ticking away like an awkward heart, the hands whirling around over the surface and pointing everywhere and nowhere all at once.

"Doesn't make sense," I said, once I could speak again. "What's it supposed to be pointing out?"

"The dragon piece is still too close for it to do anything other than that, unfortunately," Malahide said. She smiled so much like a fox that if Thom hadn't come forward at that moment, I would've actually gone after her, just to wipe that expression off her face. There was just something about her that rubbed me all the wrong ways, and I didn't want to look at her any more than I absolutely had to.

"It's close," Thom said, repeating things the way he liked to when he was about to come up with some kinda hypothesis or thesis or whatever applied out here in the desert. "But we don't know what direction to take, and if we choose the wrong one . . . Well. It won't stay close very long."

"Thanks for that, Professor," I told him, antsy for a whole lot of reasons, the most important of which being what fucking direction we were supposed to head in now. "Real helpful."

I caught Madoka giving me a look like maybe she wanted to get her hand back, but I couldn't stop staring at the compass. Even if it wasn't pointing toward what I needed, it was still a real part of my girl. It felt weirdly too private, like I was looking at her insides or something, which I guess I was. I had a feeling she wouldn't've liked it—she wouldn't've liked any of it—but then, there wasn't much I could do about it now.

"That *would* be our dilemma, if the compass was the only tool at our disposal," Malahide admitted, smiling at Thom like a woman about to reveal she wasn't just getting fat on account of eating too much. She'd get a lot further with that act on Thom than she would on me, but I was still gonna have to knock her one if she took it too far. If *this* turned out to be the kind of woman Thom fell for, then we were done. Family was family, but in-laws were a fucking life sentence.

"Lucky you," I said flatly. If they thought they were going anywhere without me, they had another think coming. "What's that?"

"Now, now," Malahide trilled, in her arch little voice. "A lady never reveals *all* her secrets at once. Far too wanton, don't you think, Rook?"

"A *real* lady, maybe," I countered. Madoka said something I didn't understand. It sounded like a question, though, and then right on cue like I'd asked him, Thom translated.

"She wants to know if we can get going," he said, standing at my side like a living, breathing dictionary with too much personality for everyone's good. "The fighting's all but stopped, and she believes we are wasting our time by just standing here. Though the words she used weren't half so polite."

I snorted, and Madoka shot me a funny little smile. I didn't usually like women smiling at me unless I knew the reason for it, but I figured I could make an exception at least once. A sudden flurry of hoofbeats on the sand gave me enough time to drop her hand and grab my knife, whirling around ready to finish whatever some bastard had decided to start up again.

Except it wasn't some bastard. It was Kalim.

"My enemy is dead," he said, sliding off his camel as everyone fell silent. I guess a desert prince was enough to shut up even as weird a group as I'd managed to gather. Even the way he walked made it obvious he was somebody important, as compared to the rest of us, and that kind of attitude could sew all kinds of mouths shut. "Before I killed him, he told me that the magic was in the possession of a witch, and that she planned to unleash it for him. Now I see that he did not lead me astray. He would not let strangers into his camp lightly, and yet here I see three of them."

"Pleased to make your acquaintance," Malahide said smoothly, dipping low into a Volstovic curtsy. She really did have a move for every situation. I was starting to think she might even've outmaneuvered Adamo in a chess match, but she'd've won by being sneaky, not by being clever. Probably the way I'd've won at chess, if I ever wanted to play chess—which I didn't. Too fucking boring. "I must admit, it's something of a shock to hear my native tongue spoken out here, as far from home as possible."

"Are you the witch he spoke of?" Kalim asked, striding right up to her the way I might've done if she didn't creep me right out. He hadn't washed the blood off his face yet—hadn't had the time, or maybe this stuff was fresh—and the look on his face would've sent any *real* noblewoman from Volstov into a dead faint.

Madoka hid her hand behind her back, and I didn't exactly blame her. If I was on anyone's side at the minute, I guess I'd have to say I stood with Kalim, but more than anything else I was always on my own side. I'd wait, same as Madoka, to see which way this shook down.

"I am a witch," admitted Malahide. Not only didn't she bat a single dark eyelash, but I could practically see the hen feathers in her fox's mouth. "And *so* many other things besides that. I am called Malahide."

"And I am Kalim," Kalim said, one hand still on his knife. He had to stoop a little to look her in the eye. "You are the witch he spoke of, but you do not have what I am looking for."

"Regrettably, no," Malahide said. "It was stolen from us."

Next to me, Thom was watching with both eyes peeled wide open. Even in books, he'd probably never read about a scene like this. We made a pretty odd group: the prince of the desert; Madoka with a dragon compass buried in her hand and her Ke-Han bodyguard; Malahide, the penny-fee freak show; my brother the professor; and me, whatever that was. We were all after the same bastion-damn thing, and someone'd up and stolen it from *all* of us, which meant there was one more person in our little gang who had yet to show his face and be counted. It wasn't nice of him not to introduce himself politely like everyone else.

"*Stolen*," Kalim repeated, savoring the sound of the *l* on his tongue a little too long. He turned to me. "Is this true?"

"Yeah," I piped in, seeing my chance to remind everyone that I was still here and this was my bounty before it was anybody else's. "But there's good news, too. This one here says she's got a way to track him," I said, nodding toward Malahide behind her back. Given the right motivation—my motivation this time being to tie that bitch's hands behind her back for the good of my cause and to the *detriment* of hers—I could be as helpful as a schoolboy. "A real trump card. She's the only one who knows how to do it, too. Being a witch and all, guess that makes sense."

Malahide's head snapped around like a snake's and I grinned. I didn't know what she'd been planning, but I'd just done a real good job of ensuring the odds were three-on-three. A fair enough fight for a Mollyrat.

"I see," Kalim nodded, thinking over what I'd told him. "My men are heading back to camp now. I have killed the man who stole from me, and the rest is personal." He looked at Malahide a moment longer, giving her a real once-over, like a man looking to buy an expensive horse. Then he seemed to come to some kind of decision, so whatever he'd been looking for, I guess he'd seen it. "For my part, I will accompany you to find this thief. To think that my home should allow so many *rakhman* past its borders of late . . . I must be the one to carry out this duty. Magic is well and good, and gifts from the gods do recognize a true leader. But I am a man as well, and do not wish to have other people prove my worth for me. I will go."

"Truly," Malahide began, "that isn't necessary—"

"He has started out ahead of us," Kalim said, cutting her off. Another thing I liked about him: Once he'd made a decision, things happened real quick. "We will need to ride swiftly after him. I will not have my progress impeded by witches who walk."

He whistled sharply, a strange little trill that cut off just as quickly as it'd started. I heard a strange, scuffling kind of sound, and out of the dark came a string of seven or so camels, all fully kitted out for battle, though their masters were conspicuously absent.

"Take your pick," Kalim commanded, with none of the easy air he usually had about him. This was an order and we were meant to follow it. One day I'd have to take him to task for assuming he could boss me around like anyone else, but for now, going along with Kalim the leader suited my needs well enough. Let him be the one to deal with the horseshit, and let me be the one who took the final prize. "But be quick about it. Witch, you ride with me."

I couldn't have planned it better if I'd been some kind of master strategist. Maybe I wouldn't have been half-bad at chess after all. I took up my piece—guessing anyone could've called that Rook—and prepared myself to ride fast and straight. A compass that half worked and a sneaky witch who *could* work.

We'd make it, all right.

CHAPTER FIFTEEN

MALAHIDE

For the first time in my life, I was riding a camel. At least it wasn't bareback.

I couldn't say I was particularly grateful for the experience, even despite the comfortable saddle. Of all the surprises I'd run across in the desert, finding myself face-to-face with one of the Esar's infamous airmen definitely ranked up near the top. I certainly hadn't expected to discover that he'd formed an alliance with one of the nomad tribes, either, which was how I'd wound up riding the camel in the first place. And, I suspected from his attitude, Airman Rook was threatened by me and therefore did not like me very much.

All in all, bouncing along on the sand, pressed up against a stranger with princely airs as I tried to pick up the scent of the dragonsoul above the odors of blood, sweat, and camel, I was quite ready to lose my temper. Indeed, I might have come to the edge of my patience at last had I not detected the one smell on earth guaranteed to quicken my pulse and set my blood to burning.

It wasn't only the dragonmetal I could taste upon the wind.

The thief in question was the very man I'd been following across the mountains. More than that, he wasn't alone.

I took the reins from Kalim, spurring us around in a sharp turn to the right. I'd never ridden a camel—when would I have had the chance?—but I *was* practiced on horseback, and the basics were essentially the same. I even felt a slight kinship toward the beast, lumpy and ungainly as it appeared next to the sleek, more desirable form of a horse.

Next to us, the airman Rook kicked his own mount up to speed, matching our pace with his own. He wasn't giving me an inch, which was a trait I normally liked in a man, but just now—so close to the conclusion of this saga, and my prize—his relentlessness was getting under my skin. Since Kalim was behind me, I couldn't even check to see how Madoka was doing with one bad hand, but she had Badger to look out for her, and the other Volstovic was hardly a threat. In fact, I barely bothered to remember his name.

I had rather shamefully lost track of time somewhere between the sun's set and our prize being stolen right out from under Madoka's nose, but now I could tell that the sky was starting to lighten. The pure dark was lifting, and the moon had already passed above our heads long ago. We had a few hours left, I could only guess, but it was a clumsy assumption, based on nothing but my own hope and makeshift calculations.

It didn't matter. I would ride through the day, if I had to. No one else could stop me.

At least the prince behind me was not foolish enough to try to make idle conversation with me. He did not trust me, same as Rook, which was why he kept me close—a little too close, perhaps. It was behavior that would not have passed even in an Arlemagne court, but his reasons were different. While Rook's fur was ruffled by my power—the sort of man who did not appreciate the idea that a woman could do something he could not, nor the concept that women came in all shapes and varieties of beauty—Kalim was cautious of me, and wary, because he was respectful. Magic seemed to be a currency favored in the desert. And why not? It made absolute sense. No vein of Well water had been found here in the desert. The only magic one could observe was the tireless strength of constant riding. No one here seemed to grow weary of all the sand, the heat, the inability to feel like one's skin or one's belongings were ever truly clean.

In summation, Kalim respected me and I respected him, for the sole reason Rook did not respect me: because we were very different.

I was still breathing in deeply, a rhythmic pattern that suited the bump and jostle of the camel beneath me. After all, I had to adapt to my current surroundings, and what better way than this? An hour or so ago—it was difficult to keep track of time, and the sand had long since destroyed the mechanisms of my prized pocket watch—Madoka had told me the pain in her hand *was* growing substantially worse. This meant we were on the right track. The scent grew stronger. We approached our quarry, but his party was substantially smaller, and he was riding fast.

I wondered idly if they would stop to rest. We could draw up to them while they slept. In broad daylight, with no shade or shadow nearby but the ones our own bodies cast before us, we would put an end to this charade, once and for all.

And I did so want to meet the man I'd been following.

If some of us more rational folk could keep him alive for long enough to squeeze a few answers out of him—questionable because of the dark, murderous rage I scented, among other less savory things, from Airman Rook—then he would prove just as valuable in mind as the dragon piece he carried.

It must have been something special, if so many were after it. Our numbers were almost humorous by this point, and I did have to wonder who would come out victorious in seizing the physical object, claiming "success" as their own. I also wondered what the Esar would do with this item if and when it was returned to him. No doubt he would destroy it—the grandest irony of all—so that no one else could ever possess it again, and he himself would see it only as a haunting specter in his darkest, most uncertain of dreams.

Indeed, it was enough to make a woman jealous that so many here chased the object in question for their own personal reasons, and were not merely envoys of another man. Madoka, Badger, and perhaps the quiet Volstovic were all pieces similar to pawns; I was a bishop, and Kalim and Rook were the knights. How quaint that we had made our chessboard the vast and inescapable planes of the desert.

"You think hard," Kalim said behind me.

I paused in my task. Thinking and working came hand in hand for me. As I scented I thought, and both enhanced each other. I could more easily chase a thing the better I understood it, and the only way to understand was to analyze. Still, I had found the direction. I kept my senses keen, but by the same token, I did not wish to be rude and alienate a potential ally.

"It is necessary for my work," I explained.

"By which you mean your magic?" Kalim asked.

I glanced over at the other riders. Rook's companion was having trouble with his camel, whose face was a pure, blissful expression of spite if ever I had seen it. Rook himself saw that Kalim and I were conversing, and his hawklike gaze was fixed upon us so unwaveringly that I had to wonder whether or not sand even got in his eyes or if it bypassed him completely, sensing another more violent storm. Madoka and Badger were still riding steadily just a few feet behind us, and I sighed, having to trust that they would do well enough on their own. If anything, Madoka was stubborn beyond the normal limits of strength.

She'd be all right. On top of that, she'd see Badger through, as well.

I smiled faintly and murmured my confirmation. "Indeed," I said. "My magic."

"You breathe in deep like a camel," Kalim told me, laughing. "But you do not snort out again like one."

"What a charming comparison," I said. It was better than some comparisons I had received before, the most frequent of which were cur, hound, *mongrel*. "How very quaint."

"Quaint," Kalim repeated, rolling the word upon his tongue. "This means charming?"

"Something of the sort," I replied. "It is more nuanced . . . Would you prefer we spoke your language?"

"No," Kalim told me honestly. "I need practice."

"Oh, I see," I said. "So you are using me?"

"In many ways I am," Kalim said. He tightened his arm about my waist and, though he was not a man whose nature I could immediately guess—it was far too natural to be summed up so easily—I allowed myself to flutter a gasp of surprise. "No pretenses, please," he said at that, and now I could tell he was scowling. "I am not lying to you. Why should you lie to me?"

"My apologies," I said. "I mean no offense."

"Perhaps lying is your nature now," he told me, clipped and short. I was offended, but he was also quite right.

I spared a look at his face: I could only see one half of it, but it was hard and handsome and very dark, his nose straight, his chin sharp.

His brows were thick and there were many lines around his mouth; tanning from the sun and laughing at jokes and all manner of vibrancy collected in those little wrinkles. He was clearly a man who lived life every day—or every night—to the fullest, and the kind of man it was difficult to woo. I had my work cut out for me, but I needed a fourth ally for myself, Badger, and Madoka. It would turn the tables and the tides in our favor.

After that, it was every last man for himself, or so the saying went.

"Do we approach our man?" Kalim asked me. "How do you tell?"

"It isn't something I can very easily explain," I began, with the usual excuses. Then, because I could see the corner of Kalim's mouth frowning, I went on, which was very unusual. "I smell him, one might say," I explained. "And the piece he is carrying—I can smell both."

"This is an admirable talent," Kalim said. "How did you come by it? Or were you born this way?"

I thought back to my unimpressive and uninspiring youth. I was not one of the lucky creatures born into money and power, destined for intrigue and idle fame. Talent was by no means rare, but I had none of it, and it had been worth it to me at the time—and still was worth it—to trade away pieces of myself to enhance other pieces. Tit for tat, it might have seemed to anyone else, but I was clearly bargaining with fate to the point of cheating nature itself.

"I was not born this way," I replied.

Kalim snorted—like a horse, himself. "No you were not," he agreed.

I didn't much appreciate *that* implication, as it came far too close to the truth of the matter for my own liking, but it would not do to clutter my impassioned thoughts by allowing my own fur to be ruffled. My clear head was one of my finest weapons, and I planned to use it to the fullest extent of its capabilities. "Now, Kalim," I replied, as prettily as I could manage. "What *is* that supposed to mean?"

"You know well," Kalim told me. "But it can be our little secret."

He spurred his camel faster, and Rook drew up beside us, not giving me time to ponder that peculiar statement. "If you're making plans between yourselves, then shit, Kalim," Rook said, "how desperate are you? You come to Volstov with me and I'll find you fifteen women prettier than this one."

"I have no need of pretty women," Kalim replied. "I prefer my companions to be beautiful."

"This ain't beauty," Rook said, and spat savagely—grossly—downwind. "Just some nasty shadows masquerading." Kalim smiled widely and Rook rolled his eyes. "Guess there's no accounting for taste," Rook snarled. "Just be careful she doesn't cut your dick off. Snip snip, you got me?"

"This is universally understood," Kalim agreed.

Rook fell back to confer on something with his companion, and I was left with a whirlwind of sand against my boots and thoughts ricocheting from my chest to my mind. I had lived with many secrets in my time, but Kalim himself was intimating he saw through the most deftly kept secret of all.

It was impossible. My showmanship was impeccable. Even Dmitri had never guessed, and we had known each other since childhood. I would not have said Dmitri knew me better than I knew myself—my particular nature required that I know myself better than I could ever allow anyone to know me—but I had always assumed it would be he who realized before anyone else.

This was confounding.

"Do not let it distract you, in any case," Kalim suggested lightly. But there was something in his eyes that suddenly frightened me. "How close are we now to our prey?"

The wind picked up, and I scented something dark upon it. Magic, I realized all at once, and I grasped the camel's reins, pulling him up short.

I couldn't afford to be distracted now. Kalim was right about that, at least.

"Do you sense something?" he asked, his light air of a moment ago completely vanished.

"Magic," I told him, quite honestly. I breathed in deeply, and nearly regretted it, so potent was the reek of spellcasting that washed over me. "Foreign, perhaps. But there's something familiar about it, too."

I wasn't in the habit of thinking aloud—I'd rarely had the opportunity, since losing my tongue—but I felt almost compelled to do it now. Kalim didn't trust me, and I needed him to. If honesty was the trade I had to peddle in order to win him over, then so be it. Old Nor would've been proud of me to see me in action.

"Perhaps they seek to rebuild what was lost," Kalim suggested. "To use this magic now for their own ends?"

"I wish you hadn't said that," I told him. It was one thing to entertain my own private concerns about our enemy's intents. It was quite another to hear those same concerns uttered aloud. "Honestly, is there no sense left in the world? One would think that you men *might* have better things to do than chase a sentiment into the desert."

"Watch your mouth," Rook grunted, coming up on our side with his companion. "It's *rude* to talk about things that have nothing to do with you."

"It's ruder to eavesdrop," I pointed out.

"So why'd we stop?" Rook asked, instead of rising to the bait. Our relative progress across the desert was apparently the only thing that penetrated his thick skull.

"Malahide says there is magic afoot," Kalim explained, just as I'd opened my mouth to do so. It hadn't been so very long ago that I'd needed someone else to speak for me, but no one had ever done it of his own free will before. It was strange, and I was entirely sure that I did not like it.

Nevertheless, I was about to elaborate when I heard a shout from behind, and Kalim turned us around just in time to see Madoka drop from her camel like a sack of new potatoes fresh off the back of the cart. Badger was down by her side in a flash, with the swift necessity of a soldier's movements, and I found myself struggling to dismount as well. Kalim let me free and I fell to the ground, somehow managing to keep from twisting an ankle—these bastion-damned boots were useless in the sand—and I hurried over to her.

The scent of the magic was thick in the air now, a heady, intoxicating aroma that made it difficult to sort out anything else. Almost a blessing since I could no longer smell the rotting in Madoka's hand, but it meant that I would have to work much harder to detect the now-elusive scent of the dragonmetal, and my own quarry, beneath all the rest. Layer upon layer, like a fine lady's evening gown, with the truth of her body hidden underneath so much silk and brocade and lace.

I took Madoka's hand—the good one—in mine.

"Hurts," she muttered through clenched teeth. Though the light in the sky was quite dim, I could still see that she was growing increasingly pale.

"We're getting close," I told her, the wind picking up around us. I felt almost guilty, using her pain as a kind of compass itself, but I'd been trained to make use of every tool at my disposal, and I couldn't afford to forget myself, not even now. Not when I'd finally come so close. When we grew too near to our target for the machinery in her hand to work properly, it was Madoka's relative threshold for pain that I followed, alongside my nose. There was nothing else to it.

The breeze gusted up into my face, and my nostrils flared, drawing in the scent of my surroundings. Everything paled against the magic, but there were little hints of other things: Madoka's fear and pain, Airman Rook's furious impatience, the corrosive tang of dragonmetal in Madoka's palm, and something else. Something *quite* familiar, in fact. That I hadn't recognized it sooner was a matter I would later scold myself for. It was as plain—for lack of a better expression—as the nose on my face.

"Madoka, my girl," I began, with some urgency in my voice that was neither put on nor exaggerated. "Would you like to know what I have just discovered?"

"Sure," Madoka said, humoring me as she struggled to sit up in the sand. Badger put a hand behind her back and steered her upright. "Why not?"

"The smell of magic that I've run across just now—the air positively *stinks* of it here, so I can only imagine he thinks himself safe— shares a certain odor with that nightmare in your hand, as well. It's a signature, if you will. All magicians have them, because all magicians have more ego than brains. Call it a shared trait."

I watched her closely as the realization sank in, the emotions on her face as evident as if she'd been a mechanical compass herself: all the gears shifting and moving to create a new sense of purpose. She no longer looked as though she was about to shuffle off into the afterlife. How could she possibly, when the man who'd done this to her rested so close at hand?

She got to her feet, and I saw a new resolve burning in her eyes. She would reach our destination, I knew that much, and bastion help any man who tried to stand in her way. Feeling rather proud of myself, I stood a moment later and nearly stepped backward into Kalim, who'd crept up on us without warning.

"You have the gift of many tongues," he noted, his face entirely impassive, so that I couldn't tell what he was thinking. The wind whipped the sand around us and I winced as it stung my cheek, then drew my shawl tightly around my face to avoid a second occurrence.

"Just not my own," I answered, and I couldn't have said what *I* was thinking just then either. The smell of the magic was inebriating me. It was the only possible explanation. "Come," I added, in more serious tones. "If we linger here, we may inadvertently alert them to our presence, and I do so enjoy the element of surprise. Especially when there is only one magician among us—or should I say witch?—and my Talent is abstract rather than physical."

"Let's *crush* them," Madoka said, with a good helping of the fire I'd seen in her when we first met. "It is . . . 'them,' right?"

"You're much smarter than you look," I said, all too aware of Rook's companion standing nearer to us, and translating what I said in the Ke-Han language back to the airman himself. He was useful for something, then, after all, and I had underestimated his abilities. Well, it would not happen again. "I believe there is more than one magician."

"I don't care if it's a whole *army* of fucking magicians," Rook snarled, and I got the distinct impression that he was being completely truthful. "We're going in there and taking back what's mine."

"Hmm," I said, allowing a small smile to play about my lips. "I wonder if it will truly be that simple."

It was going to be *incredibly* interesting to see what came of our little expedition, nearly everyone in it for his own separate reasons and all of us intractable to a man. Again, I found myself the odd one out, with no personal stakes beyond professional pride in the matter. Kalim had his tribe; the airman had his dragon; Madoka's troubles were deeply personal; Badger had Madoka, I supposed; and the translator seemed to have his own reasons—it certainly wasn't for the adventure of the ride. I'd never been bothered by such a thing before, but it niggled at the back of my mind like a splinter, small yet insistent.

I studied the camel for a moment before mounting it with relative ease. It *was* rather the same as riding a horse, if slightly more uncomfortable. Swiftly, Kalim was behind me again, and I twitched the reins quickly, setting us off before he could say any more troublesome things. Now was not the time to theorize. There was a storm cloud ahead of us and the dawn was an eerie gray.

The sun was coming up more rapidly now, staining the desert a rosy yellow and taking the cold sting out of the night breezes. Magic was thick in my nostrils, guiding me like a banner's wave to meet our goal. The air itself was pale and shimmering—or perhaps it was my eyes watering from the stench, and I myself was hallucinating, like a child drugged before the removal of a rotten tooth. Whatever it was our opponents were doing, they were so engrossed in it that they hadn't taken the time to set up proper perimeters—no watchmen or scouts. Perhaps my quarry, having slit that man's throat, had presumed it sufficient to sneak away in the chaos between two warring tribes. Or perhaps, like me, he was simply feeling the weight of time on his shoulders, what he'd spent and what he had left behind. A man pressed for time could be engrossed in what he was doing to the exclusion of all else. We might well ride right up to his doorstep in the open sunlight before he noticed anything amiss—or so I hoped and planned.

As long as we moved swiftly, I could be sure we wouldn't lose the advantage of surprise, which we sorely needed. This magic was a brand more potent than my own; it must have been, for what it had done to Madoka's very body. I certainly could not contemplate the trick this man had pulled, nor how our magicians back in Volstov might undo it. And, on top of that, my own magic was by no means combative. Airman Rook and Badger were soldiers, but physical strength against this more violent strain of Talent was not a match on which I could bank good money for *my* side winning. The question in my mind now was, What in bastion's name were they doing? All this desert, I thought, and all that power inside that dragon part. If they were unleashing a storm, I truly did not wish to be caught in the middle of it.

Rook kicked his own mount into a pace with ours, and Kalim wrapped his fingers around the shaggy fur in the camel's neck. On our other side, Madoka appeared, and after a moment, Badger alongside her. It was certainly the largest—not to mention the strangest—group I'd ever traveled in. My inability to trust such a large collection of individuals was why I had never chosen to be a true soldier. And so I was somewhat out of my league, wasn't I?

What we were traveling toward would almost certainly dissolve us, but for the time being, I could allow myself to relish the bizarre and unfathomable feeling, rare as it was, and passing strange.

"You smile like a jackal," Kalim told me. "In my homeland, this is a sign of good luck."

"Let's hope it's *my* good luck," I said, and set us going even faster.

THOM

The sun was coming up over the desert, and we were following the Esar's agent to the dragonsoul.

It wasn't exactly the way I'd envisioned our quest drawing to its close, but then I presumed it was the sort of thing that Sarah Fleet would've found monstrously entertaining. Had she been with us—I was relieved all over again that she was not—her barking laughter would have signaled our approach to our enemy. And yet her Talent might have proven somewhat useful in our current situation. Magicians: always a boon and a bane, never quite one thing without being its opposite.

At least I'd finally found a way to make myself useful for my brother, even though impromptu translator hadn't exactly been the position I'd had in mind. It was something I could do, and it was *clearly* driving him insane that the woman Malahide could switch between languages the way he switched between moods, just as quickly and just as naturally. We'd have to keep an eye on her. Rather, we'd have to keep an eye on everyone, since we were only working together *now* because it suited everyone's purposes to do so. I held no illusions about what would happen once we reached the dragonsoul and put paid to the men currently holding it.

It was going to be ugly. For my part, I knew exactly where I stood— Rook and I were the only two bound together by blood—but I was less certain of the others. Would Kalim hold fast to preestablished loyalties and take our part, for instance, or would he decide to claim the dragonsoul as his own? Was Malahide in deep enough cahoots with the Ke-Han man and woman that she would stand with them, or would she be setting out on her own as soon as she'd located what she believed was hers? It was the most complex mathematical problem I'd ever tried to sort out, and in all likelihood it was a waste of time trying to put two and two together, but I wanted to be prepared, no matter what happened. It was the most I could do.

I twisted the reins around my wrist and squeezed the camel's sides with my heels, spurring her onward while trying to close the distance between myself and Rook. Only Malahide seemed to know how close—or how far—we were from the site of this mysterious thief, and I had no intentions of being caught off guard.

I'd long since given up the idea that she was lying to us about what she "smelled." Even I—and I was no magician—could taste the strange colors of the air. My tongue burned, and my throat was tight around every breath I drew in. At first I'd wondered if it was simply the way the desert felt when one was about to ride straight into a sandstorm—just our luck, wasn't it?—but Kalim wore an expression now that he would not have for a simple storm, something to which he had been accustomed all his life.

Unfortunately, I could not consult with him. He was too close to Malahide for that, and as Rook refused to trust her, I couldn't ruffle his feathers by appearing to do so. It was a paranoia that almost appeared jealous, depending on the light.

Riding blind into the center of the storm, at least, was the sort of thing for which my brother was built. No one was born to be comfortable in a situation such as this one, but Rook *had* been groomed for it. He was ready, even if I wasn't.

"Just don't fall off your mount," Rook muttered to me, quiet enough that, presumably, neither of our Volstovic-speaking counterparts could hear us.

I drew up alongside him as quickly as I could, feeling marginally embarrassed when he had to slow his camel so that I could do so with less difficulty. Still *trying* to learn, in any case. I was stubborn as all bastion-blessed, and I wished more than ever that Rook could appreciate determination as much as he appreciated results.

"I haven't yet," I replied.

"What the fuck's happening?" Rook added, with less venom than I'd expected. The curses themselves held no bite. They were merely rote expression, and I wished again I had some talent—like his—that would prove useful in a bind.

"I don't know," I admitted unhappily. "There *is* magic. But I don't know why."

"What sort of stuff's inside the soul, do you think?" Rook asked.

It was a very deep question, especially for him, and I thought about the best philosophical way to answer it before I realized he'd meant what was physically inside Havemercy's soul, and that it wasn't as deep as I'd thought. More suited to the moment, though. I sighed and shook my head. "I can't say for certain," I replied. "Sarah Fleet seemed to indicate it was some combination of Well water and personal magic—blood, sweat, and tears, perhaps without the tears part. A little bit of pure magic and a little bit of personal Talent, and there you have it."

"But it's powerful enough to bring something alive," Rook said, and then added quickly, "to bring *someone* alive. Right?"

"Sarah Fleet seemed to indicate as much," I reminded him. I wasn't an expert on dragons, but I did at least know the answer to that. "And if the magicians in possession of the soul plan to resurrect her, then I'd assume they're thinking along the same lines. Whether or not she would be the *same* as when you knew her, I couldn't say. It's complicated, but the basic principles . . . Well, it's an animating force."

"Real powerful," Rook said.

"Mm," I agreed.

I didn't like the color of the sunrise now. It was bright and sunny at first, but the higher the dawn crept the less colorful it felt, as though there were some half-transparent substance between us and the horizon blocking off the full source of the light. The air itself felt thick—countless sand particles swirling up with the quickening wind—and I'd long since forgotten about the marginal discomforts of sand getting here, there, and everywhere now that I realized it was becoming more and more difficult to see.

"Hey," Rook said. His voice was calm but a little urgent. "Whatever happens, I wanna—"

Then the wind picked up so ferociously that even Rook's camel reared.

Mine tossed me from its back so easily that I wondered if it had even been trying, all those times before, or if it had simply been toying with me. My wrist yanked against the reins as sand flew in from every which way, forming a barrier between us and the sunlight. In my confusion and fear, I managed somehow to wonder if Rook had, with his impeccable instincts, sensed this coming. He might well have been trying to say his good-byes to me, or at least he was trying to impart some last piece of wisdom in hopes of keeping me alive. A fool's hope, I thought wryly, and hit the sand in slow motion, with a solid *oomf.*

Either the men we were pursuing knew we were here for them, or they were just very lucky in dismantling our pursuit with their own private actions.

I heard my camel run off, and counted myself lucky that it did not trample my head as a parting gift before it went. It *did*, however, kick up sand into my eyes, and my wrist hurt very badly from where it had been wrapped within the reins. I could hear nothing else, only the sound of the sand whistling and howling all around me. At one point I called out for my brother, but the words barely left my lips before they were thrown back into my throat, along with so much sand I nearly choked. After that I learned not to open my mouth and pulled my arms over my head to keep the sand from clogging my ears and nose. I squeezed my eyes shut. It was possible this would last forever—or at least for long enough to bury us all here in the darkness. I tried to calm myself, repeating a few passages of my favorite books over and over to distract my mind from the certainty of death. Maybe, in a thousand years, someone would find my notebooks, and my writings would live on: the undiscovered works of a long-lost scholar. Or something like that. As of now, it was the only legacy for which I could reasonably hope.

And then someone touched my elbow.

"You just gonna lie there like that forever, or are you gonna do something about this shit?" Rook demanded, right next to my ear. He must have been close, since I could actually hear him, and felt his breath more than the cut of the sand.

I was as relieved as a little child, but also ashamed. Had I really given up? Why was it so easy for me and yet so difficult for him?

"Don't open your mouth," Rook continued, still shouting against my ear. "Just follow me."

I searched out his hand, groping blindly through the sand with my own, and when I found it, I squeezed it, just to show him I understood. He grabbed it tight and pulled me forward, and I crawled after him. At least he felt guilty that he'd taken me all this way, only to land us smack in the middle of magic we barely understood and a storm we barely had the means of surviving.

All of it was for Havemercy. I'd hardly even known her. I certainly hadn't loved her. In fact, I'd never had anyone to love—which perhaps was why I was incapable of understanding my brother's determination right now.

I was jealous as well as baffled. I wondered, in a mean and angry rathole of my heart, if he would ever have fought this hard for me. Not back in Molly—when we were still really brothers—but *now*.

"Stop thinking!" Rook shouted, right up next to my head, so loud that it might well have shattered my eardrum. I didn't know how he could tell what I was doing amidst all this mess, and in my own head, not to mention, but he was right. This more than anything was his area of expertise, and I'd do well to listen to him. The sand and the wind were so strong I could barely move, but I *was* trying, dragging myself forward and after my brother. I felt him move more than I could see him, and then the howling of the wind died down somewhat. He'd placed himself between me and the direction it was blowing from, and I would never be able to thank him for it. He'd simply never allow it.

A monumental ass, I thought wonderingly, and tucked myself against his body, allowing him to rescue me in this small way.

"What about the others?" I asked, up against his jaw. Some sand made it into my mouth, but not much, now that he was between me and the source of it all.

I felt him shrug, and I knew well enough what his answer would have been, if he could speak. *Fuck 'em.*

He was probably right. There wasn't much we could do in the middle of the storm to save ourselves, let alone four relative strangers. Kalim, I reasoned, could probably handle himself next best to Rook— he'd been born into this sort of climate, hadn't he? And as to the others, I would have to harden my thoughts. Leaving them to fend for themselves didn't sit well with me, but what else could I do? I was as useful as a eunuch in a whorehouse—I had my brother to thank for that comparison—clutching to Rook's hand and following him as *he* followed only bastion knew what. His own innate sense of direction, or whatever extrasensory perception he had for the dragonsoul's pulse, calling out to him even across the most deadly of manufactured storms. Or pure stubbornness, when all else failed him.

I held close, plugging my nose and mouth with my free hand. My eyes I kept slitted open—even that stung them, but Rook almost certainly had *his* eyes open, and I wouldn't make myself any more of a burden than I absolutely had to.

Gradually, because I had nothing else to turn my attention toward, and because I *couldn't* stop thinking, no matter what Rook had told me,

I noticed the ground was beginning to slope downward beneath our feet. It was a small thing, perhaps completely insignificant, but this mildest of changes gave me hope. At least I knew we weren't simply wandering around in circles, which had probably been precisely our enemy's intent.

They hadn't counted on dealing with someone like my brother. With his particular set of skills, not to mention the formidable will he always exhibited, he certainly wasn't the sort of man I'd have liked to imagine coming after me. My brother was exactly the kind of stubborn bastard Molly was so proud of churning out. He was more tenacious than most species of vermin, more terrifying than a childhood nightmare.

A fierce wind kicked up and I ducked my head behind Rook's shoulder, holding him steady as the sand whipped around at our clothes and faces. He leaned back against me, taking my support as he tried to decide whether to head straight into the sudden gust or around it. Ke-Han wind magic had been a big part of Xi'An's defense against the Dragon Corps; I remembered that. If anyone knew the best tactics for bypassing it, it was Rook. I stood as still as I could manage, trying to cultivate solidity where there hadn't been much before. We were in this together, and even if he never thanked me for my help—what little there was of it—I was here to give him exactly that.

It was only a brief respite. Shortly, he began to move again, cutting a path through the rush of sand and throwing an arm up in front of his face to protect himself from the worst of it. There were a dozen things I wanted to ask him, but I wasn't about to choke myself on sand just to speak. There was no space even to part my lips—it felt almost as though sand had replaced the very air around us.

Then, just as abruptly, we were through the worst of it. Rook stumbled forward, his momentum overcompensating in the sudden vacuum, and I fell straight into him, my bones turned to sand themselves. We must've come to the center of the storm—the relative eye of the cyclone, if it could be called that—and I breathed in painful, gasping gulps, taking the chance to fill my lungs while I still could. Rook coughed, and I brushed the sand from my eyes, taking great care not to rub it in. We were entirely covered in the stuff, I realized, now that I could see, and my brother looked more like an ancient statue rising from the dunes than a man of flesh and blood. He shook the sand off like a dog, then he was Rook again, if a little dustier than usual, all the sand crusted in the corners of his mouth and eyes, clinging heavily to his hair.

"See?" he croaked, licking his lips and spitting out sand into more sand. "Nothing to it."

"Oh, I wouldn't quite say *that*," said a not-unfamiliar voice, causing me and Rook both to whirl around almost in tandem. "Selling yourself short is such a mistake, after all."

There was a slender, dark-cut figure standing against the backdrop of the swirling maelstrom. His face was thin and clever, and I immediately knew that I'd seen it before. It seemed like ages now, but it had only been a few weeks, less even than a month, since we'd last exchanged unpleasantries. Afanasiy. Fan. But what in bastion's name was he doing here, and now?

Rook snarled, starting forward immediately, and I only just managed to catch him by the arm before it was too late. With some atavistic strength I'd never exhibited before, I hauled him back, keeping him from attacking out of anger, without thinking and, worse than that, without planning things through. Fan *seemed* to be alone, but if he was responsible for conjuring up a sandstorm like this one, then there was no telling what other tricks he had up his sleeve. Also, and this was more to the point, I couldn't see the dragonsoul anywhere. Either he had an accomplice, or he'd stashed it somewhere he thought safe for the time being. None of this made any sense with the information I currently had, and that made me wary. Neither of us could afford to throw ourselves senselessly into the center of action.

My brother, however, had evidently considered none of this, and the look he shot me when I held him back was akin to a blow.

"Get the *fuck* off me," Rook said, trying to shake me off like deadweight, which, at that moment, I supposed I was.

"Easy there," Fan said, his tone light and breezy, the same as it had been that night at the countryside camp. "I'd take your brother's counsel if I were you. He seems like the smarter one. No offense, of course. Just an observation."

"Yeah, well I'd start observing a little more about your own situation if *I* were *you*," Rook said, fighting against me less than he had been before. Never one to listen to counsel, of course, but never one to let anyone outsmart him, either. "Two against one doesn't exactly scream 'you're a winner,' and even if you are a fast little motherfucker, I'm willing to bet I could put you down."

"Please," Fan said, almost entreating. The condescension in his tone offended me, but that was beside the point. He was wearing a heavy coat in direct contradiction of the early-morning sun that now beat down overhead, and there was a curious light in his eyes that gave me less offense and more fear. "You don't truly believe me to be that stupid, do you? By now, your little party is scattered across the desert, and the odds are entirely in my favor. This sandstorm was a neat trick, you must admit. Appears entirely natural to the untrained eye."

"What have you done with it?" I asked, feeling like an intruder on the conversation. My voice didn't sound nearly so sure as Rook's or Fan's, but I would have to make do. "Where's the dragonsoul?"

Fan smiled in reply, a sickly grimace that looked like it'd been carved by a sculptor with a crude knife. I recognized it on the statues in the desert: a smug certainty, that air of immortality portrait artists often captured, which later generations come to understand as deeply ironic. Fan, however, did not seem to be one such deep thinker. "Do you know, I almost feel sorry for you?" he said, putting his hands behind his back. His stare was intent and malicious, but I couldn't allow myself to look away. "You want this thing, this *dragonsoul,* for sentimental purposes. Because you can't let go of the glory days, or you long for a memento. Something to stick up on your mantelpiece so you can look at it and remember a time when you were actually of use to the world around you, when you were more than relevant—when you were *necessary.* But you've got no imagination, no *idea* of the power contained in something like that. You can only see what it was: a part of an antique, as useless and outdated as the broken statues you passed along your way. But we . . . we have true vision. We're the ones who will take the potential nearly *destroyed* by the likes of you, nearly lost to the desert or even shattered by your own hand, and put it to a better use."

"That's real nice," Rook said. I could practically feel his pulse racing, and I held tight to his arm. I didn't have any illusions about my strength compared to his if he *really* lost his temper, but I certainly wasn't about to let go without a struggle. "You sound just like old Jonas down by the Mollydocks, reading fortunes for a ha'penny and spewing all kinds of shit-nonsense to anyone dumb enough to listen. Don't think you've got an audience here. I don't care what your stars said when you were a fucking tyke; I don't care what you think you're going to do with her. She's mine, and that's the way of things. I'd give you a chance—fight it and die or some better option—but you lost that a long time ago. You've only got one fucking choice now and I don't give a flying shit what ace you've got tucked up your sleeve."

Fan tilted his head and arched an eyebrow. The light in his eyes did make him look rather mad, I realized, or perhaps it was something to do with his close-set features. If we were lucky, he would have no Talent.

If we were not . . .

"I didn't expect you to listen," Fan said with a deep sigh. "Men like you are always so stubborn, for better or for worse. Or perhaps you can't bear the idea that your precious 'girl' would be turned against you—just like this."

"Where is it?" I asked again, steadier this time. Fan talked about his plans with the same bluster and fastidious detail with which many of my professors had attacked their specialties. I knew how to talk to people like that, how to flatter their vanity and make it seem as though even in defeat I admired their cunning, understood the intricacies of their peculiar genius. I had no confidence that it would work under these circumstances, of course, but it was the only chance I had. The principles were essentially the same. "What *do* you plan to do with it? With . . . her? And how can you be sure it'll work, to begin with? No one to date has ever dismantled and reconstructed a dragon—you can't possibly know that the parts will function as you've planned."

"Why*ever* do you think we've come out here in the first place?" Fan asked, spreading his arms wide as if to encompass the desert itself. "It's the perfect testing ground. No inconvenient buildings in place, no tiresome patrolmen to keep an eye out for. In fact, you merry rovers are the only obstacles we've currently run up against, but that's all right. Onto every parade, a little rain must fall. Unless of course one comes to the desert," he added, giggling thinly at his own joke.

"You're not alone?" I asked, just to make sure. There was always the chance that he was speaking as the Esar did—Fan seemed far removed enough from the real world to assume that air—and I didn't want to rush into things. Especially when I'd come so far in keeping Rook from doing just that.

"Oh dear," Fan said, shaking his head. "And here I called you clever. Well, no matter, perhaps I can *clear* things up for you."

He raised both hands, and I tightened my hold on Rook instinctively. The shifting miasma of sand at Fan's back howled and began to part like a golden mist. There was a shape behind him that I couldn't discern, impossibly large, too delicate to be one of the stone columns that had surrounded Kalim's camp and somehow . . . familiar. I glimpsed an elegant neck, the cruel hook of a talon, and the stark, metallic outline of a rib cage.

Rook snarled and dragged me a full foot forward before I recovered myself, hauling back at him with all my weight while praying to anyone that might've been listening that now would be an *excellent* time to grant me just a bit of added strength.

I'd known what it was before my brother moved, of course. It was difficult to forget a face that'd left such an impression on me.

"I imagine she looks a little different than when you last saw her," Fan said, and the sound of his voice made me want to hit him right between the eyes. "It's a shame really. We had to make do with what we had, and as you can imagine, after the war it was difficult to get our hands on *too* many parts without looking suspicious. You could call this a collaborative effort though. She'll carry Havemercy's soul, but I wouldn't be entirely shocked if there wasn't a piece of all the dragons in that body."

"You're a real son of a bitch," I said, both because I was unable to help myself, and my brother seemed too shocked to move. "I hope you know that."

"Let's not bring my mother into this," Fan said. "The mere sight of you has already ruined my day *quite* sufficiently."

"But you led us right to Sarah Fleet," I protested, as Rook shifted slowly, with less anger this time and more calculated intent. "What possible reason could you have had—unless you meant for us to come here all along?"

"Well, not all of you," Fan drawled. "The only one we really need is your brother."

"Sucks to be fucking you," Rook replied. He hadn't even taken his eyes off the dragon—I couldn't call her Havemercy, not in her current state—and I hadn't *really* been sure that he'd even been aware of the conversation. "I ain't biting."

I could feel the tension in him, and for the first time I truly appreciated how much it was taking for him to remain still. He was waiting, no doubt measuring the distance between himself and Fan, weighing his options, planning his next move. If he hoped to stick a knife through Fan's heart and exorcise him in that way, then he would of course wish to make sure his blade hit the mark. It was pressed between us currently, and I shifted, stepping away from Rook just enough that he would know he could remove it now without fear of somehow injuring me. Whether he noticed or appreciated my efforts was unclear, but Fan clicked his teeth together.

"Ah ah," he tsked, holding up one hand. In it was a small vial of clear liquid; I had no idea whether it was something as simple as water or a substance far more potent. Rook's jaw was hard. "No planning between you, please. No sudden movements, either." He paused, licking his lips. The vial was important—perhaps that was his trump card. "Don't recognize it, do you?" he added, after a brief moment. "Or, I suppose I should say, don't recognize 'her'?"

"Everybody changes," Rook said harshly.

"Don't do anything rash," I cautioned—as though somehow my words could affect Fan's decisions at all. I was still trying to talk him down from whatever madness he hoped to indulge in, here in the desert where no one from Volstov could see. If I could only manage to make him grandstand just a little longer—posturing enough to give me further clues as to his confederates, his desires, his *motives*—or at least distract him for long enough to give Rook a clumsy opening . . . As ridiculous as both plans were, they were all I had.

I squeezed Rook's arm and his muscles tightened beneath the touch.

If only we might have worked together.

"It's a good plan, actually," Fan explained, gentling. He held the bottle up, but there was no light for it to catch, only solid walls of sand every which way, sunlight barely managing to filter in from far, far above. "We took this from the source itself, the guts of the soul, so to speak." He shivered, but I wasn't expert enough to tell whether it was feigned or genuine. "Opens you up to all sorts of theological philosophies, doesn't it?"

"There is a magician in the desert, you know," I said, testing him. "She created this particular dragon. The part you intend to test is her creation. Wouldn't it be better to go directly to the source? Rather than be here, working with a power you can't possibly understand fully . . . To have that knowledge—"

"Unnecessary," Fan said, clipped. "As I've said, it's not her we need. It's Rook. Mix his blood with this, return it to the soul, and the bond between dragon and rider will be broken. Terribly inconvenient, her having imprinted on him in the first place, since it introduced all *sorts* of complications into the initial plan. All we have to do now is mix your blood with the woman's, to create a transference of that loyalty. You've no idea how delighted I was to encounter you on my travels. I've never had much reason to believe in fate before, but that was truly an indication of some higher power."

"Fat fucking chance," said Rook, but I could see him eyeing the vial with considerably more care than he'd first paid it.

I thought hard, harder than I ever had and more swiftly—I could practically hear the gears of my brain grinding in protest—but I couldn't come up with anything. Silence and the wind. I didn't dare to close my eyes, though they were burning with the heat and the sand. Somehow, because of the immediacy of direct sunlight from overhead, it was burningly hot in our little prison, and the sand crusted on my skin was not helping matters in the slightest. The wind at least cooled my body down somewhat, enough for me to think things through.

Fan was working with at least one companion. That much I knew. And it would have to be someone who knew a great deal of magic— perhaps even the cause of the Ke-Han windstorm we were currently experiencing. I cast my mind back to my initial assessment of him, back when we had only first met. Part Ke-Han, I had guessed then, and now I wondered if I wasn't so far off. If he was part Ke-Han, and this magic had at its source a Ke-Han wind-magic element, then it stood to reason that Fan's purposes—his interests—lay with the Ke-Han.

I had a motive. Perhaps.

"The Esar would be willing to bargain with you," I offered tentatively. "For this piece, you *know* he would offer you a great many things."

"Bargain?" Fan said, and laughed. "I don't need to bargain."

"You probably want him to beg," Rook said.

Fan's silence explained everything, and I realized with grim certainty that my guesswork had led me to the proper conclusion. QED, as it were. We were at a grave disadvantage, and Rook must have known it too; it was why he wasn't acting yet, or even acting at all. He stood as still as an alley cat waiting for a mouse—all muscles coiled and primed, tense and ready to pounce. But no mouse had yet presented itself, and Fan was watching us with that same smug delight. Or perhaps the idea of a resurrected Havemercy was one that Rook didn't find so disagreeable now that he was confronted with it. Face-to-face, so to speak, with one he'd loved and assumed gone forever.

I couldn't allow myself to doubt his motives though. I had to trust my brother.

"What about us, then?" I asked, sliding farther away from Rook. I had to give him *some* kind of opportunity to act. At the very least, we might be able to use Fan as a hostage—that is, if we could locate his counterpart, the other agent in this dangerous masquerade. "Do you intend to kill us?"

"Perhaps," Fan said. "You've been very troublesome, following me all this way."

"We haven't been following you," Rook said. He wasn't watching me, but I could tell he was painfully aware of my every movement. "Guess you're getting a little paranoid there, huh?"

"No matter," Fan said, shrugging lightly. "If the storm does not take care of all my enemies, it will certainly neutralize them. I am used to being pursued."

"There certainly is a lot of sand, isn't there," I said, lifting my hand to wipe at some of the grit that was crusted around my mouth. "How do you tolerate it?"

That brought Fan up short. He stared at me as though I'd lost my mind. "Beg pardon?" he said.

"And the camels," I added. "Have you been riding them? Beasts. In fact, I think I'm going to sit down. This is all tiring me out tremendously. I'm not at all the adventuresome type."

"Don't move—" Fan began, but I'd given Rook all the time he needed. He went after him with a howl and then—much to my horror—they both disappeared with the force of impact, falling straight through the wall of sand at Fan's back.

"John!" I shouted, but only the wind answered me. I was alone.

CHAPTER SIXTEEN

MADOKA

When the wind started up like a wounded wolf, our shit luck didn't even surprise me anymore. At least I knew this kind of magic—and I knew it pretty damn well. Even growing up in a piece-of-shit village that was nowhere near the contested border—the one where all the action happened—I still knew what it was like to feel the sharp wind on your skin and know that it didn't have anything to do with nature. The emperor's magicians liked to fiddle with things most sensible people knew were better off left alone, and the weather just happened to be the most convenient trick they had up their sleeves for when the dragons came calling. No one cared that sometimes a storm got out of control and blew down a few shacks, tore up a few rice fields. The war effort was what was important, and the rest of us had to be good little patriots and suck it up.

The only difference between this and the storms I was used to was that the latter didn't usually involve sand. But there was a first time for everything, wasn't there? This whole trip just proved it.

The wind bit into my cheeks and the sand cut into every inch of exposed flesh, but this time I wasn't about to let any Ke-Han magician get the better of me. That certainty gave me something to cling to, a fire to bolster my spirits. I'd never thought about killing someone before—

leastways no one had ever made me mad enough to—but I had a feeling all that was going to change.

I didn't care about what my ancestors would've thought. If I found that magician before any of the others did, he was going down with my hands around his throat.

"Madoka!" I heard Badger shout, and he grabbed for me while our mount bucked. We'd come a long way from him skulking along behind me in the shadows, that was for sure. I held firm to the reins, and even dug my fingers into the camel's shaggy neck fuzz, but it was only a matter of time before we lost our hold. The beast was going crazy along with the weather. I couldn't say I blamed it, but it was stronger than me.

I tried to answer Badger, but when I opened my mouth sand flew in, and I was too busy to say anything what with all the choking. I felt my fingers slipping—couldn't concentrate on holding on *and* breathing at the same time—and I hit the ground hard. But I didn't let the impact daze me for even an instant. I had new strength way down to my bones, and I hadn't hauled my ass this far only to wipe out right at the finish line. I had a purpose now and it was right in front of my nose—just past all the sand, anyway—and I was so close to freedom I could almost taste it.

Except that was probably sand too.

I cleared my throat and spat—trying to improve my situation a little—then realized I was totally fucking alone in the middle of the desert, no mount or anything, the storm swirling all around me and threatening to swallow me up. Wind magic was a mean, shifty little trick to play at this point, and I couldn't help but wonder if they'd seen us coming after all. They'd sure as hell chosen the most effective way of evening out the odds, and confusing the shit out of everyone, to boot. Where the hell had Badger gone? It wasn't like I needed him around or anything, but he'd disappeared trying to get to me. I didn't want to owe a soldier any more than I had to. And where the fuck was the rest of the party?

Maybe they were dead. Hell, it was more than possible.

I couldn't even grope around in front of myself. My hand was throbbing worse than ever, and I didn't want to know how much worse it could get if sand got into my veins, but that pain was good. The pain meant I was near to that dragon piece, and if I was near to that, then I could follow the aching in my palm straight to the man I was looking for. Then I could end him. It was my only shot at this point, since I couldn't hope to see the hands on the compass.

Against my better instincts, I closed my eyes—I was going to need them later, and it wouldn't do me any good to go sand-blind before the real shit went down. Besides, in this situation I was probably better off than the others since I didn't need to see in order to reach my goal. All I had to do was follow the throbbing in my hand, and even though it was hurting bad enough to make me want to scream, I could tell myself *this* time it'd be worth it. With each ridiculous, shuffling step I took through the desert, I was drawing closer to the magician who'd done this to me. That knowledge was the only thing that made it bearable. I was every woman wronged by a man who thought he could be clever enough to cheat the fates. Every lonely ghost conscripted to wander the loneliest corners of the land until she closed in on the one who'd mistreated her. Every cautionary tale whispered in a young child's ear at night to make 'em shut up and go to sleep.

Those stories'd scared the shit out of me as a little tot. Now they seemed about the same as all those heroic legends I'd gobbled up—everyone got what was coming to them, and justice was served.

Justice with a side of sand.

All of a sudden my hand pulsed something fierce and I straightened up quick as shit, eyes squeezed shut, shirt pulled up over my nose and mouth to keep all the sand out of my lungs. All I could hear was the wind howling, but the pain in my hand was telling me that wind wasn't the only thing close by. The sand whipped sharply at my face, like I'd fallen into a nettle patch, but I held myself still, breathing shallow and close against the fabric of my collar.

As I stood there, the wind started to sound more like voices—loud angry voices and thin, shivery voices all rolled up together. On top of the fever, I was probably just losing my mind in the heat, the way people said happened once the sun came up over the desert. Not that I could see the sun behind all this sand, but I knew it was there.

Where are you going? the wind sighed, hard against my face but soft on my ears. *Wouldn't it be simpler just to lie down and rest? Let the sand cover your tired bones?*

I didn't know whether the voice was real or imaginary, but to my mind it sounded an awful lot like that rat-faced magician from the capital. I couldn't tell what direction the words were coming from though, so that didn't help me. All I had to go by was the feeling in my hand, like someone'd stuck an arrow straight through it.

As a kid, my favorite stories had been the ones about the blind warrior—the one who won out against impossible odds every time, even when you thought his goose was cooked. I used to imagine what it was like to fight blind—to go into every battle knowing you were at a huge fucking disadvantage and not to let your guard down even after you'd thought you'd won. I'd go out back of the house, shut my eyes tight, and listen as hard as I could while one of my kid brothers tried to sneak up behind me. Sometimes I got him, and sometimes he got me. There didn't seem to be any rhyme or reason to it, and eventually I decided I was sick of playing blind warrior.

What kind of idiot gave up an advantage she was lucky enough to have in the first place?

That magician bastard was somewhere close now. I knew it as sure as the throbbing in my hand, and I was stuck in the middle of the desert playing blind warrior again, only out here the stakes were a lot higher than bragging rights or who got first crack at our mama's fried dumplings.

Breathing in slow, I forced myself to focus on the pain. It hurt enough to make me feel a little crazy for even trying it, but it was my only shot at getting the drop on this asshole. I took a step forward. Nothing happened. I shifted my weight to the right and got a blinding flash of pain all through my hand and up my arm for my troubles. That was the way, then, and he was a lot damned closer than I'd thought for me to be feeling this bad.

Screwing up my courage, not to mention my eyes, I took another step in what I already knew was the right direction. The voices started up again, louder than before, though they echoed strangely, sounding faint as they whisked past my ears.

What can you possibly be thinking? Even an animal knows to lie down when it's been beaten. Surely you have more sense than something that goes about walking on four legs?

If that was the best they could do, I thought, gaining momentum against the shallow incline of the dune I'd come up against, then I was going to get through this, no problem. Every girl with a couple of brothers learns to build up a tough skin against being called animal names, and those desert voices had made a pretty big mistake in piping up again since I was almost positive at this point where they originated. Cheap insults had nothing on the shit I was living right now.

My palm flashed white-hot pain as I crested the dune, and with the last of my strength I threw myself forward, hollering like any blind warrior worth his salt. Maybe I should've kept the element of surprise on my side, but there was only so much I had planned out before my future became crazy with revenge.

I connected hard with something good and solid, and for a minute my head swam like I was maybe going to pass out right there. But then me and whatever went over together and hit the ground with a thump that knocked all the wind out of my lungs—and there hadn't been much in there to start with, what with me breathing hot, thick air in gulps through my shirt. I opened my eyes just long enough to see something bright and silver go flying in an arc through the air before it disappeared behind more sand, and I had to squeeze my eyes shut again or risk going blind.

The thing I'd hit shrieked like an animal caught under a cart wheel, and after that it started to struggle real good. I struck out at it blindly—at *him*, I hoped—hitting soft sand, then something hard and bony. My hand was hurting bad enough that I half expected *it* to start screaming, but I was caught up in some kind of madness, and nothing could tear me away from my purpose. He threw me off, but I was bigger than he was, and I definitely didn't land as far away as he'd hoped. I sucked in a gasp when I landed, then realized that I hadn't gotten any sand in with my air.

Tentatively, I opened my eyes, just in time to see a flash of blue clothing, and a pale, spindly arm heading straight for me.

"Idiot girl!" the owner of the arm shrieked, and if I hadn't been sure before, that voice cinched it. I rolled away just in time to dodge the magician's blow, and was on my feet—with my eyes *open* this time—before he could rally to get the better of *me*. "What if you'd broken it?"

"Well, considering it's been doing its best to break *me* ever since you put the damned thing in my hand, I figured I'd give it some payback," I told him, a little bit of my own madness in my voice now, from the heat and the anger and the fever pulsing in my blood. "I'm a pretty simple person. Don't know anything about magic in the first place, so I couldn't tell you one way or another what you're doing either. Just that I don't like it and I *want my hand back.*"

He stamped his foot like a child, and I swallowed the urge to laugh in his face. *This* was the man who'd caused me so much pain and suffering? He was about as angry as a little boy who'd lost his favorite toy—and then I realized my hand wasn't hurt as bad as it could've been, or should've been, if I was face-to-face with not my tormentor but the object causing all my torment.

"Shit," I said.

"Exactly!" the magician cried. "That contraption in your hand is the final piece. Without it, everything else will fall to pieces. You can't possibly understand its importance. The *planning* that went into this."

"Guess you shouldn't've let me wander off on my own, then," I said. We were in a pocket of air maybe, but the wind was coming in strong, if not the sand. What'd just moments ago been a shelter from the storm felt like it was closing in on us—it was possible I was hallucinating, but just then, I wasn't really sure. I had to assume everything and everyone was hostile to get the job done. Safer that way—if anything *could* be safe, at the moment.

"But you're an incompetent," the magician said.

Sure as shit, it baffled me too.

"So then why the hell'd you ask me to go after the piece in the first place?" I demanded. "Did you already know where it was?"

"Only the general area," the magician said. "I had more important things to do than drag an ill-mannered pack mule down to the desert and use her as a divining rod. Easier to follow you once you'd homed in on the soul, so I could take care of other pressing matters. I hope it doesn't offend your womanly pride to hear that you were not the *only* thing required for my plans."

"So are you gonna take this gods-cursed thing out of my hand or not?" I asked. I figured I was going to kill him either way, but there was no harm in asking.

"In a sense," said the magician, scratching his cheek as he stared at me with those ghostly eyes. "When we join you with the soul." He sounded irritable. I was gonna have to wring his neck. I pressed my fingers against the inside of my elbow, trying to soothe the pulse.

"I'm supposed to pretend like I know what that means?" I asked, like it didn't scare me one bit to have some creep deciding things about *my* body.

"I wouldn't expect you to," the magician sniffed. "You're an uneducated fool from a backwater outpost. Only someone who'd dedicated themselves to the study of dragons could possibly hope to comprehend my plans."

"Great," I said, fighting the urge to go for his throat then and there. If I could keep him talking, I might be able to figure out what the hell I was going to do with this hand of mine. Lucky for me, he was an arrogant prick, and there was nothing arrogant pricks liked more than explaining their plans to stupid women. "What's that mean?"

"It *means* that the only flaw with the Volstovic dragons was their volatile nature. Only certain men could ride them, and it had to be men of *their* choosing. A very quaint arrangement, to be sure, but I cannot afford such a capricious nature. I require a vessel, in crude terms. If we activate the dragon's soul within a *person*, however, then all I need to control is you."

"Sounds like you've got that all worked out," I said, talking now because if I thought about what he'd just said, I'd lose my mind. I hadn't come this far and fought this hard just to sign up to be a slave.

I'd die first. And I was damn well going to take him with me.

"Come on, then," he snapped, and tried to grab me by the arm, which wasn't his first fucking mistake. His first mistake was getting me involved in the first place. All the rest was plum sauce on the shaved ice. I lunged at him—no weapon but my bare hands, or *one* bare hand, anyway, but that'd be enough once I got at him—and he was gonna be a split second too late to block me, when something rocked the foundations of sand beneath us. He went down to his knees. I didn't.

"The hell was that?" I demanded.

"That *idiot*," the magician howled. "He can't have started without me!"

It seemed like he wasn't in the mood for all his plans to be going to shit. Too bad, because that's what I had in mind. I ducked away from him, but my reaction time wasn't what it should've been. Maybe if I'd trained more as the blind warrior, I might've been better at this. As it was, my magician friend grabbed me by the wrist and pulled me up. He was using me, same as ever, trying to get that compass to tell him where the remains of the dragon were.

I brought my knee up, right into his balls.

That sure as hell stopped him and he shouted in pain, letting go of me like I was on fire. Funny I should think that—seeing as how I was—

but I didn't let the humor of the situation stop me from taking control. I grabbed him by the hair and pulled his head up, then punched him good and hard across the face with my bad hand.

Fucking mistake, I realized right after. The pain was so awful that suddenly it was me who was screaming, and the only pleasure I could get out of the situation was noticing that the face of the compass had left a mark on his cheek before he flipped the tables and was over me, one hand at my throat.

"Don't try me, gutter pig," he said.

He was an idiot because he'd left himself open, and I got him in the balls a second time.

There was no grace to it whatsoever: just me kicking and scratching and screaming, and him maybe realizing that he'd fucked with me one time too many. Adding insult on top of all the other insults—not to mention all the injuries—was just enough to make me act without regard to my own life, without thinking about what he could and would do to me.

That was when he pulled out his magic.

Wind blasted like a solid wall into my chest and threw me back against another solid wall of wind *and* sand. I was bleeding from one corner of my mouth and my eyes were full of tears—pain and the sand smarting underneath the lids—but I forced myself to keep my eyes open and my gaze on him, even when I fell. He was coming toward me, and grabbing my arm again, and when I tried to kick out at his ankles wind pinned me down and kept me there.

"Don't think I'll let you do that again," the magician said.

"Guess two times were enough for you," I replied.

He brought his face down close to mine. I could see him a little too well—the mole on his chin and his sharp, dark eyes, his nose pressed up against mine. Hell, I could probably smell what he'd had for breakfast.

He sure had me. Stubborn as I was, I'd've even been the first to admit that. He had power over me that my gutter-pig brain couldn't even imagine, and now I'd forced him to use it. I'd shown him I was a real threat and he'd taken me up on that. All my actions to that point were just scratching at the bars of my cage. I wished briefly, violently, that I'd known the rat bastard's name, so that when I came back as a ghost I could cry it out in the middle of the night and get the haunting done proper. I'd do a damn good job of it too, until he was nothing but screaming and pissing and crying in a corner of his fine house—the kind of place I imagined where all rich bastards lived, with quiet sliding doors and fine carving on the lintels, eating full meals every night they didn't even have the decency to finish every last scrap of. Didn't they know how hungry some people were?

Probably never crossed their minds. And that was what made us different.

But what also made us different was that I was down below and he was up above, the weight of magic pressing me down, my body telling me there was no reason to struggle anymore.

Then the ground shook again, like something enormous was thrashing around. A dragon flashed through my head, weak and struggling, making a halfhearted attempt at life. The magician's concentration wavered—whatever was about to happen, he was scared of it—and that was another difference between us. Because I wasn't scared enough to do anything but take the opportunity for what it was. I balled my bad hand up into a screaming fist and I punched him with everything I had.

He stumbled back, his eyes wide. He looked shocked too, and for the first time our eyes met. In fact, I might've been able to say that he really saw me. I dragged myself to my feet and I lunged for him, closing both hands tight around his neck quicker than he could blink, the compass digging into the soft hollow of his throat. He struggled like a drowning rat, but I was bigger than him, and used to the pain now shooting through my palm, up through my arm. Just his bad luck this whole trip had made me tougher, but that was how poor people survived. You either grew calluses or you gave up young, and I'd crossed giving up out of my own personal vocabulary.

Hell, I didn't even know how to write it.

His face was turning red, eyes bulging, the ghosts over them flitting back and forth faster and faster. He made a choked sound and I *pushed* all my weight down, squeezing harder than I'd ever done doing the laundry. This motherfucker had wanted to turn me into a dragon. He'd tried to take my life away from me and now I was gonna do him the same favor. It was only fair.

I felt his body go limp underneath my hands and I drew them away slow, just in case he was pulling a fast one on me.

His eyes were glossy, the ghosts in them still, and his arms lay flat at his sides, spread out like a kid making a sand angel. I wanted to close my eyes, but I forced myself to look at him. It was no good killing someone—even someone who'd really deserved it—and showing your yellow belly afterward. I started to stand up, but before I could the air bubble above us collapsed and sand came roaring down on top of me.

"Madoka!" someone shouted. I knew it wasn't the magician. I wanted to reply, but I was buried—buried like the voices said I would be—and all I could do was fight or be lost.

So I fought, of course. But I was pretty sure I was already dead.

ROOK

I didn't know where the fuck I was.

In the desert, sure; that much'd always been obvious. Except I wasn't with my brother, and I wasn't fighting fair, and the sand was so thick around me by then that I didn't even know if I was hitting the dunes or hitting Fan when I struck out. I could've stumbled right into that thing Fan was calling my girl and not even known it until I tore myself open on one of her claws. Simply put, we were tussling like two mad fucking dogs, and at one point I was pretty damn sure he'd bit me, so I bit him back, and both of us were spitting sand for our efforts in the end. All we were doing was swinging at shadows, and only occasionally were we hitting the man behind 'em.

Fan probably knew right now that I didn't want answers like someone else would've if they were in my boots. Revenge was the only thing I was looking for now, and it was wearing a Fan suit. He was probably regretting having shown us the dragon too, since in case he couldn't tell, that was what'd gone and pushed me over the edge once and for all. The only problem was getting my revenge pinned down. I didn't even care I couldn't see him; you could kill a man without seeing him. I'd had enough of beating around the bush and wasting my time, so I wanted to get this over with even if the circumstances weren't fucking "ideal." I was gonna show him what happened to someone who so much as *suggested* breaking the bond between me and my girl. He needed blood? I'd give him blood all right.

Sure, it was possible that just maybe, what with all the magic flying everywhere right now, I was in over my head. The last time I'd fought magicians I'd been way up high and I'd had my own kind of magic to work with. As always, it wasn't the same fighting solo on the ground as it was in a team up in the air. But as long as Thom stayed put—real fucking likely, except not—then I could deal with this bastard Fan, find my brother again, and deal with the whole dragon mess. But those were a lot of ifs, and the sand was starting to move so fast that it was hurting me more than anything Fan managed to land.

We were in the middle of a fucking shitstorm. Literally.

I'd've laughed out loud if I hadn't been busy.

This man'd fucked with us one time too many; he'd gone and made something that was already personal even more fucking personal still, and he didn't know when to give it up and beg forgiveness from the merciless fucking god that was me. I was bigger than he was and I damn well had more fighting experience than he did—it showed in his technique—but even if he was a slippery little snake, there was still no way he could turn this fight against me.

I landed a punch somewhere square on his nose and he grabbed my arm, so I grabbed his. It was a damn foolish mistake because now we each knew exactly where the other one of us was. I brought my knee up against him where it counted and I could hear him grunt. I wanted to let him know how happy I was we were finally seeing things the way they were supposed to be but I couldn't even do that—no chance to get chatty when the sand could've finished me off better than Fan could—so I started raining blows down on his body with everything I had left. I was saving using Kalim's knife, which was my knife now, for the very end.

Everybody could be a little prideful sometimes.

Maybe I should've used it first, before anything else—or maybe I'd been lying to myself saying I didn't want answers. Maybe I just wanted the bastard to suffer a little, like he'd've made my girl suffer, and something told me if we were in each other's boots, that's what she would've wanted for me too. Fair was fair and all that horseshit.

But I'd lost track of where everything was, and when he yanked me forward hard, my face smashed right into a big metal bone. *There* she was, my girl and not my girl, and I was going to get him *good* for fucking using her against me like that, only he'd used the distraction to peel away from me. I could hear him scrabbling along her body in the sand,

and I lunged after him, quick enough to see that damned vial in his hand. Part of Have's soul, the part he'd wanted to mix with my blood, except I guess I'd pressed him into a corner. He pried open something on my girl with his bare hands and I went for his throat, getting him a split second *after* he'd smashed the contents of the vial inside.

Fan screamed a word I didn't even fucking understand, but I was through with listening to his trash. He started coughing like an old woman for all his troubles—served him right for opening his mouth in the sand—and that was all the opening I needed.

My fingers brushed the handle of my knife and a sudden flash of light burst wide across my vision—bright enough that I could see it against my eyelids. I had just enough time to wonder what the shit before the screech of metal filled my ears, groaning through the sand. Something heavy hit the ground and it quaked under me, knocking me clean off my feet and sending me sprawling backward into the sand. I had to hand it to Fan, that rat bastard. He sure knew how to make it difficult for a man to kill him. All that sand stung my back like hitting a brick wall, only worse, because all the hard gritty bits of the wall were moving like they wanted to tear my skin off my bones. Fan'd slipped away from me in the mess, probably exactly like he'd planned.

I was gonna do a lot worse than cut him up when I finally got to him. I was gonna tear every limb from his body and that was only gonna be the opening act.

I'd've cursed his name, but breathing was suddenly a lot more difficult than it'd been a minute ago, and so was everything else. Because I could see what'd caused the quake now—a long metal tail swished sharply though the sandstorm—and I could see the outline of her head before I had to close my eyes or risk going blind.

There was no mistaking what I'd seen, though. Have was moving.

I couldn't let that shit fuck me up now. Now if *ever* was the time to be just a little like my brother and look at all the fucking facts. Fan hadn't done anything with the dragonsoul *or* my blood. He'd just panicked and shot his load too early, sprayed Well water or whatever all over her insides.

Maybe he'd brought a dragon to life, but she wouldn't be Have. At least, that was what I was telling myself now just to make sure I made it through the rest of the day alive.

I was gonna need all my concentration to make sure that *other* people didn't.

There was blood in my mouth and I spat it out, the wind whistling all around me like it thought this was *real* funny, and sending the blood right back into my face; I was just lucky my eyes were closed. Something was trickling warm down my cheek too, and I could only guess that was more blood. My gift to the desert, and I guess it was pretty much the only gift I had to give, by this point. Meanwhile, my chest hurt like Have'd stepped on it, and maybe that was how I was supposed to feel, considering the blast'd been from a part of the lady herself. Maybe if I'd been able to talk right about then, I'd've had some real pointed questions for Fan about that fancy little maneuver he'd just pulled. He'd answer 'em—he was that kind of blathering moron who couldn't keep his mouth shut even when it was in his best fucking interest—and then I'd be able to pin him down like a roach under my boot. I wouldn't even stoop so low as to pull the same trick on him he'd pulled on me, because my girl was better than that. If you killed scum, you were scum. It was good enough for me but she was too good for it—too good for me—and always had been.

I pulled my sorry ass to my feet, still fighting mad, but warier now. Getting blasted across the desert could do that to you, and I had no idea where Fan'd landed, or where my girl was, though I could hear the sounds she was making over the howl of the storm, clicking and groaning and metal scraping up against metal like whoever'd put her together had done a real shit-poor job.

Wherever Fan was, I hoped he wasn't hurt too bad, because he was giving me all sorts of reasons to take my sweet time with killing him.

I heard a shout, quickly swallowed up by the wind, and I whirled around blindly, forcing myself in the direction it'd come from. I hoped the blast from the dragon waking up'd knocked him off his feet at least. Doing what he'd done—waking up a dragon halfway, as far as I could tell—was either stupid or desperate, and as much as I hated Fan, I wasn't about to call him stupid considering how quick he'd outwitted us the first time. At least it meant he was finally wising up to exactly the kind of pain and suffering he'd called down upon himself—first by trying to use me to his advantage, then by trying to get between me and my girl.

There'd always been an understanding between Havemercy and me: that we'd kill any man who came between us. I was just holding up my end of the bargain now that she couldn't uphold hers.

The wind changed on my right side—the airflow interrupted, compensating for something in its space—and I had just enough time to whirl and face it before Fan threw himself at me.

He'd probably been scouting me out after the blast, and I was too fucking stunned to do the same in return.

For the second time in too fucking short a space of minutes, we went down hard. I hadn't been expecting the sudden force of Fan's attack but I should've known better. I'd backed him into a corner, and now he was fighting mean and hard, snarling like a rabid animal that'd been hunted within an inch of its life. He bit my fucking ear, and that was another mistake since it told me exactly where his face was. I hit him hard and square in the jaw and he howled, the sound cut off sharp when I got him again good in the stomach.

"*Pathetic*," he gasped, part of a longer phrase that got lost in the sand. I rolled to get up and he kicked me right behind the knee, sending me flat on my back again. Apparently I wasn't the only dirty fucking fighter around. ". . . you *really* so blinded by *sentiment*?"

I rolled quickly onto my side, lunging for him before he could get to his feet. He made a choked noise when I plowed straight into his chest, and we really were fighting like animals now, on four legs instead of two and no speech between us. I couldn't get my knife out without it being turned against me with all this blind flapping and I was pissed about that, but bastion, at least it resembled some kind of even fight. Fan grasped blindly at whatever he could reach, yanking hard at my braids and scratching at my face. He smashed my nose with his own fucking forehead and it made a real good crack. Lucky for me, my nose knew the score, since it'd been through this and worse. It hurt like all bastion fuck, but I didn't let go of my good friend Fan, even when he got me a lucky one right in the damned throat, and I had to hope that the crack'd hurt his head just as much as it'd hurt mine. Fact was, I was hurting all over, but none of that mattered in light of the unshakable truth. This time I had him, and we both knew it. He wriggled and twisted and nearly threw me off him more than once, but the simple fact of the matter was I'd stayed on top of fickler mounts than some skinny little magician's dog, and I wasn't about to let him go that easy. I managed to get my hands around his neck and could feel the vulnerable pulse—flickering wildly like an out-of-control flame—right under my thumbs. Fan coughed and I could feel that too—the involuntary spasms of his lungs trying to pump sand out and air in, and not quite able to do a full job of it.

"Not sentiment," I told him, leaning in real close to keep the sand out of my fucking face for two seconds. "I just *really* don't like you."

Fan's answer was something I recognized a split-hair second too late, just *after* his knife stuck me right between the ribs. I hadn't even known he'd had the damn thing, but that was my own fault and no one else's, and I deserved what I got for it. Punishment: the only way a Mollyrat knew how to learn.

Back before Adamo'd put a ban on fighting in the Airman, he'd given me all kinds of lessons on what he liked to call my shit-stupid mistakes. Now that was back when I'd been more anger than brains, more muscle than menace, and I guessed after everything I still kinda was, but I liked to tell myself I'd learned a *few* things. Number one was supposed to be never letting your enemy out of your sight. Somewhere a little lower on the list was never letting your enemy's *hands* out of your sight, since you always had to assume anyone you were tussling with was fighting dirtier than you were, but I was willing to bet even Adamo'd never expected me to be brawling out in the middle of the desert, right in the center of a bastion-damned sandstorm, over something so precious we were all prepared to kill for it at the drop of a ha'penny.

I could hear my girl rumbling somewhere in the sandstorm, like a newborn kitten searching blindly for its mama. Hearing her like that made me sick, but I couldn't think about it now.

Still, didn't really make much difference. I squeezed down hard on Fan's throat with both hands and he twisted the knife, the pain coursing sharp like a poison through my body, throbbing in back of my molars and right low in my gut like I was about to be sick. When he twisted my arms got weak, and then Fan threw me off and scuffled around like he was stumbling to his feet. I cracked my eyes open—I had to risk it now since I'd lost the advantage of being faster. He'd done me the favor of leaving his knife in me, at least, so I didn't have to worry about bleeding out. What I did have to worry about was how the hell I was going to get to my feet since I was having a little trouble keeping my head on straight.

At least I could see him now, the barest outline of him, that mangy little fuck. I hauled myself up into a sitting position, light-headed but thinking as hard as I'd ever done. *Get it fucking together, Rook,* and all the usual shit. Have'd be *laughing* at me if she could've seen this spectacle, me sitting on my ass in the desert when the one who'd caused us both so much suffering was still standing upright. Not to mention there was still my brother, fucking *Hilary,* who could probably talk a man to death, but that was about it. He was waiting for me, back in that quiet place inside all the sand, probably sweating like somebody's grandmammy and muttering about the heat, and bastion damn me if I was about to leave *him* alone to take care of business when everyone knew he couldn't.

He wouldn't even know where to fucking start.

Slowly—*painfully* slowly—I dragged myself to my feet. Fan's outline didn't change, but I saw him take a blurry step forward. At least I'd winded him, but that was about all I could claim.

"Come now," he hollered, his back against the wind. "Don't embarrass us both. Have you forgotten what I have in my possession?"

The soul, I thought, but didn't say. Let him wear himself out on taunting me. That was how I'd gotten the drop on him the first time.

"I suppose it would be a quicker end than bleeding to death, wouldn't it?" Fan yelled, clearly not at all put out by having a conversation with himself. "I *had* intended on saving the actual soul until my brother arrived, but he seems to be taking his time. Not something you'd know anything about, I'm sure."

There was more than one person in the group I'd rode out with that I could imagine being shit stubborn enough to take down a person in a sandstorm. I had my money on Madoka.

"Does it console you to know you may well have wasted all our planning?" Fan shouted, but I could tell the bastard was just taunting me. "I've no idea what the soul will do on its own, without a vessel to control it. That was never my specialty, but you've pushed me into a corner. You or me, I'm afraid, and I'm *very* attached to myself."

He was starting to move away from me. I could tell by the sound of his voice, even over the raging wind. If I was going to get him, it'd have to be soon.

I couldn't waste my chance. Didn't really think I was gonna get more than one.

"It's quite a shame," Fan said. He just couldn't shut up, and that was going to be his final fucking downfall. I risked a look—I had to—and caught sight of something glimmering in the sand. That was what he was heading for. I was just gonna have to stop him before he got there. "I don't at *all* fancy being the one to break the news to your brother. I actually rather like him—more at least than some—but the irony of killing you with your own precious beast is all too—"

Things happened real quickly all at once—the way they always fucking did when shit got down to the wire. Fan went for the soul, I went for Fan, and something came crashing through the impenetrable wall of sand from Fan's right. It hit him before I could, tackling him like one of Provost's champion wolves and holding him to the ground. They knocked into the dragonsoul and sent it flying, bright silver disappearing into the sand.

I lunged for it, and a horrible sound ripped through the air, like a dragon roaring, only her mouth hadn't been put on quite right. The earth shuddered again—she was moving—and it sprayed dune dust everywhere. Probably would've blinded me if I hadn't managed to shut my eyes in time.

"Rook?" someone called, a little choked and a little reedy, but un-fucking-mistakable all the same.

I'd better be fucking dreaming, I thought, and risked opening an eye again.

There was sand everywhere, nearly impossible to see through it, because whatever wind'd been holding it out in pockets was completely fucked by the dragon thrashing around. Sand came sniping in at us from every direction, and I didn't know much about the way this shit worked—or the way anything worked, really—but I had to wonder what in bastion's name was keeping the sand from pouring down on us like a landslide in the mountains. The ground was still trembling, or maybe it was just me; either way I could barely keep myself on my feet. The only thing that had me going still was Thom, who was staring right at me. And if *I* lost it, he would too.

"Bastion fuck," he said, eyes going wide. He was gonna get sand in them and go blind, just for me. I could tell. "Is that a knife in you?"

No time for stating the obvious, I thought dizzily, and wasn't that just the plain old truth, because Fan took that moment to kick Thom in the gut and scramble away—looking for the dragonsoul again, I could only guess.

Well, now he'd gone and done it. He'd hurt my baby brother, and I was going to *waste* him.

Fan reached out in the direction the soul had gone flying and I had my own knife out, faster than anything. I couldn't even trust my own fucking body to get there in time so I threw it, sharp and clean, and at least my aim was good. It pierced clean through his outstretched hand and he screamed—that I heard.

Fan was scuffling in the direction Thom'd gone—I couldn't look at him, because it'd fuck everything up—and I started toward Fan, aiming to get my knife back. Shadows passed over my vision and I figured I was close to blacking out, so I'd have to get this done quick. No more wasting time. I'd put too much in danger shitting around and fighting like a 'Versity boy, and now I was serious.

I knocked Fan down and grabbed the special hilt of my knife, ripping it out of his hand. He screamed again and I grabbed him by the back of his neck, the knife against his throat.

He laughed, that little snake, but it didn't go all the way up to his eyes.

"Funny what one's willing to do for family, isn't it?" Fan said, pulse pounding like a jackrabbit's. "I take no pleasure in saying this, but we *aren't* as different as I thought."

"Don't be so fucking sentimental," I told him, and the blood was already flowing when Thom shouted.

"Stop!" he said.

Fan's eyes jerked up and I heaved, wondering why he hadn't just run, wondering if I was always going to be afflicted with him until the end of my days—which, fuck, might be pretty soon depending on what happened when it came time to take this knife out of my body. Fan didn't know all the special places to slide a knife *between* the ribs, which he would've if he'd grown up in Molly, so I didn't think he'd gotten me so good that I couldn't pull through if I clung to my usual good fucking luck, but there was always room for complications. And we were in the middle of the fucking desert, not to mention, which meant we were far away from good Volstovic doctoring that I could—sometimes, sorta—trust. No healing Talent around here, and I was willing to bet good money that the magician Fan was working with—his own brother, apparently—wasn't exactly the type for that, either.

I heaved, blood coming out my mouth, blood covering Fan's hand and Fan's knife and my knife, blood soaking through my shirt, and sand getting everywhere the blood wasn't.

Slowly I turned, but I kept the knife pressed firm into Fan's throat just in case he tried anything. No matter what, he was getting his throat slit here today.

"Don't do it, John," Thom said carefully, his face unrecognizable, crusted in sand. "I've got it—see? I've got it."

Something sparkled. He was holding the soul like a fucking newborn, cradled up against his chest like he planned to start nursing any minute. I'd've laughed, but it would've come out all bloody.

"You don't know how to use it," Fan grunted. "To bring her back. *He* was the only one who could—he'll be here, just you wait."

I nearly cut his throat then and there, just so I wouldn't have to fucking listen to him talking anymore. The sand was what saved him in the end—or rather, the sand fucking *falling* was what saved him, coming down over our heads without any warning and blocking out all the light. The dragon let out another wail, heavy, awkward steps sounding along the ground. I fell forward and I felt something wet and hot against my hands, pouring over my wrists; then the knife in my side glanced off one of my ribs as I fell forward, crushed under so much sand.

I just hoped what was left of Havemercy didn't kill what was left of my family. That'd be a real peach, wouldn't it?

Hilary, I thought, and then I really conked out.

MALAHIDE

I wasn't entirely certain, but I was *almost* positive, that Kalim had fled the scene. If I was lucky, he might have died amidst the chaos—a terrible thing to say, but I would have preferred my secret to die with him, and it would make things much easier if I did not have to kill him myself. In any case, he was no longer nearby. Whether or not the sand had devoured him or he had taken this as some sign of godly wrath against which he could not hope to prevail, I had no way of knowing. Simply put, I could not smell him any longer, though I *could* smell the others—scattered scents dancing helplessly and poignantly, carried to me by the sand and wind.

Next to me, Badger grunted.

He'd been very brave and had thrown himself between me and the brunt of the storm—a magical effect on the weather if ever I'd seen one, and definitely Ke-Han in origin. Scent alone was indicative of that, but I had studied these very effects and needed only common sense to determine the source.

I was grateful for Badger's help since I was dizzy and trying to piece together the locations of our various quarries: where Airman Rook was, nearby his companion; my own friend from the mountains; Madoka and her diseased hand; the dragonsoul itself; and a new scent, obviously belonging to the wielder of this sudden power.

We were trapped quite nicely between walls made entirely of sand, and I pressed myself against Badger's broad back as I attempted to make some sense of all of it, my own compass thrown for a loop.

"Where is she?" Badger demanded.

"Hush," I told him. "Don't disturb me. I *am* working on it."

Sand filled my mouth and I scowled, disgusted. Such dirtiness was loathsome in and of itself, but now it distracted me, the magician's scent carried to me upon each grain and confusing all my senses.

So our task was very clear, I realized. We had to find the source and take this monster out. Once the weather itself had calmed, when our most dangerous foe was eliminated, then we could turn our collective attentions toward what had brought us all here in the first place.

The question was simply how we would kill him.

"Have you ever killed a magician?" I asked Badger.

He shook his head no, sensibly choosing not to waste his breath. I pressed my face against his shoulder and spoke into the fabric of his shirt in order to avoid choking to death on all this horrible sand.

"No matter," I told him. "I have."

Granted, that was under special circumstances, and I'd certainly had "the drop" on them, as the saying went. They hadn't been *fair* fights, in any case—more like quiet assassinations gone uninvestigated and unexplained, negating any potential trouble the Esar felt might arise in the future. Such a circumspect man! One day I too would become rebellious—it was inevitable, given my liege's mercurial whims—and he would have to find someone to negate *me*, but all that was neither here nor there.

In this case, if anyone had the drop, it was almost certainly the man behind this frightful sandstorm.

"Are you armed?" I asked Badger. I felt him nod. "Excellent," I continued. "Will you help me kill a man?"

He hesitated, probably trying to understand my motives—I felt that, as well—and I patted him lightly on the back, nudging him in the proper direction. The stench was overwhelmingly pungent and I was having difficulty breathing. Pressing my face up against Badger's back made it hard for me to smell anything over the odors of his own skin and sweat and shirt, but if I were to try to breathe without that cloth covering, too much sand would enter my nose.

I was lucky this magician was so powerful, the magic so prevalent. What made him strongest was the very thing leading me straight to him, with Badger as my handy weapon. He didn't seem altogether delighted to be in his position, but a soldier was nothing so much as a tool, meant to be used at an appropriate occasion—and none was so appropriate as having to confront an unknown magician with none of my usual wiles about me.

Even if I'd thought to bring a pistol, all this sand would've rendered it useless in short order.

"I believe this is the man who put Madoka in her current position," I told him, as incentive. "Does that assuage your qualms any?"

It seemed to. His back stiffened with resolve, and the square cut of his jaw hardened.

We were both equally contemptuous of this man—and no one hated him more than Madoka. I felt bad that I was not trapped here with her—for truly, she was the one who deserved to force him into a corner and laugh in his face. I only wished she could have been given that chance, but fate had preordained otherwise. It was strange for me to have cause to think about anyone's motivations other than my own, but I couldn't allow such thoughts to distract me at such a crucial interval. It was pointless to even wonder what the *Esar* was thinking, though I'd done a fair bit of it on this trip. Not exactly my usual style.

I pushed Badger onward, the sand whipping around my boots and sending my skirts in all directions—yet another reason to be glad that Kalim was not here, or for the moment, at least, I'd lost the scent of him. I pressed myself up against Badger for shelter as we moved, tugging on his left arm or his right when we needed to make a turn. We made a fine team in silence—neither of us being much for words when there was serious work to be done—and the next wall we broke through flooded my nose with the thick spice of magic. It was nearly overwhelming and I smiled grimly; we were drawing closer. Our pace was something to contend with: one step forward, two steps back, it seemed, and my legs were screaming. No doubt things were worse for Badger, taking the brunt of the wind as I supported him from the rear. At least he was trained in soldiering. All I had to do was allow him to shield me and to keep up my own fierce pace.

We were at a distinct disadvantage, but it was my sole purpose now to nullify the magic's effect. How I had come to the point of helping others to get the job done in my stead, I would never know—but after this, I swore to myself, I was done with it. I worked best on my own, as all true agents of change. Allowing myself to become engrossed in the curious, baffling lives of others—their whims and their wants—had more than distracted me from my ultimate goal.

It had changed so much in recent days that it was difficult to keep track of it. My missions from the Esar were always straightforward—almost childishly clear, bastion bless him—so that I had never had cause to call my purpose elusive. Now, with the wind at my back, Badger at my front, and, somewhere out there, a magician I had to kill, I couldn't quite escape the feeling that I'd somehow lost sight of the duty I'd been charged with.

Simply defeating the magician was not enough, and neither was freeing Madoka. Those were both goals set for my own personal satisfaction, and nothing close to my true duty. No doubt the Esar would have laughed to see me now, a grown woman tramping around in the desert with his erstwhile enemies, all of whom were as good as struck blind by all this blasted sand. Meanwhile, he sat enthroned in our beloved country, enjoying the comforts and pleasures of home. At least it was clear his paranoia-inspired nightmares had been based in some real truth, but still, it seemed hardly fair at this current juncture. I could only hope that what I brought to him at the end would be more than just a handful of sand.

A sharp gust kicked up without warning, blowing straight into our faces and bringing with it the honeyed overtones of some sweeter magic, more pleasing to my nose. It was a part of the dragonsoul; I recognized that quite easily—I was willing to stake my life on what I smelled—and I paused to note, with some curiosity, that it was *not* in the same place as the magician, when a terrific crack broke through the sound of the wind and sand, followed by a deep, shuddering rumble that passed beneath our feet and through the entire dune. It was followed by the scent of something spicy, and though foreign, it seemed strangely familiar. I fell into Badger, and Badger fell into the sand.

Quickly I pulled myself to my feet once more, stretching my hands out to help Badger do the same.

"What was that?" he yelled against my ear once I'd tugged him up.

"I don't know," I told him, not for the first time wishing I'd had something more to give up for the as-yet-undiscovered Talent of omnipotence. The smell was more my concern than the earth's rumbling, but I couldn't tell him that either. "We aren't heading in that direction."

"If Madoka—" Badger began, squinting off into the distance.

"She's not over there either," I said, raising my voice. The curious quality it held—tinny, Madoka called it—became more obvious when I shouted. I sounded a little like the wind itself, sharp and strange. Lucky for me, the wind was devouring all it came across now, and the tone of my voice was the least of Badger's concerns. "Trust me—I would know!"

In truth, I had no idea where Madoka was, since I'd lost the scent of even her hand in the wake of all this other magic. It drowned everything else out, to the point where I felt rather blinded by it. The explosion had made things worse, and not just because of the wild roiling of the sand. At present, I needed Badger to stay on course, and if he needed to hear that Madoka had not been caught up in whatever minor earthquake had just occurred in the middle of the desert, then I was doing us both a favor. In the past, I had done far worse in order to get what I wanted. The only difference was, it had never bothered me before.

Badger squeezed my hands, though, and straightened his back once again. The walls of sand had shifted, collapsing in on themselves with the force of whatever had erupted in the distance, but they still held strong. I drew in as deep a breath as I could dare, one hand pressed over my nose and mouth. Sand found its way in, but at least there was still some air left for breathing.

We were so close now that the stench was burning my nostrils—a sharp pain that made my eyes water. The wind whipped my tears away as quickly as they formed. In fact, our sheer proximity was what made it difficult for me to choose our next move since the magic on the air was overwhelming no matter which direction I turned in. Much like Madoka's compass, I could not operate when I was too close to the source.

I could be sure, at least, that we did not need to head toward the direction of the explosion. That much was certain. Its cause was beyond our present concerns. And if we stood here for very long, we were all too likely to become too tired to fight any longer against the fierce winds and sands. I would simply have to trust my instincts—those, at least, were always good—and follow them for the time being, instead of my nose. I knew what direction I *had* been heading in; in this storm, it seemed impossible that even the man controlling the winds could navigate all that quickly through them. It was a safe assumption to make: that he had not gone far from when last I'd been certain of his whereabouts.

I tugged at Badger's shirt and gave him a little nudge in the direction I'd chosen, hoping he wouldn't decide that now of all moments it was time to do something foolish. I'd underestimated his soldierly training, however, and he did nothing of the kind, simply starting off through the sand the way I'd indicated and leaving me to scurry along quickly in his wake. He didn't like me, but he was willing to work with me for Madoka's sake. People could be so funny when they were trying to be decent.

I clutched Badger's shoulder as we walked, and the scuffling sound of the sand beneath our feet coupled with the shrieking of the wind— much more intense than it had been moments ago—covered up any further conversation we might've indulged in, about Madoka or otherwise. Of all of us, including the men from Volstov as well as Kalim, I understood Badger's stake in this quest the least. I would have liked to ask him more about it, had there been ample time and opportunity. It had been my experience, of most of the soldiers I'd known, that their loyalty to country far outweighed their loyalty to themselves, but his behavior wasn't that of a man acting out of duty. I'd suspected he'd had feelings for Madoka, but to see it in action now had startled me. I had never allowed my own personal feelings to take precedence over my missions.

I'd never had personal feelings strong enough to warrant it.

Unfortunately, fate seemed to be rather short on both time and opportunity these days. I could trust his motives. They were not fickle. That was all I needed.

I'd only just adjusted to the inundation of magic flooding my nostrils, a heady brew that made my brain feel lazy as I followed along tightly behind Badger—when the quality of the air around us changed once more. I tensed, unsure of what to expect, when another boom shuddered through the sands—this one much stronger than the first and stinking to the heavens of a new brand of magic. Sand sprayed everywhere, like someone had overturned a giant hourglass, and ahead of me, Badger pulled up short. For the first time, I felt the sand falling as a weight against my shoulders instead of pulling at me right and left. Realizing what it meant, I had time only to give my companion a firm push as I threw what remained of my energy into a speedier pace.

"Run!" I shouted, the sound of my voice nearly swallowed by the sand now hailing down around us. A blizzard of sand, one might call it; but whatever the name, it was a terrifying and unnatural expression, perhaps the landscape's reaction to so much torturous manipulation.

We had no choice but to escape it.

Badger broke into a sprint behind me, though I couldn't exactly promise I was the best person to be following at the moment. Like everyone with a bit of sense still left in them—and I did have that, despite what everyone had always told me—I had an inordinate fear of being buried alive, and the way the sandstorm had turned on us, I was beginning to fear that might be the result. I was running toward the direction I'd chosen, but I no longer had any guarantee of what we would discover once we arrived there.

I stumbled through the soft dune sands, and at one point Badger even hauled me back up to my feet, the pair of us running blind through the sudden downpour. My heart was pounding, and my lungs ached from the lack of air they were receiving. I could only hope that somehow—despite all the odds, which seemed to have turned against me as of late—we would break clear of the sand before it covered us. Already, every step I took was sinking a little lower into the ground. The sand sucked at my ankles, pooling around my shins and threatening to tear my boots off the more I struggled. And behind me I could hear it, roaring like a wave. We had to outrun it as it chased us from the center of the storm. As for our comrades, it was more than possible they would be buried beneath all this madness. The very desert had turned against these insults and was reclaiming itself from us. So much for Kalim's theory that his gods were behind the appearance of dragonmetal in these parts. A more suspicious person would have suggested this was the gods' revenge against the very piece in question.

At least this would make an excellent story for Dmitri, if I ever saw him again.

Then, just as I was all but ready to accept the almost certainty of my final resting place, unmarked and unremarkable in the midst of the desert sands, the air pressure lifted from my shoulders. I stumbled forward with the sudden lightness in my feet, falling onto all fours on the ground, the sand scorching hot beneath my palms. I could feel the sun, and hear Badger's boots on the sand behind me, and—feeling acutely foolish—I risked opening my eyes.

The deluge had stopped completely.

Good girl, I thought privately. Even among Ke-Han magicians, the quickest solution to stopping a spell was killing it at the source.

All I saw was sand, sand for miles, the shapes of the dunes shifted but unmistakable. Blank and impenetrable, as well. My eyes stung with the ferocity of the sunlight. It must have been about midday.

I drew in a deep breath, daintily picking myself up off the ground and dusting off my skirts, trying to regain some semblance of self-respect. The smell of magic was still potent in the air, but it hung about my body like an aftereffect—nowhere near as strong as it had been before. There was still that other scent I'd detected, tickling in my nostrils like strong pepper, and I followed its direction with my eyes. A great dune in the desert was shifting. At least, that was what it looked like from here.

"What's that?" Badger asked abruptly. I assumed he was talking about the same thing I'd seen, but when I turned to look at him, he was facing in the exact opposite direction.

Some few feet away was a funny little mound, not at all natural to the area, with something glinting off the side of it. I couldn't be sure from this distance—all that peering through the sand had done some damage to my eyes—but it very *nearly* looked like a compass. At least, it was metal, polished to exquisite brightness by the force of wind and sand.

"Madoka?" I asked, a little wonderingly, and Badger was across the distance in a flash, using his hands as blunt shovels to clear the sand off her.

Somehow, her body had made it through.

I let Badger go for her. It seemed to please him that he could. I had been under the assumption earlier that they had not known each other for very long, but soldiers often grew attached to their companions. I was a little jealous, but I could hardly begrudge them their closeness. It was almost sweet.

He grabbed her under her armpits and hauled her up out of the sand, shading her with his own body—again, a small thing that was, to me, quite touching. In the meantime I undid the laces of my boots and dumped the sand out of them, and as I redid the laces I scented the air. The magic was still there, simply muted, as though all the sand had deafened me—or it. But it was fading fast.

At least now my boots were much less painful to wear, though my stockings were torn and my heels and toes made rough with little pin-pricks, each grain of sand nothing on its own but quite painful when working in tandem.

I glanced at Madoka again. She was moving, as were the hands upon her compass. She was still alive, then, and Badger was attempting to coax the sand from out of her lungs, two hands pressed flat against her chest as he heaved his considerable strength against her. But it was not Badger's sweet, futile emotions that caught my attention most. It was the compass in Madoka's palm.

All at once, the hands went still—they hadn't been moving as wildly to begin with, I realized, the meaning of which I could not entirely comprehend. Was the dragonsoul buried? I would certainly be com-pelled to dig for that.

"She's alive!" Badger called out to me. Perhaps he expected some-thing of me. I should have gone to him and taught him the proper ways to coax breath back into aching lungs, but instead I drew up my skirts and turned my head back over my shoulder, in the direction toward which the compass hands—all three of them at once—were pointing.

Something, very far in the distance, moved.

"Can she walk?" I asked.

Badger opened his mouth—no doubt to tell me she could not.

"I can," Madoka croaked. "Where's the fucking magician?"

I paused to sniff the air. "Dead," I said, and I was certain of it.

"I know," Madoka said grimly, then, "Shit. How'm I supposed to get this out of me?"

"I promised you that Volstovic magicians would take a gander at your predicament," I reassured her, all the while not taking my eyes off the compass. It was still pointing straight in the same direction. I sniffed again, but the air was so still I could smell nothing at all beyond the stench of blood and rot and metal in Madoka's hand.

"You're dreaming if you think I can make it that far," Madoka said, and privately I rather agreed with her.

"Well," I said slyly, "there is one more option."

All three of us looked at her hand at the same time.

"Help me up," Madoka said.

Badger was going to protest again, then thought the better of it. He stood, bringing Madoka with him, and she was sure on her feet. The sleeve of her dress was torn and I could see red lines traced with green tangled all up the length of her forearm—I could not imagine how it would be to have your body turned against you so thoroughly, and the man behind the magic dead and buried beneath the dunes. Yet there *was* one option left to us, and the compass made the direction all too clear.

"Don't care what you do with it now," Madoka told me. "I just want this thing gone."

"We can only hope it's three against two," I replied. This time, I would be the one to lead the way, not Badger.

And, I added privately to myself, I hoped the odds were even more in our favor.

CHAPTER SEVENTEEN

THOM

The wind had stopped. It was painfully quiet. Whatever Fan had done to animate the body of the dragon, she had wound down, or perhaps all the sand had fouled up her workings. In any case, she was silent, the air was still, and I was alone. My chest was aching, but it wasn't because of the sand.

Rather, it was what the wind and sand had given me—thrown against me in one last dying blast. I'd tried to get it to Rook. I remembered that much. It'd hit me so hard that I felt my heart stop, and I wondered if this was yet another earthquake—if this one would finish me off—before I lost consciousness. It was brief, however, and my heart soon regained its usual rhythm.

And so I awoke with my arms wrapped around the dragonsoul, as though it were a baby cradled in my lap.

It was beautiful. Despite the heat, the glass and metal were both cool, save for a tender warmth that pulsed at the very core of the glass tube. The metalwork was intricate, and even the cogs here and there had been bent into such shapes as to look like crown jewels. There were nubs of metal that reminded me of the mechanisms inside music boxes, and the liquid magic itself glittered like fireflies were caught inside. All the rest was made up of gears and workings I had no way of comprehending. There was even some ancient, polished wood mixed in with the metal, and despite the ordeals it must have been through, the polish remained glossy—not even a single edge was blistered or burned. Only one part of the whole looked incomplete, or imperfect. There was a spot on the side where a circle of metal had been sheared off, the glass beneath cracked but not shattered, and I ran my fingers against it wonderingly. A shiver ran down my spine.

This was what we had been looking for, all this time.

It truly was as glorious as our mad search warranted.

If I give this to John, I thought, *he really will be happy.*

But he was somewhere underneath all the sand. I'd seen him buried underneath it, and here I was, clinging to some inanimate object—one he'd been looking for, not me. If I let go of it he'd be angry, but he wasn't here to rebuke me.

It hadn't even been long since the wind had stopped howling and all had fallen still. There was a chance Rook was still alive under the sand mounded up before me, but I was afraid—afraid that if I began to dig I might discover that he wasn't. As long as I did nothing, I still had hope.

And what kind of pussyfoot thinking is that horseshit? Rook would have demanded. I would have stiffened, scoffed, frowned, fought off the insult, then kept it privately within my heart as a secret wound for the rest of my life. If I didn't change now, then I would never be able to.

Still, I couldn't drop the dragonsoul. We'd worked this hard, come all this way, fought with one another and beside one another—in a manner of speaking, if whatever *I* had done could even be called fighting—just to get our hands on it. I held it tighter, then loosened my grip, afraid of its power as well as the fissure in the glass. If I broke it open, what horrible power would I unleash?

More important than all that was this: The last time I'd seen my brother, before the sand came down around us all, there'd been a knife sticking straight out of his rib cage. I knew anatomy very well, and I knew that such wounds could look worse than they really were. It all depended on where he'd been hit, but that injury on top of the sand-storm . . .

I felt sick.

"Shut up, Thom," I said out loud. It sounded like Rook, and it jolted me out of my idiocy more quickly than sitting on my ass mourning my assumed losses had done. I stood, hauling the dragonsoul with me, and stumbled in Rook's direction.

I couldn't be certain that this was where he'd ended up, but it was the last place I'd seen him before the sand had come crashing down around him, and it was the best choice out of my limited options. The desert landscape had gone back to its natural state of eerie barrenness after the eruption of the storm, and, frankly, the sight terrified me. There was no trace of my brother, nor was there any of Fan, though the latter was hardly my concern at the moment. With shaking fingers, I set the dragonsoul down in the sand, where it wouldn't be in the way but where I could also keep an eye on it. I'd remain mindful of it. I owed that much to my brother—a final vigilance, if all was as hopeless as I feared—but, perhaps not surprisingly, it was not my foremost concern, either. It seemed strange to have sought so long for something only to have it matter so little now. The soul was a beautiful piece of work, both powerful and strange, but all its magic amounted to nothing if I had to bear it alone.

On my knees, in the middle of the desert and sweating under the blaze of the noon-high sun, I began to dig.

For once I didn't allow myself to think about anything except the task at hand, how best to clear the sand away from the site of my excavation. It was horribly disheartening work, the sand so dry that it seeped in where I'd been digging only moments before, making my efforts seem almost worse than futile. The only way to beat it was to stay on top of the flow, digging a wider radius as I went deeper, so that the very center was never covered by any of the sand as it spilled in around the edges. It was troublesome enough a task that it kept my mind occupied, giving me no time to think about my brother's capacity for air while trapped under the ground, or the knife that had been stuck into him. I should have trusted Rook's initial assessment of Fan and allowed Rook to do away with him as he pleased. My brother was paranoid and violent but, as much as I hated to admit it, he was so often *right*.

But such thoughts would only bring me to ruin or despair, and I required all my energy for digging.

Rook was the most stubborn person I'd ever met, and I knew he would cling to life with the same tenacity he chose to exhibit for all the other activities and objects most important to him. Havemercy was the one thing about which he'd been most passionate, but over the course of our journey I was beginning to understand some of the others as well. Rook liked his freedom—he'd taken to the desert like a native, comfortable in ways I could never hope to approximate even after years of trying to settle down—and he seemed to like traveling. Reason should have dictated that he was happiest with nothing and no one to answer to—he'd chafed considerably under the Esar's command, after all, which had caused all our mutual grief in the first place—but something gave me the sense that this initial assessment wasn't quite accurate. There was some valuable piece of the puzzle that I was still missing, and I scrambled to uncover it just as I was attempting to displace an entire desert in order to find my brother.

The sand was hot—it burned my fingers—and the sun was growing almost intolerable. I tore my shirt off, winding it around my head as a makeshift protection from the heat—my back and arms would be less lucky, but these were small losses against a more immeasurable one—and I kept on digging, mindless of what discomforts the desert might visit on me. I dug until my fingers grew numb, chapped and red from the heat, the skin under my nails beginning to bleed.

My brother hadn't come all the way out here, chasing a phantom of the past, because he liked things best on his own. He'd come because what he *really* wanted was something—or someone—on which to constantly test his teeth. He wanted someone who could roll with the punches and give him as good as they got, in return. Someone who, bastion help them, could in all likelihood keep him in line, though the relative position of that line might have to be moved every so often in order to keep him from being garroted by it.

Rook no longer had Havemercy, but he still had me.

Without warning, my fingers brushed up against something smooth and hard in the midst of the little sinkhole I'd created. I froze, my heart picking up sudden speed like the unsteady thundering of my camel's hooves. But I couldn't afford to falter now, and I plowed back in with renewed vigor, trying to extract sand from around what I'd hit. Further digging revealed a shoulder, clothed in dusty blue—my brother for certain, then, and not Fan. A revolt started in my stomach, all the way down to the tips of my fingers, now cracked and messy with sand-dried blood.

Even as I continued to dig, clearing the sand away with feverish need, I was still afraid. I was afraid that I was about to haul my brother's lifeless body out of the dunes, afraid that then I would truly be alone. I was so terrified of this that it nearly froze my blood in my veins.

I stood quickly, bracing myself against the ground to pull at Rook's shoulder, towing him up under the arm I'd managed to clear. It was horrifically difficult, the sand heavy and Rook even heavier, and when I'd managed to get him up some of the way I tucked my arm firmly around his rib cage for better leverage. I pulled him back against me and hauled with all my might.

When he finally did come free, the sand sucking and popping against and around his body, I stumbled over backward, dragging him with me. We collapsed back onto the surface of the dune, in the shadow of Havemercy's frame, the impact knocking the breath from my lungs. I could see the dragonsoul out of the corner of my eye, winking merrily in the sun like the most beautiful of desert jewels—a true diamond in the rough. The sand beneath us burned my back and the sun overhead was so hot as to be nearly unbearable. I was being baked alive, but at least I *was* alive.

Rook, however, didn't move, neither to lift his head nor to swat me with his hand, all in order to tell me what an idiot I'd been. He looked worse than I'd ever seen him, pale beneath the sand and the front of his shirt soaked in dark blood. The knife was missing, probably lost under the sand along with Fan, though the damage it'd done remained. There were things I had to do—measures I had to take to be *sure*—but my heart was already sinking. Part of me wanted nothing more than simply to lie here and wait for the end to come and finish us both off. I was so tired that I felt as though there couldn't possibly be anything left within me. I couldn't even lift my own hand to shield my eyes from the sun. And I was angry with Rook, because so many things in the past had failed to kill him. How dare he leave me now? How dare he let something so small become something so large? If I'd only put my foot down, I might have made it clear to him that he was only chasing a dream through the desert. Desert wind whistled through the metal bones at my back. There it was, the last remnants of a war he'd won, and—irony of all ironies—this was what had finished him off.

I hadn't finished my task, though, and I knew that I'd never be able to look my brother in the eye if I admitted defeat now. If he *was* alive, of course.

Besides, it wasn't in my nature to give up on a lost cause. We *were*

Mollyrats, after all. Lost causes and refusal to give up even when thoroughly beaten were a part of our blood.

I fumbled for a moment, then grabbed Rook by the wrist. There was a pulse there, faint but real. I had no way of knowing how long it would continue to beat before it thumped its last.

With monumental effort, I pushed Rook off me, rolling into a sitting position myself. He looked more like a statue than ever, coated in sand and still as stone. I pressed his chest in hard compressions with both hands, leaning my head close to see if I could hear or detect even the faintest signs of breath.

"Ridiculous," I found myself muttering, continuing the rhythm of pressure against his chest as best I knew how. "This isn't the proper way of things at all, do you know that? *I'm* the one who gives up; *I'm* the one who makes everyone worry when there's hardly any cause for it. Don't tell me you mean to switch places, because that's hardly fair at this juncture—I don't think I'd be able to adjust at *all*. That's your strength again, do you see? I'm not adaptable. You've gone and gotten us all mixed around so I can't make heads or tails of it anymore, and you don't even have the *common decency* to stick around and clean up after the mess you've made? I suppose I shouldn't have expected anything better."

I'd really done it now. I'd held on to it as long as I could, but now I'd lost my mind at last, and there I was, babbling to myself like an asylum inmate in the middle of the desert.

My throat caught, then I no longer had the heart or the breath for words beyond my increasingly desperate mutterings as my ministrations grew in turn more frantic. I was *furious* with him. He was the one to engage in such dangerous activities, and yet he had the gall to reprimand me for attempting to partake in them?

Yet *I* was clearly fine. *He* was the one who needed looking after.

To one side, the dragonsoul was glowing, even in the bright light of midday. I didn't want to look at it, but I found my eyes hopelessly pulled in its direction. It was like a siren call, too lovely to resist, and yet drawing everyone around into ruin. As far as I knew, it had killed us all. I was the only survivor, while the others had been dashed upon the rocks, lured in by her promise and charm, and destroyed by their own desires.

A mere object, like the soul before me then, didn't have that kind of power—I knew this logically—and yet I was forced to draw my conclusions from the circumstances around us. Rook and I were the only ones left, and we were just two broken bodies in the middle of all this sand, sheltered by a relic from another time.

Then I heard a slight sound, almost like a cough, and I whipped around to face Rook so quickly that it made the muscles in my neck scream out in protest.

Rook looked exactly the same. Any movement I thought his chest was making had to be a hallucination, a trick of the heat. But, stubborn and hopeful, I leaned over him closely, my eyes scanning anxiously over his body for any sign that what I'd heard had been real and not some aural mirage of the desert.

"John?" I whispered, my face inches from his own.

For a long moment, he had no answer for me. It was so painful to wait that I wished to find that knife and demand a response from him.

Then he let out an explosive cough and sand sprayed me directly in the eyes. Blinded, I grabbed him by the shoulder and rolled him onto his side, thumping him hard on the back as more coughing followed the first pathetic burst. I pushed the hair from his face as he choked, trying to brush him off as best I could before I attended to my own eyes. His entire body was tensed with the force of his expulsions—his body doing everything it could to take in the air now available—and I kept my arm around him tight, my hand against his back.

I wished I had some water to offer him, but I'd lost all our supplies along with the camels. Everything was gone.

Yet we were alive—though a few more hours of this heat would finish us both off.

"Do we have it?" Rook demanded, still choking.

No "Are you all right, Thom?" or "Am *I* all right, Thom?" It was the one question I should have expected, and the one question I was the least prepared to hear.

I thumped him again, a good hard one, on his back, and felt him wince.

"Bastion," I said. Now I felt like a cruel bastard, and then some. "You're hurt—"

"Something like that," Rook muttered, waving me away, as though I wasn't trying to help him. "I asked you a fucking question."

"We have it," I said. Resigned to my place, I turned to retrieve the dragonsoul.

Only it was gone.

In its place were a pair of boots. A shadow fell over me, and I told myself then that every insult Rook had flung my way—every phrase that began as a compliment and quickly turned sour, every exasperated "I'll just fucking take care of it"—was probably justified. And yet *I* was justified, as well—more concerned about my brother's life than the piece of magician's work that, though it may have been called a soul, was no more than a capsule housing a splash of this and a dash of that, all of it as simple as a little bit of magic.

How had I missed *this*, though? Three backlit figures stood before me; all I could make out from the shadows was the sudden glint of sunlight upon the soul.

"You boys *have* been busy," Malahide said, taking in the rebuilt form of the dragon behind me. "It hardly seems fair to take this from you when you're in such a state."

Rook grunted. I had no way of knowing if it was from pain or rage, though I settled on grasping his hand, just in case it was the former.

"Ain't that nice," Rook said. "We do all the fucking work, then you waltz in here after the storm's cleared and take what we fought for. You and th'Esar . . . you're all the same." Something told me he had more to say, but there was too much sand in his throat for him to say it. A small blessing, perhaps; there might have been a chance that, by degrading myself and begging for assistance, our lives would be spared. Rook would of course never forgive me, nor would he ever speak to me again, but at least I would have the knowledge that he was alive and well— somewhere—which was more than I'd had once, and it would have to be enough for me. I tried to tell myself that it would be all right, that I could not live in the desert nor probably make it to Eklesias if *these* were always to be the terms of our travels, but that was a blatant lie, and I was too tired for lying.

"Assumptions, assumptions," Malahide said, clicking her teeth. "I came to ask you if I could borrow this, not keep it."

"And give it to your fucking master?" Rook snarled. There wasn't even true vehemence in his voice. He sounded beaten. I wanted to beg *him* now—to stop talking, and save his breath—but it would have been selfish of me to ask that. My motives were less than pure. I just couldn't bear hearing him like that.

"Things happen in the desert," Malahide said easily. I envied her her composure and wished she would stop flaunting it. "It *will* be the first time I've failed to accomplish a task outright, but if I bring him proof of its destruction in place of the dragonsoul itself, that should cover things nicely. That is, of course, presuming you *do* still plan to destroy it."

"Bitch," Rook said.

"Rook," I snapped.

"No need," Malahide told me. "I'm well accustomed to gratitude phrased in similar ways."

"But what about your . . . friends?" I asked. "They want it too. Are they relinquishing their claims?"

"It's a complicated matter," Malahide replied, in a way I didn't quite appreciate. "There's something they must do with it, and then, I suppose, it's all yours—if you promise not to be idiots and to destroy it." Rook squeezed my hand and I winced. His grip was quite tight. "I leave that last honor to you," Malahide continued, nodding to Rook, "because, as you so eloquently pointed out, you *did* do all the fucking work."

I looked at my brother. His eyes were squeezed shut almost all the way as he squinted up at Madoka; beneath all the sand, his skin was deathly pale. If we continued to discuss the terms of our agreement, he was going to bleed out all over the desert floor and I refused that end with every fiber of my being. I squeezed his hand back, and hard, and suddenly the corner of his mouth twitched up into some haggard semblance of a smile.

"Madoka needs it, huh?" Rook asked.

"Indeed," Malahide replied.

"Fine by me," Rook said. It might have seemed like nothing at all to anyone else, but I knew what it meant. It was the return of Rook's mean-spirited, shit-slinging, offensive grin, and if he was able to joke about a woman where Havemercy was concerned, then he'd finally let go of her. I breathed out, very slowly, my lungs afraid to hope along with everything else in my chest.

"Are you sure?" I asked him.

"Anything for a real lady," Rook replied, and I knew he'd spit more sand at me if I pressed the issue any longer.

"Then it's settled," Malahide replied, and began to turn to her companions.

"Well," I said, "actually, my brother—"

"This'll only take a moment," Malahide said. "And then we'll see about getting the wounded out of this sun pit."

"Don't ever let a woman talk to you like that," Rook told me raspily. "I mean, if you can call that horse-face a woman."

"I'm glad to see you back in such fine spirits, Rook," I said, and meant it with all my heart.

MADOKA

At last, we were together. Me and the dragon-thing, and no magician standing between us. We weren't alone, and for that I was kinda grateful, although if shit went down after all the rest—the sandstorm and the crazy magician and the almost being buried alive—or if I made a total ass of myself when it came down to getting my end of things done, then I might be feeling a little less gratitude. Only time and the shakedown could tell.

Malahide'd as good as admitted to me she didn't know if this trick I'd agreed to pull was gonna work, but it was the only shot in hell I really had, and I knew as well as she did—even as well as Badger did— that I had to take it. I wasn't going to make it back to Volstov, we all knew it, and this thing sitting in the middle of the sand was pretty much my only shot—no matter how much I really didn't want anything to do with it.

And at least I could console myself by saying I wasn't as bad off as the Volstov bastard was, the one lying in the sand and bleeding all over the place. Actually, I probably *was* as bad off as he was, maybe even worse, but at least I wasn't sweating and puking and shaking and passing out like I had been the last time I'd been face-to-face with the thing my compass was pointing toward. And that was a good start for me. Boded well. *Auspicious,* the priests would say.

The main problem was, I was still afraid of it.

"Guess it's kinda dumb to ask if this is gonna rip my hand off along with everything else, right?" I asked, glancing over at Malahide. She looked small, but she must've been pretty strong to carry that thing without breaking a sweat—and wearing those fucking impossible shoes, not to mention. She didn't even stumble or waver, whereas just looking at those high-heeled Volstov boots made my legs cramp.

"I suppose it might be," Malahide agreed. "Never a dumb question, really, but you already know I can't possibly tell you the answer to that."

"So it *is* a dumb question," I said. "Let's leave it at that."

Not exactly comforting, that Malahide.

"I don't like it," Badger said, looking between me and the dragon like he was afraid he'd blink and we'd switch places.

"You think you're the only one?" I snorted, which was easier than letting him know I was shook up. He was kinda sensitive for a soldier, and I didn't wanna give him another reason to worry, on top of everything else.

Hell, I didn't blame him for worrying, after what that magician had said about his true plan, or whatever. So I should probably have been even more afraid than I already was. But given the choice of fucking myself over worse while trying to take steps toward improving my situation, and not doing anything at all, I knew my answer was pretty clear. Like I'd said, there was no way I could make it back in one piece to Volstov. And besides, I wasn't letting more magicians fuck around with me. *Definitely* not Volstov magicians who—like Malahide—hadn't ever seen magic like this before.

Madoka wasn't anyone's experiment. Not anymore.

"Okay," I said. "Everybody wanna stand back or something? Since we don't know what it's gonna do?"

The friend of the Volstovic guy bleeding all over moved between us and him and said something to Malahide I didn't understand.

"He wishes to know what, exactly, we're doing," Malahide translated for me. She drew closer and added, in a quieter voice so only me and Badger could hear it, "And he knows what he's talking about, so lying to him probably won't do. Shall I tell him the truth? It's possible he might not let us, with his wounded companion so close to all this. But we can't take any risks; we *certainly* can't bring this back to a more populated center of civilization. We'd risk countless more lives, not to mention having the dragon piece stolen right out from under our noses a second time."

"The desert's best for it," Badger said grimly. That whole sit-down-and-shut-up mentality soldiers had was doing wonders for him here.

Mostly I just appreciated that he wasn't showing how piss-terrified *he* was. As much as I didn't like soldiers, there were still a few tricks I could learn from this one. I patted him on the shoulder and he touched my hand, and somewhere in the sand I heard the wounded Volstovic snorting.

"Pity he's not choking," Malahide said dryly.

"We'd better stop all the private conferencing," I told her. "Just tell him we've got no idea what it's going to do but we're gonna do it anyway."

"How comforting to hear it spelled out like that," Malahide said. "I'm sure he will not be amused." But she straightened and pulled away and turned to explain—I assumed—whatever we'd just gone over. I saw him pale and wipe the sand and sweat from his brow. He asked his wounded friend something, and his wounded friend just laughed at him.

Malahide returned to us. "They seem to agree that if anything worse happens now, they should just accept it and succumb to their cruel fates," she said. "How poetic. I concur."

"Great," I said, nodding like I even *almost* agreed with that crazy statement. I'd gotten pretty attached to living, after I'd fought for it so hard and all, so I wasn't really sure I wanted to go along with the idea of succumbing to anything just yet, cruel or not. And probably cruel, given my recent streak.

I just had to look at this like it was my one big chance, or else I might've ended up chickening out completely.

I stared at the dragon-thing. The dragon-thing—even though it didn't have eyes—stared back at me. It was the strangest piece of work I'd ever seen—not at all like the twisted wreckage I'd pulled out of the capital in those first hectic days after the end of the war. That stuff had all been junk, but it had also looked real to me, like it fit in with everything else. Scraps of metal torn clean off, pieces of wood and stone scorched by fire, splintered pieces almost polished by the debris. Even the compass had made some kind of sense, because I'd seen compasses before. *This* piece of work sitting in front of me now shimmered and danced like a heat dream, elusive and made-up and way beyond my station. Even though it'd been dragged across the desert for days, it showed no signs of wear and tear like the rest of us—even Malahide. That said something. Hell, as far as I understood it, this thing had been riding its whole life in the belly of a dragon, and you sure as spit couldn't tell it'd been through the war. I guess that all went to show how little I knew about magic, though—Volstovic stuff at least.

If I could've, I'd've probably touched it, just to say I had and to spook the kids back at home—that is, if I'd ever be able to tell stories about this.

Maybe it was better to leave it all buried here in the desert.

I didn't need to understand it any more, though, which was good, 'cause I still didn't. But things were pretty simple: I had something it needed. I could even see the small, flat groove where the compass had come loose from the main body of the mechanism; next to it was a little groove in the wood canister, and the glass up against that was cracked. It was obvious to anyone with a brain and two working eyes where the compass went; less obvious what it'd do once it went there. I wondered if the palm of my hand would look the same way as the dragon piece did—different or incomplete somehow—once I'd gotten rid of it.

You could waste a lot of time with wondering, though. And it wasn't *only* the dragon piece that was staring at me just then. As much as it gave me confidence to have people standing at my back, even though most of 'em weren't exactly people I could call friends, it made me nervous too. Somehow, though we'd all ridden out here racing to be the first to capture the prize, we'd managed to agree long enough for me to get a minute alone with the thing. That made a girl feel important. And as someone who'd spent all her life having it ground into her just how *unimportant* she was, it was kind of like turning the skies on their head.

I didn't want to waste it.

"You don't have to do this," Badger said, like he thought someone ought to remind me, just in case. I patted him on the shoulder with my good hand and he patted me right back, like we were two old buddies from the war. I guessed we kinda were.

"Yeah, I do," I said, then—while I wasn't thinking, like I really believed I could trick myself—I lifted my hand and pressed it up close to the dragon-thing. As close as I'd never been able to get.

No warning for me, no warning for it. That was my thinking.

It fought me a little, just at first, like holding up two pieces of metal that didn't want anything to do with each other, and the thin space of air between me and the mechanism suddenly felt as thick and solid as a wall. I gritted my teeth and dug the balls of my feet into the sand— much good it'd do me if the thing decided it didn't want to be whole again, but what else could I do? My jaw so tight I could hear the bones grinding, I *pushed* as hard as I could. Then, without any warning, the polarization changed, and what'd once been fighting me tooth and nail was now switched to tugging hard at the compass and pulling me in close. It hurt something fierce—bad enough to send black and red and white lines crisscrossing all over my vision—and I fell forward with the sudden force of the pull, one hand on the ground and the other sucked up tight against the smooth, hard surface of the dragonmetal.

Good thing Malahide wasn't holding it anymore.

It felt more like glass to me than metal, and its surface was faintly warm—though nothing at all like the sand underneath me, or even my own skin, which felt like it was about to roast and peel off at any minute. It was too smooth for that. Something made a *clink* like the sound of a heavy glass being put down onto a table, then there was a screech like metal being sheared in half by more metal. My hand pulsed, but with warmth this time instead of pain, and it was a welcome change from the usual. In other words, I wasn't begging for mercy. Not yet.

I gripped tightly to my wrist with my other hand, praying that whatever happened next, it wouldn't rip my arms off. Through the haze over my eyes, I could see—or thought I could see—the liquid inside the dragon parts begin to glow, like the river of starlight that stood between the moon princess and her beloved, separating them forever in the sky. It swirled up from the bottom of the capsule, lapping like ocean waves at the clear walls of its container, and I felt another faint tugging in my hand, from somewhere deeper.

It still didn't hurt, but it felt so strange that I gasped, and both Badger and Malahide came forward at once, like choreographed dancers. Out of the corners of my eyes, I saw their shadows move. *Cute,* I thought.

"What is it?" Badger asked.

"Are you in pain?" Malahide elaborated.

"Mm-mm," I said, and shook my head. The feeling traveled up my arm, cast like a fisherman's lure to draw out some deepwater prey. It was invasive, but not the same blinding pain I remembered from being brought to the desert rider's camp and subsequently to his tent. By contrast, this was nothing—a little tickle instead of a hammer's blow. It felt different from your regular run-of-the-mill pain, but I couldn't hope to describe it. It tickled, all the way down to my elbow, where it hummed warm and slow. Still looking, peeking and poking through my very blood.

Behind Malahide and Badger, I could see the Volstovics arguing, the wounded one trying to get up and the not-wounded one somehow keeping him down. He muttered something sharp as an addition, and the wounded one grunted, settling back into a sitting position with a sour look on his face. I could definitely sympathize with the wounded one, since I'd been on that side of things more often than not these days. Sucked to have your body not working the way you wanted it to, and you lying on your back with no way to make it listen up.

I feel you, brother, I thought to myself, trying to remember his name, and right then was when the smooth surface against my palm got *real* hot real fast. I shouted, yanking my hand back on instinct, only to find that I couldn't. Of course not. Whatever magic I'd set into play wasn't finished with me yet. *Rook,* I remembered, though I wasn't all that sure *I* was the one doing the remembering. Well, at least I could console myself with the knowledge that *I'd* done this, and no one else, so whatever happened, I only had myself to blame. The silvery contents swirled more fiercely now, glowing like a second sun and not more distant stars, and I had to look away or risk going blind. Malahide covered her eyes and turned to one side. Badger—apparently not possessed of enough soldiering sense to stay back when danger was at hand— lunged forward and put his hand on my shoulder, squeezing it as he quickly shut his eyes, his face pressed to the inside of his elbow.

What a freak. Maybe he had a thing for sty pigs, after all. Well, to each his fucking own. I wasn't in any place to judge right now, myself. Would've been too cruel, after all we'd been through.

The feeling in my arm had climbed as high as my shoulder and was even heading into my chest, all tingling and soft like spiders' webs running along between my veins, when all of a sudden it stopped moving. It latched into place—exactly like fishhooks—and then it started to reverse. I shivered all over, though my hand was still burning, and Badger's fingers dug into the muscle in my shoulder, right around the bone. That hurt a little too, but it was a good kind of hurt. It gave me a distraction from the rushing recession in my arm—a feeling like the tide going out all at once, ebbing to reveal the wet and muddy sand beneath.

The glass was vibrating faintly now, and the worst headache of my life was starting up smack between my eyes. But it was nothing in comparison to how my arm felt: like the skin or muscle or even bone was being peeled away, but I could see that it wasn't. My pulse hammered loud against my temple and in my chest, reminding me of the repair work being done on buildings in the capital. Every morning it started so early you couldn't sleep much past sunrise, and every night it ran until late. Yeah, that sounded about right. I was getting some repair work done right now, by invisible fingers, reaching up *through* and *into* my own, visible hand.

Someone else shouted—one of the Volstovics, since it was a word I didn't understand—and my arm shuddered all over like the rest of it *was* about to be torn off. The pain in my head doubled, and the dragon-thing let out a high-pitched whine—like even *it* thought all this was way too much. I heard a groan of machinery, the dull scrape of gears moving one against the other and a *pop* of suction being released, like the stopper being pulled from a tub of water—a fancy bath, the sort I'd never get.

For a moment there, I even thought I might've passed out. I heard a voice—not the same one as the voice on the wind telling me I was crazy, telling me to give up. It snickered at me and said something in Volstovic I couldn't understand, but it was faint as a whisper, the wind against my face. And then it was gone completely. My eyes were still glued shut, but the bright heat on my face had faded. I wondered if it was safe yet, or if I was still dreaming, or what.

At some point when I'd had my eyes closed, I'd moved. Either that or the dragon had gotten closer to me, and the wounded Volstovic—Rook, I remembered—was staring up at me from the sand.

I knelt, still cradling the soul in my other arm.

"Hey," I said, and his eyes went wide like I'd stung him.

"I thought you only spoke . . ." his companion began, trailing off.

"One of your eyes changed color there," Rook grunted, his face tightening in pain as he lifted his hand to point. "Might wanna get that looked at."

"You always *were* a little slow," I said, only it wasn't my voice that was coming out of my mouth. It was something from the soul. "Guess it'd be too much to expect something less than a constant disappointment."

Rook shook his head. He even chuckled, but his face went dark and the man sitting beside him put his hand on his chest to keep him from doing *that* again.

"Sorry, baby girl," Rook said. "Guess I'm not exactly at the top of my game."

"Didn't ask for a bunch of excuses," Havemercy said. "You see *me* making excuses for why I look like a big pile of shit some kid knocked together back there? Look at that; that's not even my *wing*. They don't even match."

"Some people got no eye for design," Rook agreed, with a crooked smile.

"Listen," Havemercy said, and I could see him sit up a little straighter. "I don't wanna hear anything about *you* trying this bullshit somewhere down the line, you hear? Or else you'll get a knife somewhere a lot worse to go with the one you've got now."

"So," Rook said, eyes flicking over my face as he tried to process that, "you're sticking around? Gotta be clear with me, sweetheart; I'm dumb as manure right now."

"Sure, 'right now,'" Havemercy said, and I felt myself smiling. "I'll be . . . around. Not like this, of course. More like an observer. This woman's stubborn as dirt, and I don't much fancy the idea of taking anyone's freedom away. Call me sentimental."

A look of such resignation passed over Rook's face that for a minute I almost felt like telling her, *Sure, go ahead, set up camp.* He'd made me laugh when I was feeling pretty low, so he couldn't've been all that bad. The only problem was, I'd never know if he wanted me for *me,* or Havemercy. And the chances of the former seemed pretty slim.

"Better get going, then," Rook said, not as harshly as he might've under the circumstances. "I hate long good-byes and everybody's staring."

"Always a gentleman," Havemercy sighed. Then—despite me doing everything I could do to stop it—she leaned in close and kissed him on the lips. "Learn some manners, you rude little fucker."

"Stick around and teach me," Rook murmured.

"What do I look like, a professor?" She chuckled, wiping the sweat from his forehead with my hand.

Then, just as abruptly as she'd come, she was gone.

The heat in the glass beneath my hand began to fade immediately, and the pain in my head followed. I squeezed my eyes shut. I heard Malahide come up behind me—the sharp *click* of her teeth, which she used to make noise instead of pushing her tongue off the roof of her mouth like the rest of us. Her version of *tsk*ing. For the first time in a long time, my head felt clean, and clear, not like it was so heavy it was going to drop off my neck, and the muscles in my arm were aching—not out of a deeper, poisonous pain, but because I'd been favoring it for so damn long.

I didn't want to open my eyes, but I did it anyway.

"Shit," I said, which wouldn't have been my top choice for some first important words, or whatever, but I couldn't help it. "What the hell was that?"

The dragon-thing was sitting in the sand, neat as you please, only where before it'd been filled with soothing, silver-white liquid like a million pearls all melted down, its contents were now angry and red. The mixture swirled darkly against the metal-hammered glass, making the whole contraption look more sinister than beautiful—a giant container of somebody's watered-down blood. Was she in there?

"I wouldn't worry about that just now," Malahide counseled, leaning forward on her knees to examine the dragon piece curiously. I probably wasn't interesting anymore, considering I was no longer a part of it.

"Can you move your hand?" Badger asked, giving voice to the one thing I really didn't want to find out about. It was cowardly of me, sure, but I really didn't think I could take the disappointment if it'd worked but hadn't worked, or if I was fucked for life now because of all this.

Malahide looked at me expectantly, her hands already on the dragon-thing to pull it away before I could tell her not to, and over her shoulder those two men from Volstov were watching too, their eyes glued to me like they'd just seen one hell of a show. I guess they had.

"Your eye," Badger said, looking at me appraisingly.

"Wish you hadn't said that," I muttered. There was a part of me that'd been hoping whatever'd just happened was a dream. "What's it look like?"

"Gold," he said, and he was smiling even though I couldn't think of any reason he'd have to be doing something like that.

"Great," I said. "Just what I need. One brown and one gold."

He reached out and put his hand over mine—the one I'd been too scared to move up until now.

"I think it suits you," he said, and I didn't have a smart retort for that one.

Guess I really was some kind of desert witch after all. It was just too bad I didn't have a bigger audience to see it anymore.

Gingerly, I lifted my hand from the cooling surface of the glass. My whole body was tensed, expecting the worst: That pain could return at any minute, or maybe the compass would rip out of my hand when I moved it, or maybe I'd be sucked inside to swirl with the bloody liquid. Badger was holding my hand, though, and I didn't think he'd let anything like that happen to me. Not now, when we'd taken care of that piece-of-shit magician once and for all.

"Your arm!" Badger exclaimed, startling me.

"Shit," I said again, "you'll scare me out of my skin like that." The joke was kind of ironic, all things considered, but it put me in good enough spirits at least to look down at myself.

So I did, and I wasn't expecting what I ended up seeing there. All the angry red lines had vanished, and there was no sickly, pale green color to the skin, either. That little sliver of hope was all I needed, and I pulled my hand back with certainty now, flipping it over palm up so I could force myself to look at it before I chickened out.

The compass was gone. In its place was a scar, pink and fresh and perfectly round. I wouldn't be able to tell my future by reading the lines in my palm anymore—just my past—but I figured I could live with that.

"Nice," I said, looking up at Malahide. The world began to move around me and I was pretty happy that Badger was still there, because when I keeled over from all the stress, he'd catch me when I dropped.

I was sure of it.

I'd never had anybody like that before, someone to watch my back for me. I guess you could call it a friend and I guessed I *would* call it a friend. I had my hand back and I probably could've caught myself, but I'd done enough of that for one lifetime, landing on my own two feet in the middle of so much shit. Gutter pig, yeah, but even sows had sty mates. There wasn't any reason for Malahide to stick around, and despite being grateful to her, I was glad she wasn't going to. Life could get back to the way it was but a little bit different, at that. I looked back over my shoulder at Badger and he was smiling at me, his face all crooked with the scar.

"Me too," I said, meaning my hand.

It was getting embarrassing, the number of times I'd passed out. But this was my last. I was finally done with it.

CHAPTER EIGHTEEN

MALAHIDE

We'd all assumed it was going to be impossible to find our way back to immediate medical help. After all, we had two almost deadweights on our hands—Madoka and the airman—the first of whom was out stone cold, and who could blame her after such a barbaric ritual, and the second of whom obviously could not walk, despite all his protestations to the contrary. No matter how hard or how loud some people protested, they were still no closer to convincing *me* of an untruth, and that was exactly how things were with Airman Rook. Some choice phrases were exchanged, with his traveling companion attempting to mediate the damage—needlessly; I certainly wasn't going to be offended by empty words slung at me from a wounded animal—before Badger commanded all of us, with diction even those who did *not* speak the Ke-Han language could understand as a soldier's order, to shut the fuck up and sit the fuck down. He held Madoka in his arms like she was a fallen comrade, and I was fond of them, but my attention really was directed elsewhere.

The item in question rested before us, forever altered. It reminded me of myself in some ways: The outer vestiges of what it once had been had been blown clean away, and now it was as much a part of Madoka as it was a part of a dragon at all.

No wonder she was all tired out.

It had to have been the dragon's core—its heart, or perhaps more accurately, its soul. Whatever magician had wrought this beauty would never know the spectacular display it had given at its last—more than even a simply fiery death in battle could have allowed. I was so proud, even though it had never involved me directly. As a spectator, I had participated in such a beautiful exhibition that it would leave me changed for life. Even if parts of it turned out to be things Madoka might prefer to forget. *That* was something we all could appreciate.

It might take years; it might take an entire lifetime; it might exceed my capacity for understanding at all. I had been through certain magical experiments myself, when I was young but not too young to remember all the details, and this surpassed them all. The sun was slowly beginning to set, and yet it had been brighter than the sun itself at full burning capacity, above us and unbearable in the desert sky. How had anyone managed to create such a wondrous thing, with full knowledge that it was to be used for destruction?

Bastion bless the Volstov, I'd thought to myself, and even had the capacity to laugh at my own precious little joke.

But that hadn't left us in any better straits—they were, in fact, rather dire. Alone in the desert, no transportation, no water left, no knowledge of where we were: It all pointed to trouble. Yet *more* trouble. It was no sandstorm I could outlast nor desert tribe I could outwit. I'd never been the praying sort, but I was almost embarrassingly close to it. I could even see Badger was participating in a few prayers—perhaps he assumed his gods could hear him all the way out here, so far from home. I would never understand the deeply religious. I had never been the sort of person to give up in any situation, no matter how grim—I considered myself something of an opportunist, and a lucky one at that—but even I couldn't see my way toward strolling free of this one. No amount of gumption or wit could charm the desert itself. We'd ridden this far from the oasis by following my nose, and not any natural landmarks, so that no one in our ragtag little gang even knew which direction to start in.

We were, to put it shortly, quite doomed. But fate had a funny way of repaying me for services rendered—among other things I'd given up—and it seemed she'd decided not to allow the ink on my tale to dry, just yet.

When we'd least expected it—indeed, I believed Badger himself had fallen into some sort of meditative trance—we were saved. Not by a stroke of luck from above, as I'd imagined, but by my favorite and least favorite man on earth. Well, currently, in any case. But nonetheless my *intimate* friend, Kalim.

"You will ride!" he told me, meaning me and the others, after one of his men had dismounted to bring both Rook and Madoka some water. He'd had the good sense to ride out with a solid entourage, whether hoping to bring help or simply to show off the magnificent display of the desert magic, I would never know. In a moment of rare simplicity, especially for me, I found that I didn't care one iota.

They were efficient, very well trained, and I was unable to fully appreciate all that they had to offer, as I felt Kalim's eyes on me the entire time. It put a decided cramp in my style, and I smoothed my skirts with fingers that were genuinely unsure. He didn't think I was dangerous—he wasn't trying to test me, to see if I would make the first move. In fact, there was an almost jovial camaraderie in his expression. I trusted it even less for that assumption. To him it might well have been nothing, but for me, it was the world.

After drinking a few greedy gulps of the proffered water, Airman Rook finally *did* manage to draw himself to his feet, despite his companion's adamant disapproval and insistence that he should absolutely not do so.

"Can I ride with this?" Rook asked, limping proudly and foolishly over to the dragonsoul.

"It appears cursed," Kalim said. "It is changed. You should leave it here."

"There's something I gotta do with it," Rook said, leaning down and grunting. He looked like he was very near to coming apart at the seams, but it wasn't my place to mention anything. I knew—call it womanly intuition—that my concern would not be appreciated. Somehow he managed to pick up the dragonsoul, then stood there swaying like a dead man. I admired his success, if not his motives. His companion ran over to him, as though to help, and after a moment I thought I saw the tension in his shoulders ease as he shifted—not half, but *some* of—his burden. "Get outta here, Thom," he added, but there was no passion in it.

"I will not," Thom said.

"Enough, enough!" Kalim said. "We will take you back to Karakhum. Are you sure you wish to bring that with you? You are hurt, and there are men there who would steal it."

"I'll take care of it," Rook said.

He was a ridiculous man. Impossibly stubborn and set on what he wanted. I couldn't admire him, but I did envy his conviction. Just a little.

Others could deal with him now; I would have to keep an eye on him and make sure he got rid of it, so that I could make my report back to the Esar without being contradicted by the evidence. I could at least tell that he did not intend to cling to it as some memento, as though it were really as simple and benign as a lover's token. There was little left I had to worry about, save for incompetence. At least there were two of them; their separate brands of intelligences almost made them as clever as a single clever person.

I turned to Kalim.

"We shall ride," I told him. "That man is wounded; the woman, weary."

"I saw a great deal of magic here," Kalim told me, still looking cheerful, but also overawed.

"Yes, well, I had very little to do with it," I replied, feeling put out. "How far is Karakhum?"

"We ride through the night," Kalim replied, "and reach Karakhum in the morning."

And that is exactly what we did.

I had never been to Karakhum, having passed through the Cobalt Mountain Range on my first trek out to the desert and bypassed the famous desert city quite entirely. It seemed a lonely and mean path when I thought about it now, though at the time it had been perfectly satisfactory. My mind had been solely on the chase, following a man who'd ended up buried beneath the dunes—I had never even gotten to meet him at all. Truth be told, I was a little disappointed that he'd been dispatched so easily. I would have to continue my search for my equal— someone who would not let me down when push came unequivocally to shove. This one, like all the others, had disappointed me.

Such was the conclusion to this particular chapter.

I rode the entire way to Karakhum on my own camel, thank you, keeping pace with Kalim's out of choice and not because I was a witch under suspicion this time. A few of his men shot me curious looks, but looks had never bothered me before. I was a creature entirely unique. Not in the sense that every young woman with more powder on her cheeks than sense in her head thinks herself special, but *truly* different. If they wished to stare, they could; at least they did not consider me with the same comprehension as Kalim, for which I was grateful.

As was often the case, I appeared different to them. They could not put a finger upon why, nor could they articulate the difference they observed. I was and was not the "typical" woman—or whatever facsimile they expected from their own comprehension of womanhood—for the simple reason that I was not born a woman at all. Nor, I suppose, did I have the requisite parts to receive their blessing as a woman even now. But that, as always, was beside the point.

I'd made the decision when I was much younger, as contrary as ever to the current state of things. It was no secret among anyone in Volstov that a woman's place in society was below a man's, and though I was nothing but a forgotten orphan and therefore less than worthless to begin with, I somehow considered it my little joke: to be worth more than anyone else when I was at once a woman *and* an orphan. Contrary, indeed, but I knew the tales as well as anyone. There were ways to buy Talent with your own talents, to offer something to the earth and the sky and receive something from it in return. It was not so simple as drinking from the water and receiving the blessing—the strength, the power—but the one burr in my side was that I could not choose with what I would be gifted.

I could, however, choose the form that would receive it.

And besides which, it suited me better.

I put myself in the hands of the Esar's personal magicians—a blank slate, upon whom they could practice their designs without remorse; no one would notice I was missing. The experiments had been conducted while I was *much* younger, when I'd been deemed a suitable candidate for the process and had offered no protests to the contrary. I'd had very little in common with other children of a similar age and background—no parents or family at all to speak of, no one to protest or demand I be one way rather than another, and I'd imagined that perhaps I might find my way more easily through the world if I made this my purpose in life. Simply put, it was right for me. I was a little girl and, back then at least, my eyes were very innocent. Who would ever suspect me of any darker thoughts, any plans of my own or deeper designs?

At that time, the Esar had been in need of an agent—a female agent—who could be trusted in Volstov and afar. It had to be a woman, for women were so often considered benign little jewels of the court, and for all their restrictions, the lack of consideration they were afforded allowed them, in some regards, greater mobility and greater access. I had nothing to say one way or the other about the injustice of this. It was the way Volstov was, and in my own way, I had subverted it. There were other women, magicians or widows, who managed to make a place for themselves among the men—whereas I had managed to make a place for myself among the women—and their strength and determination was that upon which I modeled myself, even at so young an age.

The sacrifice of my freedom had seemed to me very small indeed, and I'd given it up much more easily than I had my tongue—a decision with which I'd made peace years ago. It hurt less, to begin with, and while losing my tongue made my body something less than what it once had been, this new change quite obviously did not. I'd hidden my true identity for as long as I could remember—there were some things the experiments had *not* done away with, and it took the utmost vigilance to keep them as intimate a secret as I wanted them kept. My clothing did a great deal of the work for me, and carefully trained body language did the rest. I had never allowed another man—or a woman, for that matter—to observe me in an undressed state, and I had never felt before that I was missing out on much. Riding beside Kalim now, however, made a strange memory rise to the surface, of another ride through the desert, when it had been cramped and hot with his arms around me and the wind kicking up ahead.

It was the closest I'd ever been to another person. Even my old partner had never come so near. And yet I still felt as though it was too far, by some measureless standard that I'd never before anticipated using.

How curious I was.

The sun was rising again when we reached Karakhum. By then, I was more than ready to see the backside of my camel. I was a trained rider, but our travels of late had been quite intensive, and I was looking forward more than anything to a good soak in a *private* bath and perhaps the leisure of riding sidesaddle upon a sweet, properly trained *horse.*

As always, though, I had some business to attend to before I could reward myself with even the simplest of pleasures. I couldn't properly relax until I was sure that Airman Rook had destroyed the dragonsoul, and I could not be sure that Airman Rook had destroyed the dragonsoul until I saw it shattered with my own two eyes. As I watched his companion—Thom, he'd called him—ease him down off his camel, I had a feeling my presence wouldn't be much welcomed by Rook's bedside. There would be some recovery time required for both Rook *and* Madoka, and I might just be able to slip some personal time in during it. I could catch up on my correspondence, send the Esar a letter—carefully devoid of any more private details, of course, for despite what he thought, what the Esar did not know would not *always* harm him—telling him that I would be on my way to Thremedon very shortly, my foray into the desert successful. If my news was to his satisfaction, no doubt he would need the time to prepare for me a very warm welcome, and I wished to give him as much advance warning as possible.

Then there was the matter of Dmitri, who always did fret so when I didn't write him for months at a time. It put him in a frightful mood, pinned as he was to the city, and I didn't think much of wishing that fate on his fellow wolves, not to mention the hapless criminals he caught, unlucky enough to run afoul of him during such a time.

"This is where we part ways," Kalim announced, sliding off his camel with an ease that I envied. "My men will not stay in the city."

"And what about you?" I asked. A desert breeze eddied around my boots, kicking up the dusty hems of my many-layered skirts. They would already be out of fashion in Thremedon, and I would have to buy new ones before I returned to the Esar's court. For once, I found that I had nothing to do with my hands—no hair to twirl, no coy motions of the wrist. I was tired, I was hot, and I was—in all likelihood—sunburnt to within an inch of my life. I had never found myself so far removed from my element, and I had never been stripped so clean for all the gritty sand I felt everywhere.

I ought to have known. Rumor had it the desert could separate a man's flesh from his bones. It shouldn't have surprised me at all that it had found no trouble in infiltrating the layers in which I'd cocooned myself.

Kalim laughed, a hoarse, rough sound that was nonetheless pleasant to hear. "I took my schooling in this city," he said, "and I like its buildings and its windows. But I go where my men go. If I did not, I would find myself a very lonesome man, do you not think so?"

"They should go where you lead them," I said, stubborn and more peevish than I might have liked to seem—especially as an ambassador of my liege. The wind whipped a long, awkward piece of hair into my face, and before I could move, Kalim was there. He brushed it to one side, his fingers coarse as the sand itself. For once I looked him straight in the eye, even though all I wished to do was to drop my gaze. There was no artifice in the troublesome rhythm of my heart—simple adrenaline, I knew, but it had never reacted so over something as straightforward as this. I could smell him. Just as the sand was clean, so was his scent—the sweat and the sun and the camels a bare whisper over the skin beneath. "It doesn't trouble *everyone* to be alone."

"Perhaps not," Kalim said, shrugging his shoulders easily. He glanced over his shoulder as the Volstovics passed us by, the dragonsoul—and Rook, whether he'd admit it or not—in tow. We were lucky we had arrived early; there was no crowd to gawk at us. The dragonsoul might yet make it indoors without causing a commotion. "It seems to me that all creatures of warm blood desire some form of companionship or another. Even lizards and snakes seek mates. And, as you know, lizards and snakes are cold inside despite all this sunlight. But maybe that custom seems strange to one whose home is not the desert."

"I'm quite content with my walls," I said, the words sounding hollow to my ears. My heart wasn't pounding with excitement, but fear. I *needed* walls, just as Kalim needed the open space of the desert. We hardly knew one another. The safest, not to mention the simplest, thing to do would be part ways now. It would seem difficult at first, but in the end would prove much easier than whatever mad things were currently racing through my mind.

A real girl at last, I thought. But I knew as well that this feeling, desert or no—woman or no—was a worldwide experience. An equalizer, one might call it.

I was humiliating myself.

"Contentment is quite a different thing from pleasure," Kalim said, and without warning, without even so much as a *handshake,* he put his arms around my waist and kissed me upon the mouth.

I fought it, of course. It was uncalled for and invasive and there were people *everywhere.* I could hear Airman Rook's derisive snort, and a catcall that sounded *distinctly* like it'd come from Madoka. It certainly hadn't come from Badger, thank bastion and all else. But Kalim's arms were quite strong and sure. From this close the scent of him was overpowering, smelling more like the sun than the desert itself ever had. His shoulders were sweaty when I rested my hands against them, and taking that presumably as a sign of consent, he lifted me clean off my feet. Not exactly how every woman pictures her first kiss, but then I'd gone long beyond the stage of ever picturing *anything* of such a nature. Not even a dirty little orphan had dared to pull this manner of stunt on me. It was entirely a surprise, and it was entirely too much. What made it even more difficult was that I had no tongue at all—but if this lack of proper anatomy surprised Kalim, he gave no indication of it. The kiss was deep, as though I had everything it could require.

"Put me down," I said at once, when our lips parted. Our faces were still far too close, our bodies pressed together in a way that left very little to the imagination. Was he mad, I wondered? Perhaps there was a little madness in all the people of the desert—too much sun did much to desiccate the brain.

Kalim complied, grinning like a jackal, and even when he'd set me back on my feet I didn't feel as though I was properly on the ground.

"Hate to fucking break up the party," Rook snarled, though the bulk of his energy was clearly going to keeping himself upright, "but if we're getting Madoka to whatever excuse this place has for a clinic, it oughta be sooner rather than later. You all can continue the freak show behind closed doors where nobody's gotta look."

"Also, it might be a good idea to get out of the sun," Thom added, ever the conciliator. "We've been standing in it probably much longer than is strictly healthy. I think I'm getting a headache, and some of us . . . Some of us are worse."

He put a hand against the dragonsoul in Rook's arms. It was quite evident to me, if no one else, that Thom's concern was *not* for himself.

It was also evident that I was going to have to wrangle all these wild horses—converse in the language only I, apparently, knew; call for medical attention; keep an eye on the dragonsoul while Rook was being tended to; procure food for Badger and Madoka, to keep their strength up. Apparently a bath for myself was out of the question.

I was by no means a caretaker. But neither was I the sort of woman who ran off into the desert following the whims of a strange man.

At least, not the whims of *this* strange man.

"Merely consider it," Kalim said with a smile. "You are still young, and you have impressed my men with your skills at riding."

"Have I?" I replied. "Unfortunately, the desert does *not* suit me."

Kalim mounted up, with nothing more to say to me than that, and I shielded my eyes against the climbing sun.

My skin had the propensity to freckle. No, I would not be living in the desert, ruining my complexion, living without running water, and without all the comforts that I had earned through cleverness and steady determination alike. I had not come all this way only to abandon everything that mattered as though it had meant nothing at all. What, then, would be *my* worth?

"Perhaps I will come to you, then," Kalim suggested. "I have always wished to open talks with the Volstov."

It felt as though the Cobalts in the distance were about to grow legs and move, all on their own. Then Kalim spurred his camel quickly into a trot, to follow his men out past Karakhum's city walls, and did not turn to look behind him as he left.

I had found something in the desert, something that I had not been looking for—something that I would have to keep for myself. However, I intended to write first thing to the Esar and tell him there were tribes in the desert disposed to friendly relations between our peoples.

Or perhaps I would not.

I had chosen to be restricted by Volstovic practice. This way, Kalim would never become entangled in the webs I made my living spinning. He could never be used as a bartering piece to get to me, and by extension the Esar. I could be very happy with that.

ROOK

It wasn't the first time Thom'd sat vigil at my bedside while I was recuperating, whereas I'd never once stood over his. And I sure as bastion didn't like the implications of that.

Sure, it was just dumb beginner's luck that I kept getting the short end of the stick jammed in my eye and he didn't even get scratched, and that was the way it had to be, I guessed, since if Thom was the one in bed and I was the one sitting next to him, I'd've been long gone already. Not even a note on the table—just some money, and the assumption that he'd use it to drag his sorry ass home for good and keep himself out of trouble. He could read for the rest of his life, sit in some professor's armchair, talk until his jaw fell off, and not get in anybody's way. Especially not his own. No arguing about it, no questions asked. And the second any of his blood spilled while we were together, that was gonna be the way of it.

He'd been dragged around for long enough.

I slept for a while, getting my energy back and trying not to think about how much my ribs hurt, and I let the desert doctors look at me like a good little boy while Thom stayed out of the room and kept the dragonsoul hid good and proper. Couldn't let anyone else see it, even the medics—my girl had this bad habit of attracting too much attention, good and bad—and I didn't want anybody to see her when she looked like this. Everyone had a whole lot of advice for how I should and shouldn't feel, what I should and shouldn't do, and just what she was and wasn't anymore, but in the end, only I knew the down-and-dirty truth of it.

Which was: Havemercy was gone. At least, the parts of her that'd been lingering in the soul were, since those'd gone into Madoka. I couldn't hold on to a *woman* like a memento, and especially not one like Madoka. Besides, she'd made her choice, and now it was up to me to do away with the remains of the soul. Not because I wanted to, but because I had to—and I could fucking man up and accept that.

If only for her sake.

At least everyone else had fucked off, Malahide spending time with her Ke-Han buddies and smelling of desert perfumes and being exactly the kind of woman I didn't want to have anything to do with—and because of that, I had to keep away from Madoka, exactly the kind of woman I *did* want to have something to do with. Not that there was much I could've done all bandaged up like a present. That was probably for the best, since her soldier friend kept looking at me like he knew what I was thinking. But the thoughts I was thinking about Madoka were far away and mostly unimportant. I could get back to 'em later, on lonelier nights, and keep myself nice and warm, but right now I couldn't, since that'd cheapen it. And I guess I'd come to that point where I had to distinguish the women in my life, or at least I had to put one kind before the other.

It was a weird feeling, but I could adjust. I wasn't some kind of rigid 'Versity professor who couldn't tell which way the wind was blowing. In fact, I'd always had a pretty good nose for the wind.

I'd made up my mind, and because I *wasn't* gonna pussyfoot my way through this like it was somebody's prize daisy garden. I was just gonna do it. Rip the bandage off and deal with the consequences after that. Thinking about it too much was only going to drive me nuts, and I couldn't let that happen, because what was Thom supposed to do with his brother in the nuthouse? If I had dreams about it while I slept, then it was because of getting my guts nearly sliced out in the desert, and if I had dreams about it *later,* then it was because I was a piss-poor excuse for an airman or even a man who couldn't let a good thing go because he knew he'd never see anything that good again.

At least I wasn't gonna *cry* and share how I was feeling with my brother, which was what he was waiting for, all this time, just sitting by my bed and staring at me like he was expecting something. A word or two that would explain everything—like words could explain anything. The problem was, someone'd told him that they did, and he'd had it beat into his head so hard that he couldn't quite see his way around to any other kind of thinking.

Wasn't my job to figure him out, though. That was *his* deal, analyzing. And if he wanted to waste his time with figuring me out instead of himself, then that was his problem.

"Guess I'm gonna smash her," I told him, late one night, just to keep him on his toes. He was nodding off in the chair by my bed and I startled him good—which I almost felt bad for, except then I didn't. I'd told him to sleep in his own bed and that I'd had worse scrapes than this one, but he was being stubborn and there was no fucking arguing with him when he got like that. So there he was, shitting himself the second I spoke up, and I had to look away not to let on that I'd planned it that way all along.

"You're going to— Oh," he said, waking up real fast at least. Faster than he did most mornings, green eyes all bleary and hair that definitely wanted cutting. He was learning, even if it was slow going. "Oh, I see. Do you think that's appropriate?'

"Can't burn her, can I? She was made to withstand that kind of heat. Part of her makeup. And I can't bury her, either, 'cause someone's bound to dig her up and we'll be back where we started. I've been thinking about it, anyway. So that's the only fucking way."

"I suppose it is," Thom said. "I'm sorry. When do you want to do it?"

"Tonight," I told him, wondering if that would slide.

Instead of giving me the usual dance-around about how I *shouldn't* and he *couldn't* and we *wouldn't*, he clenched his jaw and looked somewhere else, far past me.

"John," he said, and oh, I knew I was in real trouble then—not even the kind of trouble you could argue with or ignore, but the kind of trouble that you had to face head-on and it made all your teeth hurt. "I don't really remember anything."

"I noticed," I said.

He sighed, frustrated but not angry. "That isn't what I meant," he said. For once, my little brother, at a loss for words? Unfucking believable. "What I mean is, about you. Before all this. I wish I did remember."

"Why, 'cause you'd like me more?" I asked.

"Maybe," he said.

"Probably not," I told him. "And if you think you're gonna distract me with all this hoopla about who I *used* to be and bastion knows what else, then you're fucking mistaken."

"I've already decided we can go," Thom said. "I was just trying to ask you a simple question. Not *everything* is a battlefield."

"Fuck you," I said. Then, because I couldn't say "help me up," he saw right through my horseshit and helped me up anyway.

It was slow moving, and the muscles in my chest did hurt, but like I'd said, it could've been a lot fucking worse. Fan hadn't known where to stab and he'd been blind-crazy with trying to defend himself by that point; I'd gotten lucky, and he hadn't. Somehow it'd all turned out to be simple as that. His move'd missed everything vital and it'd glanced off the rib cage, and so my own fucking bones had saved me. I'd have to thank 'em sometime, do something nice for 'em for a change. I'd heard they had baths in Eklesias, public ones, where everybody got naked, men and women together, and just spent time steaming and relaxing. I could use some of that, to finally get all the grit out of my heart.

"I suppose you're going to want to carry that by yourself?" Thom said, giving me one of those looks.

I tested the weight of my baby's soul. It was pretty damn heavy, just like I remembered, and parts of me were pretty pissed that I was even trying it. But I just snorted and ignored 'em.

"You suppose pretty damn right," I said. "Got any suggestions on how to smash this thing?"

He looked up at me like that was the greatest question I'd ever asked him. And maybe it was, since I didn't mind if he came with me, didn't mind if he watched, didn't mind if we walked back together in the end. I wasn't gonna look up at the stars and tell him about how much I missed it. He already knew all that.

"We could drop it from the roof," he said.

"Just like flying," I agreed.

Thom grinned. "So long as you don't fall off."

We made it up to the top of the building, the wind cold up there in the darkness. The moon was a neat little sliver in the sky and too far away for me to look at. I remembered all the things Have used to say and I squared my shoulders, lugging the soul up past the final step and pausing to catch my breath. Thom had the fucking decency not to ask me if I was doing okay, because I was just fucking fine, thanks very much, and he sat there with me while the wind cooled off my sweat and made me feel like I was alive again.

"We could always stay here," Thom offered softly. "In the desert."

"You hate it here," I said.

"I do," he agreed.

"Don't do me any favors," I warned him, not angry, just wondering why he was so fucking bell-cracked.

"It's just that you seemed to enjoy the camel racing," he explained. "And since I know it's difficult to find things in life you truly enjoy, I simply thought—"

"It's not the same," I said flatly.

Thom stared at his hands. "I suppose it wouldn't be," he said at length, and thank bastion he didn't bring it up a second time.

I could've been okay in the desert, but Thom wouldn't be. He'd be complaining every morning and hanging back at watering holes staring like a lost soul at the pools, dreaming about books and cities and crowds and crazies. We had to find somewhere in between or we really were going to lose each other, and as much as I wasn't about to admit it to anyone, I worked best in a team. Not that I couldn't pull through on my own if I had to.

I stood and lifted the dragonsoul after me, then moved to the edge of the roof. It was about five stories up and the alley below was narrow and quiet. Had to check and make sure no one was wandering around down below, because my brother'd never forgive me if we accidentally killed someone in the explosion.

Blowing up part of a city street was enough to get us thrown in jail, but if we planned things right we could actually steal some horses—no more camels, not ever—and race out of there, heading back to the mountains, and back in the direction of Eklesias too. I didn't want to answer any questions about what we'd been doing in Karakhum with explosives anyway.

"You can do it," Thom said, trying to be helpful and achieving about the same level of success as usual.

"Shut up," I warned him.

He held up his hands in defeat and I breathed in deep and long and slow, probably just putting off the inevitable like I knew I couldn't for too much longer. I wished I was alone but I was glad that I wasn't, and when Thom came up behind me I didn't shout at him, or make him back away, or anything like that. He put his hand on my shoulder, and I didn't even shrug him off, which said a lot about just how fucking doomed I really was. But then, it was Have who'd spotted some kind of resemblance between Thom and me in the first place—almost like she'd known before either of us, though I didn't go in for that kind of spooky crap. If anything, I figured she wouldn't mind him being here now.

It was a weird thought, but kinda nice—my girl's soul in front of me, and Thom at my back, like that one crazy night we went up into the sky all together and my own brother nearly squeezing me in half with how tightly he was holding on. Already it seemed like something out of another life, but it *also* seemed like it could've happened yesterday, and that was what had me so mixed up. I didn't know where I was coming and where I was going, and Havemercy would've told me to just get it over with, stop being so sentimental, and grow a pair while I was at it.

So that's what I was gonna do.

With a grunt, I lifted the dragonsoul up over the lip of the roof, effectively ending the conversation. Even if it was a lot damn heavier than it looked, the dragonsoul had a nice heft to it, and maybe someday we'd come back to the desert just so I could tell Sarah Fleet what a piece of work this thing was—almost as much a piece of work as the creator herself, and that was saying something. We should all be lucky enough to make something in this world half as fucked up as we were ourselves, something we could leave behind.

Behind me, I could hear my brother's sharp inhale, his hand tight against my shoulder. Even in the dark, the soul glowed—the most beautiful thing I'd ever seen. Moonlight glinted off the edge of the glass, and I held my breath. Just like the first time I'd ever seen her—*my girl*—it was almost too hard to look at her.

Then I threw the dragonsoul over the edge of the roof, sticking out an arm just in time to catch Thom as he stepped forward to watch it.

Havemercy arced through the sky like a big red shooting star—like those comets that came once every seven years and astronomers all shit themselves, marking it down as a portent of doom and disaster. Terror flying bright through the skies, coming a little too close to earth.

As a dragon, my girl had been just that. It only seemed right that she go out in the same fashion.

Thom held tight to the arm I'd used to keep him back, and we both watched for the split-second turn when flying became falling and you knew it was all gonna be over soon. The soul crested the height of its arc—at least I'd given her one last flight—and then plummeted sharply down like a stone.

"I hope that doesn't kill anyone," Thom said, but his tone was quiet, almost reverent.

"I checked," I told him, figuring I could let it slide just this once.

It landed seconds later with a *bang,* and a ferocious *crunch* on top of that—sort of like a lightbulb exploding, only magnified by ten at least. A bright light flared up from the streets, then immediately went out, like it'd burned too brightly for whatever fuel was left to sustain it. We were probably lucky we hadn't triggered some explosion. Or *I* was lucky—because I had to be with her at the last, no matter what kind of *boom* and *crash* followed.

From below, someone shouted, and I could see dimmer lights turning on, torches and oil lamps, doors opening and people staring out of their windows.

I drew back from the edge of the roof, pulling Thom with me.

"Come on," I said, and before my brother could say anything stupid to ruin the moment, I grabbed on to his arm, wheeling him around the way we'd come.

Sometimes I didn't give him enough credit, though, 'cause he didn't seem to be all that surprised. Instead, he just had that resigned look on his face, like he thought that'd fool anyone into thinking he wasn't anything but happy at being dragged off to our next destination. Wherever it was.

"Are you well enough to ride?" he asked, like *he* wasn't the one stumbling after *me*.

"I'm fine," I told him, and if he wanted to take that in both directions at once, he could. *I* knew he wasn't just asking about my injuries, anyway. I was either too smart for him, or he wasn't that subtle to begin with. Or we just knew each other a little bit by this point. "Job's done, anyway. Hate getting sidetracked."

Thom craned his head around to see if he could make heads or tails of the commotion taking place below us. Everyone's lights were on now, and I could hear angry shouts mixed with more excited ones— probably the opportunists who'd noticed the precious metals laid into the shards of glasswork. Those would've survived the fall, I imagined, but that wasn't my concern. My stake in it was over, my work was done, and I wasn't interested in looking back. Neither of us could protect each other anymore.

There were all sorts of horses stabled outside the place we'd been staying. It made me feel a little low-down to be stealing from sick people, but then we'd be leaving our camels behind, so as far as I was concerned, it was a fair trade. Thom didn't even pipe up once to complain about it, either, which gave me some idea of just how bad an influence I was turning out to be. He did a neat job of prepping the horses, checking the bridles and making sure the saddles weren't too loose. I didn't know where this sudden burst of competence had come from, but if I had to guess, I'd have said it was pure fucking gratitude at getting the hell away from his camel and back onto an animal that made more sense to him.

"Did you have a destination in mind?" he asked, leading my horse up to me, neat as punch, like all of a sudden he was some kind of cindy mind-reading animal savant.

"Still have to get to Eklesias, don't we?" I asked. I eyed the horse for a minute, trying to decide on the best approach, only while I was doing it, Thom was suddenly at my side, pulling my arm over his shoulder and hefting me up onto the horse, like I was a sack of vegetables or something equally useless. I sure as bastion shit didn't like *that* feeling very much. Oh how the tables had fucking turned. I'd've hit him in the head if it'd even looked like he was *thinking* about laughing, but he didn't.

We'd have to pretend that never fucking happened.

"There's nothing to remember," I said, taking him off guard again and before he could start back to his own horse.

"Pardon?" he asked, fiddling with my reins before I yanked them out of his hands. He looked like he *might've* known what I was talking about, but he wanted me to say it first. Just so he could be sure.

You know what they say about assumptions, I thought, and figured it couldn't hurt to do him one good turn. So long as he didn't get too used to this.

"You and me," I clarified, going along with his little game. "There wasn't much, and what there *was* wasn't any good to begin with, so you're probably better off not knowing about it. Dear old Mom and Dad skipped out on us both pretty early so it's not like I can tell you much about them. She looked like you; he wasn't even around. As for the rest, you were a pain in the ass then, and you're a pain in the ass now, so it's not like much has changed. Just in case you were thinking it was any different."

"I see," Thom said, wearing a quiet smile on his face. "I suppose I'd rather expected as much; a starved toddler doesn't exactly make for the fondest memories."

"Doesn't matter," I told him. "Anything you dig up from the past's always gonna be just that. You can't hold on to it, and you can't go back to it, so it doesn't seem to me like there's much damn point. Better to focus that big brain on something that'll make a real difference—at least that's what I think. Can't change anything from back then. Better just to keep your mind on what's next so nothing gets you in the nuts, you know what I mean?"

Maybe it was some of the stuff I'd managed to sort out for myself so far, lying in my bed of pain, and maybe that made me a bit of a hypocrite, passing it off like a rule I'd always known to live by, but I didn't care. If I couldn't use what I'd learned to kick Thom out of doing something stupid, then what was the point of learning anything at all?

"Focus on the future," Thom repeated, one hand stroking the sheen of my horse's neck. Then he looked up at me with those big eyes of his and I knew I'd made some kind of fatal error. "Our future?"

"I meant *in general*," I told him sharply, nudging his shoulder with the toe of my boot. "You want to have another long conversation in the middle of stealing horses? Don't think I won't ride off and leave you. You could write letters to me *and* Balfour from a desert prison, having just blown up a residential area, and wouldn't that be just peaches and fucking cream?" My horse stamped her hoof in agitation, wondering why she suddenly had a rider who didn't seem to have any intention of going anywhere. I agreed wholeheartedly.

"Well, sometimes," Thom said, and took something out of his pocket, handing it up to me, "it's not that terrible to remind yourself, occasionally, of what once was. I took it before we brought the soul up to the roof. I thought you might want to keep it."

I would've recognized it anywhere. It looked like a pocket watch but it had four hands, and none of them were moving. Stopped in time forever, I guessed, without anything left to point at. She was all gone, and this was the only thing that was left behind. Not even in working order, but just enough to let me think: *Hey, beautiful.*

"Sentimental asswipe," I told him, but I put the compass in my own pocket, right over my chest. "Don't expect me to thank you. Someone'll probably steal it, then you'll be sorry."

Thom shook his head quickly and scampered off to mount his own horse. At least he managed to look halfway respectable while doing it. No more camels; that was the only promise I could give him.

"Eklesias, then?" he asked.

"Sure," I said. Wait until my brother got a load of those fucking baths.

He squeezed his heels around the horse and she took off like a shot, leaving me to bring up the rear, which was an okay change from what things had been like in the desert. I *was* going to miss it, kind of, but it wasn't like I was about to grow old and drop dead anytime soon. We could come back. It was all a matter of waiting just long enough for Thom to forget how much he'd hated it here. Might be a long time, but I was willing to be patient about *some* things. I might not've been looking forward to returning to the way things'd been before either, but Thom'd gone and lost his journals in that sandstorm—everything he'd been recording up until this point—and when I'd asked him about it, he'd admitted he wasn't that keen on starting up again from scratch.

"You miss out on a lot when you're writing things down instead of looking at them," he'd said. "I think I'd rather have the experiences now and leave the memories to my head for a while. That doesn't mean I won't come to write about it later. And maybe I will take a few notes, so I don't forget how things really were . . ."

I gave it a week, maybe two weeks tops, before he broke down and changed his mind, but it was a nice thought all the same. I'd take all the peace and quiet I could get.

We drew even with each other at the white gates of Karakhum, bright and imposing, even in the dark. I had no fucking idea which way Eklesias was from here, but I picked a direction and took it. If it was the wrong way, we'd find out soon enough, and at that minute it didn't really matter. I had my brother with me, and as far as I was concerned, we had all the time in the world to get things right.

ABOUT THE AUTHORS

JAIDA JONES is a graduate of Barnard College, where she studied many things, most of which have found their way (in some unrecognizable form) into her writing. A poet and a native New Yorker, she had her first collection of poetry, *Cinquefoil,* published by New Babel Books in 2006.

DANIELLE BENNETT, from Victoria, British Columbia, studied English literature at Camosun College. She has passed through a collection of odd jobs, including Starbucks barista, McDonald's grunt, consignment shop worker, and jeweler's secretary. She likes this job best.